JOURNAL OF THE
PLAGUE
YEAR

An Abaddon Books™ Publication
www.abaddonbooks.com
abaddon@rebellion.co.uk

This omnibus published in 2014 by Abaddon Books™,
Rebellion Intellectual Property Limited,
Riverside House, Osney Mead, Oxford, OX2 0ES, UK.

10 9 8 7 6 5 4 3 2 1

Editor-in Chief: Jonathan Oliver
Commissioning Editor: David Moore
Cover Art: Sam Gretton
Original Series Cover Art: Sam Gretton and Pye Parr
Design: Sam Gretton and Pye Parr
Marketing and PR: Michael Molcher
Publishing Manager: Ben Smith
Creative Director and CEO: Jason Kingsley
Chief Technical Officer: Chris Kingsley
The Afterblight Chronicles™ created by Simon Spurrier & Andy Boot

ISBN (UK): 978-1-78108-245-4
ISBN (US): 978-1-78108-246-1

Printed in the US

A POST-APOCALYPTIC OMNIBUS

JOURNAL OF THE
PLAGUE
YEAR

C. B. HARVEY // MALCOLM CROSS // ADRIAN TCHAIKOVSKY

WWW.ABADDONBOOKS.COM

INTRODUCTION

It was about the beginning of September, 1664, that I, among the rest of my neighbours, heard in ordinary discourse that the plague was returned again... it was brought, some said from Italy, others from the Levant... others said it was brought from Candia; others from Cyprus. It mattered not from whence it came; but all agreed it was come again.
— Daniel DeFoe, *The Journal of the Plague Year*

IT'S HARD TO imagine, in our pampered world of antibiotics, vaccinations and modern hygiene, how terrifying plague must have been, in years long past. How unstoppable and overwhelming the threat, how uncertain the future. In the understated terms of his opening lines, DeFoe quietly conveys a panic so general it hardly bears explaining; the widespread gossip, the frantic guessing as to where the disease had originated, and in the end that simple statement: *all agreed it was come again.*

That isn't to say that we're strangers to dread, in this day and age. Economic collapse, environmental disaster, social breakdown, religious fundamentalism; these are the real, believable dangers—in many cases, dangers that DeFoe could barely have imagined—of our age. And in a way, the raw simplicity of a true apocalypse is almost preferable. Because the terrors of our time are so nebulous, so hard to engage with, to even pinpoint. Who are the villains? Who the heroes? Does the threat even exist, or are we (as some insist) being lied to, by the wealthy and the powerful with agendas of their own? How can downfall be averted, if it can be at all?

There, then, is the appeal of post-apocalyptic literature, the reason for its flourishing, even decades after the Cold War that ushered the genre into the mainstream has ended. Because the problems in those stories seem so *simple*. In the end, calamity—nuclear war, plague, global winter—takes all of that anxiety and uncertainty away, and boils everything down to a single, very straightforward problem: survival, at any cost.

There's a reason it's called *post*-apocalyptic. The disaster itself almost doesn't matter; it's scenery, the reason why our heroes have to fight to survive. It gives us modern characters, but takes away the complexity of the modern age, and with it the protection of society. It gives us warlords and killers, striving to clamber to the top of the heap in the aftermath of the end. Nice, simple villains to despise and oppose, in a time of nice, simple problems to overcome. Even as we indulge ourselves in a world of our fears, we diminish it, make it into something to fight.

And it's an injustice. How can you really do credit to a world of destruction, if you relegate the destruction itself to a backdrop? Take a leaf from DeFoe's remarkable journalistic work! Show me that terror and that dread, that sense of the world come apart and the shock the survivors feel at suddenly losing everything they once depended on! It's always been a core theme of the *Afterblight* books: Lee Keegan, Rob Stokes, the nameless hero of *The Culled* aren't walking over the cooling body of a civilisation long-dead, but running through its death throes, trying to hold onto something not quite lost.

JOURNAL OF THE *Plague Year* rewinds the clock, takes us back through the first year or two of the Cull. Our heroes see a world still collapsing, new powers just beginning to rise; one actually watches the collapse from the outset, from the dubious safety of an orbiting space station. It shows us, if my authors and I have done our jobs right, that creeping dread, and rising panic, that DeFoe reveals in just a few bald words.

But it does more than that besides. I wanted to see the world. Four of the *Afterblight* books are set in North America; six in the former United Kingdom. We've heard hints of the rest of the world—a little about Japan, a hint of France and Germany, a suggestion of Russia—but (aside from *Blood Ocean*'s floating city in the Pacific) the stories themselves have largely stayed in the bounds of the Special Relationship. So I asked my authors: where else can you show me?

Malcolm Cross set himself two near-impossible goals. First, to tease together the many different snatches and glimpses of *what* the AB-virus actually *is*—by authors who, if we're honest, aren't biologists—and tie them into some coherent, plausible explanation (damned if I can tell you if he achieved it, since I'm not a biologist either, but I applaud the attempt). Secondly, he set out to tell a post-apocalyptic story set in the remote, clinical environment of the International Space Station; and this, I am proud to say, he delivered in spades. *Orbital Decay* is a tense, gripping thriller that somehow manages to be both claustrophobically isolated and terribly vulnerable to the chaos outside. Malcolm is a talented, hardworking young author who deserves to be better known.

I'm a bit of a sucker for old-school Ozsploitation stories—an Australian by birth, I watched a lot of really terrible movies as a teenager—and CB Harvey's *Dead Kelly* brilliantly captures the mood of this very bleak, bloodthirsty subgenre. The wasted Outback always seemed, in these movies, packed full of leather-clad gangs, shooting and stabbing each other and doing awful things to each other's girlfriends (it's not, though; I checked), and "Dead" Kelly McGuire's revenge drama is no exception. Colin got his break when he won the first Pulp Idol storytelling prize issued by *SFX* magazine and Gollancz, and it's a real pleasure to publish him here.

I'm both a fan and a friend of Adrian Tchaikovsky, and I was thrilled when he offered to contribute to this omnibus, and intrigued when he wanted to step outside the safety of the Anglophone world and take us to his ancestral Poland. *The Bloody Deluge* not only forced me to go on Wikipedia and investigate the seventeenth-century war it's named for (a fascinating period about which, I'm embarrassed to say,

I knew nothing), it also perfectly captures the mood of hope amidst adversity at the heart of the series, and does it all with a distinctly European feel. He also offers a fresh, thoughtful take on the faith-versus-rationalism theme; delightfully, the staunchly atheist scientist running around after our heroine turns out to be not much less of a pain in the ass than his fanatical counterpart in the enemy camp.

Herein, then, three short stand-alone instalments in the post-apocalyptic world of the *Afterblight Chronicles*, shedding light on corners of the globe (and above it) you've never seen before. I hope you enjoy them.

David Moore, Editor
May 2014

ORBITAL DECAY
MALCOLM CROSS

CHAPTER ONE

"Hi. My name is Emily, and I'm eight years old. My question for Alvin is, are you safe from the bird flu pandemic in space?" The transmission ended, leaving only a static-eaten silence.

Two hundred and fifty miles over Emily, and travelling at a little under twenty-eight thousand kilometres an hour, Alvin froze. He nudged the ham radio's tuner just a hair, giving himself another second to delay before answering Emily's question.

Kids were meant to ask 'How do you go to the toilet in space?' He had an answer for that. But this? All he had was the canned response Mission Control had given him.

"Well, Emily, before we were launched to Space Station, we were held in quarantine to make sure none of us were sick. But if we do get sick, we have the training and equipment to take care of each other, and if we need to we can even get advice from doctors on the ground. Thanks for your question, Emily." He swallowed back a tense, tin-foil taste in the back of his throat. "We have enough time for one more question."

A moment passed while microphones changed hands, and

then a far more enthusiastic voice came across the radio. "Hi, my name's Oliver and I'm ten years old and I want to be an astronaut and my question for Alvin is can you please tell us how to be an astronaut because I really, really want to be an astronaut!"

Alvin smiled. At least you could count on kids to want to be astronauts when they grew up, no matter what was happening on the ground. "Thanks, Oliver. What a great question. The most important thing is to find something you love doing, something you can practise until you become real good at it, but studying math and science help a lot! I'm sure your school or parents can help you look up more about that on the NASA website, and good luck with achieving your dream, Oliver."

Oliver's 'thank you' came through fuzzy, burned with radio hiss. It took just a nudge of the tuner knob to correct— Space Station's orbit was fast and low, fast enough that radio signals between Station and ground receivers Doppler-shifted across radio frequencies depending on the alignment of orbit and Earth. Even corrected for, though, Alvin could hear the trademark bubble and pop of ground interference.

"I think that's all we have time for. Station's probably about to pass over the horizon from your perspective."

"Well, thank you, Alvin, for talking to us down here at Bannerton Elementary in New Jersey," one of the teachers said, so grave and formal he must have thought he was part of a historic broadcast to the moon landings, his voice torn to bits by static. "The Amateur Radio on the ISS program is a fantastic opportunity—"

"Thank you for the opportunity to talk to all the kids," Alvin cut in. "Our transmit window's closing, so this is NA-One-SS signing out. Good luck and God Bless to all the kids and staff at Bannerton Elementary. Out."

No matter how hard he listened, adjusting the dial, all the static gave him were a few warbles that *might* have been a class full of kids yelling an enthusiastic 'bye!' at him. It had been a short window; from the ground, Space Station had streaked across a corner of the sky in just twelve minutes.

Alvin Burrows hooked his toes under the handrails on the surface he was treating as a floor, to anchor himself down while he turned the amateur radio set off. The silence in Zvezda, the Russian command module, was broken only by the ever-present humming of the airflow fans. As far as Alvin was concerned, after five months and one week in space, that just about qualified as pin-drop silence.

"Space Station, this is Houston. You've finished with the ARISS event?"

Alvin unhooked his toes and pushed away from the radio set, turning and twisting to re-orient himself toward the ceiling, and the communications panel. He leaned in to touch 'transmit' on the microphone. "That is correct, Houston. All went as scheduled."

"Okay, Alvin. That was your last piece of volunteer work for today. For next week's session you're going to be in contact with the school in Reims, France. Any issues?"

Alvin shut his eyes and tried to picture the path that Space Station took over Earth. On a flat map it looked like a sine wave, bobbing North and South in long curves, although in reality it was just a regular orbit around the Earth, tilted away from the equator and making a full circle every hour and a half, while the world rolled sedately beneath. If France passed below, before that they'd either be coming in from the direction of Spain, or Britain... "Will the orbit let us fit in that private boys' school if we start early? Have the session with them, then the French, one after the other?"

"I think so, Alvin. We'll check into that for you. Any other business?"

"No." Alvin stopped, staring at the photographs the Russians had stuck up on the bottom end of Zvezda. He was alone in the module right now, but it was part of the Russian living space. They, or their predecessors from earlier expeditions, had turned a wall into a shrine to rocketry, with photographs of Yuri Gagarin and other Russian heroes of their space program, but his crewmates Matvey and Yegor had colour photos of their children there, too.

Their children on the ground.

The taste of tin-foil in Alvin's mouth was overpowering. He swallowed. "Actually, Tom, what's the news on the pandemic down there?"

It was okay for the kids to ask, Mission Control had a rehearsed answer for them, but if Alvin asked about the pandemic there was always a thirty second pause before Tom transmitted an answer.

It wasn't officially a pandemic, of course. Officially it wasn't anything except this year's bird flu outbreak. But whatever it was, officially or unofficially, the plague simply hadn't *existed* when Alvin had launched on his Soyuz from Baikonur to Space Station. Now, people were infected everywhere from Alaska to Azerbaijan to Australia, and in the past few days victims were beginning to die. First, one or two; then dozens. Now? *Hundreds.*

It felt like Tom took far more than the usual thirty seconds to come up with an answer. "Not much different than in the news this morning. What's the problem, Alvin?"

"I just don't know what to keep telling these kids, Tom. They all want to know about the bird flu, whether we're safe up here, if we've got a cure. They're scared, and it's heartbreaking, it's just real heartbreaking, you know?"

Another thirty second delay ticked away, but it wasn't Tom's fault. Tom was another astronaut, assigned as CAPCOM on one of the communication shifts from Mission Control at Houston. He was older, though Alvin knew him well on a personal basis. Tom invited him over to barbecues and church fairly regularly, even though Alvin was still fresh blood, this his first mission. Hell, Marla—Alvin's wife—traded baking recipes with Tom's eldest daughter. Tom Rawlings was good people; Alvin *trusted* Tom. But that thirty-second delay put a sick, half-electric tinny taste down the back of Alvin's throat.

"Well," Tom said, "if necessary we can cancel some of the amateur radio sessions until the pandemic settles down and things start cooling off."

"I'm coming home in three weeks, Tom. There aren't that many ARISS sessions left."

"Three weeks is a long time. I'm sure we'll start hearing some good news about all this before the end of the week."

Now it was Alvin's turn to remain silent for a stunned thirty seconds. He shook his head slowly. "Well, I hope so, Tom. I guess that about does it."

"Okay, Alvin." No delay at all, now. "Once again, thanks for volunteering some of your free time. We all appreciate it."

"No problem, Houston. Station out."

Giving up free time was a big deal. On Space Station, free time meant time to clean, eat, and sleep. Thankfully, so far as sleep went, Alvin had found himself needing less and less since coming up to Station. His usual seven hours a night had dwindled to six, then gradually to five and a half. He hadn't lost that last half hour of sleep a night until the pandemic had started.

Seemingly, it had popped up everywhere at once. There had been speculation that the pandemic started spreading at an airport, either Heathrow or JFK, but the news was calling it bird flu. Every recent bird flu outbreak, like SARS, had started in China, and spent months passing between humans and farm-bred birds before making the jump to human-to-human transmissibility.

The pandemic wasn't bird flu, and wherever it had come from, it was global now. It started with the sniffles and a dead tired fatigue, usually accompanied with a fever. In the supposedly rare cases where someone had died, a cough started and got worse and worse, eventually turning bloody.

Alvin didn't understand the first thing about it. Just knew he didn't like what he heard on the cut-down news segments Mission Control sent up. Just knew he wished he was on the ground with his wife Marla, taking it quiet and easy in a cabin in the woods somewhere far away, like having a do-over of their honeymoon.

He missed her. At least he could call her, there was a laptop in the Cupola. They didn't have a whole lot of bandwidth on Space Station, but there was enough for the internet phone. On weekends the whole crew got a slot with a private, or at least semi-private, video conference call home, but Alvin really didn't want to wait that long to talk to Marla, no matter how badly he wanted to see her face.

He bent down—in orbit, it was more like pulling his legs up toward his chest—and pulled his socks straight and snug over his feet. As usual, the surface over his toes where he hooked in under handrails was a little dirty, but he'd be okay with this pair of socks for another three days at least. Some engineer who'd apparently mistaken Space Station for a party-oriented college dorm had decided it'd be acceptable to wear the same clothes for a week, then just throw them out. After all, doing laundry in space was hard.

Doing just about anything in space was hard, except for moving around. Once you got used to it, anyway.

Turning himself over, he got his feet pointing away from the long drop 'down' from Zvezda along the long line of modules that formed Space Station's spine. After all, Alvin was just a little afraid of long falls, so he turned over instead and faced the drop head-on, turning it into a narrow sky above him. He flew up into it, with just a tug at the handrails.

Space Station was a maze of smaller modules breaking off from the main 'spine' of the station, like the crossbars on an orthodox crucifix, a world of orderly right-angled bends. Alvin spotted Rolan in the first side-module he passed. Rolan Petrov wasn't the easiest man in the world to stay friendly with—he was a little too detached, that flat-iron face of his seldom breaking into any expression, let alone a smile—but Alvin waved anyway, and Rolan looked up briefly from the book he was reading to wave back.

Alvin kept going 'up,' past Rolan's module, the hiss of air loud in his ears while he squeezed his way through the dark, bent Pressurized Mating Adaptor. The PMA was a goose-necked tunnel that separated the Russian and American sections of Station, linking the Russian Zarya module to Station's crossroads—Unity Node. Storage bags layered every wall of the PMA, all strapped down with bungees, making the already narrow gap tighter still. It was dark, and the bend of the PMA blocked line of sight until he finally got into Unity, which was effectively Station's kitchen and living room, in addition to being a giant airlock holding the two halves of Station together.

Alvin grasped the edge of the next side-module's hatch, and swung himself through into Trinity—primarily a living space and life support module, where the biggest window on Space Station—the Cupola—had been installed. But someone was already in the Cupola's niche.

Charlie Milligan was nestled in the blossom of her ruddy brown hair. Loose, it stood out at all angles, a foot long and slightly frizzy, as though she had a colossal afro. A hairband was floating beside her, and she was drifting in front of the Cupola, silhouetted in the light reflected up from Earth.

The module's laptop was open in front of her, drifting at the end of its cable, and from its speakers Nate Milligan was crying for his mother. "M-mommy, everyone's wearing plastic and we're not allowed to leave the neighbourhood!"

"Shh. It's okay, sweetie. Mommy's here. It's going to be okay, it's just for a little while."

"A plastic man said I wasn't supposed to be in the yard and he yelled at me and then dad yelled at him but I don't want to wear plastic mom I want it all to be normal like it was I'm scared—"

Alvin didn't wave this time. He just shut his eyes and silently pushed himself back out of the module, trying to forget what he'd seen. He and Marla didn't have kids yet, but he knew he wouldn't want one of his crewmates intruding on a moment like that.

Poor Nate. He might have to wait for his mom for a very long time. Charlie and Alvin were on slightly different expedition shifts—the Soyuz craft that took them to and from Station only carried three people, and there were six crew on the station. Every three months, three of the crew left, and three new crew members came up. Alvin was due to go home on the next return launch, but Charlie was going to be up here and away from her family for at least another three months. Maybe longer, if this pandemic thing impacted the launch schedules.

Alvin wouldn't be able to stare at Earth through the Cupola's glass like usual while he called Marla. Not the biggest sacrifice to make, even if he preferred pretending he could spot her, somewhere down there. Instead he crossed over into Harmony and went to his sleeping station—a closet bolted to the 'ceiling' packed with a sleeping bag, his few personal things, and one of Station's laptops—and found his pictures. He wasn't allowed to bring much up to Station, no personal electronics, so Marla had gotten his pictures printed on glossy photo-quality paper.

He pulled out his favourite photo from the thin stack, leaving the rest in their Velcro envelope stuck to his bunk wall, and smiled at Marla's smile. In the photo he was standing next to her, and they were close to the same height.

Alvin finally got ahold of his privacy in the JEM—Japanese Experiment Module—and settled himself down with the laptop from his sleep station in front of him, and the experiment airlock door behind him.

He had to wait for the internet phone to load up, and his request for a call took another minute to go through the system before he got permission to use the bandwidth. Then it rang for a little longer still, until Alvin started to worry, jiggling himself lightly from his perch, one foot hooked under a handrail, the other foot pressed down on top.

At last the fuzzy sound of her phone ringing gave way to the fuzzy sound of her voice, sweet as ever. "Alvin?"

"Hi, Marla. Do you have time to talk?"

"Of course I do. But do you?"

He laughed. "Well, I should get something to eat, but I'm not real hungry. What time is it over there? Four?"

"That's right."

The clocks and schedule on Space Station were set to GMT. Back home, in Houston, it was six hours earlier. Sometimes Marla didn't have much time to talk, even if her husband *was* an astronaut. After all, sometimes she was with patients... Alvin frowned. "Hey, aren't you supposed to be at work?"

Marla grunted noncommittally, in the way she did, with the cute little squeak at the end. "Meh. They're talking about extending the quarantines from downtown to the whole city, so Lil closed the office early. If the quarantine extends it's not like anyone's going to keep their dental appointments."

He carefully tucked the photo against the screen, and let the laptop drift in front of him while he tried to massage the tension out of his skull. "Well. Is it an '*if* it extends' or a '*when* it extends'? It—uh. It sounded like the Milligans are caught up in a new quarantine extension."

"Yeah? What did Charlie say?"

Alvin bit his tongue. "She didn't say anything. I—I pretty much overheard things with her kid."

"Mmm. Hm. I haven't heard anything on the radio, but they're on the other side of Houston, so I don't know. Why's the government being so cagey about this, honey? There are so many conflicting messages and nobody's really certain about anything... I heard one thing on CNN that said not to drink tap water, to drink bottled water only? Then Fox said that tap water's fine, it's more of a risk to go out and buy bottled water."

"Do you have masks?" He folded his arms. Hugged himself, really.

"Yeah. I have surgical masks. I stole a box of them out of the supply closet." Her smile came through in her voice. "Enough for me and enough for you, when you get home, assuming this isn't all over by then."

Smiling back at her picture, Alvin shook his head. "I'm sure the Russians will give me plenty of masks the second the Soyuz pops open."

"Mmm. But will theirs smell of perfume and whiskey?"

"Hey, if you're going to talk dirty at me, let me double-check I'm alone..."

"Oh, I'm sure everybody up there's *dying* to know that after a couple of drinks you like me with a dab of Chanel and nothing else."

His nose was a little stuffy—yet another problem of life in zero gravity—but he could just about smell the floral tang of her perfume mixed with the edge of aged alcohol on Marla's breath. Alvin turned his back to the experiment airlock, kept half an eye on the module's entrance, and quietly murmured, "To be honest, honey, I think I'd rather keep your sweet-talk *all* to myself."

"Aw. Does that mean you'll read me sweet little French poems? Or will it be Italian ones, now?"

"I was thinking about trying to learn Mandarin, they've got lots of poets..."

Marla laughed. Alvin did too, and for a little while home didn't feel all that far away.

LATER, AFTER HE and Marla's bandwidth had run out and they'd said their goodbyes, Alvin grabbed packets of barbecue steak, shrimp sauce and tea along with his chopsticks from Zvezda, then settled in with Charlie in Tranquillity, the two of them taking a meal above the Cupola. Charlie was shaking her head, accepting a clean pair of scissors from Alvin, using them to clip open her food packet.

"I don't even know what's going on anymore." She clamped the packet shut before the pink, plasticky looking crumbs floated out, and squeezed a little water into her 'Clam Chowder,' giving it slow and careful shakes to rehydrate the food. "Rudy"—her husband—"he... fuck. Just... fuck. Rudy almost, *almost*, got quarantined out of the neighbourhood, and Nate was alone at home. He was driving home with the groceries just as the army, the fucking *army*, were putting in quarantine checkpoints."

"Jeez."

"Apparently one of the houses two blocks over—*two blocks*—is wrapped up under a giant cover, like exterminators are going to fumigate it for termites. A whole fucking *house* in plastic." She shook her head again, and sucked from the open corner of her food packet. Champed the mush between her lips, pulled a face, and massaged the packet to mix it up a little more. "Fuck. It doesn't even taste of anything."

A flick of the finger sent the shrimp sauce slowly in her direction. Alvin nodded at it. "Try some of that." Being in space was a little like having a head cold, no gravity to pull the fluids down out of your head. It dulled the senses, but sometimes the shrimp sauce managed to taste of *something*.

"Thanks." Charlie plucked the sauce out of the air and squirted some into her food. Started mixing the pack all over again. "Anyway." The expression of disgust for her food was replaced by utter misery. "Rudy and Nate caught up in that shit... Whatever this is, it's just not influenza. It's just *not*, and I can't understand why everyone keeps pretending it is."

"It's not?" Alvin tentatively caught a square of steak with his chopsticks, and nudged it against the bubble of shrimp sauce clinging to the plastic sheet he'd duct-taped to the wall for a 'plate.' "I mean, I don't really think it's regular *bird flu*, but I don't know what it is. The bloody cough doesn't sound right."

"You can wind up coughing up blood with influenza if your

throat's raw, and you cough hard enough to rip the lining."
Charlie knew more about it than Alvin did. Alvin knew about
computer viruses, Charlie knew about real viruses. She'd
studied microbiology before entering the astronaut corps, and
Alvin had done systems design for satellites. "But that's clearly
not what's happening to these people. Just about all the cases
of deaths in non-infants and non-elderly, the ones out of the
three hundred and fifty-ish cases that are public, anyway—"

"Three hundred and *fifty*? Christ."

"I know, right? Anyway, they're almost *all* haemorrhaging
somehow. Coughing up blood, bits of sloughed off lung tissue,
like, like…"

"Like Ebola?"

She frowned, wagging her head side to side. "Kinda, not
really, sort of."

Alvin sucked up some of his tea, staring at her. "This isn't
the thing those people you know at Galveston had the accident
with, is it?"

"No, no, no, *no*," Charlie stuttered. "They were working
with *actual* Ebola Zaire at the Galveston National Laboratory.
And that was six months ago, it can't be related to this. This,
this bird flu thing, it's not a filovirus like Ebola."

He kept watching her. Watched her steadily go paler and
paler as she thought about it.

"Ebola sits in your liver, the virus digs into your liver cells
and hijacks them, makes them replicate more and more copies
of itself until the cells burst. Then the organ breaks down,
literally *breaks down* into pieces, and it spreads to the rest of
your body, and it's absolutely not the same… The pandemic
isn't killing *nearly* that many people, even if less than ten
percent of sufferers are recovering from the chronic effects."

Alvin sipped his tea, looking down at the Cupola. "You
know, when Tom and I were talking earlier, he mentioned that
they'd cancelled leave for about ten percent of the astronaut
corps."

She frowned quizzically at him. "Ten percent?"

"Yeah. Tom figured it out, mentioned it while we were
chatting. They're pulling in everyone who's O-negative. They
pulled in Greg Manley and Josh Thursten, he was in the same

graduating class as them, and the NASA docs with them on survival training used to tease that they'd have to provide blood transfusions for everybody else. Think it's related?" Alvin asked, shepherding floating steak squares with his chopsticks.

She hesitated, then shook her head slowly, ducking her head forward to keep the mass of her hair out of her face. "Blood type… it's not very relevant, immunologically. Not usually."

"What's your type? I'm O-positive."

"B-negative." She kept frowning, staring down at the Cupola. At Earth.

"So this thing isn't why they're pulling up all the O-negatives? It's something else?"

"Probably. Well… I don't know, there's viral envelopes, around the capsid."

"Capsids?"

"A capsid is the virus's coating, its skin. And some viruses kind of… wrap their capsid up in a sheath of material they pull out of a victim's cell walls." She squeezed a little chowder out of her packet, a big floating globule. "So if the chowder is the cell wall membrane, a virus kinda…" She snatched away one of his steak squares and nudged it against the watery surface of the chowder.

Surface tension immediately bonded the steak to the chowder glob, but the chowder wasn't entirely liquid, it was thick, slow. Bit by bit the glob pulled the steak into itself, like a drop of water on a window swallowing another droplet. Gradually the glob enveloped the steak, leaving only the evidence of an oily sheen of shrimp sauce on the now misshapen globe of pinkish chowder.

He blinked at it. "So it pulls part of the cell wall out to use as camouflage."

"Yeah." Charlie sucked her fingers clean, then lunged over and slurped the steak and chowder mix out of the air. She patted her mouth dry and stuck her napkin back against the exposed duct tape on the wall. "That's one theory for why we have distinct blood types. So our bodies can defend themselves against viruses with envelopes pulled out of other people with slightly different blood types."

"Huh."

"Yeah. And that's probably why if we had to try and transfuse my blood into you, or if we gave you a transplant from someone whose tissue didn't match yours, your immune system would attack the foreign cells. Not very useful for us."

"Mmm." Except Alvin wasn't paying full attention anymore. That thing about blood types... it was almost familiar. He was sure he'd read something about that, and recently. He struggled to remember where, but before he could think of it, Charlie pointed down at the Cupola with a gasp.

"Look! It's night."

The Cupola was huge. Seven panes of glass, six around the circular centre, forming a rough dome you could stick your body into and look outside, look around at Station and Earth and space.

Naturally, as the spot with the best view and always angled towards Earth, it was where everyone tried to get a photograph of their hometown from orbit. In fact, Alvin and the other NASA astronauts had all spent a couple of weeks training with professional photographers specifically for making sure their holiday pictures from space would be as striking as possible.

Privately, Alvin didn't think that amateur photographers would need all that much help to make photographs from Station *striking*. Below them—above them, as he flipped over to join Charlie at the glass—the faint glow of the sunlit sky formed a slender blue band in the distance. The moon was barely visible as a greyish freckle of reflected light on the Atlantic Ocean to one side of Africa, turning the streaks of clouds a glowing silver. Speckled dots of light clustered around Africa's coasts, faded and wandered across the continent like rare stars, and bloomed into fire at the base of the Nile, racing up its course to the Mediterranean, ringed in golden light. Above that, Europe was compressed into a glowing, glittering band of sparkling pinpricks vanishing over the horizon.

The sight of Earth at night, and the glitter of the cities below, pulled Alvin away from his worries and made him focus on the simple wonder of where he was. Of how small the world seemed, of all the people down there, of the vast *distance* he could take in with just a glance.

Charlie gently cranked open the shutters on the six side-panels, turning the knobs beneath the windows one by one. Opening up the view, giving Alvin a glimpse of Madagascar at the horizon and the dark gulf of the Indian Ocean beyond, the dark bulk of Space Station around them, light spilling from the few small windows in the other modules.

"Such a clear night," she murmured.

They'd only be over it for another forty minutes or so. When everything below them was so very fleeting, there only a moment before it vanished, it was hard to look away.

ALVIN FORGOT ABOUT his troubles until the next morning. He woke up to the hum of the ventilation fan pulling air through his sleep station, and muddled his way through the first moments of consciousness by trying to remember what was real and what was just a dream. Sometimes the sense of weightlessness, the absolute and total comfort of floating free, felt too much like he was still asleep. After all, most people only got to fly in their dreams.

He'd been dreaming that he'd been walking along the station's spine, from Zvezda down toward Unity. Not floating, walking, under gravity. And that once he'd struggled through the narrow canal of the PMA, brushing aside bags of water that had floated away from him, he'd been in a long dark corridor, like a deserted hospital, and that he couldn't find Marla. But his father had come by and given him Marla's medical file, and he'd seen that her blood type was AB-positive, not O-negative, and something about that had made him afraid.

That was when he remembered his conversations with Charlie and Tom. When he remembered the nagging feeling of not quite remembering something. And in the calm, relatively quiet warmth of his sleeping bag, lightly anchored to the wall of his sleep station, he remembered exactly where he'd seen it. The mice were AB-positive, A-positive, B-negative. And none of them were O-negative.

He fumbled around, trying to find where everything in the little wardrobe-sized cabin had floated to during the night, and unfolded the laptop in there with him against the wall.

He left it there to boot up, silently unzipped himself from his sleeping bag, and slipped out still in just his underwear.

The lights were on, but Space Station was still. The doors of the other three sleep stations, flimsy and curtain-like as they were, were still shut. It was still a little while before the wake-up call came, but as usual, Alvin had woken earlier than anyone else in Harmony.

He edged over, just a few feet, tumbling gracelessly, grasping at the handrails and bungee cords strung up against the walls until he'd lined himself up right. Then he kicked off a rail, shooting from Harmony, through Destiny, and up towards Unity. He lightly patted the module wall in Destiny, kept himself on course, and stopped himself in Unity, just short of the twisted throat of the PMA.

The PMA's interior was one of the few dark places on Space Station. To his sleep-fogged eyes, the bundles of white packages strapped along its sides seemed like organic, cancerous lumps. Alvin shuddered, despite himself.

If he was going to face down his problems, first he needed tea.

With a packet of tea stolen from the clear plastic binder it was held in, he tucked himself through the hatch into Tranquillity to get a shot of lukewarm water from the purification machine beside the toilet. With the water recycler's help, yesterday's tea was going to become today's tea.

He scuttled back into his sleep station with a guilty thrill of secrecy, as if he'd raided the fridge at midnight, and sank back into the warmth of his sleeping bag to suckle tea and go over his schedules for the past few days to look for what worried him, now that his laptop had finished booting.

Space Station was, in essence, a colossal flying laboratory. The goal was science, and almost every surface of Station not dedicated to supporting life and station operations was covered in racks. The racks were simple places to slot in and operate scientific equipment and self-contained experiments, providing them with power and cooling or heating or water or whatever it was the experiment required. Some needed tending, some were almost automatic, the astronauts aboard Station slotting them in and out like modular components in a computer.

It didn't take Alvin long to find what he'd been trying to remember the previous day. It was about the mice. Or more properly, the AAMICE.

Antigen Altered Microgravity Immune Cell Experiment.

He'd had to check its status a few weeks earlier. The mice were an experiment in a sealed box, mounted on an external pallet outside the Japanese Experiment Module. Among the thirty or so other experiments he'd had to interact with—some of them with fanciful acronyms like JEXTER and EXERCISE, some with more prosaic strings of letters like BKCE and VDMM—the mice were the only experiment that he needed to bring physical samples home from. In fact, he knew just the spot in the cramped Soyuz capsule he was supposed to stick them into, a little nook just three inches wide.

It hadn't interested Alvin for any reason beyond having to prep it himself before bringing it home. He'd only scanned the experiment's details long enough to make sure he didn't need to practise any procedures for it beforehand. Looking at it again, the details made his spine prickle. The sealed box contained a colony of mice, an infectious agent, and their life support.

The mice had been genetically altered with retroviruses to produce human blood group antigens on their red blood cells—a significant undertaking by itself, since mice had completely alien tissue. But as he scanned the list of compartments in the life support box, one thing became clear. Of the eight major blood groups of the ABO and Rhesus system, only seven were represented in the transgenic mice. AB-positive and -negative, A- and B-positive and -negative, and O-positive.

Not one of the little mouse astronauts was O-negative, like the astronauts on the ground that Tom knew, all with their leave cancelled.

But what the hell did *that* mean? Were they trying to make sure O-negatives couldn't mix with the rest of the astronaut corps? Trying to make sure no O-negative mice could foul up their experiment by infecting the rest?

Alvin thought about it in the minutes he had until the first strains began to play of music that Houston piped through the station's speakers for the morning's wake-up call, but he didn't have the time to concentrate on it for longer than that.

At breakfast proper, while Alvin surreptitiously discarded his empty tea-packet, Krister Munson—the crew's commander, a Swede from the European Space Agency—pulled a thin sweater down over his buzzed-down hair, pushing his free-fall fattened face through the neck hole. He turned to Alvin, only to grumble, "The flight computer crashed, *again*," in his thick, Nordic accent.

"Zvezda's?" Alvin asked, making space for Matvey—one of the Russian astronauts who slept in the station across from Alvin's—to get by on his way along Station's spine. "Or ours?"

"Of course Zvezda's. And it brought down ours with it. So that's your job for today."

"Well… Well *gosh-darn*," Alvin mumbled hesitantly.

Krister and Charlie both laughed; Alvin went beet red. He hadn't ever really picked up the habit of swearing healthily, like Charlie had.

It only took Alvin a few minutes to eat his breakfast and check with Houston about what the computer crash had done to his schedule for the day. More than half of his original schedule had been pushed over to tomorrow, and then some of tomorrow's work into the day after that, everything toppling like dominoes until his free time had been chipped down to the bare essentials of eat, exercise, excrete and pass out with exhaustion.

"You built it, so you better fix it, hm?" Krister kept on laughing, after finishing his coffee.

Alvin shook his head. "I only helped design the *replacement* boards and system software."

"Still! You better fix it before we fall out of the sky."

Falling out of the sky was an exaggeration. The occasional lost atmospheric molecules that hung around in low orbit slowed Space Station down only fractionally, but the two flight computers—which were supposed to work independently and check themselves against each other—were tied in to Space Station's power and atmospheric systems. Urgent, extremely urgent, but not an emergency. Yet.

For now he had to forget about the mice. But they'd come up again.

After all, they were on his schedule.

CHAPTER TWO

AFTER THE TROUBLE with the flight computer, Alvin got roped into helping the three Russians troubleshoot Zvezda's electronics problems for days. Zvezda was Space Station's service module, the ship's bridge in a sense, and even though Alvin was comfortable reading Russian, the Cyrillic forced him to concentrate on double checking the procedures manuals.

But forgetful as he was, the mice did come back to him, although it took almost a full week. A week after his not-quite nightmare about Marla. A week of steadily worsening news-clips from the ground.

But even if thousands, even *tens* of thousands of people had died as the pandemic worsened, the mice burned back into his consciousness like a meteor hitting the sky beneath Station. What made him notice the mice this time wasn't the nature of the experiment, but the fact it had been *prioritized*.

Station repairs got prioritized, trouble with the CO_2 scrubbers got prioritized, experiments? Experiments got torn to pieces to fix Station's systems or ignored or unplugged. Experiments were, for all their importance, very seldom the priority when living in a set of pressurized cans strung together two hundred and fifty miles over the ground. In his five and a half months on board Space Station, Alvin had never seen an experiment leap up his schedule and wind up marked as a *priority*.

It was slotted in for the afternoon, and he had the plans in his hands, but the first thing he did with his thirty minutes for eating lunch was find Charlie.

"I'm running late. Can this wait a minute?" Charlie was floating with a medical monitor strapped to the inside of her wrist, checking the monitor's screen and making entries on one of the computers.

"Yeah." Alvin ran his hands over his neck. He was still, barely, on schedule. He could find time to suck down a meal later.

"Okay," Charlie said after finishing up, taping the monitor's cables down against her arm before turning herself around to face him, with a quick twist of the body so that her face was aligned with his. "What is it?"

"Remember the blood group thing?"

She squinted for a moment. "Yeah. Yeah, Tom told you something and you were asking about viruses."

Alvin nodded. "About *the* virus."

The news still coming up to Station, filtered by Mission Control, was still terrible and alien enough it seemed like something happening in another country—on another planet. The National Guard had been called up all across the US, something similar was happening in most of Europe and China. The authorities were begging for calm in the face of rising public panic. The pandemic had gone from the first death to the first hundred in days, and a week later the official count of the dead was up past forty thousand. Around the globe, people were fearfully waiting for it to hit a hundred thousand, while hospitals in every nation were crammed full of sufferers.

"Here. Look at this." Alvin held out the folded print-out he'd made of the AAMICE project details. He figured Charlie could get more out of them than he could. After all, microbiology was her field.

"Mmn." She accepted the pages with a lack of grace, a hint of *this-is-a-waste-of-my-time*, but her expression calmed, became focussed before she'd even finished reading the first section. Without looking up she said, "I didn't know you could do that to mice."

"Hm?"

"I figured that any kind of genetic modification that extreme would fail. Result in cancer, that kind of thing. As much as playing with retroviruses is a precise art, significant gene modification is tricky and this... this sounds tricky."

"How tricky?"

"I haven't been reading the journals lately, but when I graduated, this would have been impossible." She turned the pages over with a rustle. "This experiment brief doesn't seem right to me. The research objectives are murky; 'observe the results of incubation in microgravity' doesn't tell me much."

"I thought it seemed okay..."

"I'm not bitching at you, Alvin. What you have to do with the experiment's straightforward, but this doesn't tell me what they're doing. What results they're looking for. It *looks* like they're testing the transmittability of some kind of infectious agent, but it doesn't say what the agent *is*. And why the hell is it in a box *outside?*"

Alvin folded his arms and frowned. "Shouldn't they be doing this kind of work on the ground? A real biocontainment lab?"

"Well, you'd think so, but up here bacteria can divide faster... microgravity sometimes seems to flip a switch in cells that's like, hey guys"—she snapped her fingers—"go nuts."

He hesitated. "How nuts?"

"Division rates go up tenfold. More. There was a virus experiment up here a few years ago that turned a petri dish into an absolute viral factory—some viruses just *love* microgravity. You think this has to do with..." She covered her mouth for a moment, before jerking her thumb in the direction of the module's Earthward wall. "What's going on back there?"

"I don't know." Alvin shook his head. "This just got pushed up on my schedule for today. Has priority over everything else."

"That's weird."

"I'm taking the samples home with me, too."

"Huh." Charlie frowned, reaching back briefly to pull off her hairband and shake out her hair to let it float free while staring down at the pages. She looked up at him. "You mind if I keep this? I want to look it over again when I've got more time."

"Go ahead." Alvin smiled briefly.

"Thanks," she said, turning away, scratching at her scalp. "And Alvin?"

"Yeah?"

"Be careful when you haul these mice in. *Real* careful."

"STATION, THIS IS Houston. Do you read?"

"Houston, Station receives you loud and clear. I'm powering up the remote manipulator's cameras now."

Alvin licked his lips, and gingerly touched the switches on the control panel in the JEM. One by one the monitors flickered into life, displaying a long slender white arm stretching into the distance, still folded in on itself.

The remote manipulator system's robotic arm was mounted over the 'porch'—a flat plate on the exterior of the Japanese Experiment Module, specifically for holding experiments that needed to be exposed to space. The mice were on the underside of the porch, shielded from sunlight and the radiation produced by experiments like the JEXTER laser.

"Okay, that's good, Station. We're receiving the feed. Do you have the dead pixels on monitor two, or is that on our side?"

Alvin squinted at his screen. "No, I think that's the arm's camera telling us she's growing old." The radiation count was high in space, and it wasn't just from the experiments. The sun's radiation was brutal without the atmosphere as a buffer; it was more than enough to gradually burn out the cameras on Station.

Alvin went one by one through the slow careful steps to power up the robotic arm, double-checking himself at every turn, even if Tom at Mission Control was supposed to be handling the checklist for him.

Tom was CAPCOM again. He usually was, on the day shift. One small reassuring piece of familiarity, even if everything else was changing. Usually Alvin would be talking to the control centre at Munich for research operations, but the Munich centre had been closed as part of the German quarantine effort.

Going through the warm-up procedures for the manipulator

arm, making sure the lubricants in the arm's actuators were smoothly spread, Alvin wet his lips again and dared to ask, "So how you doing, Tom?"

"Pretty good, Alvin. Wife and kids liking their trip up to visit the cousins at Muir Beach in California. Real quiet up there, still. They're liking the seaside."

"That's good." With any luck, they'd be away from the pandemic.

"Marla?"

"Mad as a cat on a hot tin roof about not being able to go in to work, but she's good." Alvin kept an eye on the screens. Wet his lips yet again. But it didn't matter how often he licked his lips, if he didn't ask. "So what's the news like, Tom? Anything on the quarantines?"

The air fans hissed at him.

Silently, the insulation-wrapped steel out there in space wobbled back and forth, as though the spindly arm was doing its own little mechanical tai chi routine.

Alvin sucked down a breath, swallowed down his spittle, and asked, "Tom?"

"Sorry, buddy. It's all rolling along, you know how it is. How's that warm-up going?"

So the thirty-second rule was still in place. Alvin sighed. "Yeah, it's going. You know how it is." He laughed mirthlessly. "So is there anything we can talk about? How's everyone doing with their leave cancelled?"

"Huh?"

"Greg and Josh and all them?"

"Oh. Them. They got taken out to Sheppard Air Force Base. Don't know much about it; nothing I could talk about, anyway," Tom said, with a subtle edge to his voice.

Alvin blinked, quietly thinking that over. "Uh-huh."

"Yup."

"Well give them my best if you see 'em. Houston, I'm starting the procedure now."

With that, Alvin delicately started moving the manipulator arm. While the mice were the point of the exercise, Alvin was scheduled to get in as much useful work with the manipulator as he could while it was warmed up.

There were canisters to remove and exchange, a non-functional gas spectrometry experiment to unbolt, which he lifted off the porch and relocated to an unused sunny spot where the radiant heat of the sun, when Station wasn't in Earth's shadow, wouldn't matter any. And of course that opened up a shaded space to move another experiment into…

All told, it took Alvin close to an hour before he got his first look at the mousebox.

Two thick metal bolts held it to the underside of the porch. The box itself was a cube about ten inches to a side, with slender extrusions where a gas cylinder was screwed into it.

It didn't seem very big. Especially not for a mouse colony to fit inside, with all its life support and food.

In the dark of Space Station's shade it was hard to make out the corners, wrapped up in yellow reflective tape, like an industrial hazard strip. The closer the manipulator got, reflecting sunlight off its white insulation, the brighter the mousebox got.

Alvin leaned over to the small window in the module's hull. The manipulator looked like an anglepoise lamp trying to make itself small and hide, bent over with its head hidden under the porch. Maybe like someone awkwardly stretched to check down the back of the couch, where something had been lost and forgotten.

Looking at the mousebox on the monitor, Alvin had the feeling he was the first to look at it in a long, long time.

The camera shuddered side to side as he brought the arm's head in closer, close enough to read the letters engraved in the box's white skin. *Model organism colony support apparatus 656.* And beneath that, pasted over a biohazard seal, written on a white sticky label that had dried and curled away from the box in the absolute dryness of hard vacuum, was the hand-pencilled word 'Pandora.'

Alvin stared at the monitor, the bitter taste of tin-foil bubbling up in the back of his throat.

"What the devil are you, then?" he whispered.

STEP ONE IN the procedure for removing the mousebox required that he use the manipulator to twist a control on the box's exterior, triggering the remote euthanasia mechanism. He'd expected step one to result in a puff of air, venting out of the box, but the box remained still and inscrutably silent. Step two specified five minutes to wait for the mice to die, and that wait didn't sit right with Alvin. He toggled the internal battery (step three-point-one), disconnected the power feeds (step three-point-two), and waited for the computer to confirm the box's systems were ready for removal (step three-point-three). Finally he made it to step four—pulling the mousebox off the porch and bringing it into the experiment airlock.

He stared at it, slowly bouncing around in the lock, after he'd shut the external door and powered down the manipulator.

The cube turned serenely, then a little faster, buffeted by the air filling the airlock. The handwritten label blew off, flicking against the hatch window, sticking fast and filling the window with the word 'Pandora.'

Alvin stared at it, hesitating, hand on the hatch. He looked over his shoulder, as if he was doing something foolish, something frightening. He wanted someone to come by and stop him, but Alvin was alone.

'Pandora.' The box just *had* to have 'Pandora' for a label.

"Great," Alvin mumbled under his breath. "Real great."

He opened the hatch, and the world didn't end. It didn't even wobble when he picked up the label—through surgical gloves, naturally—and pasted it back to the sickeningly warm box's side. It had a living warmth, at least on the side where it had been facing the sun on the way into the airlock. The shadowed side was cool, almost dead to the touch.

If there had been more stowage space on the Soyuz, he wouldn't have had to open up the mousebox, but he had to separate it out into smaller samples that could be taken home. Thankfully, he could do that in the sealed glovebox.

The glovebox wasn't anything special, just an airtight box with a window and set of rubber gloves built into the side to safely handle hazardous materials, complete with its own separate air supply. The only real difference from any glovebox on Earth was that this one vented into space if he pulled the right valves. It was standard, theoretically safe, though now that Alvin actually had to use it he didn't feel very safe.

He sealed it up, tucked his hands into the sleeves of the gloves, and anchored the mousebox to a piece of double-sided Kapton tape on the inside wall. One last check to make sure all the seals were secure, and he set about opening Pandora's box. He had to force the lid-latches on all four sides with a hard shove of his thumb until he felt the click. One by one, until air hissed with the fourth click.

The lid exploded out with a blast of pressurized air, spinning madly, sending razors of panic raking down Alvin's spine with every bang of the box lid against the glass in front of his face. He caught hold of it with a reflexive grab and searched desperately for a crack in the glass, but, nothing. Everything was still sealed, safe. He forced down a breath, and did his best to ignore the sick tin-foil taste in his mouth.

The mousebox was full of dead mice, pinned between wire grates in cages no more than an inch tall. They floated in a congealed mixture of their own shit and piss.

Even spared the smell, Alvin retched.

Their white fur was stained faecal brown in places, some had licked themselves cleaner than others, some had torn out clumps of their own fur, leaving bloody little marks on their bodies. They didn't look sick, though. They looked like they'd all been alive until Alvin had turned the control that killed them.

There were twenty-eight mice packed into a small section of that ten-inch cube, cramped into cages crowded out by the far larger mass of their life support. One by one Alvin took them out of their battery-farm cages, tucked them into plastic pre-labelled envelopes, and transferred them into a three-inch-wide sample cylinder that had been in storage for the duration of the experiment.

Thank God he didn't have to touch them. Not with his hands, at least. He used a set of long-handled tweezers, and did his best not to look at them.

When he'd finally finished, the sample cylinder sealed up and wrapped in two layers of tape and another plastic envelope, he sealed up what was left of the mousebox and stuffed it into an airtight biohazard trash container. He taped up the container, and vented all air from the glovebox's interior. Even so, and even with a filter mask over his face, when he opened the glovebox back up he could have almost sworn he could smell death in the air.

He stuffed the sample cylinder into the MELFI storage freezer, and welcomed the opportunity to try and forget all about it.

AFTER THE COLD loneliness of packing away the mice in the JEM, the bustle and warmth of Unity at dinner time almost had Alvin wondering if he was dreaming.

Matvey and Yegor were smiling at each other, playing chess with a set made from Velcro and fabric swatches that they could fling back and forth to make their moves in the midst of the crowd of six. Even Krister was hanging out from the ceiling, manoeuvring spoonfuls of paste back and forth before catching them in his mouth. Rolan floated below him, using a new pair of scissors to cleanly open the food packets after getting them out of the toaster-sized warmer.

Alvin accepted his brisket with a smile, and carefully bumped his bag of tea against Charlie's bag of orange juice. "Cheers."

"You should try the orange juice again," she said, with more of a smile than Alvin expected. She'd had another call from home today.

"Okay." He squeezed out a careful blob of tea into the air, reddish and almost clear, blew it lightly in Charlie's direction. "I'll swap you some tea for some orange juice."

She gulped the tea out of the air, sent a blob of orange juice heading back, and Alvin caught the blob between his chopsticks, struggling for a moment to keep from flicking his traded beverage away, but with a little care he got the juice in his mouth.

"Still doesn't taste of much of anything to me," he said, as cheerily as he could.

"Bah!" Matvey stuck his head into the conversation, giving the board a flick back across the node to Yegor. "*Our* food still tastes of something in orbit, even if Roscosmos gave us sand instead of coffee!"

Charlie managed to laugh. "Hey, do you have any of those cans of honey? Want to trade some American peanut butter for it?"

"Sure, sure! Give me a minute." Matvey pulled himself over to the rack of plastic binders with their food packets, and searched through Unity's small stockpile of Russian food.

At the folding 'table' mounted to the wall, just a board angled to form a ledge, he held the can down with his thumb to keep it from floating away, and levered it open with a camping-style claw opener before giving it to Charlie. Charlie had her own supply of peanut butter, part of the small number of personal foodstuffs sent up with each resupply on the Progress vehicles. She unscrewed the tub, took Matvey's spoon from him, and pulled out a lump that would never have balanced on a spoon on Earth. It didn't drip, just hung on.

"There you go," she said.

"*Spasiba!*" he said. *Thank you!*

"*Puzhalsta,*" Charlie replied with a grin. *Please, it's nothing.*

A regular little feast and celebration, 'family dinner' on Space Station. Alvin smiled, glancing back down at the movie everyone was ignoring, playing on one of the laptop screens. Some box office bomb; *Tank Girl*, Alvin thought.

Alvin watched Matvey spread peanut butter on one side of a piece of toast from the bag on the table... but only one side. He lifted his finger and pointed at the dry side. "You should butter both sides."

"Hm?" Matvey quizzically turned the bread around, looking at both sides.

"No gravity, no bottom side of the bread. You can put peanut butter on both sides, there's no plate for it to smear off against." Alvin popped a piece of brisket into his mouth, kept talking with his mouth full. "Got told about it at NASA. One of our guys up here a few years ago figured it out."

"Hm!" Matvey massaged his spoonful of peanut butter onto the dry side, too, holding the toast at the edges carefully. "Interesting. Another fine example of international cooperation!"

They both laughed.

Alvin cast a worried eye in Charlie's direction a moment later. She'd drifted away from the group a little, while putting her peanut butter away. Was looking thoughtfully at the other personal food items she'd gotten. A lot of them were packed up and chosen by the astronaut's families, and Charlie's family were still stuck in the Houston quarantine.

The quarantine had expanded, as expected. More houses in her neighbourhood had apparently been wrapped up in plastic sheeting marked with biohazard trefoils, doctors in hazmat suits making the occasional journey through the suburban homes, soldiers delivering Red Cross packages with food and essentials. No one in or out.

Little Nate was apparently okay, but her husband Rudy had been coughing at her over the phone. No other symptoms, though, and even though the quarantine had been broken—a couple of neighbours breaking through their plastic wrap only to wind up getting tasered and handcuffed by the patrols within minutes of their 'escape'—there was every reason to believe he just had a regular cough. Or at least, every reason to hope that.

Of course, Alvin hadn't been the only one to notice Charlie going off by herself. And bit by bit, instead of talking about comfortable nonsense like food and complaining about how things didn't taste of very much in space, the conversation edged its way onto the subject of the pandemic.

"*Several districts in Moscow are going to be evacuated,*" Rolan said, voice low, keeping it in Russian, even though the others had learned it to at least a conversational level, Charlie included. "*Not that we were told. Do you know how the kids are?*" he asked Yegor.

Yegor shrugged, a surprisingly full-bodied motion as he drifted. "*I've heard little. They'll tell me what they think I need to know,*" he said, before peeling a cloth chess piece off the board with a Velcro rip

Yegor was the veteran in the room. Now in his late fifties, as a younger man he'd been in possession of a luxuriously Stalin-esque moustache. He'd shaved it off after *perestroika* and the fall of the Berlin Wall, and since then had been a mainstay of the Russian space station programs, having clocked in close to four hundred days in space. He was the type to be happy with what he was told. But Rolan, and especially Matvey, were younger men. A little more interested in the world.

"*This plague is only going to benefit the criminals,*" Rolan muttered. "*Isn't that right? All an evacuation will do is get the police out of the city, leave it to the ruffians who stay behind.*"

Matvey caught the chess-board, once Yegor finished his move and threw it over. A thoughtful look at the state of the game, and he stuck it to his shirt for later while he finished off the toast. Another shrug, more expressive than Yegor's. "*I don't know. Maybe the plague will kill them if they stay behind. Then only the law abiding citizens who left will be safe.*"

"*Pfah! As if this plague could do any good at all.*"

"It's an ill wind that blows no good," Alvin murmured. He didn't know if there was a similar expression in Russian.

"*It could be for the best,*" Krister rumbled, his Russian accent better than his English one. "*We are all using too much oil, too many natural resources. The natural consequence of overpopulation. Tens of thousands have died so far, but even hundreds of thousands is too little. If millions died, then, then perhaps the problem could be solved.*"

No one answered that.

No one could, all of them staring at Krister.

Krister turned a little red in the face, uncomfortable. He was in Earth sciences. Weather patterns, pollution, global warming. All the ways in which man was destroying the planet. "I'm sorry," he said. "I didn't mean it like *that*. My mouth ran away with me."

Charlie glared at him. Shook her head, leaning back. The motion hid her face in the floating cloud of her hair.

Rolan and Yegor shared an awkward look over the silence. At last Yegor looked away when Matvey returned the chess set.

"They're probably partway to finalizing a vaccine for it anyway," Alvin said, just to hear someone talking.

"Why say that?" Krister asked, relieved that the conversation was moving again.

Alvin let go of his chopsticks and spread his hands helplessly before recovering them from the air. "They're smart with viruses and immunology. It just takes time, right? I was just preparing experiment samples today that go home with us in two weeks. I don't understand it myself, but they're doing this real advanced stuff with mice."

"What stuff?" Krister demanded.

"Oh, well, they have these mice genetically modified to display human antigens on their cell surfaces..." Alvin explained it as best he could, but he knew he fumbled it. He wished Charlie would step in and explain, but all she contributed to the conversation was that the research documentation looked incomplete, or maybe even false.

"They haven't listed what infectious agent they're studying, they haven't explained why they have every blood group represented except for O-negative... It really doesn't make any sense." She grimaced. "There's something seriously wrong with it."

"Haven't you asked the research coordinators about it?" Matvey asked, amazed.

Charlie shook her head. "It's not my project, it's Alvin's." She stared at him, almost accusingly.

"I wouldn't have thought to ask," he said, meekly. "If it was an electronic engineering project, I might have picked it up, but, I don't know what the 'normal' procedures are in biology. Sorry."

"Well." She kept shaking her head. "I did try and look up the university and department the experiment's being conducted for, but apparently it's just this office that gets private funding, so, who knows? That thing could have been sent up by almost anyone."

"If you tell me what I need to ask, I'll get Tom to ask for us as soon as I can."

"Shit." Charlie palmed at her face. "Tom. Tom's O-negative friends."

"Yeah?"

"Are they sick?"

"Not so far as I know."

Charlie kept rubbing at her face. "Are *any* of the O-negative guys sick?"

"What's this?" Matvey jutted in to ask, chess set floating forgotten beside him. "O-negative guys?"

"Apparently NASA ordered part of our astronaut corps into quarantine at Sheppard Air Force Base," Alvin explained. "We think they're all O-negative."

"And none of the modified mice are O-negative?"

Alvin shook his head. "Not one."

"Are the Russians doing anything similar?" Charlie asked. "Rolan? Yegor?"

Yegor simply shook his head. Silent. As he had been since the conversation shifted. He was staring intently at them, his arms folded. Rolan, floating beside him, was just as tense. Just as quiet.

As Matvey caught their gaze, he turned pale. Shook his head, and that was all.

At last Krister said, "I don't think any of the quarantined ones are sick. I haven't been getting any responses to e-mails from them—I remember Josh saying he was being relocated—but the other astronauts I keep in touch with, both in ESA and NASA, they haven't been called up for anything. Some of them are in hospital."

Charlie, Alvin and Krister compared notes. Gossiped about who they knew who'd wound up in hospital, who they knew who might have been relocated to Sheppard. All while the Russians ignored them and watched *Tank Girl*, following Yegor's forceful example, silently staring at the screen.

LATER THAT NIGHT in Harmony, when Matvey finally made his way up from the Russian section, he looked over his shoulder a dozen times before settling into his sleep station. Went to the bathroom twice.

Nervous as hell.

So, floating in his sleeping bag and gazing across the gap as Matvey returned for the second time, Alvin called out, "Hey. What's up?"

The young Russian shook his head miserably. "Nothing is 'up.'" Then he smiled, thin-lipped and pale. "We are in space, remember? No up, no down."

Alvin snorted out a half-laugh. "True, true."

Krister floated by, sticking his tongue out after brushing his teeth. "Bleh! I *still* can't stand swallowing my toothpaste!" Of course they all had to swallow, no drains to spit into on Space Station. No faucets to run a brush under, either, so Krister sipped some water to rinse the brush in his mouth with.

Matvey and Alvin both laughed, but Matvey's laugh was weaker than Alvin's.

Alvin watched him. "Yegor got you down?"

Matvey started to shake his head, but stopped. "Yegor. He... He is into some heavy shit, you know?"

"I don't know." Alvin blinked. "Like what?"

"Like FSB, KGB before the dissolution of the union." Matvey smiled weakly. "You know, he wasn't in the air force before he became an astronaut. Not the proper air force, anyway. He flew spy planes in the 'eighties. Yegor has connections you would not even want to imagine."

"Christ," Alvin muttered.

Charlie pulled open the thin doors on her bunk, above Alvin's, from Alvin's perspective. From hers, he was above hers. "Are you serious? Does he *know* something? Is that why he shut you guys up?"

Matvey grinned nervously, pushing his arms through the slits in the sides of his sleeping bag and hugging himself. "I don't know. I shouldn't have said anything."

"Shit. I bet he *does* know something," Charlie said, leaning out to lock eyes with Alvin. "Maybe not about the mice, but about this whole mess."

"Maybe..."

"Don't ask him, *please*." Matvey held out his hands. "I am not even supposed to know these things about Yegor. I just pay attention to rumours, maybe too much attention, you know? They are just rumours."

"Rumours like *what?*"

"Rumours like, during the war in Afghanistan, the pandemic was deployed there on KGB orders." Matvey just got paler and paler. For him, 'the war in Afghanistan' was the Soviet invasion in the 'eighties. "But you know, that's one that my daughter heard on the school ground, and I had to write to her, Kalinka, that is silly, and besides, if it were true they would have censored your e-mail to me, so there is your answe—"

Keeeeeeeeeee!

The alarm cut Matvey off.

"Fuck!" Krister yelled, kicking off from the wash stand and

hurtling across the module to grab onto the small emergency panel near the hatch.

"What is it?" Alvin asked, struggling his way out of his sleeping bag. "Air leak?"

"Transmission failure." Krister banged his hand against the array of warning lights on the panel. "Didn't you fix that damn flight computer?"

"I thought I *did!*"

Charlie was already up and out, going through the emergency procedure manuals rattling around on their shelf. She found the right one, dodged around Matvey making his way to his station in the Russian section, and handed the manual up to Krister. He splayed it open, and Alvin moved in beside him to check the instructions.

The voice from the communications panel crackled with interference. "Station, this is Houston, do you read? Over." It was Tom, barely audible.

Krister wrestled with the communications panel before he got the microphone out of its cradle. "Fucking thing... Station reads you, Houston. We have a transmission failure light blinking at us here. We are still investigating the problem on our end. Over."

"Well, Station, the problem isn't on your end, it's on ours. One of the satellite ground relay dishes has been destroyed."

"What?"

"Uh, Yeah. Station, be advised that communications from Houston are going to be spotty for awhile." Even through the static, Tom didn't sound right.

Alvin shouldered in next to Krister, that sick feeling in his gut back again. "Tom! I *know* that tone of voice. You haven't sounded like that since you had to tell your kids the dog died. What the hell's going on?"

The seconds ticked by, waiting for a response. "Well, Alvin, I'm afraid I have to tell you guys that the Houston Space Center is under terrorist attack."

CHAPTER THREE

THIS WASN'T A procedure anyone had ever thought would be needed. Alvin told himself that, the second time he burned himself with the soldering iron, and resigned himself to fouling up again before getting it right.

Houston was never supposed to go off the air. There was supposed to be a signal just about every moment of every orbit. Occasionally Station went into a blind spot between satellites or over an ocean, but *Station* went off air, not Houston.

Houston was off the air. Tom's voice had faded to nothingness with a crash of static as another relay dish was destroyed.

Space Station was served by the TDRSS satellites, usually referred to as the Ku Band satellites, which kept data and bandwidth pouring into Station for all but five to ten minutes of each orbit. Then there was contact with ground stations, and a more reliable but less useful satellite constellation that just shunted voice communications back and forth between Space Station and the ground. But everything went through Houston to the satellites, and from there to Station, and had ever since the Russian communication network's final two satellites had given up the ghost.

"Here." First came the circuit board, then came Rolan sticking his head and shoulders into the space Alvin was working in. It made the narrow gap behind the wall panel even more cramped, but after handing over the board, Rolan took the flashlight hanging in the air and held it steady on Alvin's work.

"Thanks," Alvin murmured, and dug back into the forest of connections and exposed electronics boards behind the Ku band antenna's internal links.

The system, and the antenna, had only been intended for a simple data uplink/downlink, using the satellites like radio repeaters and reflectors—space-based internet routers that passed data between Station and Houston. It was all routed through sealed units and chips remotely programmed by teams on the ground; Station wasn't supposed to need access, and they didn't have it. No direct control of the satellites, and no direct control of the antenna. Not until Alvin finished soldering in a direct crosslink between the antenna's system and their computers, anyway.

Krister peered in critically at Alvin and Rolan, Alvin occasionally asking for a tool before finishing up the crosslink by feel and instinct. He'd never worked like this before—it was almost as though he was drafting up a design for a circuit, but instead of using software he was simply building it piece by piece, checking voltages with a multimeter until at last he'd cobbled together a connection into one of the laptops with pieces of the SPHERES robotics experiments.

When he came up for air, he found out he'd been working for barely forty minutes. He sipped water in Unity and washed the scent of solder out of his nose with deep breaths — with no fans pushing air behind the panels, and no gravity to make heat rise, the vapours from soldering had built up into unmoving bubbles of hot gas.

Krister continued to watch him contemplatively, almost calculatingly, until at last Alvin shrugged at him, not sure what he wanted. Krister shook his head and turned his attention to Yegor and Rolan, the pair of them struggling to manually establish a connection to the satellites.

They'd made progress even without Alvin's help, querying the satellites' onboard systems enough to make them ping diagnostic data at them—power levels, remaining fuel, and so on. With Alvin helping, it took them only a few minutes more to command them to orient their dishes to preset ground coordinates in their memory. Nobody had any idea what the coordinates represented, but Alvin gambled that they were backup ground stations.

On the third preset, the satellites relayed up a slow stutter of gunfire in response to their call of, "Houston, do you read? Houston?"

No answer, but they could hear gunfire over the link as someone triggered the transmitter.

"Tom, are you still there?"

"Y-yeah, Alvin." Tom was breathing heavily, now. "We're still here. It's good to hear your voice. I thought we'd lost contact with you. Did someone bring the relay dishes back?"

"Maybe. We rewired the Ku antennas and got the satellites pointed at a different ground station."

"Heh. Without us to help? Nice work."

"Tom. Is Houston still under attack?"

"Yeah, we are. They broke into the building about twenty minutes ago." Gunfire, again. A lower thump that fuzzed the transmission. "Security went down to barricade the doors, but we haven't heard from them since. The National Guard are coming..."

"That's good. Who are the attackers?"

A pause. That thirty second delay. Alvin smiled weakly, though only he got the joke, looking around at the other astronauts clustering around the communications panel. The delay ended about twenty seconds early.

"I don't know. They've been shouting something about the pandemic on bull horns. I think... I think they blame us for the quarantines."

"Why would they blame NASA?"

"I don't know," Tom murmured. "That gunfire's getting pretty close, now."

"I'm praying for you, Tom."

"Thanks. We're all praying for you guys up there, too."

"I'm sure the National Guard is going to get there any time now," Alvin said.

Matvey looked sorrowful, staring at the microphone in Alvin's hands. Krister had gone up to Zvezda, but Charlie was still there, fumbling the procedures manuals back into their rack.

Alvin cleared his throat, spoke a little louder. "Hey Tom, I'm sure the National Guard's going to get there real soon." He waited a moment. "Over."

He waited a moment more, unwilling to let thirty seconds elapse before holding down the transmit key.

"Tom?" Alvin exhaled slowly, waited. Waited, repeated his friend's name, and at last let the microphone go, dragging his hands back through his hair. "God damn."

Matvey touched his shoulder. "I am sure it will be alright. I am also praying."

Alvin nodded uncomfortably. The taste of tin-foil was back. That deep, inner discomfort that left him feeling sick inside. Alvin wasn't too sure about the power of prayer, but Tom believed in it. So all the same, Alvin prayed, staring at the radio.

It remained resolutely silent. Checking on the computer systems, though, there was still a carrier signal—the station on the ground still had power, could still transmit, but nobody was transmitting.

"We should double-check that we still have contact with Moscow," Matvey said, after a few quiet minutes.

Moscow was the Russian ground control centre. Their round-the-clock communications were routed through Houston's systems; if Houston went down, Station would be limited to direct line of sight radio communications while over one of Moscow's antennas. When they switched the communications panel over to channel two, they heard Krister and Yegor speaking with one of Moscow's ground control officers.

"*—Ridiculous that you cannot check! Are there no copies of the American documentation there?*" Krister barked.

"*Ordinarily we would use the hotline, but no one is picking up at the other end. We simply do not have the protocols for linking directly into satellite communications, there was never any need for it!"*

"Do not make excuses," Yegor said. *"Are you in touch with any of the Americans?"*

"We are in contact with Kennedy but they say they do not have their engineers in the facility yet. You must wait!"

Charlie pointed at a blinking indicator on the panel. "Look! Someone's talking on channel one."

Matvey switched it over.

"Tom?" Alvin asked, taking the microphone from Matvey.

There was no gunfire in the background. Just a long, drawn out hacking cough, voices in the background, and the unfamiliar twang of a Texan good ol' boy's accent. "Where's the movie set?"

"Houston, this is Station, please identify yourself. Over."

"I *said*, where's the movie set? We found the pool, but none of y'all were in there. I'm speaking to the movie set, right?"

Alvin looked to Charlie and Matvey for support, but they were both staring at him, wide-eyed. Frightened.

Alvin cleared his throat. "Who is this, and who do you think you're speaking to? Over."

The good ol' boy laughed knowingly. "I'm Jerry L. Brentford, one of the sumbitches who busted in on your sorry ass to tear down your factory of lies. Now if you get out of that movie set where you film the Space Station hoax, and get on your knees in the corridor, we'll arrest y'all like good citizens and ain't none of you gonna get shot. Now how's that sound to you?"

Charlie whimpered. "Oh, Fuck."

"What is he talking about?" Matvey looked away from her, shot Alvin a desperate glance. "I don't understand. What is this?"

"Jerry seems to think we're a hoax."

"What?"

The radio crackled. "Y'all making up your minds? I ain't a patient man. You coming out and cooperating, or not?"

They all stared at the panel.

Finally, Alvin cleared his throat. "He thinks the ISS is faked."

"But what is this! That is *mad*," Matvey stammered. "You can point a telescope up and *see* us, who is he, how can he be that *stupid*?"

Alvin licked his lips nervously. "Go get Krister."

"What?"

"*Go get Krister!*" Alvin spun, tearing Matvey from his perch and *throwing* him up the station, toward Zvezda. "Just get Krister, damnit!"

Reeling drunkenly, Matvey caught himself against a wall. Blinked with frightened betrayal at Alvin, then turned to pull himself into a single long soaring glide up Station.

Alvin drifted backward in a slow tumble. Equal and opposite reactions. Newton's third law. He clutched at his head, twisting away.

"Look, I ain't in the mood for games," Jerry told them across an audio background of men screaming at each other. "If you don't come out of whatever hideyhole you got yourselves dug into, I'm going to have to start killing your friends over here. Now you've got to the count of ten to start talking. One, two—"

"*Alvin!*" Charlie screeched.

He grabbed at the nearest bar and yanked himself back to the communications panel. She fumbled the microphone at him as if it was an adder, and he grabbed it tight.

"Five... Six..."

"Jerry you've gotta believe me, please. We're not at Houston, we're real far away."

"Yeah? *Where?*"

Looking at Charlie for help got him nowhere. She was staring at him, scared.

Alvin was scared, too. "I can't tell him we're up here," he whispered. "He'll shoot Tom."

Charlie bit her lip raw. "Russia. Tell him we're in Russia."

Alvin held down the transmit key. "Jerry. You there?"

"And fuckin' waiting, boy."

"We're at the Baikonur Cosmodrome. Star City, in Russia. It's—it's where they launch the Soyuz from."

"Huh. Makes sense to keep it remote and out of the country, I guess."

"Jerry, please—please don't hurt anyone, okay? It's real important you don't hurt anyone."

The man snorted. "Real important *I* don't hurt anyone?

How about it's real important *you* don't hurt anyone? That's rich, that's fucking rich. You ain't got no room to speak, boy, not when you and yours have been spreading the Cull!"

While Jerry continued his ranting, Krister caught Alvin's eye from the hatch. The Russians were with him. Silently they climbed and floated down to listen. And the longer the crew listened, the worse it got.

"We know you government bastards been pumping the Cull into our homes, it's cuz of *you* our kids are getting sick, putting that shit in drinking water and spreading it in chemtrails after planes, using satellites to *rain* the Cull down on us! And why? Just so's you can control us? Make us line up for vaccinations and get the mark of the beast slung on us or *die?* That ain't no way to live! God *damn* you faggots!" He punctuated his statement with a gunshot. And another.

It was the first time Alvin had heard the pandemic called 'the Cull.'

"This ain't God's retribution upon man! It's *man's* retribution against man! And we will not take the deaths of our sons and daughters laying down, we'll fight and put these bastards in the ground—"

Gunfire, and the transmission went dead. Alvin prayed that all Jerry had struck down in his anger had been the communications console, but after fifteen minutes of panicky consultation with Russia, they lost all signals entirely. Every ground station the Ku band satellites knew about was down.

Space Station was off the air.

"BUT THERE *IS* no procedure for this emergency. No one thought Houston could just *vanish*. We have to start preparing the Soyuz capsules to go down!" Charlie stumbled over the words, rushing to get them out before catching her thumbnail between her teeth, gnawing, ready to rip it right out.

"I agree," Yegor said in slow, careful English. "We should start running the checks on the Soyuz capsules."

"We are not evacuating," Krister growled. As far as he was concerned, as Crew Commander, this was the closest thing Space Station could have to mutiny. "We are not in any immediate danger and can safely continue the mission. Communications have been lost before, this is nothing to be unduly concerned about."

"I didn't say *evacuate*, I said run the start up checks." Yegor glared at Krister. Yegor was scheduled to take command of the next leg of the expedition, when Krister, Alvin and Matvey returned to Earth in two weeks. *If* they returned. "I am not suggesting we get into our suits. But if the emergency escalates, we must be ready."

"It already *has* escalated! We need to evacuate, without Houston the mission is *over!*" Tears were starting to glob up around Charlie's eyes. Not falling, just clinging to the corners of her eyes in the freefall. She wiped at her face with her sleeve. "We can't do this without a connection to the ground."

Krister gritted his teeth. "There have been blackouts before."

"We need the engineering help." Alvin grabbed the bar behind him to keep from floating into the centre of the group. He didn't want too much of the spotlight. "We need the teams on the ground to help us keep this thing in orbit. We're up here, but there are hundreds of technicians down there, and... and now they're *not* there."

"I am sure that ground control can be transferred to Moscow if the situation demands it," Matvey pointed out. "We also have flight engineers and expertise, they can be briefed by NASA—"

"They *can't!*" Charlie yelled, as though raising her voice would put more force behind her argument, make up for her panicky worry. "Don't you get it? Those crazies who attacked... they're infected with the Cull. They're talking about their children dying, they're infected! They've broken every quarantine between wherever they started from and Houston, the entire Johnson Space Center is infected, the American half of this effort is *dead*."

"The Cull—the *pandemic*," Alvin corrected himself, "isn't that lethal. Millions have been infected but only forty thousand or so have died—that's less than one percent."

"Seventy-six thousand," Yegor grunted. "It was forty thousand this morning. Seventy-six was the last official number I saw, just after dinner."

"Still, though..."

"It's not a normal virus down there!" Charlie held her arms against her face, eyes squeezed shut, damp tears spreading. "A week ago it was no more than six hundred. Three days ago it hadn't broken ten thousand! The number of dead are almost doubling every day, Alvin. *Doubling*. The infection is spreading even faster than that, and in another week the number of dead will be in the millions."

They were all staring at her. Even Alvin. She whipped her head around, meeting their gazes in turn, tears flicking off the edges of her eyelashes and into stilled raindrops in front of her eyes. "Almost no one clears this infection after they catch it, and once it's got you it always gets *worse*. They're all going to die. *All of them!*"

Silence met her, until Krister hesitantly spoke. "We... we don't know that."

"We don't, but my husband and child are caught in a fucking quarantine and now I *can't even fucking call home to check they're okay!*" She started shaking with sobs, whirling away from the rest of them to grind her eyes into her shoulder.

After a moment, Matvey said, "My children are safe, but I am worried about them, too. Perhaps Charlie is right."

"We all have people back home we're real concerned for," Alvin said. "I haven't heard from my wife in a day or so. Our families are important to us, but the mission's important too. I agree that we need to evacuate, get home, but let's do it safely, huh? We need to get Station's systems shut down and remote control established at Moscow—"

"Those are not our orders," Krister pointed out.

Yegor stared him down. "It is true those aren't our orders, but I agree that we need to be ready to leave if the situation deteriorates. Thankfully it has not deteriorated yet."

Rolan shook his head slowly. "There is another problem. None of us are O-negative."

"What?" Yegor asked.

"Alvin's mice, the NASA astronauts pulled to their air base. It is all connecting together, isn't it? You said very few are beating the infection, yes?" Rolan tugged at Charlie's shoulder until she faced him, her eyes raw red, tears building again. "It's the O-negatives, isn't it?"

"I don't know. I don't think that's being investigated. Fuck, if I could just read the medical papers from the ground…"

"None of us are O-negative," Rolan repeated. "And we do not even know if that gives immunity. When we return to Earth, what then? We will be infected like everyone else. Up on Station we are, at least, quarantined from Earth."

"That's fine for you, Rolan," Alvin snapped, "but I'm scheduled to go home with Krister and Matvey in another two weeks anyway. I'm not quarantined from anything for long."

"Then stay. We should all stay on Space Station until the situation resolves," Rolan said.

Alvin stared at him. "You… You don't *have* anyone to go back to, do you?"

"Yes, I am the only one of us unmarried." Rolan's expression hardened. "So what?"

"So you don't *care* if you get home or not, do you?" Alvin looked at the others. "All of the rest of us have wives and kids and *family* to go back to, people we love, people in *danger*, but Rolan Petrov is too good for—"

"*I have family!*" Rolan howled, face scarlet, snarling as he lunged out at Alvin, restraining himself from actually striking, body shaking with the effort of only letting himself scream in Russian. "*You shit-eating bastard! I have my family and my nephews and nieces and just because my career came before marriage does not make me heartless!*"

Alvin recoiled away in fear, spattered by the droplets of spittle hanging in the air, tumbling toward him from Rolan's lips.

Yegor didn't quite hold his comrade back, but the older Russian did edge himself between them, glaring at Rolan judgementally.

"The mission. Is more important. Than the six of us," Rolan growled out in brutally accented English, past Yegor's shoulder.

Alvin covered his mouth with his hands for a moment, staring at Rolan, the pair of them both breathing hard. At last he said, "I'm sorry I said that." He sucked down a long breath, and made himself say the words slowly. "I'm angry and I want to see my wife. I'm worried and I don't see how we can do our jobs without Houston. I spoke without thinking, I'm sorry."

Rolan grimaced at him. Shook his head, still red in the face. "*Fucking American conflict resolution.*" He laughed mirthlessly. Waved his hand at Alvin. "Da, da. Is fine. We are all unhappy."

Charlie edged back up to the conversation. She'd dried her eyes. "Alvin's right. We can't do this without Houston. We're going to have to go home sooner or later, and I want that to be sooner." Her voice was hoarse. "We all know they can keep Station flying from the ground if they have to. There are procedures for safely evacuating and leaving Station prepared for control by ground crews."

Rolan held up his hands, taking a breath, *thinking* before speaking. "I disagree. I think that Houston's functions can be taken up by Moscow, and that the mission can continue. We are here for the mission, the mission must continue."

"*What* mission? We are at the cutting edge of science, theoretical physics and microgravity research, but there are *much bigger* problems on the ground," Matvey snapped.

He was rewarded with silence, the time to shake his head and silently back down, before Charlie spoke up.

"You don't *know* that Moscow can take over," she said.

Rolan folded his arms, considering that. "This is true. But I am confident it is an option."

"Evacuation is another option."

Krister, mostly content to watch, eyes flashing judgement at them all, shifted his accusing gaze from Rolan to Charlie. He cleared his throat. "Is your opinion influenced by your personal situation?"

She stared back at him icily. "You mean because I'm a mother?"

"Yes."

She narrowed her eyes at him. "I may be a woman," she said evenly, "but I'm also the only one here whose family is directly quarantined. Matvey and Yegor's kids are *safe*." She looked at them, face carefully neutral. "Don't you two tell me that you wouldn't share my concerns if *your* children were stuck in a house two doors down from people sick with the pandemic and willing to break quarantine."

Matvey and Yegor shared a glance. Matvey looked away first,

and Yegor spoke. "I agree, Krister. Her judgement is no more suspect than mine, or Matvey's, or even Alvin's." He gestured across at Alvin. "Your wife is also in quarantine, isn't she?"

"Her place of work is," Alvin said.

"I won't pretend that my 'personal situation' isn't clouding my judgement, but even if things are a little more difficult for me than they are for the rest of us," Charlie said, "I don't believe my judgement is any more suspect than yours. This situation is difficult for us all."

Alvin nodded. "She's right. Krister, all of our opinions are being influenced by our personal situations. If we put it to a vote…"

"We will not *act* on a vote," Krister said, much too quickly. "But at least it would be helpful to make our opinions clear. Those in favour of an immediate evacuation?"

Alvin put his hand up before checking on the others. The only two abstainers were Krister and Rolan.

Krister looked at Rolan, blowing out a sigh. "And for staying aboard…"

Rolan nodded, lifting his hand. Stared questioningly at Krister. "Isn't that your 'vote' as well?"

Krister hesitated, shook his head. "I am not sure what my opinion is. Charlie, I apologise for questioning your judgement."

"Apology accepted," she said, blowing out a last, tense breath.

"I do not agree with the evacuation of Space Station in the short term. We will wait to establish direct radio contact with Moscow. Our first chance at it should be"—he glanced at his wristwatch—"in ten hours, fifteen minutes. In the meanwhile we return to our schedules. Physical fitness training, systems maintenance on the station, *sleep*. We'll ignore the science until we're sure of what's going on, and in the meanwhile, Yegor, running a check on the Soyuz capsules would not be unwise."

"Very well."

As the group began to draw apart to get back to their routines, Alvin saw a strange expression flicker over Charlie's face. She stared at the back of Rolan's head for a moment. "Krister, shouldn't we have two people working on the capsules, one for each of them?"

"There's no urgency," he replied. "Yegor can handle it alone."

"Okay," she said, voice carefully neutral again, and looked away. For a moment, Alvin caught her eye. She shook her head, leaning back until her hair wafted around her head, hiding her expression, and she turned and sailed away from one module to the next.

CHAPTER FOUR

THE RUSSIAN RADIO station in Zvezda was better designed than the amateur radio set a few feet away. All Rolan and Yegor had to do, stonily silent with one another, was compute the path of their orbit, set it into the station's controls, and the dials began to slowly turn themselves, compensating for Space Station's speed and the radio signal's Doppler shift.

"*Moscow, Station. Do you read? Over.*"

Rolan ignored Yegor and pulled himself closer to one of Zvezda's small windows, staring out at the ground far below them with intense scrutiny.

Yegor repeated himself. "*Moscow, Station. Do you read? Over.*"

This was their fifth pass over Russia. Each orbit passed a little further east than the last one, and after this final window of contact, Space Station would be all alone again for almost a day, as long as it took their orbit's alignment to come back into line of sight with Moscow's antennas.

During the first pass, things on the ground at Houston were still up in the air. Moscow hadn't re-established contact with

Houston, but they were in touch with what was left of NASA elsewhere. Kennedy Space Center was already trying to take over Houston's role. The National Guard had surrounded the Lyndon B. Johnson Space Center, and had lain siege on the attackers who had overrun the Houston control buildings.

The attackers were, as the Moscow controllers read to them from an internet news article, 'Something of an ideological mix between Texas's independence militias, survivalist conspiracy theorists, and the Ku Klux Klan.' They'd been calling themselves the 'True Patriots' since shortly after the pandemic had come along, and were the unfortunate result of quarantines that had trapped domestic terrorists together with right wing maniacs and people too desperate to think straight.

Or, as Charlie darkly murmured to Alvin after they'd heard that, people who *couldn't* think straight anymore. People incubating the pandemic inside them, the disease mysteriously bubbling away in their guts and brains and blood.

"*Moscow, Station. Do you read? Over.*"

"*Yes! Moscow reads you, Station!*" It was still a relief to hear those enthusiastic words, even for the fifth time.

Yegor smiled at them before settling in to business. Reporting the situation on Station, the current air mix, the few vital statistics that Mission Control could use to try and diagnose potential problems before they became anything to worry about.

Then Moscow shared its news. "*The siege at Houston was concluded forty minutes ago. The American Army's Delta Force assaulted the True Patriots as planned and have secured the grounds and main buildings.*"

They all wanted to ask questions about that, but in the limited time they had to communicate, there was a little more business to get through first. The standard details about Station's operations, not just the essentials. What part of life support was acting up, reporting and confirming what they'd achieved in the time since last contact—Alvin had gone through the checklists to ensure none of Station's systems that could be remotely controlled from Houston had been acting up, or been sabotaged, and he took the microphone to read that out, until they'd gotten through enough that they had time to ask a few personal questions.

Matvey asked about their families. All their families. The answers were brisk, and painful, for some of them.

"*Matvey, your children have been notified. They are fine, Liliya wants to tell you that the dog is behaving.*

"*Rolan, there are no messages*"—Rolan gritted his teeth, not looking at any of the crew—"*but your siblings and parents have been notified.*

"*Yegor, your eldest daughters could not be reached, but your wife has been contacted and says they are travelling, and all is well.*

"*Krister, your wife has been notified, she sends your family's warm wishes.*

"*Alvin, Charlie, we have been unable to contact your spouses or families. Kennedy were unable to provide their contact information but are attempting to make contact.*

"*Are there any short messages the crew wish to send home?*"

Yegor looked around the crowded space of Zvezda, from face to face. He almost offered the microphone to Alvin and Charlie, but hesitated. At last he asked, voice as gentle as the rough old man could ever make it, "Just our love and reassurances?"

"Yes," Krister said.

Charlie nodded mutely.

Alvin stared at her, as if for support. Surely she'd want to say something, anything? He wanted to tell Marla everything would be alright, that he'd be home soon, that he hoped she was safe... He bit down on everything he wanted to say, and nodded weakly. "Yes," he whispered. "That sounds good, Yegor."

"*The crew send our families and friends our love, and reassurances that all is well with us, and that we are safe. That is all for the moment, Moscow.*"

"*Good. We have a few minutes left for the radio window. Are there any questions?*"

Of course there were. Yegor held out the microphone, first to Matvey, who looked pointedly in Charlie's direction. Yegor nodded, and held the microphone out to her, instead.

She leaned forward, and cleared her throat before speaking in careful Russian. "*Are there any news reports about the Houston quarantine?*"

A pause. "*We will research this for you, but there are no changes we are aware of.*"

She hesitated, about to speak again... but then glanced at Alvin. Ushered him forward to Yegor, thinking he'd want similar news.

But instead Alvin asked, "*Was anything said about the staff at Houston? Are they safe?*"

There was a nagging pause. Slow, and heavy. Almost like speaking with Tom about the pandemic, a thirty-second wait that dragged on and on, until at last Moscow responded.

"*The True Patriots executed their hostages in the main buildings before the assault began. I am so sorry.*"

Praying hadn't been enough.

"THIS IS BE-SIXTY-SIX-KL. Is IG-Twelve-TK out there and listening? Over." Alvin clung to the amateur radio set like an anchor. It had been two days. Two awful, awful days.

Charlie had been right about the pandemic's mortality rate. The first night after the assault the tally had gone up to an estimated hundred and sixty thousand. The second night it edged up to the nice round number of four hundred thousand. Tomorrow it would be eight hundred thousand, the day afterward, one million six hundred thousand. And every day after that... Alvin didn't want to think about.

Kennedy had re-established contact. Given them the Ku band satellites and given them time to call their families, read the news, read and respond to e-mail, stare at the photographs of bodies piled like cordwood outside a hospital crematorium in London, a man in yellow hazmat gear torching the bodies with a flamethrower, because the crematorium would be just too damn slow. And, of course, read about the rioting as what was left of the True Patriots rampaged through suburban Houston, burning down power and phone lines.

Marla's cellphone had stopped ringing the day before—just out of charge, Alvin prayed—but it left her out of contact, and the quarantines had been extended to their part of Houston.

"This is BE-Sixty-Six-KL. Is IG-Twelve-TK out there and listening? Over." Alvin stared at the set, and dared hope. He didn't use the station's amateur radio call sign, NA-One-SS. Even on a night like tonight, with the streets burning in a dozen cities across the United States, as people who thought the True Patriots had the right idea screamed and rose up against the government, Space Station's call letters drove the ham radio operators down there into a frenzy trying to make contact.

At last, the signal buzzing, Alvin heard an unfamiliar voice call back to him. "BE-Sixty-Six-KL, this is MT-Seven-One-LW. I have a message to relay for you from IG-Twelve-TK. Do you read? Over."

Alvin's core went frozen, his heart not quite stopped as he bit down on the side of his tongue, fighting the nervous crackling ache of tin-foil at the back of his throat. "I read. Go ahead, over."

No thirty second pause, just the brief delay of someone reading a note out loud. "IG-Twelve-TK relays to BE-Sixty-Six-KL: Neighbourhood has no power, Lenny sick but will keep trying to transmit. Marla yelled message over fence, she is not sick yet, loves Alvin very much. End of message. Over."

Tears brimmed over the corners of Alvin's eyes and built up, thicker and thicker until they wobbled like jello over his eyelids when he blinked, left him just about blinded and unable to do more than pull up his shirt and wipe them dry, only for the tears to build all over again.

He sobbed, spluttered. Shook his head.

Leonard was a saint. An ex-astronaut in a suburban neighbourhood full of them, a good neighbour, an amateur radio buff, and a saint.

There wasn't time to cry, though. He had no idea who or where MT-Seven-One-LW was, and the transmission windows between Station and the ground for amateur sets were fifteen minutes long at best. "Thank you, MT-Seven-One-LW. Can you relay a message back?"

"I can try. Go ahead."

"Thanks to Lenny. To Marla, Alvin loves Marla back, and will come home as soon as he can." He held his shirt's hem against his eyes and, for a moment, let himself cry. "Promise."

*   *   *

CHARLIE WAS STAGING a strike.

Until the ground staff at Kennedy and the Air Force got her family out of their quarantine in Houston, she was refusing to work. No lab experiments, no repairs, no checking on her bone density, nothing. She'd asked Alvin to join her, get more of the crew behind it until they got Marla out too.

He was tempted. Matvey was, too. His daughters may have been safe, but they could have been safer. Russia hadn't reacted peacefully to the news that the pandemic was worsening. But in the end, Alvin had chosen to stick to his schedule and trust that NASA would do what it could for Marla.

This was Alvin's first expedition, his first flight. He had decades left, and if Yegor was still in space while chasing sixty, Alvin didn't want to give up the possibility that he could be part of future expeditions to Space Station. Maybe the hoped-for mission to Mars...

"There isn't going to be a mission to *anywhere* ever again, Alvin." Charlie sucked her soup through a straw, before glaring at him. "The space program is over, everything's over, we need to be ready to pick up the pieces back on Earth."

"When the crew of Skylab mutinied for a day, well. *None* of those guys ever flew again. Not one of them. It didn't matter that they were right about being overworked, they never got another mission."

"We're not going to fly again, Alvin. And even if we were, we're going to do more good on the ground. It's not going to be about pushing the boundaries of science after the pandemic's over, it's going to be about practical engineering—rebuilding society. Dealing with new problems."

He stared at his bag of tea, trying not to dwell on the fact that Leonard was sick. Right next door to Marla.

"Problems like what?" he asked.

She sipped up her soup quietly. "Like stopping the inmates from taking over the asylum."

"What are you talking about?"

She shook her head. "I've been reading up on the pandemic research from the ground. There's talk about neurological damage, psychosis, it's... not pretty."

Alvin bit his lip. "Could you do me a favour?"

"What? Now that I'm on strike and don't have anything to do, you mean?" She smirked at him.

He didn't feel her levity. "That thing with the mice is still bugging me, and I don't have the time to look into *anything*..."

"THE PANDEMIC IS following a pattern," she told them all as they gathered at the end of the day in Unity. Even if it wasn't the pleasant feast of previous nights, the crew still gathered to eat, and Charlie was still part of that crew, even on strike. "It's getting worse the longer it goes on."

She held up one of the laptops. She'd been reading research from the ground on the pandemic's viral agent, and used the snippets she'd copied out like a crude slideshow for them. "The first deaths were in the young. Children. Fevers, mostly. But it didn't kill the elderly like that; the elderly victims first fell to cardiac problems. These were the outliers, incidental deaths, people who were already vulnerable. But a viral strain analysis showed that the virus had been around a lot longer than that.

"By comparing lineages, taking into account how fast the virus changes and mutates, the Galveston National Laboratory estimated that the two most widely divergent strains they could find, from southern Spain and California, had split off from each other anywhere between three to six months ago. The first news reports referring to it are from two months ago, *weeks* before the first death."

"Which means we might have it," Krister grimly pointed out. "Your launch to Station was a little less than three months ago."

"I don't think so. None of us have shown any symptoms." Her response earned raised eyebrows, so Charlie went on. "Exposure to the early pandemic strains resulted in an initially mild case of infection, fevers and fatigue, and in some cases a heavy course of antivirals cleared it. Not all cases, but some of them. Since then, nobody's cleared an infection without being O-negative. And honestly, it doesn't sound like that many people with O-negative blood were infected long enough to develop symptoms. Most never contracted it in the first place."

She looked around. "Judging by the pattern on the ground, if the virus were on Station we'd either all be sick by now, or dead. We're not O-neg. Even if the virus was spreading before we launched, we haven't picked it up."

"Mmmn," Yegor grunted. "Okay. And this pattern?"

She snapped her fingers, pointing at him. "Right. Back on track. Okay, so the longer the pandemic's been active, the longer it's infected a population, *the more lethal it gets*." She looked around at them expectantly, but none of them had her background. She had to explain. "This isn't how viruses work, it's not how they evolve.

"The faster a virus spreads, usually, the faster a natural equilibrium emerges, so the virus can spread through a population without killing. It wants to spread in a population of healthy hosts—particularly lethal diseases are generally new to human populations. After they've been around in us a few hundred years, they settle down, become benign. The pandemic's doing it backwards.

"By the time we found out it existed, it was so mild that it'd spread globally without anyone noticing. By the time we found out it could be *lethal*, by the time we started quarantines, it'd gone airborne and had been mixing in the global population for weeks." She looked at them expectantly, and this time got worried understanding for her efforts. "And all of these individual strains, no matter where they were, all independently started turning lethal. It wasn't that a single strain somewhere had turned lethal and spread; no, in every afflicted population the virus did it spontaneously.

"Worse still, the symptoms leading to death are getting progressively worse. From the blood pressure spikes that killed the elderly, it went to haemorrhage in the lungs, that bloody coughing that's been on the news. But a freak case in Arkansas early last week was worse still, a patient named Nicholas Boone's internal organs began to suffer runaway liquefactive necrosis—he almost literally shat out his guts. The same thing's happened in Ohio and Oklahoma, with no possibility of cross infection. The pandemic developed new strains with the same effects, in locations hundreds of miles away from each other."

Yegor continued to stare at her. He was pale. Jaw clamped. No longer making his musing grunts. And beside him, Matvey was staring at the old man with nervous horror.

Matvey looked across to Alvin, almost pleadingly. Touched his fingers to his lips while Yegor's attention was elsewhere. *Shhh.*

Just what kind of 'heavy shit' was Yegor into?

"That sounds... bad," Krister said, at last.

"It is. The longer this pandemic continues, the worse it gets. We have to stop it as soon as we can. And we may have the answer to stopping it on Space Station."

"What?"

Charlie gestured at Alvin. "The mice."

Alvin folded his arms uncomfortably. All he'd done was ask her to look into something he didn't understand. She'd done the actual *work*.

"Not only are they genetically altered to produce blood group antigens, their immune systems were altered." She smiled, nervously. "Changed around and spliced to fit a risk profile we *know* exists for the pandemic. The experiment's documentation doesn't tell us *what* they're infected with, but there are no O-negative mice in the group, the experiment was launched with one of the Progress craft four months ago, well within the time margin Galveston thinks the pandemic emerged in, and those mice? That experiment's designed to turn them into farms to cultivate a single virus in their blood. I'm sure it's an early strain of the pandemic, and they're *swarming* with it."

The nervous taste of tin-foil sizzled between Alvin's teeth. "You're talking about a vaccine?"

She nodded. "Cellular division can accelerate under microgravity conditions. If I had a new, unknown virus on my hands, and I wanted a vaccine for it *fast?* I'd get it into orbit as soon as I could. After having isolated the virus, the first thing you need are clean samples. You can't just take it out of victims, that gives you the wild strain. You need to get the virus clean, to get a population infected with a single workable strain, a *seed* strain. Ideally the earliest ancestor you can catch.

"They've been struggling to achieve it on the ground. Trouble getting it to grow in the lab, and they've had repeated failures trying to breed the wild strain down to something usable. But up here that work's been *done*. It's in the mice. They've been raised in a sterile environment, the only viral loads they'll have in them are the pandemic itself and the remnants of the retroviruses used to modify their immune systems.

"We can take them *right now*, pull a serum from them and dose it with formaldehyde to kill the virus, and we could inoculate ourselves with it."

"That doesn't sound entirely safe." Rolan pulled himself back down against a wall, looking at her from an awkward angle. At last he let his food go, reoriented himself to face her properly, and reclaimed the floating packs. "You're telling us to inject ourselves with formaldehyde?"

"Very little. Think of it as more like washing the viral material with it — just enough has to be used to break the virus down so that it can't replicate, but the antigens remain intact."

"Antigens? I though those had to do with blood type."

Charlie grimaced, shook her head. "Antigens are anything the immune system learns to produce an immune response to. The antibodies generated are tuned to cling to a specific part of a virus, or proteins forming a cell wall, anything foreign to the body. That's the antigen, if it's biologically active. If it's relatively inert, it's usually termed an allergen. It's the same biological process.

"The trick is to keep the virus fragments whole enough that the body recognises them as antigens, and then produces antibodies that respond to the complete virus just as effectively."

Rolan stared at her levelly, digesting the information. "What risk is there if the viruses are not broken down enough by the formaldehyde?"

"Then we've injected ourselves with the live virus. With luck, the strain they sent up with the mice was stabilized and asymptomatic. It's what you want in a seed strain. I hope that's what they did. But I'm more worried about the retroviruses they used to make the mice transgenic—I don't have a good way of filtering those out while we're up here. Gene therapy to play with the ABO antigens... the literature talks about pancreatic cancer and tumours causing brain damage akin to schizophrenia in rats." She smiled tightly. "So if anything, the risk is going to be that I'm too thorough breaking the viruses down and the fragments left will be too indistinct for an effective inoculation."

"How many doses can you make up here?" Alvin swallowed back the tinny sting in his mouth. "You can't mean we could make enough vaccine to protect the entire world, do you?"

"No." she shook her head rapidly, a sharp flick of her hair, a halo around her. "There isn't remotely enough material for that. But I could make a handful of doses. Enough to keep us and a few others safe long enough to manufacture a proper vaccine once we get to the right facilities on the ground."

Rolan locked eyes with Yegor for an intent moment. Neither said anything, but Rolan broke away first, turning to Charlie. "You're talking about saving the world."

"Maybe. I hope so. It can take weeks, months, to manufacture a vaccine in the quantities required once it's at this stage, but it's possible we could make enough before it's too late."

Krister blinked at her, his eyebrows raised, shocked, as if he'd been slapped. He took a breath, putting on the calm face of their crew commander. "If it's the correct strain of virus," he said, voice betraying worry, excitement. "And if it is, it sounds like this experiment is *critical*. Something that takes priority over everything else we're doing here."

Alvin was staring at one of the pastel pink walls of Unity. An absurd colour, but calming, and that's why it had been used. That's why he focussed on it, gently chewing the sides of his tongue, trying to banish the tin-foil taste from his mouth. A handful of doses? Those would have to be used on those working to cure the virus. There wouldn't be any way to justify vaccinating non-critical personnel. Could dentists qualify? He doubted it, Marla didn't have anything like the right experience for this. But Rudy, Charlie's husband, was a retired industrial chemist.

He watched her face, waiting for eye contact, until at last she smiled at him. Her smile lost none of its excitement, none of its righteous hope, but Charlie's attention returned to Krister and Rolan, ignoring Alvin's sick worry.

"We need to confirm the details of this experiment. If it's true, wasting even a week could be critical," Rolan said.

"We may need to send Krister, Alvin and Matvey back down immediately, rather than in two weeks as scheduled."

Krister nodded back at him. "If Charlie's theory about the experiment is true. Let's call the ground."

"THAT'S A HARE-BRAINED theory you guys have," the CAPCOM at Kennedy said over the link. It was a new voice, one Alvin wasn't immediately familiar with—Kyle Gilder, an astronaut who flew a desk and keyboard these days. "I'm looking at the listing, but the experiment documentation we've got just lists the strain introduced to the mice as the 'Ten-Zee' subtype and doesn't specify *what* it's a strain of..."

"Can you get in touch with the laboratory concerned?" Krister looked up at Charlie, and nodded once. She hadn't been able to find anything to the laboratory running the experiment beyond a front office in a small university.

Kyle hesitated, though it wasn't anything like the thirty second pause, just the flick of pages turning as he looked through a file. "There's a lot of documentation here, guys, I'm not sure I'm getting all of it. The file here is huge, and it's mixed up with a lot of other projects..." He trailed off.

Krister waited, until impatience took over. "Kennedy, do you have anything for us on the AAMICE project?"

The microphone clicked off, dead air. And Alvin found himself counting the seconds, very nearly all thirty seconds of that old pause, before Kyle Gilder murmured over the miles, "I'm real sorry to tell you guys that, looking at the file, we don't have any information on that. Other than loading up the samples to return with the Soyuz as scheduled, there's nothing else in here that Station needs to be informed of."

Even though Alvin didn't know Kyle, he could hear the worry and fear in his voice.

Worry and fear that was repeated in Charlie's voice when they returned to Harmony to bed down for the night, after the crew's slice of private personal time. "Where's Matvey?"

Alvin hadn't expected to get much sleep that night—his five and a half hours were slowly shrinking away to four—but still, the intrusion was unwelcome. He popped open the slim doors of his sleep station and peered out. Charlie was leaning out of hers, hovering upside down in front of him as she held open the doors to Matvey's space.

Empty.

"Where's Matvey?" she repeated. "Krister, Matvey hasn't gotten to bed!" She glided through the space to the station opposite hers, reaching out to push open the doors—for a moment, Alvin expected Krister not to be there either, for this to be the setup for some confused nightmare, but Krister pushed the doors to his bunk open just before Charlie touched them.

Krister examined Matvey's empty bunk, with enough attention and focus that Alvin didn't think he had been sleeping much either. He checked his watch, and murmured, "Give it five minutes. He might just be taking a little more personal time…"

If they wanted more personal time, unless they were deliberately going against their schedule like Charlie, they had to give up time taking meals or time sleeping. But even then, usually they just stayed in their sleep stations and shut the doors for privacy; they didn't wander off.

"Did you check the Cupola?" Alvin asked, rubbing at his eyes.

She shook her head slightly. "That's where *I* was all evening."

"I'm sure he'll come to bed when he's ready," Krister said.

Charlie frowned at Krister, and launched herself off at the nearest communications panel. She tapped it over to internal communications. "Matvey? Can you get in touch?"

Her voice echoed lightly, repeated in all of Station's modules.

The delay lasted a lot longer than thirty seconds, with Krister pulling himself back into his sleeping bag dismissively, while Charlie waited for a response. "Matvey?" she repeated.

Finally, Rolan came onto the intercom. "He's not here. He is not on that side of Station?"

"No." She turned. "Krister, he's not reporting in…"

Krister hesitated, rubbing at his face. Waited, taking a deep breath. "Okay," he said, finally. "We'll search for him."

Two minutes later, while Alvin was searching in the PMM— Permanent Multi-purpose Module—his nerves churning away in his gut, he heard Yegor shouting in Russian on the intercom, *"Bring the medical kit to Rassvet!"*

Before Alvin had even gotten himself out of the module in a tangle of adrenaline, the intercom clicked back on. Yegor sounded tired. Broken. *"Never mind. Just... just bring the stretcher and body bag."*

CHAPTER FIVE

THE DEAD SHOULD never be so alive as they were in orbit. Matvey rolled serenely. His eyes were shut in what could almost have been sleep, expression soft. Drifting, he bounced into one of Rassvet's walls, his body crumpling against it in a way Alvin had never seen a person move before. His arms and legs slowly twisted until his shoulder hit a surface, and his body slowly bounced away, legs gradually flexing almost straight. Life returned to his limbs, arms curling, hands waving. His pants were marked with spreading stains of damp, and spittle drifted at the tip of his tongue, between teeth held stiffly open a fraction of an inch.

It wasn't the first corpse Alvin had ever seen, but it was the first one that seemed to be trying to say something.

A laptop with a black screen bumped against the walls from the end of its cord, making the only sound in the module besides Alvin and Rolan's breathing. No hiss of air. The ventilation fans were silent. The air was still.

The scents refused to mix. In one spot, Alvin couldn't smell anything. Move his face slightly, and then his nose was caught in the wet warmth of exhaled air, gathered up in a bubble of carbon dioxide so thick it gave him a headache with just a single breath. To get a lungful of oxygen he had to pull away from where Matvey had been found, where Matvey had asphyxiated on his own exhaled breath.

Matvey slowly drifted, still turning. Rigor mortis was pulling tension into him piece by piece. First the face, the jaw, the neck. Soon, the limbs wouldn't crumple anymore.

"*Pass the stretcher,*" Rolan murmured, holding his arms out to the hatch.

Matvey's skin was chill, when Alvin caught his fingertips. Warmer, close to the elbow. There was only a hint in his hands of the tension that held his face rigid. His arms resisted motion, slightly. It was like moving a training doll in an emergency procedures training session, Alvin told himself, and nothing at all like fighting with the first onset of rigor mortis in a friend's corpse after he'd died because of something so damn pointless as *asphyxiating for the lack of a breeze.*

Alvin bit down on the inside of his cheek, trying to stop himself from crying, and fought with Matvey's body. They had to get his head in line with his spine, so that Alvin, Rolan, and Krister could strap Matvey to the stretcher, wrap him in the station's single body-bag and put him in the hurriedly emptied single cupboard that was Station's only morgue. And Matvey fought back, stubbornly holding his head at an angle, refusing to let himself simply die and be stowed away, as though afraid of being forgotten.

"AT FIRST *I thought he must have been alive.*" Yegor tugged at his short hair, his hands wandering over his face as if searching for the moustache he'd shaved off twenty years before. "*He looked to be asleep. He didn't answer when I called him. I gave him a shake and he was... he was limp—It was then, I think, I noticed how quiet the module was. That the fans were off. That close to him the air was stale.*"

The microphone was open, relaying every word back to the ground.

"*When was the last time you saw him, before?*" Krister asked, as gentle as he could.

"*He had been watching the end of one of the DVDs. Some film he'd been watching in fifteen-minute chunks by himself now and then; to calm down, I think. I heard it when I went past earlier… he could have been in trouble then, without my noticing. He had the DVD playing so very loud. By the time we found him, the film had finished.*"

Alvin leaned close to Charlie. Whispered, to keep from interrupting the brief investigation. "If he dropped off to sleep…"

She nodded fractionally. Murmured back, "Maybe."

If Matvey had been asleep, by the time the carbon dioxide had built up around him enough to have given him some sign—shortness of breath, a headache—he might have been unable to regain consciousness. Gone straight from sleep into stupor, and from there, slowly to death.

Rolan, next. Moscow Mission Control asked the first question. "*What did you see, when Yegor called you to the module?*"

"*Matvey, unconscious. Yegor was trying to find his pulse, but… I thought he might have been alive, but when Yegor went to inform the crew that he was dead, and I tried to find his pulse myself, I felt it. No pulse, and rigor mortis in his neck muscles.*" Rolan paused and shut his eyes. Shook his head slowly. "*But earlier, when I was leaving to use the water-closet in Tranquillity. Maybe… half an hour before we found Matvey. I saw someone leaving Rassvet.*"

Everyone froze, staring at Rolan.

Even Moscow remained silent. The hiss of static went on and on, until at last ground control asked, "*Who?*"

"*I do not know—I was in the PMA, it's too narrow to turn around. I thought it was Matvey, all I saw was the movement behind me…*"

"*No, Rolan. The question I meant to ask was to the whole crew, you are all listening, aren't you? Who was it who left Rassvet? They would have been the last to see Matvey alive.*"

Yegor had given his version of events. He and Rolan looked first to Krister, and Krister turned his accusing stare on Alvin and Charlie, lingering to one side.

Alvin took a moment to register the full meaning of that look. It hit him in the stomach, with a foul taste at the back of his throat. "I was in the PMM writing e-mails before bed. Trying to get someone to run batteries to my wife with the quarantine supply deliveries…"

"If it wasn't one of us," Charlie said slowly, carefully, "then maybe it was Matvey."

"But where were you, Charlie?" Krister's eyes were icy. "What were you doing?"

"I was in Tranquillity, over the Cupola, reading the research notes on the pandemic my friends are mailing me. And, of course, same as Alvin, whining at NASA to do something to get my kid out of that *fucking* quarantine." She met his gaze with fury, her teeth gritted. "What about you, huh, Krister?"

"It was my turn on the exercise bike; check the schedule if you want. It must have been Matvey, then," Krister concluded, looking back at Rolan. "So we know he was alive shortly before the accident."

"It doesn't make *sense*," Charlie hissed. "That much carbon dioxide doesn't build up in *a few minutes*. If he was awake, he would have *noticed something*. You were there, how thick was it?"

Alvin paused, clinging to the rail beside Charlie, in the quiet of Unity, now that they were alone. He looked up, briefly, at the PMA—the passage linking the Russian section to Unity. That gooseneck bend, the walls of it thickened out with white supply-bags all bungeed down. No, Rolan wouldn't have been able to turn around in that tight space. Not easily.

He cleared his throat. "A lungful gave me a headache. It was… rank. Not from Matvey—just, hot. Real stale."

"Yes, but was it enough for Matvey to have asphyxiated on?"

He thought about it, frowning.

"Was it?" she asked again, tone sharper.

"Probably," he said. "It shouldn't take much, in still air, if you don't move."

"But you'd move, wouldn't you? That headache, that tight feeling in your chest. That shit would wake *me* up." Charlie bit her lip. Uncertain, but not so uncertain she gave up on the thought. "And besides, just breathing hard, and taking deep enough breaths, that'd make the air circulate, *surely*."

"You don't like the idea that Matvey was moving around that soon before his accident, do you?"

She nodded. "If it *was* an accident."

Alvin took a breath and swallowed. Trying to dispel his nervous energy. "What bugs me," he whispered, even though they were alone, "is that the first phase of rigor mortis is supposed to take around half an hour to start."

"How do you know *that*?"

Alvin smiled awkwardly. "Marla has a ton of *CSI* box sets at home."

With a half-amused, half-disgusted smirk, Charlie just shook her head. Her smile vanished fast enough. "So…"

"Either Matvey went in, fully conscious, and somehow died just after Rolan saw him, or it was someone else," Alvin said.

She brought her hands to her face, pulling back her hair and clutching at her scalp. She struggled to say it, but did anyway. "Someone who killed Matvey."

"But no one's admitted they were the one Rolan saw."

"Unless Rolan's *lying*."

"Bull," Alvin whispered. "Why the *hell* would he lie about that?"

She gritted her teeth for a moment. "I don't know. But he might have been lying." She glared at him. "I know I didn't do it. Did you?"

"God, no!"

"So it was Rolan, Krister, or Yegor. And Yegor is into *heavy shit*, remember?

"Charlie…"

"Yegor's KGB and FSB and all that bullshit, and Matvey's not even supposed to know any of it, and you *saw* how Yegor clammed up when I was talking about the pandemic." Charlie's eyes were raw and angry, and full of challenge.

"That's *insane*. Don't, don't let this run away with you. Calm down."

"I'm… mostly calm."

Alvin palmed at his face. "Good for you. I'm not even slightly calm."

Charlie laughed half-heartedly at him. "I want to go and ask Yegor about this. Back me up?"

"Ask him if he *killed Matvey?*"

"No," she said, voice low, so icy Alvin could just about believe her claims to calmness. "Ask him about the 'heavy shit,' and see if it's the kind of thing worth killing Matvey over."

THEY PASSED BY Rolan in Zarya, picking obsessively through spare parts lockers for something to get the air vents in Rassvet going again, and slipped down through the hatch into Zvezda. Yegor hung in front of one of the Soyuz consoles, frowning at the data and referring to a pre-flight manual over and over.

Alvin wasn't sure if Yegor was being thorough, or if he was forgetting what he read the moment he'd finished reading it.

Charlie glanced back at Alvin, her fire quenched by the vulnerability of the older Russian, hunching over that manual and hardly seeing it, body limp with grief, but she pressed on, dragging herself down beside him. Close... but not within arm's reach, Alvin noticed.

"Yegor?"

It took him a moment to look up, but not because he was concentrating. "Yes?" He blinked at her, slowly.

She hesitated. "A few days ago, before we lost Houston, before Matvey died..."

Yegor frowned. "Yes?"

Charlie grimaced, looked to Alvin for support.

He gnawed his lip. "Yegor, Matvey was talking about your background, your career, he said you might know people... people in the government who might know something about the pandemic."

"I wouldn't know about that," Yegor muttered, turning back to the display.

"When I was talking about the pandemic's effects, you got this expression on your face," Charlie all but pleaded. "A difficult expression, and—and Matvey was so nervous about you, like he wasn't supposed to know something..."

Yegor's face went scarlet. "*Nervous!?*" he roared, whirling around to face the both of them. "What the fuck are you accusing me of? I made Matvey *nervous?* So that means I killed him, obviously!"

Charlie blinked, backing away with a push. "I'm not saying anything, we're not saying anything, Yegor; it's just—"

"Don't play coy!" He bared his teeth, like a cornered animal, swiping an arm out at her in a single violent gesture that could so easily have been a blow. "Obviously one of us killed him! *Obviously!* Are you *stupid?* Since the fucking Mir fires we have air flow sensors on all the hatches, if there is an air flow problem an alarm goes off! I go and check the alarm, what do I find? The alarm was fucking *switched off!*"

"Jesus," Alvin breathed.

"Now you accuse *me?* I know it wasn't me! I was alone! So it was you, or you, or him"—Yegor swept his arm up at Rolan in Zarya—"or a suicide, but now you find a motive because the idiot boy cannot keep his mouth shut! You know who I think it was? I think it was Alvin!" Yegor stabbed a finger at him. "You want to go home to your wife, so kill Matvey and you know that you and Krister have to return in the Soyuz immediately!"

Charlie had her hands up, palms flat. "Yegor…"

"*There* is your motive! Don't you pin this on *me*; Matvey was my friend!"

"Yegor, he was our friend too—"

"Hey, hey!" Rolan had pulled himself down to the module hatch, and was staring at all of them. "Stop arguing! What is going on?"

"It is just another American argument, Rolan. *American conflict resolution*," Yegor grunted. "We are talking and we are shouting and that is all. It is alright. Don't worry yourself."

With a nervous glance from face to face, he backed away slightly. "This is true? Alvin, Charlie?"

She nodded mutely, but Alvin found himself staring at Yegor, still.

Alvin couldn't imagine him killing Matvey. He couldn't. Finally he nodded slightly. "It's alright, Rolan."

"Okay. If you need me to intervene I am just in the next module." Rolan gave himself a push, and drifted back to his work, looking back over his shoulder at the three of them.

The old man struggled to get his breathing under control. He shook his head, wiping his face with his sleeve. "I must blow my nose," he announced, and pushed away to grab a wipe from the small secondary eating area in Zvezda.

Alvin and Charlie waited for him to finish going through three tissues, all with his back to them, shoulders shaking quietly, before at last he drifted to his small bunk in one of Zvezda's niches, then returned with his face damp, his eyes red.

"I didn't kill Matvey," he said. "You know why he is nervous about me? Because I am Station's next commander, and because he was present when I was given *this*." He held up a thickly wadded plastic envelope covered in Cyrillic-lettered seals. There was a stack of DVDs inside, bound together with something very much like a handgun's trigger-guard lock — a bolt that went through their middle, with a lock at one end, bolting them together, making them impossible to use without undoing the lock.

He offered it out to them. Charlie was the one who took it, carefully turning over the package. "And... what is it?"

Yegor lowered his voice. "Long before any of us launched to the station, *long* before we are told about the pandemic, while we were all on the ground last year? They bring I and Matvey and Rolan into an office, and they say, 'Yegor. You are to be the Russian Commander, but in case you are killed or cannot complete your duty, the others must be briefed as well. In the event that the whole Russian government collapses after a disaster, these are the codes to control our satellites, and these are the radio codes to destroy or launch the parts of our nuclear arsenal that can be given remote commands.'"

The old Russian threw his hands apart and shrugged helplessly, horror digging into his features. "And here we are. And you are talking about a virus that will almost certainly collapse not just my government, but *all* governments. What the hell am I to think? Nothing like this has happened, not even during the Cold War."

He stared at them bitterly, demanding an answer, but neither Charlie nor Alvin had one to give him.

"What am I to think? Hm? I certainly do not think of killing Matvey." With that, he took the envelope back, and held a handkerchief to his eyes.

YEGOR'S PREDICTION, THAT Alvin would get to go home, proved true. In the few NASA emergency procedures manuals that said anything at all about deaths on Station, they only got as far as step three-point-five, finish securing the crewman's body, before hitting step four—wait for further instructions from Mission Control.

The instructions were to begin immediately prepping the Soyuz that would have carried Alvin, Matvey and Krister home a week from now. They got their sleep, though. No panicked hurry about it, they first had to wait for the process of rigor mortis to end.

Matvey's clenching muscles had to tire after their death-spasm, so that his body-bag was flexible enough to be manoeuvred into his seat on the Soyuz, and back out of the hatch when they were on the ground. That was why the body storage closet wasn't chilled—it had to be warmed, so Matvey's body could go through the process of rigor mortis as quickly as possible.

Alvin didn't sleep very much that night, nauseous little fragments of tin-foil swirling around in his gut. He had another nightmare, that he was waiting for Marla to answer her phone and call him, just waiting, for hours and hours and hours... except when his eyes fluttered open again, he wasn't sure if it had been a dream, or if he'd really been waiting all night to hear her voice instead of sleeping.

In the morning, nine hundred thousand people were dead. The virus was getting enthusiastic about its slaughter.

Mission Control informed them that the entire crew was evacuating. Not just Alvin and Krister, with Matvey. Perhaps it was the situation on the ground, or more likely the result of Alvin, Charlie and Yegor quietly informing Mission Control about the airflow alarms, after which they had all separately denied having done it.

Alvin's routine was close enough to normal. Point one on

Alvin's list of tasks before going home on the Soyuz was double checking his vital signs to make sure he could survive the trip back. That was no problem, it was the second item on his list, marked 'priority,' that gave Alvin trouble.

The canister he'd stored in the MELFI freezer, full of dead mice, was missing.

"It hasn't been mislaid! Things we store in the MELFI don't just wander off like a lost pen until we find it on the air vents a week later!" Alvin was yelling, and he knew he was yelling, and he knew that yelling was counterproductive. Especially when yelling not only at Krister, but over the intercom at the others, too.

"Are you *sure*," Krister repeated.

"Of course I'm—"

"I'm sorry," the intercom buzzed. Charlie.

"What?"

"I took the samples, Alvin. Who the hell else would?"

He grabbed the open microphone. "Charlie..."

"I made the vaccine. Just like how we discussed. There's plenty of material left for a seed strain, but we've also got twelve doses."

Krister hissed between his teeth. "We don't know what they're infected with, we don't—"

"We *do* know, Krister." Her voice was eerily calm. "I haven't been able to run *all* the same tests as the ones on the ground, but I've compared it with the notes I've gotten from Galveston, and it's either the same pathogen, just as we thought, or one very similar. This thing is so fucking insidious. Do you know what this virus does? Those maniacs were right to call it the Cull. Although 'AB-positive virus' might be a better name..."

Krister clicked off the open microphone, jaw set at a desperate angle, his teeth clenched. "Where the hell is she?" he growled.

"I don't know," Alvin said, staring at the intercom as she went blithely on.

"...Down on the ground? It mutates. But it doesn't just mutate. Viruses have genetic recombination events. Kind of like our chromosomes… little spots in the genetic code like hinges or brittle chain links, where the whole code breaks apart into pieces and comes back together."

"Make a *guess*."

He stared at Krister, half listening to Krister, half listening to Charlie. "Uh…"

"The virus's genetic code… it has a head, and that's very, very stable. But there's a long, long tail to its genes, and it's very brittle, full of fragile chain links. It breaks into dozens of pieces that come back together almost randomly, every time it infects a cell and makes that cell build copies of itself."

"*Where?*" Krister demanded.

Alvin swallowed. "She'll have been working somewhere with a glovebox. Maybe the JEM."

"It's so precise," she murmured into the microphone. "Each little piece of its scrambled genetic code needs to link into the next bit to do anything, otherwise it's almost inert. But when it does? When one random little scrambled set of genes finds the next piece in the chain, links up correctly?"

"We have to find her. Come." With that, Krister twisted around, kicked off a railing, and shot through the nearest hatch. Alvin struggled to keep up.

"Occasionally, just occasionally, it *bonds*. It doesn't break up anymore, it kicks out the recombination zone, and then that part of the genome's stable too. And these stable chains, they're tiny, and it can take them weeks, months to find each other, to stabilize, to unlock another chunk of itself. It's like rolling dice… and if you roll a six, and then another six, and then *another* six in a row, another little piece of the virus is unlocked…"

Krister pulled ahead. *Far* ahead. Alvin struggled to keep up, grabbing the bars in quick hand-over-hand yanks, building up speed and momentum.

"And there's a little piece that breaks down your lungs, and that's in all the strains where people are coughing up blood until they die, and then there's another piece that attacks the gut, and another that causes muscular degeneration, another and another and another, and there's another piece that attacks the brain. A piece that will *drive you crazy*."

If anyone sounded crazy, it was Charlie. Krister had gotten past their sleep stations, was nearly at the hatch to the JEM, Alvin was behind him—

"It kind of—it kind of *eats* the cells in your frontal lobes... it makes you... irrational?" She sounded alone. Lost, scared. "Nobody's done any real research on the effects, there hasn't been time, but, I *think* it'd make a person lose focus, make snap judgements? Not think things through, act on instinct... hear voices, worship trees and fucking rocks, as if everything that made us civilized people just got *ripped out*."

"She's not *here!*" Krister met him at the hatch, swooping out. The JEM's interior was dark. No one had switched on the lights. Krister flew across Harmony and into Columbus, searching, yelling. "Charlie!"

"Whoever made this thing wasn't a civilized person." She went on, as if she hadn't heard him. "And this virus *was* made, obviously designed so that its lethal genes stay dormant long enough for it to infect *everybody*, and then it just sits there until those dice roll six after six after six..."

"Where *are* you, Charlie?" Yegor yelled down the length of Space Station, having emerged into Unity from the Russian section, a thick roll of grey work-tape in his hand.

Alvin looked up the long central row of modules that formed Station's spine, shook his head, cupped his hands around his mouth and yelled back, "She isn't down here!"

"I don't even understand how anyone could do it," she murmured over the intercoms. "Make something like this. I wonder if the ones who did were the ones who put the mice up here, with us? I had friends on the ground look into it, since Mission Control won't do anything. The university department that sent it up here? It's a fucking *storage* closet in a university building, ten miles away from Lake Erie. There's nothing there but dusty lab equipment."

Yegor's muttered response was lost in the distance. He darted from hatch to hatch, and Alvin moved up toward him.

Rolan wriggled through the choked PMA tube, looking around quizzically. He had another roll of the grey tape, tied to one of his belt-loops with a piece of string. "I don't think she's in the Russian section." The tape, Alvin recalled, was specified to be used as a restraint in the event of a psychotic or suicidal emergency.

"Of course you couldn't make this virus with dusty lab equipment," Charlie said, wherever she was hiding. Rambling. "They fucked it up, though, so maybe they weren't all that smart. There's a part of the virus that's supposed to steal part of you. Use your genes and the antigens *your* body thinks are parts of you to make your cells stop dividing and start pumping out proteins to line its capsid with... except all the strains they've found were already locked in. They'd rolled all their sixes too soon, and some Caucasian woman with AB-positive blood? The virus is using fragments of her like a ring of keys, trying each one in your immune system's locks until it finds a way in..."

The longer she went on, the more agitated Yegor got, floating across empty space up in Unity, turning around and around, as if he could follow the all-pervasive sound of her voice to find her.

At last Yegor lunged out for the intercom. "Where *are* you? Don't you understand that you've infected everyone on Station by opening that thing!?"

Her voice was cool, calm. Less afraid. "No, I haven't."

"You've exposed us all!"

"I know what I'm doing, Yegor." Her tone turned colder. Defensive. "I have the vaccine, I'm going home, and I'm delivering the seed strain."

Krister came up from his search of Columbus, shrugging helplessly. Alvin, Rolan and Yegor parted, making space for him to join them all huddling around the intercom.

"She's on one of the portable units," Rolan muttered. "No way to tell where she is."

"Split up." Krister pointed up towards the Russian section. "I and Alvin will try there, you try down here. We just keep looking until we find her. Don't hurt her. Use the intercom when you find her and we'll join you, alright?"

The other three nodded, and Alvin climbed up towards the PMA, the tense feeling of being swallowed up overwhelming as he pushed through the cramped space between the bungee-secured white fabric bags. He popped through ahead of

Krister, and silently made his way into Rassvet, where Matvey had died.

The fans were running, but the space was tight, cluttered with loose baggage and cabling that snaked through the module to the Soyuz docked beyond it.

Skin crawling, he edged up to the half-cones of the Soyuz's airlock ajar over the hatch, and called out, "Charlie?"

No answer.

He touched the cold metal of the airlock door, and gave it a shove. It bumped down into the upper part of the Soyuz's storage module, above the actual re-entry capsule. Both were empty, but the Sokol suits—light space suits to wear in the Soyuz itself on launch and re-entry—were loose.

He pulled them apart, but there were only two, not the three white suits that there were supposed to be, one for each passenger. He checked the name plates on each. R. Petrov, and Y. Utkin. Charlie's was missing.

"Shit," Alvin breathed.

Space Station was big. Big enough that Alvin lost track of Krister while searching the Russian section, spotting him once in Zarya, then losing him as he went back up to Zvezda. She could be hiding anywhere. Alvin popped his head through into Zarya and called for Krister, waving him over when he finally showed his face.

"Okay. I think she has her Sokol on." He bit his lip. "You don't think she's outside, do you?"

"Not in a Sokol, and I don't see how she'd cycle the airlock herself." It was true—if she'd just opened the external airlock door without someone running the pumps for her, the blast of decompression would have rung through the whole of Station.

"Go back to the US section," Krister said. "I'll keep searching up here."

Alvin nodded. The American side of the station was larger than the Russian side, after all. "Good luck."

Krister smiled thinly. "Good luck," he said in turn.

The baggage roped down in the PMA was starting to come loose, jostled out from under the bungee cords. Alvin was forced to push one of the tightly packed bags out ahead of him, sending it tumbling into Unity as he slipped out to search each of the side modules in turn.

The PMM, packed thick with food and yet more supplies. Tranquillity, with the Cupola's covers closed, throwing the module into darkness. The American EVA airlock, space suits limply in place and covered up in cloth.

He found Yegor in the Columbus module, his grey hair tousled, matted up around the drill bit lodged in his skull, blood winding up the furrows in the drill's sides.

Black and scarlet specks covered the walls, red droplets flying free with gore-and-pink gobbets of Yegor's brain dancing in twirling patterns of bloody fluid. The bits of flesh left smudges here and there when they bounced off the engineering work station, where the toolkits had spilled open and Velcro-tabbed tools were jostling with the gore in a slow, unhappy race to the air vents' suction.

Yegor's face was the wrong shape, now, and his open eyes were bruised, the whites mottled with blood from broken capillaries. The line of his brow, so thoughtful, had turned Cro-Magnon with the shift of the now loose plates of his skull.

Wicking surface tension was, even as Alvin watched, gradually sucking the blood and mulched brain from Yegor's skull up into a neat wet ball around the drill bit's grooves.

The taste of tin-foil in Alvin's mouth had been replaced with the tang of blood. He'd inhaled the flying spray.

Somehow, he swallowed back his vomit.

CHAPTER SIX

"YEGOR'S DEAD," ALVIN spluttered into the intercom. "Someone. Killed him." He covered his face with his hands, forcing himself to keep swallowing back the slimy feeling in his mouth. "He's in Columbus."

Rolan got on the intercom first. "*What?* What the hell have you done, Charlie?"

Her voice was hoarse. "I didn't do anything! I didn't kill anyone!"

"Bullshit! Yegor accuses you of exposing us to the virus, and now he's dead! The crazy bitch is going to kill us all!"

"I didn't do it!" Charlie screeched.

"Where are you? Come out!"

"What, so you can kill *me?*"

"Rolan, Charlie. Calm down," Krister said, cutting in. "No one is killing anyone. We'll gather in Unity. If we're all together, whoever killed Yegor and Matvey can't harm anyone else. There will be witnesses, three against one. We'll be safe."

"Okay. Okay, fine. But I haven't exposed *anyone* to the virus. I *swear!*"

"We—we need to handle Yegor's body," Alvin murmured. "Do we even *have* two bodybags on Station? Christ."

"We'll figure it out, Alvin. We'll figure it all out." Krister's voice was ice. "Let's just gather in Unity, and be careful, okay?"

"Okay."

Yegor's body drifted slowly. Alvin knew he should touch it. Stabilize it. Latch it down so the old Russian didn't float into anything. But his hands shook, so instead he crawled out of Columbus, clinging to the walls as nausea seeped into him, and carefully picked his way from rail to rail and bar to bar, stopping to breathe, swallow down his spittle until he was ready to continue into Unity.

The gentle hum of the fans greeted him. His mouth tasted horrible, filthy, so he pried an empty liquids packet from the wall rack and moved over to the small galley they gathered around most nights, and filled it at the water dispenser.

He swirled the water around his mouth, body shaking. Could Charlie have done it? He didn't think so. He didn't think any of them could have done it. Krister was trying to keep the mission going, Rolan and Yegor were friends, countrymen. Charlie didn't *need* to kill anybody. But the way she was talking... What she'd said about the virus, the brain. The way she'd been acting, the way those crazies talking about the Cull in Houston had acted.

She hadn't infected *herself*, had she?

Looking around at the carefully picked pastel pinks of Unity's walls, that very calming colour, Alvin realized that he'd been furthest away from Unity, all the way in Columbus at the most distant end of Station, but he'd arrived first. And he was still alone.

"Hello?"

The air fans hissed away, refusing to answer him.

He didn't know where to go. The PMA's throat was choked with drifting bags, an unanchored bungee slowly twirling across the gap.

Panic took him in the gut. *Idiot!* Whoever was the killer had him alone now, and everyone knew exactly where he was.

Alvin threw himself back down Station's central modules, back towards Columbus, where Yegor was dead, where the toolkits had been turned out, where he could grab the Russian EVA hammer—a vicious thing like a dead blow mallet, the head hollow and filled with a pound of steel shot, the base of the grip ending in a nasty double-pointed pry bar.

He stopped cold, grabbing a handrail and jerking himself to a stop, a cold trickle of realization flowing down his spine. There were far better weapons on Station. He looked up, staring at the dark throat of the PMA. Past that was the Russian section, the two Soyuz capsules. And in the Soyuz survival kits, all kinds of survival gear stowed in case they came down in the wilds of Kazakhstan and had to make it on their own for a few nights.

There were wolves on the Kazakh steppes.

There was a single handgun in each of the survival kits.

"Shit," he whispered.

He shoved his toes against the nearest bar, and launched himself back into Unity, past the pastel pink, and into the PMA. He fought away the loose bags, slapped the bungees aside, and fought his way through into Zarya.

"*Fuck! It's gone! They're both fucking gone!*" Rolan's voice spilled from the hatchway to Posik—the Russian EVA airlock, and the second Soyuz docking location.

"Calm down." Krister was just inside the hatch, hands extended placatively. "Put the machete back into the survival kit, Rolan."

"No. I am protecting myself. Both of my countrymen are dead." He pointed with the triangular cleaver-blade, first at Krister, and then at Alvin, as Alvin edged into view at Posik's hatch. "You had better watch out, hm? Now both of you, get out of my way."

Krister looked over his shoulder at Alvin, briefly, without concern. "Rolan, arming yourself will not resolve the situation…"

"Well unless Alvin has the guns, clearly it isn't going to resolve the situation, because that crazy bitch has both of them!"

"Rolan…"

"No! Don't get any closer, Krister. Just back off, and get out of my way." Rolan shoved the machete toward Krister's face.

Krister gave ground, but not much, backing up to the hatch and no further, body spread across it, making himself into a barrier. "Rolan, what are you going to do?"

"Get the damn guns back."

"I can't let you hurt anyone, Rolan."

"No? Two of your crew are dead, Krister." He pushed forward with the machete, lifting it until it touched Krister's face. "Now are you getting out of my way, or not?"

Krister released his hold on the sides of the hatch, unhooked his toes from their niches, and held his hands up and open, letting Rolan push him aside. "Okay, okay…"

Rolan squirmed past, shouldering Krister's gut, derisively snorting as he passed the machete from hand to hand. Neither he, nor Alvin, noticed Krister's arms snaking around his neck. At the first brush of contact, Rolan raised a hand, as though to push Krister further aside, but then Krister tightened his grip.

Krister's hands were close together, as if in devout prayer. But his elbow was hooked under Rolan's throat, and in an instant, he had clenched his hand around the other arm's wrist, and begun to choke Rolan.

Rolan swung blindly with the machete, his grunting turned into strangled choking as Krister flung himself side to side on Rolan's back, trying to evade the knife's twists and turns—suddenly Krister brought up his legs, hooking them around Rolan's chest, one heel dug into Rolan's side, knee lifted and braced under the armpit.

It was getting harder and harder for Rolan to get in a good swipe back at Krister, harder still as Krister twisted about, like a zero-g monkey, kicking his knee into Rolan's armpit. The machete was an awkward right-angled triangle of a blade, its tip a flat edge instead of a point. Not a stabbing weapon at all, more like an art-deco hatchet. Rolan swung harder, harder, but for all his effort all he could do was chisel divots of flesh out of Krister's arms with the tip's square-angled back edge.

Krister roared, twisting his body against Rolan's, releasing Rolan for an instant to ward the machete away, barely enough for Rolan to gulp down a half-breath. "Help me with him, damnit!" Krister shouted.

Alvin was frozen. Staring. He hadn't hit anyone in twenty years, since middle school.

Rolan struggled to breathe, weakening, but even so, Krister's arms were bloodied, his face scratched, and he had to twist away unnaturally to keep away from steel and fingers. That gave Rolan an opportunity to suck down another breath.

Head cleared, Rolan explosively kicked out at one of the walls, rocketing him and Krister backwards into the hatch edge. The small of Krister's back hit the metal ring first—he cried out, and Rolan carefully passed the machete from hand to hand... gripped to turn the sharp edge toward himself and Krister.

Before Rolan could go from taking divots of skin out of Krister to something altogether more lethal, Alvin leapt forward, grabbing hold of Rolan's wrist, pulling hard, planting his feet on Rolan's chest to wrestle the blade away. The machete bumped into his chest once, twice... a third time, but the chisel-like edge needed more force than that to bite into him.

Rolan blinked wounded betrayal at Alvin, and Krister tightened his grip.

At last, Rolan went limp, and released the machete. Unconscious, Alvin thought for a moment, but he croaked from within Krister's grip. Krister slackened his hold briefly once Alvin had knocked the machete away.

"I give up," Rolan whimpered.

Krister's face relaxed, although his palm against Rolan's cheek, grinding his throat against the inside of his elbow, stayed firm. He re-locked his legs around Rolan's chest. "Get the tape."

Alvin snatched away the roll of grey tape from its string at Rolan's waist, intended for restraining Charlie, and gladly wrapped up Rolan's ankles, then his wrists, panting down frightened breaths.

Krister drifted away, grabbing at the bungee loose in the PMA.

"You have made a mistake," Rolan groaned. "I am not the killer."

Alvin struggled to swallow back the acrid taste in his mouth. "You were going to kill Charlie, Krister too."

"I am *defending myself!*" he shouted, struggling for a moment, just a moment, before letting Krister wrap the bungee around his arms and chest, binding his elbows to his stomach, then Alvin helped to haul Rolan out through Zvezda and into Zarya, using the bungee's hooked ends to hold him on one of the handrails well away from any of Station's control panels.

Krister drifted back, wiping his face, the wounds on his arms. The blood hadn't really *flowed* in the lack of gravity, though it had drawn trails on his arms as he'd fought, drops clinging to his skin and rolling across it.

"Here," Alvin said, pulling open one of the bags bungeed down on Zarya's 'floor.' He passed an unopened, shrink-wrapped box of wet-wipes to Krister.

"You need to scan the bar codes, if you're taking it out of inventory." Krister laughed, faintly.

Alvin smiled back, without any enthusiasm. "I'll do it later."

"*Insane bastards,*" Rolan muttered in guttural Russian. "Are you just going to leave me hanging here while that bitch is running loose on Station? She'll kill me."

"No one is killing anyone," Krister said.

"Not so long as you get away from that hatch," she said.

Charlie hung in the dark space of the PMA. Her eyes were bloodshot, behind the sights of the Makarov pistols in each hand. The white of her Sokol suit matched the storage bags drifting out around her, her legs still wedged between them. A drill floated away behind her, modified into an impromptu centrifuge by taping cleaned-out plastic bottles to the bit.

So that's where she'd been hiding. No wonder the PMA had seemed so claustrophobic. She'd burrowed her way in behind the baggage to finish her work, undisturbed.

Clear plastic bags were lashed to her wrists. One held the sample container, the other, a sheaf of syringes held together with rubber bands.

"Get away from the hatch, Krister. I'm taking the samples home, now." She clenched her jaw, throat working slowly.

"No, you're not." He slipped between her and Rolan, hands out to the sides. Placating, just like he'd been with Rolan.

"Yes," she growled. "I am."

"You're not going to shoot me," Krister went on, nudging a foot against the wall to drift closer. "You're going to turn over the guns, and everything is going to be fine. The situation is under control, no one's going to hurt you, no one's going to *get* hurt..."

"Back *off*, Alvin." She swivelled one of the guns in Alvin's direction, pointing it at his gut... but her eyes were on Krister. Her hands steady.

Alvin froze where he was. He hadn't reached out to her, he'd just started edging towards one wall of the module, to her side. He hadn't been doing anything threatening, he'd just—

"Get away," Charlie hissed, "or I'll kill the both of you."

"See? See!?" Rolan yowled. "She's going to kill all of us."

Alvin scrambled backward. "Charlie, calm down, please, it doesn't have to be like this."

"You aren't going to shoot anyone. Are you?" Krister reached out for the gun, slowly, gently, unthreateningly.

The gunshot was the loudest thing Alvin had ever heard, louder than the rockets at launch, louder than *anything*. The blast of gunfire reverberated off every surface, the pressure wave throbbing within the pressurized environment of Station, tearing through his ears until the roar faded out on Krister's screams. He was twisting, shaking in the air, blood pouring out of his arm, feet scrabbling for purchase on the walls, trying to find something to hook against but simply pushing himself away and up and into an agonizing spin, while Charlie simply glared.

"Actually, Krister, yes," she murmured. "I *am* going to shoot anyone I fucking please. Now stay away from me."

NATURALLY, CHARLIE WAS in charge of the schedule now. The first thing she made Alvin do was check for an exit wound. The second thing, since there was a crater in the back of Krister's arm where the bullet had torn out of him, was to find the bullet. Krister, working under gunpoint, helped Alvin comb the section until they found the pockmark in one of Zarya's storage lockers, and the bullet 'safely' nestled in a blown-open package of air sampling units. Only then, certain that

Station hadn't been holed, did Charlie order Alvin to patch up Krister's arm.

Rolan had been moved down Station to Matvey's old sleep pod, given that he refused to stop shouting at them, leaving Krister to clutch his arm and watch, bug-eyed and bleary on painkillers.

"Charlie, please, I want to go home too…"

She ignored Alvin, one gun strapped to her wrist in place of her precious bags, the other duct-taped to her suit. She pulled away another of the cables hooking the Soyuz into Space Station's power supply, and shoved it through the hatch, glaring at Alvin hovering so far above her. "If you come down here, I'll kill you, Alvin."

"I didn't—I'm not going to—*Charlie*, you know me better than that."

"I don't know *any* of you anymore." She gave the next cable a shove, leaving it to twist over the Soyuz's hatch, and vanished back into its depths.

Krister sucked down a breath, and croaked, "It's the vaccine. She's injected herself with formaldehyde and infected herself with the virus. You heard what she said, the virus drives you mad."

Not Charlie. She wouldn't do that to herself. Would she?

Alvin held himself well above the hatch, where she'd left him. "Charlie," he tried. "I want to go home, too. Let me go home with you. Please."

"Take your own damn Soyuz, Alvin." She appeared at the hatch, holding the Soyuz's airlock doors open, glaring up at him. "This one's mine, the rest of you can fit in the other one."

"What about Yegor and Matvey's bodies? Rolan? That's Yegor and Rolan's Soyuz, too. Are you taking Rolan and Yegor with you?"

Charlie stayed put, watching him. Silent, now.

"Rolan's seat is in that Soyuz. His suit is in there. Krister and I can't take him with us, Matvey's a lot shorter than Rolan, he won't fit in Matvey's seat. If he's not snug in that seat when the Soyuz hits the ground…"

She continued to stare at him, cat-like.

They had all spent hours being fitted for their Soyuz seats. They were like cradles, hand-carved to fit them exactly. It wasn't for the force of the launch, but the landing. The Soyuz capsule had parachutes, but it hit the ground with the force of a car crash, even with the cushion of fire provided by the retro rockets that triggered an instant before landing. The rockets and the parachute slowed it enough to be safe. Safe, at least, for an astronaut snug in a form-fitting seat designed specifically to support them in that instant of impact.

Charlie's seat was in her Soyuz, along with Rolan and Yegor's. If she took Rolan's seat, she doomed him.

"Please, Charlie. We can take out Rolan's seat and put in mine. You're going to try and get it to land in Texas anyway, aren't you?" He could feel the desperation in his voice, and hated it. "That's where I want to be; the Russians probably won't even let me go home. You trust me. You know me. And I trust you. All I want to do is get home to Marla."

"I have a mission," she said, voice wavering. "I have to get the samples home. To Galveston. Stop the pandemic. You going to help me?"

"I want to stop it too."

Charlie scrunched her eyes shut. Shivered. "Fine. Get your suit and seat."

Alvin nodded and scrambled away for the next junction in the Russian section, to the other Soyuz.

Krister met him, smiling. "Good. You've bought time, now we have to secure Space Station..."

"No, Krister. I'm going home. Two of us are dead, both capsules have to return now."

Krister stopped, still clutching the pressure bandages on his arm, and stared at him. "We need to keep Space Station manned and flying, Alvin. She killed Yegor and Matvey, we need to get her restrained. Mission Control makes the next decision, not us."

"I don't know that she killed them."

"She wants to go home to her *family*. Killing Yegor ensured her capsule would return home."

Alvin locked eyes with Krister. "How do you know I didn't kill them? I want to go home, too."

Krister searched Alvin's eyes. "You're not a killer," he said, at last. "I know that much."

Alvin looked away first, and pulled himself into the second Soyuz.

While he suited up in his Sokol, skipping the safety checks with the intent of running through them with Charlie later, he heard her shout at Krister to stay away from the hatches. Alvin started pulling his seat free from the capsule's hull, and Krister came by to check on him. Then the Swede simply drifted off, no doubt to consult with Mission Control.

Mission Control could go to hell.

Finally, forty tense minutes later, Alvin was ready to transfer his seat. He knocked on the hatch, and Charlie stared hard at him through the narrow gap.

"Okay," she said. "We're ready here."

She pulled open the Soyuz's lock properly, and pushed Rolan's suit out first. Alvin pulled it along and left it to drift back through the docking module. Then, Rolan's seat. It was bulkier than the suit, and she struggled with it in the tight space, until at last she relented, letting Alvin get in closer to help pull it through and leave it to drift in the docking module.

"Okay," she said. "Go ahead and get your seat installed." She pulled back the faceplate of her Sokol and came out into the docking module, gun loosely in her hand.

Her eyes were bloodshot. Alvin's first fear was that it was infection, but... no. He knew those rings under her eyes. "You haven't slept, have you?"

"Not since we found Matvey." She grit her teeth. "First thing I did was grab the guns. Been thinking about it since the attack on Houston. If Rolan got to them first..."

"You think Rolan killed them?"

"No." Charlie tightened her grip on the gun in her hand. "I think you killed them."

He froze.

"You and me. We're the only ones who really want to go home. If one of the others dies, everyone on their Soyuz has to go back." She wet her lips. "And that's why you killed Matvey, isn't it?"

Alvin couldn't help but focus on the gun. There was something about the shadow inside a pistol's barrel that drew the eye's attention.

"And by the same logic," she murmured, "I'm the only one who could have wanted to kill Yegor. So one way or another, at least ground control can know the killer's off the station, and Krister can keep things going up here as long as he wants." She smiled crookedly. "So this is a win-win, isn't it?"

"I didn't kill anyone," Alvin whispered.

"After that *bullshit*, with you telling me Matvey 'fell asleep'? Fuck you, Alvin! I *trusted you* and you lied to me!" The smile vanished.

"I—I *didn't*."

"No? Then I guess it was me." She jerked the gun toward the Soyuz hatch. "They'll figure out this whole mess on the ground."

There was nothing he could do except stare at her in disbelief.

"We'll get the vaccine in you, get you on the ground, and then you can fucking go home to Marla." Her voice was strangled. "I hope you're proud of yourself, Alvin."

He stared at her, the tin-foil back in his mouth. "I didn't."

"Just get your seat secured and let's go home." She lifted the gun, face cold again.

"Okay." He let himself breathe, shuddering breaths that threatened to turn to sobs. But he had to concentrate on putting the seat in place. He pushed it through into the Soyuz, and counted his bolts one by one, like a man praying the rosary.

He pulled off his Sokol gloves while he worked, let them drift, painfully aware of Charlie hovering over the hatch, staring down at him as he worked, lost in thought. Thinking that he'd killed Matvey.

But if she hadn't killed them...

He looked up through the Soyuz. "Charlie..."

Her hand was tense on the pistol. She turned her head to look up, away from him, her hair a nimbus around her face.

Charlie opened her mouth to speak, twisted in surprise, and got out, "Kris—" before jerking out of sight with a strangled yawp.

"Charlie!"

Everything was too crowded, too cramped. His seat crushed him against a wall as he tried to move; he had to back away and lever it aside while she screamed and the first bloody *tchok* of sound was met with another gunshot, another—

"Alvin!"

Krister was at the hatch, in the process of pulling her out of the docking module. But she had the gun, had it pointed at him—he let go of her and pushed the gun aside, and Charlie was screaming, blood pouring out of a gash in her suit, the perfect white turning slick red as baubles of her blood floated free. Distantly, Alvin could hear the depressurization alarm.

She screamed.

Alvin clawed at the Soyuz's hatch door, kicked free only to jerk back to a wrenching halt, his suit snagged on the docking latches.

Krister beat the machete down into her face. The blade split her skin and exposed scarlet meat with a crunch of bone.

Charlie stopped screaming. She drifted serenely backwards, trailing globes of blood, her hair gently wafting forward to hide her face, cover her wound, and show just the machete handle sticking free.

Now Alvin screamed, like he never knew he could scream, kicking and tearing at the hatch, launching himself at Krister with just his fists and nothing else and—

A whirl of limbs, caught in a maddening tangle. Something hot on his face, as Krister swung him around—a splash of Charlie's blood. Krister's teeth gritted, arms locked around Alvin's waist. "Damnit, Alvin!" The crunch of Alvin's knee against the module wall as he lashed out. "Stop it!"

Alvin didn't stop. Alvin struggled and writhed, and the keening of the alarm came back to him as Krister barked out, "Station is leaking!"

But Alvin didn't give a shit about Station anymore. He got his fingers into Krister's arm, under the bandages and *into* Krister's arm, alive and wet, and Alvin fled the bigger man's grip as pain folded him double. Alvin kicked himself away from the whining of alarms, and the gentle drift of air being sucked into space.

Alvin fled. He squirmed through the PMA, choked for a moment in the drifting baggage blocking the tunnel, only to burst free and send himself flying-falling-screaming through

Unity and down Station's spine, plummeting straight and true until he grabbed a bar and stopped himself, just above Matvey's sleep pod.

"Rolan? Rolan, fuck, I'm sorry, you were—"

Rolan's throat had been cut. Blood lined the seam between the sleep pod's doors, drifted away in broken droplets the moment he'd opened it to see Rolan's trussed corpse drifting listlessly.

He'd done it. Alvin had helped. Had *helped* Krister do it.

Alvin cast about, he didn't know where the fuck to hide from his mistakes, from his sins. He stopped. Rolan still had everything he'd been planning to use on Charlie, didn't he? They'd stuffed the tape back into his pockets.

Alvin fought down his disgust, and started frisking Rolan's corpse.

After a moment the alarms keening from the Russian segment stopped. And then Krister appeared at the PMA hatch, far above, pushing free of the baggage-snarl.

"Alvin—"

He bolted. Down, down and away, with a kick at the wall to send him careening into Columbus.

Yegor was still there. Still dead. And so were the tools. Alvin threw himself aside, shut his mouth and tried not to inhale Yegor's congealing blood while he searched for the Russian EVA hammer.

He could *feel* Krister behind him, and just as he touched the hammer's cold metal, and turned, gripping the long handle in both hands, he heard, "Alvin. Stop. You need to stop, calm down, and listen to me now."

Heart pounding in his chest, Alvin turned, hammer raised, angled back-spike facing outward, and waited for the attack.

The attack didn't come. Krister didn't even have the machete anymore. He simply drifted at the hatch to Columbus, behind Yegor's floating corpse, hands open, placating.

Alvin had seen that before.

"It's okay now," Krister said, gently.

"It fucking isn't."

"Zvezda is depressurizing, but I have the hatches shut. It's no longer an emergency, Alvin. Now, just… just listen to me."

*   *   *

KRISTER HAD KILLED Matvey. Matvey had been watching his movie, and Krister had switched off the fans, and then put him in a headlock until Matvey had fallen unconscious and left him there to die in the still air. One of those things Krister had learned how to do in Sweden's air force.

Then, yes, he had killed Yegor. The drill was just... expedient. Krister had been worried about Rolan, but with Alvin's help it had gone alright, and, well. Alvin had seen him kill Charlie, but it was worth confessing that Rolan had died shortly after Alvin had started messing around with the Soyuz seats.

The truth was, "You're the only one who can do it, Alvin."

Alvin had both of Charlie's guns.

Krister had given them both to Alvin, and that was, perhaps, the only reason they were now speaking in Tranquillity, over the Cupola, with Earth far below them.

"What do you mean, I'm the only one who can do it?" Alvin had his finger curled over the trigger-guard, and the gun pointed at Krister.

Krister kept his hands apart. Body language open. Charlie's blood on his shirt, in his hair, mixed with some of Rolan's and the bandaged smear of his own gore around his arm, made a mockery of what Krister was trying to express. Calm and peaceful friendliness.

"Of us all, you're the only one with any involvement in the actual construction of systems on Space Station. The rest of us, we actually *need* the ground to keep Station running. We're like people struggling with DVD players or toasters or whatever overcomplicated appliance has fallen into our hands." Krister took a level breath. "We need guides that set out everything step by step, and if we were never trained to do it, we're in trouble. I saw it when you fixed the antenna—you know how these things work, Alvin. You're the one who can maintain Space Station."

The tin-foil in his mouth was steadily giving way to acid. Alvin fought down the urge to retch. "What?" His voice was quiet. So very quiet.

"The pandemic down there is going to kill everyone."

Krister breathed slowly, forcefully. Keeping himself calm. "A vaccine? It's too late, Alvin. They're all infected, down there. Tonight, it's going to be more than a million people dead. Tomorrow, more than two million, and by the end of the week hundreds of millions will be dead. It's too late to use a vaccine, even if it worked. It's too late for us to do anything, Alvin."

"But we've *got* it. She, she *made* a vaccine... She knows... *knew* what she was doing!"

"You heard her. I read the research papers just like she did. The virus covers itself in a coat of the body's own antigens. A vaccine sensitizes the immune system to react to antigens." Krister smiled, weakly. "You can't vaccinate yourself against your own cells, Alvin."

"It *has to work*." Alvin put his hands to his face, the gun cold against his cheek. "Charlie made a vaccine and it has to work, then we have to, to bring the samples to Galveston and they can make more of the vaccine and—"

"It's not going to happen. It would take months, even if it could be done, and in months *everyone* will be dead. If we go down there, we'll catch the pandemic, and we will die like the rest of them. You hear me?"

Alvin stared at Krister's legs, too afraid to look into his eyes. "I hear you."

"This plague is going to wipe out almost all of humanity. And you have to survive, because when things calm down on the ground, when there can be said to be anything like 'survivors,' they're going to be in a very different world—" Krister choked on his words. His eyes were watering, but he didn't try and clear them. "They're not going to have schools, they're not going to have telescopes, they're not going to have antibiotics, they're not going to have even the basics of a civilization left. Not unless there's someone to teach them what those things are. Someone to steward it all."

Krister squeezed his eyes shut. Bit by bit, his eyelids were covered in a film of tears. "And that has to be you, Alvin. You're the one who can teach. Who can use that ham radio to stay in touch with the ground. You know more languages than the rest of us; English, Spanish, French, Russian—you could learn more if you had to, couldn't you?" He spluttered out the words, almost begging.

"I—I could," Alvin stammered.

"There's enough time still for ground to give you the bandwidth from the Ku band satellites, upload textbooks on just about everything. This is a disaster, Alvin, but—but afterward? Clean sciences. By the time they're ready, the world will be so much cleaner. If you teach them, they can skip the polluting industrial ages, go right to clean energy sources, live in harmony." Krister smiled, eyes tight shut. "This could be the best thing that ever happened to mankind.

"And that's why I had to kill them, Alvin, because you have to survive, and you're not a killer. I'm a killer," Krister said, breathing unevenly. "I can do what needs to be done, and this way, this way you don't have that on your head. But now, now there's six times as much food for you to survive on, six times as much water, air, power, everything. You'll be able to keep things going up here for *years,*" Krister babbled, "if you have to you can store the bodies outside, in the station's shadow they'll freeze, you could live off them for months more—"

"*Shut up!*" Alvin yelled.

Krister drifted back, stunned.

Alvin shook his head violently. He couldn't take it, couldn't believe Krister was right. "They've—they've got to have prepared something like that on the ground. Somewhere safe, some—some bunker somewhere."

"Just look," Krister said, gesturing down at the Earth below them.

It was morning, still, by Station's clocks. Night, below. The west coast. California. And even as Alvin watched the world turn by, below, he could see that the sparkle of lights wobbling down the coast, from city to city, was uneven. Patches of LA and the Bay Area were dark. The Nevada desert was filled with shadows where Las Vegas should have been blazing all the vice and sin of its neon glory up at the sky.

"They're dying. Nobody thought this would happen. Call up the ground, Alvin. Ask them to put you through to the bunkers under the White House, or find someone to answer questions about those damn mice... they're not there anymore, Alvin. They're dead, they're running away... No one's there."

"No," Alvin murmured.

"I killed them so you wouldn't have to, Alvin. It has to be this way."

"*No*. I'm supposed to go home, I'm supposed to find Marla—"

Krister slipped past the pistol, and wrapped his arms around Alvin. His embrace was sickeningly warm and reassuring. "It's okay, Alvin. You're an innocent; it was all me, my sin to bear, not yours. You won't even have to put up with me, I'll be gone." Krister's voice wavered back and forth, guilt warring with a desperate childlike need to be told it was alright. That he'd done the right thing. "When things are alright, and you're ready, I can, I can just go to sleep in Rassvet like Matvey did ..."

Maybe Krister *was* right.

Maybe.

Alvin hugged him back. "Krister?"

"Yes?"

"I'm sorry."

Alvin pulled the hypodermic syringe of Valium from his pocket, and jabbed it into the inside of Krister's thigh.

Step three in the procedure manual's entry under 'Restraining a crewmate experiencing a psychotic episode,' after explaining that the restraints were for their own safety as well as the rest of the crew's (step one), and the application of restraints (step two), was the administration of five to thirty milligrams of Valium, depending on the level of distress.

Rolan, like Krister, was a man who did everything by the book. He'd had the tape to restrain Charlie ready, and the syringe in his back pocket.

Krister sagged against Alvin like a boneless sack of water.

"If you want to do this," Alvin murmured, "struggle to survive all alone for years and years just to try and teach people how to make antibiotics after the *end of the world*, eating your friend's bodies, you do it. Don't make me do it. I didn't do anything to deserve that." Alvin wiped the tears from his eyes. "I'm going home, Krister. I don't care if I die, I want to see Marla first."

Krister clawed meekly at Alvin's chest. "You can't," he slurred. "I did it for you, I killed our friends so you wouldn't have to, I'm supposed to die now—"

"Nobody was supposed to die." Alvin shook him off. "That was the point of the mission. Not *this*."

Then Alvin went home.

CHAPTER SEVEN

THERE WAS NOTHING like the roar of a Soyuz. It was, as far as Alvin was concerned, flat on his back in his seat, strapped tight in his Sokol, unique. And he was lucky enough to experience it twice. The launch, at least. He likely wasn't coming home again.

Charlie had been wrong, and Krister had been right.

In the two months since Alvin's return, the world had fallen to pieces. Nobody had a plan. Nobody sane, at any rate.

Gangs of maniacs were tearing through the dying Eastern Seaboard, from Florida all the way up to Boston, calling themselves Klans with pride as they killed and pillaged, while what was left of the National Guard and Army pulled out to 'preserve national resources.' Quarantine and clean-up teams in the United Kingdom had gone ape-shit, burning towns to the ground in an attempt to 'sterilize' the pandemic, in a misguided attempt to leave something for their children to inherit. As the Russian government collapsed, criminals took over. China was a starving, pandemic-ridden mess, Tibet finally free in the midst of governmental collapse. Japan had closed up its borders and gone quiet. Africa, South America?

As had always been the case, nobody wanted to hear what little news trickled up over the equator of the horrors in far-away places.

The world was coming to an end, and there was nothing anyone could do. Krister's plan to provide 'stewardship' had been rational.

As for Charlie… Charlie had been so sure her vaccine would work, and so certain that the pandemic, the Cull, the Blight, the AB virus, would continue its exponential lethality indefinitely. She'd been wrong on both counts.

By the end of Alvin's two months back on earth, four and a half billion people were dead, when by Charlie's predictions the population of the Earth should have died ten times over in thirty-six days. Not even the pandemic had managed that.

Corpses littered the streets in the cities and towns that ultra-lethal strains had swept through, slaughtering entire communities in days before driving themselves extinct by killing every possible host. In the few enclaves of life left, everyone was waiting for the next deadly strain to emerge, waiting for the virus's terrible internal clockwork to spin the chamber and play a game of biological Russian roulette, pulling the trigger again and again until the pandemic finally killed them all.

But the O-negatives had survived. A few rare, lucky souls—those whose genes were different enough from the theoretical Caucasian AB-positive patient zero that the virus had stolen its antigenic cladding from—had survived. And so had Alvin.

Charlie's vaccine could only save those who had never been exposed to the virus, before the virus had begun its grim work of finding its way under the body's defences. Once the virus took hold, as it had in almost every person on the planet, it formed viral reservoirs that no one but an O-neg could ever clear, no matter what vaccine was tried.

Perhaps Pandora, whoever 'Pandora' had been, could have stopped the pandemic before it began, if only the seed strain they'd farmed in that damn mousebox had reached them in time. But in all probability, by the time the experiment had launched to orbit, the pandemic had already been spreading. It had, as Krister had said, been far, far too late.

There had been some talk at Galveston that by using a massive infusion of A, B, and Rhesus-positive antibodies, all of which were native in O-negative blood, that the body could be given a temporary respite from the virus, at the risk of anaphylaxis and auto-immune disorders as the immune system fought against what would amount to a full-volume blood transfusion of the wrong blood type... but no one had been crazy enough to try it, yet. Maybe, like the mice, someone would figure out a way to change a human's blood-group from one to another... But after killing four fifths of the human race, the remaining percentage of humanity susceptible to the virus wouldn't survive past the end of the month, let alone until clinical trials for unknown procedures could be completed.

There hadn't been any hope for Charlie's family, or for Alvin's wife.

Marla hadn't been showing symptoms by the time Alvin found her, but she'd been infected, just like everyone else. Alvin had read her poetry, and she had gotten dead drunk on old whiskey, and they'd laughed for as long as it was possible for them to laugh.

It was unfair that Alvin lived and Marla died, and he would have given anything to trade places with her, but he was the only person on the planet who hadn't been infected, who could be saved by Charlie's vaccine.

Of course, there was one man alive who *wasn't* on the planet. And damn him for being right.

The final expedition to the International Space Station, made up of Alvin Burrows, Harry Stone, and Fedot Lagunov, had launched from the now abandoned ruins of Baikonur Cosmodrome. Their friends, the last surviving O-neg astronauts, stayed behind to watch them vanish into the sky on a column of flame, carrying supplies and a payload of small-print books and DVDs containing copies of just about every useful textbook it was possible to find between Alvin's return and the second launch.

Finally, two days later, they arrived and docked to Space Station. Alvin and the others vented their air, remaining snug in their Sokols, and waited for any viral particles they'd brought with them to blow out into space. With new air cycled in, certain they wouldn't infect Station, they at last opened the hatch.

Alvin drifted through the once familiar modules, reacquainting himself with the sweet sensation of freefall, even as the memories of what Space Station had become sat bitterly in his gut.

Contact with Krister had always been spotty. He spent most of his time, as he told the skeletal staff that remained at Mission Control, 'straightening up' Space Station. Making it ready for the next expedition.

They had discussed procedures for ensuring Station would remain sterile long enough to give the last uninfected man in existence his dose of the vaccine. They had read him step by step instructions, so he could repair the water reclamation systems like a man going through the troubleshooting guide for his DVD player. But in his heart, Alvin knew what they would find on arrival.

Krister, fast asleep in Rassvet, the recirculation fans and vents all still, with a bungee noose clinched tight around his neck.

In a way, Alvin was glad it ended like this. He wasn't sure he could live with what he'd done, but now it didn't matter.

He went to the Cupola, to sit and remember kissing Marla before she'd died. Stroking her hair, talking about old times, and reading her love poetry in a half-dozen languages she didn't understand. He'd had to tell her, over and over, that it was alright. That he couldn't be infected. Then she'd settled back with her whisky, sipped it, and kissed him, the taste of her sharp in his mouth.

He'd kissed her hard and long, loved her with all his heart, and then, with the taste of her still in his mouth, carefully spat as much of the virus as he could into a vial of saline solution that he'd palmed and switched for Krister's dose of the vaccine back on the ground.

Krister had been right. Alvin wasn't a killer, if only because he'd had his chance stolen from him.

Below Space Station, bit by bit, darkness fell upon the Earth. There was an occasional flash of pure, atomic-white light, and the untended factories and power generators gradually shut down and broke themselves to bits, burning and pouring smog into the skies and poison into the earth. In time, there were no cities gleaming in the night below, no light. Just shadows, and day by day, month by month, those left in the shadows below struggled and died. At last, the only lights left were scattered across the sky, gently blinking away...

"Hello. My name is Camille, and I'm twelve years old. My question for Alvin is, how can I make sure water is safe to drink?"

"Hi, Camille. What a great question."

THE END

ABOUT THE AUTHOR

Malcolm Cross lives in London and enjoys the personal space and privacy that the city is known for. When not misdirecting tourists to nonexistent landmarks, Malcolm is likely to be writing science fiction and fantasy. A member of the furry fandom, he won the 2012 Ursa Major Award for Best Anthropomorphic Short Fiction.

Malcolm's blood-type is O-positive, and he has a cough. Not long, now...

He can be found online at
http://www.sinisbeautiful.com

DEAD KELLY

CB HARVEY

CHAPTER ONE

"SAY IT AGAIN." McGuire's tone was measured, you might even say good-natured. He didn't look up, apparently fascinated by a curved scar running the length of his broad hand. Only when a moment had passed without response did he return his attention to the figure before him. The man lay crumpled on the cracked parquet floor, his limbs bent at unlikely angles. A bubble of blood issued from the corner of the man's swollen mouth, and a shallow, indistinguishable murmur followed.

McGuire stepped forward and crouched beside the figure. The man's glassy, wide eyes blinked once, slowly. McGuire very carefully pushed aside a matted lock of the man's hair and held his lips close to his scabby ear. "I'm sorry," McGuire whispered sweetly, "I didn't quite get that."

With a cough and a bloody froth, the man spoke again, louder. "Zircnosk," he hissed, his ruined body trembling.

McGuire straightened up, his thickset, grizzled features suddenly animated. He whirled around to address the squat bloke who stood propped in the doorway, arms folded, watching.

"Fuckin' Zircnosk!" McGuire exclaimed, in his excitement almost tripping over a cable snaking across the floor.

"Fuckin' A," responded Baxter, with practised nonchalance, returning to the stubby roll-up cigarette he'd been nursing for the past hour or so. When he noticed that McGuire was gazing at him he grinned, with yellow, uneven teeth. His eyes darted back and forth between McGuire, the man on the floor, and a fizzing television screen showing fleeting red and black shapes and patterns.

McGuire bounded up to Baxter and grabbed the smaller man by the face, crushing his pockmarked features together and forcing him to look directly at him.

"You've no fuckin' idea who Zircnosk is, have you?" McGuire searched his friend's expression.

"No," acknowledged Baxter awkwardly. "Sorry, Boss."

McGuire let out a full throated laugh and released the squat little man with a playful slap on the face. "Only Jack *fucking* Zircnosk."

Baxter's grin remained fixed, brow furrowed.

"Didn't you ever read the fuckin' papers, mate, or watch anything other than porn?" asked McGuire, but Baxter's expression stayed blank. The bigger man sighed. "The bloke that nailed the Montgomerys?" Still nothing. "He was a copper, mate. A fuckin' tough nut, too. Makes perfect sense."

Now Baxter inclined his head a fraction in apparent recognition. "Oh, yeah. The Montgomerys. Bastards."

McGuire stared at him. "Jesus Christ," he muttered.

Baxter's ripped black T-shirt offered glimpses of a striated burn scar that enveloped a substantial portion of the man's torso, his left shoulder and the lower part of his neck. McGuire found Baxter frustrating in the extreme, but he was loyal and normally reliable in carrying out focussed—you might even say *simple*—tasks. As he gazed at him, McGuire noted with pleasure a touch of fear entering into those otherwise empty eyes. The poor fucker wasn't entirely without sentience. Abruptly McGuire clapped Baxter heartily on the shoulder. "Don't worry, mate. The important point is we're one step closer. *Capiche?*"

Baxter nodded again, more vigorously, presumably at pains

to indicate his understanding, "Yeah, I capiche, Boss. You want me to find out if this Zircnosk fella's still kicking?"

McGuire licked his dry lips. "You got it, man. And if not him, then one of his underlings. One of 'em has gotta know something."

Baxter's forehead creased again; McGuire could almost hear the intermittent sparking of his synapses. "Um, there was a camera, boss. When we brought this guy in. Nice piece of kit. Wilcox thought we might use it for the, y'know, television station. Y'know, if we can get it running."

"Ah, right," nodded McGuire, suddenly thoughtful. "Good idea. Speak to the masses. I like it. Only..." His eyes alighted on the cable feeding from the back of the television set and disappearing beneath the man on the floor. Baxter's gaze followed the cable too, before flicking to the television. Across the screen flittered largely indeterminate red and black shapes, and then occasionally something pumping, bloody and oddly familiar.

"Oh," said Baxter, unable to contain his disappointment. "So that's where it went."

"Surprisingly good image," observed McGuire. He moved to a table upon which sat a collection of dented, bowed metal shapes, including a crude helmet. McGuire picked up one of the smaller pieces of iron and began to strap it to his shoulder.

"Good thing we got that generator running, eh?" said Baxter cheerfully, stepping forward to help. "No telly without that."

"Uh-huh," nodded McGuire distractedly. By now he'd pulled on both of the iron shoulder plates and was affixing a metal breastplate to himself.

Baxter paused thoughtfully in his attempts to secure a back plate to McGuire. "I guess that screaming was him..."

"'Resisting'?" offered McGuire. "Yeah, there was some resistance. I guess it chafed."

"It's a big camera," reflected Baxter, cigarette still hanging from the corner of his mouth.

"It's called a colonoscopy, mate. Standard procedure."

"Uh-huh," nodded Baxter. "Standard procedure. I see, Boss."

"Are you fixing this armour to me or are you feeling me up, you fucker?"

Baxter sniffed and stepped back. "Sorry, Boss. All done now. What do you want me to do with Laughing Boy here?"

By now McGuire had pulled the iron mask over his head and was carefully positioning the letter box slit over his eyes. He could feel the helmet's history in the sundry dents and bullet holes that scored and ripped its surface. A more recent addition was the stylised skull and crossbones daubed in flaking white paint on the front.

McGuire strode past Baxter, his words muffled. "I don't care, mate. Something creative, eh? And make it quick—the fucker's suffered enough." Before he exited, he swept up two Uzis from their resting place atop a dust-covered mahogany bureau.

He heard the door slamming shut in his wake and continued along the carpeted corridor through the crumbling Romanesque grandeur of the building. Simple and focussed. Yep, that was Baxter. As he clunked down a succession of staircases, his iron suit scraping and clanking with each solid footfall on the torn, dusty carpet, a familiar chant from below became gradually audible.

He emerged amidst the fluted columns atop the building's front steps. Parliament House had been built some one hundred and fifty years previously, the high, vaulted roof and covered entrance designed to ameliorate the worst effects of the Melbourne heat in days long before air conditioning. Clapped in his armour, he welcomed the marginal cool offered by the shade. The fifty or so people gathered in the space beyond enjoyed no such defence from the midday sun. Some had furnished makeshift cowls from their torn, grimy clothes in an effort to protect their burnt, scabby faces, to little real effect. When the Cull happened, sun block disappeared faster than petrol and almost as quickly as tucker.

They were chanting his name with an intensity he had come to expect. Initially he'd speculated—absently, and to himself— that starvation, illness and perpetual fatigue might have dampened it, but it wasn't the case. If anything the mantra had become more resolute, more committed over time. With each utterance of the words they thrust their arms in fist-clenched salute, just like they'd been taught, their features pinched with determination. And there, lurking at the perimeter of the group, were their teachers: muscular, tattooed men and women, hands resting on assault rifles, bandoliers strung across their scarred chests, eyes hidden behind cracked, glinting sunglasses.

McGuire marched along the top of the steps, as ritual demanded, and then back again, his audience's gaze following. As he strode, sweat trickling down his body, he reflected that he owed a debt of gratitude to that poor fucker with the camera shoved up his arse. He'd recognised the sharp-jawed, sharp-suited huckster the moment Baxter and Wilcox brought him in; his name was Danny Kline, a TV presenter host Back in the Day, back before the blight that fucked the world. He'd presented a show called *Livewire*, Tuesday nights on 13th Street. It was a sort of fly-on-the-wall mixture of shitty reconstructions and police helicopter footage, strung together with Kline's earnest to-the-camera homilies. Armed robberies, murders, the bloodier the better. Any gang member worth their scars watched it avidly. During each show Kline would sit on his desk condemning the sickening offences with a twinkle in his eye, a glimmer that told you all you needed to know about the relationship between the criminal classes and the journo fraternity.

Baxter and Wilcox had apparently found Kline wandering around town with his camera, videoing all and sundry, gibbering to anyone who'd listen about the *importance* of what he was doing. His sharp jaw looked like it had been blunted a few dozen times, and his sharp suit had been ripped to buggery, but it was definitely him. Initially McGuire had been a little starstruck, excited to meet a sort of hero. But McGuire had laughed long and hard when he'd realised Kline still spoke in that bizarre patois beloved of local news broadcasters, stringing together disparate subjects to prove some ill-conceived connection. McGuire thought it was probably as much a relief to Kline as it was to him when the torture started and it became increasingly difficult for Kline to talk at all. Ironic that it was only when the gabby fucker had been rendered virtually incapable of speech that McGuire actually extracted the information he needed.

When the shit hit the proverbial fan and McGuire had to run for the Bush, it was Kline that gave him his name, his brand.

Dead Kelly he'd christened him, invoking a title and a legend from another time. The rest of the media had apparently taken it up with drooling enthusiasm; Christ knew it had stuck. Here he was, over two years since Kline had given him the moniker, a full year and a half after the Cull that had eradicated most of humanity. TV, the internet, governance, civil society, that was all gone, but the name endured. So McGuire kinda owed Danny Boy one, and McGuire always returned a favour: that's why he'd told Baxter to make it quick.

Anyway. Better concentrate. Sure the ritual was well-established, but he liked to appreciate the sensation. Otherwise it was just going through the motions, and where was the fun in that? The people would continue shouting his name for as long as he let them, and on occasion he had delighted in making them grow hoarse with their adoration. He let rip with both the submachine guns, a short burst of fire into the air to grab their attention. It did the job, silence descending along with the clatter of the spent cartridges. The crowd panted as they looked to him atop the steps, deep-set eyes wide in anticipation. Nancy the Nun, one of his most trusted lieutenants, strode forward and relieved him of the guns, as protocol decreed.

McGuire turned, reached down and heaved a sack hidden behind one of the columns into view, like some demented fucking Father Christmas. The people seemed to sway together, as though they were one entity, and he noted with delight that some of them were smacking their lips. With a theatrical flourish he reached into the sack and pulled out the first couple of tins. They were dented, and the labels had long since vanished. Christ knew what they contained. A constant feature of life in the post-apocalyptic world was that you never quite knew what each new day would bring, or what was around the next corner. Rarely were the surprises pleasant, it had to be said, and often they were extremely fucking perilous. So somehow it seemed only fitting that the contents of a tin of food be as unpredictable as everything else.

With a sudden fluid movement, he heaved the first of the cans at the audience, and then the second. The first glanced a floppy-haired bloke in his twenties on the side of his skull, and he collapsed backward, much to the merriment of the armed guards looking on. The people scrabbled around and over the young man's jerking form, desperate to seize the prize. The second tin hit the cracked, rubble-strewn paving stones and exploded, sending syrup and some sort of orange fruit in all directions. Probably peaches, McGuire mused.

He launched a third missile. This time a middle-aged woman managed to actually catch the tin. She clutched it defiantly to her bosom, flashing scowls at the encroaching crowd. McGuire watched his soldiers, several of whom were pivoting warily on the spot. They were under instructions to intervene, but only if the situation looked like it might turn nasty. The thing of it was, their judgement couldn't always be relied upon. He knew, as always, that it was up to him to manage the situation.

He lofted the next tin in his hand, then lowered it with mock exhaustion, as though the effort of feeding his people had become too much for him. In response, the frenzied crowd grew suddenly subdued, as if they felt shameful, and the guards in their turn visibly relaxed.

McGuire smiled to himself behind his iron mask. This was what he wanted. It was what *they* wanted: the people, the guards. To be dominated, to be shown what to do, to be shown how to behave in this strange new world where nothing was certain except danger. That was his role, that was why he had become Dead Kelly. All he asked in return was that they give themselves over to him. Absolutely, and in every facet of their being.

Before he could lob the next can he became aware, even within the constraints of the mask, of someone near him, hiding behind one of the fluted columns, out of view of the desperate crowd. McGuire turned and saw a red-haired child peering out at him, green eyes wide in curiosity, stubby hands pressed hard against the edges of the pillar's base. McGuire felt the curved scar on his hand aching.

The child was Dead Kelly's legacy. As he stared at the lad, encased in his iron mask, Kelly McGuire remembered why.

CHAPTER TWO

McGUIRE LOWERED THE binoculars and blinked in the harsh light. He'd identified it as a Cessna the moment it detached itself from the cloudless sky. There was no way this was an intentional landing. The terrain around here was dramatically hilly, and those areas that weren't dominated by snowy gums tended to be rock-strewn heaths or bogs. McGuire half-wondered if the plane was trying for the Alpine Way, although given its trajectory and the way it had begun to pitch dramatically from side to side, it was more likely to end up smacking into the Thredbo.

From his vantage point, in a recess in the rock wall, McGuire listened. Only the rustling of the trees and rippling of the river reached him across the surging landscape. Nothing else. By now he should have been able to hear the plane's engine. It must have stalled. McGuire lifted the binoculars to his eyes and watched as the Cessna's undercarriage skimmed the tops of the trees before becoming entangled, forcing it into a sudden ungraceful flip. As it landed on its top, the crunch of metal reverberated across the landscape, sending a couple of maggies cawing into the sky.

McGuire pulled on his backpack, shouldered his ACR and launched himself down the slope. He hurtled across the rocks, nimble despite his muscular frame, occasionally grabbing for the brim of his Akubra. The crash site came into view some way away, the overturned aircraft suspended among the trees, rocking precariously. The closer he got, the more it became evident that the machine had only narrowly avoided smashing into the river, courtesy of the ancient gums. He could see movement up ahead; a figure on the ground, clearly injured, struggling to pull himself through the undergrowth before the aircraft finished its descent and crushed him. McGuire continued his approach, releasing his backpack and priming the assault rifle.

"Stay where you are," growled McGuire, steadying the weapon on the man.

"Oh, thank God," said the bloke, turning to look at him, offering a sweat-drenched, pallid face. His lower body was caught up in a tangle of branches he must have brought with him as he fell. He'd clearly sustained a leg injury.

McGuire appraised the situation. The fella was short and slight. He didn't constitute any particular threat. The same could not be said for the plane, which screeched menacingly above, its weight beginning to strain the branches to breaking point. After all he'd been through, McGuire was hesitant to risk his own life on a half-arsed rescue attempt. Then again, there was a reasonable chance the bloke might possess some useful information. On balance, probably worth the risk.

McGuire hurled himself toward the man, dropping to a half-kneeling squat as he reached him. He unleashed the Bowie knife from the sheath strapped to his shin, causing the bloke to flinch in horror, unsure as to McGuire's motives. The man relaxed a little as McGuire began to saw through the branches entangling his lower body, grimacing as the gradual release of the branches afforded him abrupt but painful movement. McGuire continued to extract him, his face a mask of determination. Above them, the plane's carcass shrieked like a trapped animal.

The last branch severed, McGuire sheathed the knife, grabbed the man by the shoulders and began dragging him through the undergrowth. The stranger was too injured to move himself, shuddering in pain with every step.

The plane gave an ear-splitting screech and shifted position; McGuire risked a glance upward, then redoubled his efforts. The plane was now hanging vertically, its crushed tail pointing downwards, swaying threateningly. McGuire heaved the man aside just as the Cessna crashed to the ground, its tail concertinaing, wings ripping free as its bulk flopped spectacularly to one side.

McGuire deposited the man on a rock beside the river. He'd either been thrown from the plane or had managed to drop from it after it flipped over. His leg was lacerated to the extent that McGuire could see the bone. No wonder he'd provided such piss-poor assistance in his own rescue.

"What happened?" demanded McGuire.

"It was Greg, my brother. He said he could fly the fuckin' thing. Get us away, see if it was any better in the north..." The man shook his head hopelessly. "We thought we'd be okay. Sure, he had some of the symptoms, but only mild. He said he could fuckin' well fly it. For fuck's sake. I didn't know what to do. There was nowhere to land. This place—"

"What symptoms?" McGuire interjected.

The man stared at him in astonishment. "What? What do you mean?"

"What symptoms?" reasserted McGuire. What little patience he possessed was waning rapidly.

The bloke boggled at him. "How long have you been out here? Don't you *know?*"

"Know what?"

"The fucking epidemic. My God, you don't know..." He peered at McGuire, eyes narrowing. "How can you not fucking know? How fucking long have you been out here?"

McGuire shrugged. "I've been out here... months."

"*Months?*" The bloke said the word like he could barely comprehend what it meant. Then suddenly he was garbling, the words cascading from him like he had to get rid of them, like they were fucking toxic. "We thought it was just a wind-up at first, y'know, like always. A load of Aussie tourists came back from Uttar fucking Pradesh or somewhere with some weird flu-like virus. Before you know it they're all fucking dying, and anyone who's come into contact with them is dying. This is Sydney, mate. *Sydney*. Then suddenly there are dozens more cases in Tassie and Brisbane and fucking Queensland. At the same time it's all over Tokyo and Kinshasa and London and Reykjavik, everywhere. And then it hits Los Angeles and New York, and suddenly the fucking media's going fucking *nuts*. People just fucking *dying* for no good reason. And it's like people you *know*. The bloke down the gyros shop, the receptionist at work. Some girl you once dated. Your mum, your dad, your baby son..." His wide-eyed, breathless babble came to a meandering halt, then abruptly restarted. "Like really bad flu at first. Vomiting, diarrhoea, high temperature, all that shit. But then it becomes something else. I mean, like *really* quickly. Something fucking hideous."

He reached a furtive, trembling hand to his mouth, his fingers playing absently with a wobbling front tooth. "There's so much *blood*. Bleeding from their mouth, nose, arse, even their fucking ears and eyes. Fucking horrible. Can't have been more than a couple of weeks and suddenly it's a fuckin' full blown pandemic. Like, real End of Days stuff, mate. The army had these lorries with flamethrowers. For the bodies. Jesus." The wobbling tooth came away in his hand, and he held the bloodied stump up, gazing at it in wonderment.

"If you were O-neg, you were okay, but that's so few people..." he lisped. "I mean... Mate, there's so few people left. Some guy in Sydney told me it was nine-tenths of the world. Nine-tenths of the world, mate, just *gone*. That was what—three, four months ago." The man's voice trailed off and McGuire watched his bloodshot eyes dart to the side.

A familiar *click* made McGuire smile. Whoever had snuck up on him was about four metres behind him. Evidently someone else had gotten out of the plane.

"Put down your weapon or I'll blow your fucking head off." The voice faltered a little, but rapidly reasserted itself.

"You're the boss," said McGuire, carefully lowering his assault rifle to the stony ground.

"Hands up."

McGuire nodded minutely. "Whatever you say, mate." He

kept his head lowered so that his eyes were hidden beneath the shadow of his Akubra's brim.

"Kick the weapon over there."

McGuire duly complied.

"You okay, Steve?"

"My leg's *fucked*," said Steve, confused, struggling to see the other man. "For fuck's sake, Greg. You passed out, mate. I didn't know what to do."

McGuire very carefully turned to view his interlocutor. He was about thirty. Dishevelled, sweating, barely able to keep the gun steady, lurid scabs and pustules festooning his mouth and nose—but clearly just about *compos mentis* enough to sneak up on him.

"You don't look so well, man," McGuire observed.

"That's rich coming from a dead man," replied Greg flatly.

McGuire let out a rasping chuckle. "I ain't dead yet."

"I'm not so sure about that," said Greg, making an uncertain effort to emulate McGuire's smile and in the process causing several of his pustules to crack open and weep. "'Cause I think I know who you are."

"Is that right?" breathed McGuire.

"You're that gang leader. The armed robber. The one the cops were after. He headed out this way."

"Strewth, sounds like an exciting bloke," said McGuire.

"I remember," said Steve suddenly, eagerly. "The bullion job that went wrong. The bulldozer at the airport. I watched it on TV. That was fucked up, mate." Steve gazed wonderingly at McGuire. "They reckoned the ringleader was somewhere in Namadgi. Or maybe Kosciuszko."

"Case of mistaken identity," said McGuire archly. "I'm just out for a vacation."

Greg snorted derisively. "The thing is they gave you a nickname," he continued. "'Dead Kelly,' they called you, the TV and the papers. 'Cause no-one thought you'd make it out alive. How long's it been? Seven, eight months?"

"Don't believe everything you see or hear."

"The thing of it is, the police found a body. Not far from here, as it goes. The face was cut up, but they said the corpse matched your description. I mean, they really did think it was you. As far as the media were concerned that was it. You really were *Dead* Kelly."

"Is that right?" McGuire kept his head bowed, his eyes hidden by the brim of his hat, all the while watching the trembling gun. The fucker looked wired enough to blow McGuire's head off if he was even slightly spooked.

Greg was clearly warming to his subject. "You know, I wouldn't put it past someone like yourself to pick on some poor unsuspecting tramp matching your description. All you'd need to do is slice him up a bit so he couldn't be recognised. Make it look he'd been done for by dingoes or some shit like that."

McGuire sniffed, "Uh-huh. Pretty much extinct up here, but it's a good idea."

"Of course, the cops were waiting on the DNA test. That would've cleared it up straight away, no worries." Greg's eyes played on McGuire's scarred arms. "That's why you made sure you left loads of your own blood at the scene. Anyway, turns out you got lucky. In fact, you're about the only one that did." He swallowed hard, his pronounced Adam's apple suddenly pulsing, voice straining. "'Cause that's exactly the point at which the whole fuckin' world went totally and utterly to shit."

McGuire offered a sympathetic smile. "Yeah, right. The epidemic."

Greg sneered. "Why would anyone give a flying fuck about you if most of the world has dropped dead overnight?"

McGuire let the smile hang, his hands held up, palms outward. "Look, mate, I don't know anything about any of this. And my arms are starting to hurt."

Greg looked incredulous, gesturing with his own weapon toward McGuire's discarded ACR. "Yeah, of course. That's why you just happen to have an assault weapon about your person." With what looked like a mammoth effort, he suddenly steadied the shotgun, his voice low and insistent. "Listen up, fucker. This is when your luck finally runs out. I'm gonna do what the police couldn't. I'm gonna put an end to you, you murderin' bastard."

McGuire licked his parched lips, nodding his head with slow deliberation. "Killing me means killing your brother. You're almost dead on your feet and there's no way he'd make it out of Kosciuszko alive. I'm Stevie Boy's only hope."

Greg managed an unconvincing laugh, ending in a gurgling cough. "The thing of it is," he spluttered, using his free hand to wipe a trace of scarlet-stained phlegm from his chin, "you're a mass murderer and an armed robber. I don't trust you, you fucker. I think we'd all stand a much better chance if I blew your head clean off your shoulders, to be perfectly fuckin' frank with you."

"The thing of it is," mocked McGuire. "*The thing of it is.*" He pursed his lips thoughtfully. "Okay, you win." McGuire stretched his arms with a low, heavy sigh. "Do it, then. We can all go to Hell together."

Greg chanced a fleeting look to his brother. Steve shook his head. "You can't, Greg, please. The guy's right. I'll never get out of here on my own. You're not gonna make it, you're too crook. I'm sorry, mate, but that's the truth of it."

Greg, breathing heavily, let the shotgun droop and bowed his head.

"Don't be down, old son," said McGuire with cod sympathy. "Just look on it as fate." He was advancing towards his discarded assault rifle, bending to retrieve it.

"Not so fast," came Greg's rasp. The shotgun was trained on McGuire again, and McGuire froze. "We're not that stupid."

"No," said McGuire quietly, from his stooped position. "Of course you're not." He raised his head now, so that Greg could see his face properly beneath the brim of the Akubra. McGuire could tell from the dawning look of terror that the other man had seen into his eyes, into the yawning space where his soul should probably have resided. For a moment he seemed to understand who McGuire really was. Then in one smooth movement McGuire pulled the Bowie knife from its sheath and sent it sailing through the air. It sank with a pleasing crack into the middle of Greg's face and the man fell forwards in surprise, triggering the shotgun as he fell. McGuire leaped to the side just in time, the shell roaring past his head and thumping into a eucalyptus in an eruption of splintered wood and smoke.

With McGuire reeling, Steve launched himself forward, intent on the knife. He heaved the blade from his brother's face, spinning around and advancing on McGuire, his face a snarl. McGuire raised his hands, grinning, then lunged for him. Steve lashed out with the knife in desperation. McGuire staggered back, wincing, and looked down at his hand to see a deep laceration running in a curve across the palm. McGuire lifted his injured hand up in fascination and flexed his fingers experimentally. No tendon damage.

Steve was hobbling, struggling to stay upright, dripping Bowie knife in his hand, the exposed injury on his leg oozing blood with each agonised movement.

McGuire smirked. "That was *cool*. I'm impressed, Steve. I thought your brother was the one with the balls and that you were the family pussy. Looks like I got it wrong."

"Keep away from me," spat Steve.

McGuire shrugged his huge shoulders. "Yeah, well, I'm guessing you acted on instinct, 'cause it seems to me you ain't got much of a plan beyond this point." He slowly advanced. "What with that massive fuckin' gash in your leg."

"I said keep away," said Steve, lunging again with the knife. It cut the air ahead of McGuire and McGuire came to a halt. He'd got where he needed to be, and with a flourish swept up his assault rifle from the rocky ground.

"You know what I think, Steve?" pondered McGuire as he hefted the weapon. "I think the world needs me."

"Please—"

He steadied the gun on the other man. "Sadly, mate, I don't think the same can be said for you."

THE MAN IN the top hat laughed. "You look beat, mate."

McGuire managed a laconic smile, head tilted behind his Akubra again.

"You look *dead* beat."

McGuire stopped and stared. The top hat was battered, dusty, its upper portion squashed out of shape, offset by a majestic red and black parrot feather stuffed into the band around the middle. He looked to be an Old Fella, a member of the Wurundjeri people, a descendant of Bebejan. He was also the first living person McGuire had seen since his encounter with the Cessna brothers. Not another living soul, aside from curious wildlife.

"What did you say?" McGuire's voice was low, rasping.

"You need a drink, my friend," said the Old Fella, beckoning him over to his position atop a sandstone wall. He handed McGuire a flask and McGuire drank greedily until the water ran down the corners of his mouth. He began to cough and splutter.

"Steady, mate," urged the Old Fella, retrieving the flask back from him. "Where've you come from?"

"Kosciuszko," responded McGuire, wiping his face. "Other places, too."

"No kiddin'," nodded the Old Fella. "How long you been out there?"

"A long time," said McGuire, lowering his assault rifle, loosening the backpack and slipping it gratefully from his shoulders. He propped himself against the wall. "Been walking for five days."

"Yeah, it looks like it." The Old Fella wrinkled his nose. "Smells like it, too."

"I hear some stuff's happened while I've been out there. Armageddon or some shit like that."

The Old Fella sighed. "Take it from me. Armageddons come and go, mate. The world's still turning, just with less of us on it."

McGuire looked around himself. This was Mansfield, at the base of the Australian Alps, maybe two hundred kilometres from Melbourne. Once it had been a farming and logging town, but that was a long time since, before it became a tourist destination. Hiking, skiing, hot air ballooning, that sort of shit. If what the brothers had said was true and the world really was fucked, then Mansfield would have to become something else again. Or maybe it would just return to what it was, long before the farming and the logging and the tourism. His lips curved into a grin. What goes around...

"You wanna steer clear of me, fella," said McGuire at length. "I'm a bad man. I've done bad things."

The Old Fella eyed the filthy, makeshift bandage wrapped around his hand, caked in dry blood, and the assault weapon propped against the wall. "No shit, Sherlock."

McGuire half-smirked in response. "Funny guy."

"I know who you are. You're famous, mate. You're *him*." The Old Fella made a mime of a rifle shooting. "*Boom*. They named you."

"Yeah, well. I heard they'd named me." He was too tired to pretend anything else. "Wonder which fucker thought of it."

The Old Fella stared at him quizzically. "Does it matter? One of those TV guys. Thing of it is, it sorta *stuck*. And if everyone thinks it's your name, then it's your name. Now and forever, like it or not."

"Is that right?" McGuire pursed his lips reflectively. "Didn't anyone ever tell you not to talk to dead people?"

The Old Fella threw back his head and laughed. "You'd be surprised what you can learn from dead people, mate."

McGuire studied the man's lined face, his intense, ever so slightly mocking eyes. He clicked his tongue thoughtfully. "I'll bear that in mind."

"But then, you've got a plan, ain'tcha?"

McGuire frowned, "How'd you figure that?"

The Old Fella shrugged. "You went into the Bush for a reason and you came out of it for a reason. So you *gotta* have a plan. Stands to reason."

"Yeah, well. It's been fun talking." McGuire stood upright, pulling his tatty canvas backpack up and over his shoulders and hoisting the assault rifle. "I like you, Old Fella. If I hadn't, well, this conversation wouldn't have been nearly so long." He began to plod away.

As McGuire made his way down the desolate suburban street he heard the Old Fella calling after him, laughter in his voice. "Remember, mate. They named you. That's who you are now, who you always will be."

"Sure thing, mate," McGuire called back, eyes fixed dead ahead.

The Old Fella's parting words reached him only faintly, twittering on the breeze.

"'Cause it's who you always were."

CHAPTER THREE

He trudged his way through downtown Melbourne. Initially, when he'd left Mansfield, he had doubted the apocalypse story. On the outskirts of the city, with tufts of clouds describing slow passages across the enormous blue sky and the eucalyptus gently rustling, the world had looked as suburban and normal as he'd remembered. Sure there was no-one around, but here, in the middle of a hot day in the middle of nowhere, you wouldn't necessarily expect to find anyone. It was easy to imagine the good, genteel burghers of the towns he passed through hidden inside their wooden houses, absorbing fatuous daytime telly while the air conditioning hissed soothing nothings in the background. In fact, it was so ordinary, so plain, that McGuire felt a familiar hatred blossoming in his gut. His horror was that he had been misled, perhaps even robbed: that the old order, of dull conformity, of predictable, cosy obedience, had somehow reasserted itself in the face of supposed calamity.

As he moved through the suburbs, however, the suspicion had soon dissipated. The first indication was the body of an elderly woman lying in segments on her driveway. She was drawn out, the top half largely intact apart from the arms, which had become partially detached at the shoulders and elbows. The bottom half had given way at the stomach, her abdomen and legs some way distant, attached only by portions of exposed skeleton. For the most part, the eyes and tendons had been gnawed away by birds and insects. The remains of her clothing, a floral dress and sun hat, flapped wistfully in the mild breeze. The stretched, desiccated corpse reminded McGuire of the effect achieved by pouring salt on unsuspecting slugs, a pastime he had delighted in as a kid.

The more he travelled toward his destination, the more corpses he saw. They lay in the doorways of burnt-out houses, in heaps upon the street, sometimes whole but frequently partially eaten, surrounded by patches of dried blood and decaying viscera. In some cases flies and ants frantically buzzed and crawled over heaps of bones. McGuire passed a flock of maggies picking enthusiastically at the remnants of a figure in a tattered bus driver's outfit. Rather than flying off, the birds regarded him with fleeting, imperious disinterest, before returning to their endeavours.

He continued walking, eventually entering the city proper, passing old and new buildings, some with windows and doors smashed, some daubed with portentous or simply inane graffiti, others apparently untouched, seemingly for no good reason. Vehicles were dotted around, many in perfectly fine condition, others burnt out or crumpled wrecks. Here and there were piles of rubble, while at other points the streets and roads were completely clear. Evidently this was what a sophisticated, urban twenty-first-century city looked like three to four months after the Cull. A haphazard, incongruous mix, of things unscathed and things disrupted by humanity's fevered attempts to survive, or at the very least to make sense of what had occurred.

McGuire headed up William Street before coming to an amazed halt at the junction with La Trobe. A huge animal, predominantly white with a greenish tinge, its lower body caked in mud, was toying fixedly with something—a ball, perhaps—in the middle of the street. The nearer he got to the creature, too engrossed to register his approach, the more sure he became of what it was. McGuire carefully pulled the assault rifle from off his shoulder.

It was a polar bear. He wondered how long the creature had been loose. Presumably someone had cared for it—and maybe the zoo's other attractions—since the Cull had hit. Perhaps the zoo keeper had died, or run out of food, or simply decided to let the inmates have their liberty. Whatever the reason, sweltering downtown Melbourne wasn't exactly conducive to the animal's well-being. The poor fucking creature was over-heating, judging by both its lugubrious movements and its absorption with its toy. Which, McGuire realised, as he concealed himself behind the wreckage of a crushed Toyota some twenty metres distant, was actually a human head. He wondered whether this was the same person who'd released the bear, and whether they'd belatedly seen the folly of their decision, however briefly.

McGuire felt an unusual sensation, something he struggled to put his finger on: remorse, he realised with a smile. Not something he'd felt since, well, since that unfortunate incident with his parents all those years ago. Sure, the polar bear was a killer, but that was its nature. This was a monarch amongst beasts, by dint of Nature, or of God, or of Evolution, whatever flawed system you chose to describe the universe with. He followed its listless toying with the human head through the cross-hairs of the rifle. It was beyond remonstration, beyond critique, beyond moralising. It simply *was*.

But he had a clear shot now, and even monarchs have to die. The creature had turned from playing with the head and was staring directly at him. In its mournful eyes he seemed to see an understanding, a recognition that its time was at an end, perhaps even a desire to die. McGuire pulled the trigger and a burst of gunfire rattled out, exploding into its hide with a ripple of scarlet. McGuire had expected it to roar, but instead it arched its back, pulling itself into a standing position, stretching its neck, whorls of dust billowing in its wake. It turned to him, its expression ponderous, blood oozing from the holes perforating its hind quarters. McGuire reluctantly squeezed the trigger again, and the creature collapsed backward on to the street.

McGuire moved toward the hulk, glancing around himself warily. The bear was dying, but not yet dead. He knelt by the creature, stroking its bloodied hide. Those patches that weren't matted by blood or mud were curiously wiry to the touch. Given the context, to waste cartridges was ridiculous, a soft, silly action that might come back to haunt him. And yet a thing of its power, weak and dying, was to McGuire an abomination. He stood, pointed the assault rifle at its head, and ended its reign.

He followed La Trobe, passing more inert vehicles, some damaged, some untouched, including an overturned ambulance that had clearly been looted, its contents strewn across the road, and the inert form of a bulldozer, its scoop raised in comical salute to the destruction of civilisation. Eventually he arrived at the intersection with Swanson Street, his attention piqued by a plume of black smoke hanging above a nearby building.

Intrigued, his rifle slung once again, McGuire headed down Swanson a short way, arriving at a grand building sporting fluted columns and a life-size bronze statue which the accompanying plaque identified as 'Sir Redmond Barry.' Further details were largely obscured by a sprawling graffiti tag executed in crimson and black that spelt the word 'Forever' without explanation. McGuire had visited the place some thirty years previously on a school trip, a few months prior to the unfortunate incident with his parents. This was the famous State Library of Victoria, home to over two million books, and more besides. Many of the books seemed to have been distributed down the steps and across the parched front lawn and forecourt, where they lay fluttering in the breeze like dying butterflies.

Aside from the black plume gently folding in upon itself before spiralling outward again, more black smoke was emanating from the depths of the library itself. McGuire began ascending the steps, picking his way over the debris, including a wealth of glass and splintered wood. He was mildly surprised that the place should have become a target for pillaging. He'd passed so many other untouched buildings, all liable to offer up treasures of more practical use in the wake of the apocalypse. Maybe the looters had possessed a penchant for the historical. Maybe they were just fucking idiots. As he ascended the second run of steps, the fitful noise of a failing alarm system gradually became audible.

McGuire pushed through the doors and crunched his way across a floor strewn with shards of glass and porcelain, past cracked walls with gaps in the plaster. The acrid smoke became thicker as he progressed. McGuire paused to wind a ragged bandana around his mouth and nose before proceeding, and to remove his hat. The source of the smoke quickly became apparent in the mammoth, octagonal hall at the heart of the building, billowing up toward the glass-domed ceiling. A group of people were gathered around a pyre constructed from wooden furniture, cracked computer terminals, exhibition cabinets, and yet more piles of books. For an intrigued moment he thought they were burning people too, but then he realised the melting forms he could see were mannequins, presumably drawn from various exhibits. The group were whooping and laughing, swigging from tinnies of beer and bottles of wine, seemingly unaware of McGuire's entrance. None of them looked older than twenty.

"Is this a private party or can anyone join in?" he rasped, levelling his assault rifle at them.

"Who the fuck are you?" demanded a woman with a pink Mohican, pistol in one hand and beer can in the other, her discordant voice echoing across the chamber. She probably wasn't much more than eighteen, and McGuire found himself marvelling at the amount of lacquer she must be using to keep the Mo erect. He couldn't help admiring her commitment to her haircut, what with the apocalypse and everything; clearly this was someone with a sound grasp of priorities. Around her, the others pulled themselves to their feet. A couple of them had clearly been in the midst of intercourse and were struggling to adjust their clothes.

McGuire grinned. "You're just a bunch of fucking kids. You wouldn't survive ten minutes on your own out there. Who's in charge?"

"I am," said a thick, familiar man's voice from behind him, just before a pistol butt smashed into the back of his skull.

*   *   *

A FEROCIOUS PAIN and the whiff of cooking meat brought him back to consciousness. He looked down to see the girl with the pink Mohican gleefully holding a blazing table leg to his exposed midriff, and realised it was his own burning flesh he could smell. She stepped back from him with a mischievous grin, leaving him to grimace. His hands were tied behind him to some sort of wooden pole, and his ankles had been bound together. A couple of people were holding him up, but in response to an unseen instruction they stepped away, and he momentarily struggled to maintain his stance without their support. In front of him was the pyre, into which a couple of young men and women were feeding hefty-looking tomes; possibly encyclopaedias. The fire roared its appreciation.

"Did no-one tell you?" said the familiar voice, close by. "You're meant to be dead. At least that was what Danny Kline said."

McGuire turned his head toward the bearded, muscle-bound bloke beside him, wearing a battered black leather jacket and a perpetual hang-dog expression. "Danny Kline, eh? Fuck yeah." Despite his predicament he couldn't help but feel a wave of pride. *The* Danny Kline. How cool was that. "Trouble is, Ritzo, you old fuck, rumours of my demise have been greatly exaggerated." The smoke from the fire was making his eyes water.

Ritzo pushed his swarthy face close to McGuire. "I'll say, mate. Danny Kline called you 'Dead Kelly,' and the rest of the papers and shit joined in. I mean, you can't blame 'em. The police were adamant they'd bring you down, by hook or by fuckin' crook. Then, lo and behold, a body turned up. The head was mashed up, but the cops were pretty sure."

"Maybe I'm a ghost," McGuire suggested, shifting his face awkwardly away from Ritzo, lest the stench of his rotting gums cause him to vomit. McGuire fixed on the fire again, watching a mannequin bubbling into oblivion.

Ritzo smirked, following his gaze and emitting a wistful sigh. "Yeah, well—that's the likeliest outcome of this scenario, mate." He pulled away from McGuire, pacing. He clearly wasn't sure what to do.

"But you, Ritzo," said McGuire quickly. "You're just the man I was looking for."

Ritzo eyed him sceptically. "Is that so? Fuck me."

"That final job. Somebody ratted us out. Who was it?"

Ritzo's face split into a sneering laugh. "I don't fuckin' know, man. We thought it was you. You were the one that got away. Didn't see you for dust. The rest of us poor bastards had to fight our way out. It was a fuckin' bloodbath."

McGuire clenched his fists, in the process testing his bonds, wincing at the pain from his scarred hand. No two ways about it, he was tied up pretty fucking tight. Ritzo's famed interest in kinky sex had clearly turned out to be a transferable skill. "Why the fuck would I do that?"

"Because you're a fucking psycho, man. We all knew it. All of us." He added, *sotto voce*, his face ruddy in the glow of the fire, "Even Lindsay knew it."

McGuire tilted his head suddenly toward Ritzo. "What happened to her? Did she make it?" The burn on his chest throbbed like crazy.

Ritzo shook his head. "I dunno. I remember the police leading her off. I had my own problems, to be perfectly fucking frank with you." He peered intently at McGuire. "Why'd you come back, mate? You should've stayed out there in the Bush. Now I'm gonna have to fuckin' kill you." There was the merest tinge of remorse in his voice. Something McGuire could work with.

McGuire gazed steadily back at him. "Kill me? Why the fuck would you kill me? The pair of us together..."

Ritzo waggled his finger at McGuire. "No, no, no. You don't get it. The world's changed. Not just the future, but the past too. Look at this place." He spread his arms, taking in the vast arching hall, his voice ringing out. "It's a monument to the past. No-one gives a fuck anymore. We're all too busy feeding ourselves and fighting each other. And that's a *good* thing, mate, it really is. 'Cause for most of us, the past fucking sucked big time." He stared at the fire.

McGuire nodded toward the pyre, towards the youngsters still nourishing it with encyclopaedias. "So I guess that's why you're helping the past on its way."

Ritzo smiled languidly. "I'll show you what I mean, Kelly."

He beckoned to the girl with the pink Mohican and to another girl, probably the same age, with dyed blonde hair and a ring in her tongue that glittered in the firelight. Ritzo smiled at the pair meaningfully, and they responded in kind. The girl with the Mohican kissed him hard on the lips and the blonde did likewise, then the two proceeded to snog each other. Ritzo turned, jubilantly, back to McGuire. "See?"

McGuire shook his head and laughed. "You've got to be kiddin' me. This is your gang, is it? A bunch of fuckin' teenagers?"

Ritzo pushed right up to McGuire, furious. "You don't get it, man, do you? I'm tellin' you, it's all gone." He thrust his arm towards the door. "Did you not see it out there? The rubble? The half-eaten corpses? Civilisation, fuck me, all it needed was a nudge, not even a shove, to come tumblin' down. Most people are dead. But not me, man, not Ritzo—I *survived*, and I'm gonna have a nice fuckin' life out of this." He dropped his voice to a whisper and leaned into McGuire's ear. "This is the thing, mate. Now I'm a *leader*. They *trust* me, they *follow* me. But I've gotta, like, exercise discipline, you see? They gotta see I've got the balls, that I'm the Top Dog." He pulled away, glancing anxiously toward the fire and biting his lip.

McGuire had read his mind. "So you're gonna throw me on the fire?"

Ritzo looked fleetingly surprised, then shook his head despondently. "Mate, I wish I didn't have to, really I do. But there's no other way. Shootin' or stabbin' just doesn't have the same *impact*, y'know?" He turned back to the pyre, the flames dancing in his regretful eyes. "You gotta *burn*."

McGuire smiled, nodding. "Okay, mate, I understand it. It's business. I'd do the same thing in your position."

Ritzo looked at him with something approaching affection. "That's big of you, Kelly. I appreciate it. Let's not end this on bad terms."

"Can I have a ciggie?"

Ritzo stepped away, smiling. He waved his hand dismissively. "Yeah, whatever, fuck it. Jess, give 'im a cigarette."

The surly girl with the pink Mohican pouted, then reluctantly produced a tatty packet of Camels from within the confines of her leather jacket. She pulled a half-smoked cigarette out, stepped forward and stuffed it without ceremony into McGuire's lips.

"Uh, a light?" he asked around the fag.

Sighing theatrically, the girl lifted the still-glowing table leg toward his cigarette. In that moment McGuire blew hard, so that the embers from the table leg billowed upward into the girl's face. Immediately her lacquered hair burst into flames, the girl stumbling backward, screaming in terror and colliding with Blondie. By now the other gang members were on their feet, clutching weapons, uncertain what to do, looking to Ritzo for direction.

"For fuck's sake!" raged Ritzo, pulling a pistol from his jacket. He strode towards McGuire, pulling the hammer back and raising the weapon, clearly intent on shooting him at point-blank range, all thoughts of a *Wicker Man*-style execution gone. As he stepped in, McGuire suddenly let himself slide down the pole, lashing out with his bound feet as he did.

McGuire's boots smashed into Ritzo's bollocks, causing him to buckle forward and collapse. Seizing his chance, McGuire lifted his legs up and over the dazed man's head, wrapping them around his neck and crushing his windpipe. Ritzo's eyes bulged, the gun in his hand flailing uselessly and clattering to the floor, his hands clawing ineffectually at his throat. McGuire could see the rest of the gang, frozen in indecision, save for Blondie who was emptying a stubby over the head of her Mohicanned friend in a frantic effort to extinguish the flames. The only other exception was a young bloke with high cheekbones and cracked-black spectacles, who stumbled toward McGuire and Ritzo clutching a knife.

"Release me or I'll kill 'im," growled McGuire, tightening his grip on Ritzo's neck still further. Ritzo's piggy eyes were screwed shut, the capillaries across his cheeks pulsing crimson like they were fit to burst.

The youngster hesitated, looking behind him to the other gang members, but they gazed back at him with wide, uncomprehending eyes, their gawky bodies immobile. Abruptly, the youth dropped down behind McGuire, slicing through the ropes securing him to the wooden pole. His hands and feet free, McGuire grabbed the knife from the dazed youth as he backed away. Severing the bonds securing McGuire's ankles meant Ritzo had been released too. The bearded man slumped back, gasping for air and scrabbling at his bruised neck.

Now McGuire was on his feet, rubbing his wrists. None of the youths offered any opposition.

"You fuckin' idiot!" rasped Ritzo, grabbing up his pistol from where he'd dropped it. A single shot rent the air, and the youth who'd released McGuire was thrown across the room by the force of the bullet, crashing into a reading desk. His wrecked form convulsed a few times before falling still.

McGuire wheeled on his feet, smashing his booted foot down on Ritzo's wrist with an audible snap. The bearded man shrieked in pain, the gun toppling from his grasp, and McGuire brought his foot down on Ritzo's ankle, resulting in a second sharp *crack* that reverberated around the hall. Stepping away from the writhing thug, McGuire bent and scooped the pistol up, pushing it into his belt.

He walked away from Ritzo, the gang members parting around him as he went to address them.

"Listen to me," he announced. "The world you knew has gone forever. The new world is a hard world, full of horror and misery. Don't be misled." He thrust a finger at Ritzo, who was rolling around in agony on the floor. "I know this man. He is a fool and a coward. People like him will lead you to destruction. But if you follow me, if you do as I instruct, I'll take care of you. I'll make sure you have food and shelter, and that you have security. Walk away from this place and tell everyone I am your leader now. Tell them I am Dead Kelly, and I have returned to save you."

Without waiting for a response, he grabbed one of the cans of petrol, up-ended it and started emptying the contents around the hall. The gang-members looked to each other, then broke as one for the door, pushing past each other in their efforts to escape. McGuire threw the now empty petrol can into the still blazing pyre, where it immediately started melting, then picked up another full can and began to slop it across the floor, pausing briefly to grab his discarded backpack and rifle. This time he made sure the fuel led to the prostrate form of

Ritzo, and scattered the remnants across his former friend's whimpering body.

"Please, mate," begged Ritzo. "We've been through so much together. Don't do this."

McGuire crouched beside him. "You're right, man. We went through a hell of a lot." McGuire rubbed his bristly chin with mock thoughtfulness. "How about this for a deal? You tell me some stuff and I'll help you out. How's that sound?"

"Yeah, anything," panted Ritzo. "Thank you. Anything you want. I'll tell you anything."

"My first question is this," said McGuire, casting a look back at the pyre, embers of which were starting to spark onto the floor. "Did you betray me, Ritzo? Honestly?"

"No, mate," said Ritzo desperately. "I swear on my life. It wasn't me."

McGuire nodded slowly. "Okay. I believe you. Next question. Where are the others?"

Ritzo stammered, "Wh-who? Who do you mean?"

McGuire snarled, "Who the fuck d'you think I mean? Big Foot? The Kendalls? Lenny? Trex, Baxter, Tosca, Spider; those guys. Any of 'em."

Ritzo looked in terror to the spreading flames, his reply burbling. "Big Foot's dead, Lenny's dead. Tosca too. Dunno about Spider. The Kendalls left town, I think. But Trex, yeah, I heard about him. He's gone a bit... I dunno. Religious. *Please, Kelly—*"

"Where would I find him?"

"You can't miss 'im. If you go searchin', you'll find him, I swear." Ritzo's gaze flitted to the flames, then imploringly back to McGuire. Shining globules of perspiration chased across his wretched features.

"Good, that's excellent." McGuire licked his lips. "And what about Lindsay? What about her?"

"Oh, mate, I told you, I don't know. I don't even know if she survived the fuckin' Cull, mate."

"She survived," said McGuire firmly. "I need to know where she is."

"The thing is..."

"What?"

Again the words tumbled from him. "Oh, man, you don't wanna know. They said... Well, maybe it was her. Y'know. That dobbed you in."

McGuire's eyes narrowed. "No way."

Ritzo's eyes were full of panic. "I'm just tellin' you, man, that's what some of 'em were sayin'."

"No *fuckin'* way."

"Listen, mate..." said Ritzo, his words coming in bursts as he began to hyperventilate, "I've done what you said... I've given you the answers, everything I know... I've done my part of the bargain...You said you'd help me out, mate... For old time's sake."

"Old time's sake?" mused McGuire, half-smiling, eyes playing on the collapsing pyre. The encyclopaedias were little more than ash now. He reached for his belt. "Yeah, you're right. I did say I'd help you out." He closed Ritzo's hands around something and straightened up, before turning on his heel and walking away.

Ritzo looked down in horror. He was clasping his own pistol in his violently shaking hand. "What're you doin'?" he shrieked in terror. "You said you'd help me!"

"I have," said McGuire, as he strode out the door.

THE GUNSHOT CAME sooner than he expected. He paid it no mind, gathering pace as he passed through the foyer towards the exit, feeling the heat chasing him. McGuire came to an abrupt, inexplicable halt, his attention caught by a room leading off the foyer via a short passageway. Despite the urgent need to escape the building, McGuire found himself padding along the corridor. The room itself contained various display cases, their contents intact, seemingly untouched by Ritzo's gang or any other looters. One display case in particular caught his attention, the glass cracked, perhaps by the sudden heat. It contained a crudely constructed iron suit of armour, including a helmet, shoulder plates, back plate and breastplate.

He reached out a tentative hand and pushed the glass, cracking it further until a section of it fell away. He reached in and pulled out the iron helmet. He held it reverently in his hands, tracing his fingers along the single, long eye slit, turning it over to examine the dents. It was only the roar of the heat that brought him back to the moment, and he suddenly tipped the tattered, dirty contents of his backpack—soiled laundry, decaying food—onto the floor. Then he thrust first the helmet and then the rest of the armour into the backpack, before turning and sprinting from the burning library.

CHAPTER FOUR

HE EMERGED INTO the midst of thunderous shaking, as though his theft had angered the gods themselves. Something was coming. McGuire spilled down the library steps, tucking into a roll as he reached the bottom and coming to a crouching halt behind the carcass of a wrecked camper van. Instinctively he pulled his assault rifle from over his shoulder, watching as the pavement, already cracked, began to striate further under the rising vibration. McGuire concentrated on his breathing, centring himself for what was about to happen. He pushed himself to one side, bringing the assault rifle to bear as he peeked out from behind the van.

He'd guessed right. A tank was making it way down the main thoroughfare, debris exploding under its immense caterpillar tracks. Soldiers clad in gasmasks and clutching submachine guns jogged either side of the metal behemoth, a couple of army lorries forming the rear of the convoy. He watched the turret swivelling rhythmically back and forth in its efforts to locate potential threats. One of the soldiers suddenly motioned to his fellow troops and the rest of the squad scattered haphazardly for cover; McGuire realised with horror that the turret had stopped moving and fixed its cyclopic stare on him. Turned out his hastily chosen hiding place wasn't as all-concealing as he might have hoped. Effective though his assault rifle was, it was no match for a tank. He looked wildly around for some alternative cover, and seeing nothing, simply *leapt*.

The shell smacked into the camper van and blossomed, the explosion flinging wreckage up and out in a fiery arc that blew the fleeing McGuire off his feet. He lay dazed, aching and deafened on the ground, his vision a swirl of dancing embers. He was aware of being very quickly surrounded by soldiers, who pitched him to his feet and propped him against the remnants of a brick wall. Behind him, the fire was catching hold of the museum. Acrid smoke flowed around them. He could feel the vibration of the tank fading as it continued its inexorable progress up Swanson.

The ground dipped and swayed, and McGuire struggled against the nausea that threatened to consume him. A uniformed figure had stepped forward, pulling off his gas mask. He was barking something at him. McGuire's vision muzzily focused on him.

"I said, what the fuck are you playing at, you fuckwit?"

McGuire, face dripping with blood and oil, looked up at him with amused eyes. The soldier—a captain, he'd guess—was probably in his late twenties, thin apart from some puppy fat around the jowls, privately educated, judging by his accent. Despite his injuries, McGuire couldn't help but laugh. Ritzo's people weren't the only kids trying to assert their authority. This one just happened to be a lot posher than the ones McGuire had sent packing from the museum, and wearing a soldier's uniform.

"Did you torch the museum?"

"Fuck you, Blinky Bill," McGuire growled.

"Search him," instructed the captain.

"He's carrying a lot of ammo," said a sergeant, unzipping magazines from the side pockets of the backpack. McGuire regarded his actions with a disdainful, raised eyebrow. This bloke looked way too flabby to be a soldier, his face flushed and sweaty with exertion. In fact, quite a few of the troops looked quite different from what you'd expect of professional soldiers. Uniforms, fearsome weapons and gas masks could only disguise the fact so far. "Plus this."

He'd pulled out the helmet McGuire had taken from the museum. A look of amazement crossed the sergeant's face. "I recognise this," he said incredulously, "it's only Ned Kelly's fuckin' armour."

"Souvenir hunter, eh?" snapped the boy-captain, leaning into McGuire. "Well, let me tell you something. Ned Kelly wouldn't have gotten himself caught so fuckin' easily. No way. What you are, mate, is an old-fashioned fucking looter, and probably an arsonist to boot. And in case you didn't realise, it's our job to deal with you."

"Fat chance," smirked McGuire. "You're a bunch of fuckin' amateurs."

"Yeah, well," sneered the boy-captain. An awkward pause ensued, while the kid reddened in his efforts to conjure a suitably pithy response, his troops looking to him expectantly. At a loss for anything to say, the captain suddenly slammed his knee into McGuire's groin. McGuire gasped, trying to keel over but prevented from doing so by the troops supporting him. He puked on the kid's boots.

"You fucking dickwad," snarled the captain, stumbling backward in disgust. "Ordinarily I'd have you shot on sight. But I'm not gonna, not yet, as there's an outside chance you might have some, uh, intelligence we could use." He thrust a quivering, accusatory finger at McGuire. "But I wouldn't get too fucking excited, fuckwit. Unless you happen to like torture."

And with that the boy-captain walked off, motioning to his troops. "Put the fucker in the back of the wagon."

McGuire was thrust inside the lorry alongside a collection of mute fellow prisoners, presumably picked up by the patrol for various petty crimes. Like McGuire, many of them exhibited minor injuries, including what looked like shrapnel wounds, probably following an encounter with the tank, or perhaps the bazookas McGuire had seen some of the troops carrying.

Most were emaciated, all of them looked exhausted. A woman, probably in her sixties but looking much older thanks to sunburn and innumerable sores, was clutching her arm and muttering. A couple of gas-masked soldiers sat at the far extent of the lorry, their Uzis prominently displayed.

McGuire took the opportunity to examine his own wound. He unwrapped the filthy bandage to reveal the curved scar. It was scabbing up nicely and, thanks to his own careful ministrations, it looked like he'd avoided infection.

"I know you," said a monotone voice. "From before it all happened. I *remember*."

McGuire looked up, replacing the bandage, to see a middle-aged man with rheumy eyes blinking at him. "Perhaps you do," McGuire acknowledged.

"But you're *dead*."

McGuire laughed, long and hard, and the wraith-like occupants of the lorry looked to him uncomprehendingly. One of the masked soldiers thrust a gloved hand at him. "Fucking shut up."

McGuire guessed the troops were continuing on their patrol. His hunch was confirmed when the lorry stopped and the noise of shouting reached him. The two guards were sufficiently preoccupied to enable McGuire to peek through a crack in the canvas side of the lorry. The junction of Bourke and Spring Street. Two men and a woman were being forced out from their hiding place behind the skeletal wreck of a tram. Of considerably more interest to McGuire, however, was Parliament House, which stood at the intersection of the two roads. McGuire noted with curiosity that the building was largely unscathed, except for some sprawling red and black coloured graffiti, but that it also looked derelict. He thought it odd that this building, this former site of governance, should have been abandoned. It was as though no-one had the chutzpah to claim it for themselves, not the military nor any of the gangs evidently roving the city. Not anyone.

One of the new prisoners was herded into their lorry, the other two presumably joining the other wagon, and the convoy started up again.

The pattern repeated itself another four times in the subsequent hour: individuals were challenged, apprehended and forced into the lorries. On the fifth occasion, the shouting was followed by a short exchange of gunfire, the whistle of another tank shell and a cacophonous explosion. This time, no new prisoners joined them. After another ten minutes, McGuire became aware of the lorry turning, of shouts of greeting and instruction, and of metal gates being lifted aside.

Soon after the lorry shuddered to a halt, the canvas doors were wrenched back to reveal fierce sunshine, and the prisoners were roughly extracted. As soldiers barked instructions, McGuire looked around him. In a previous incarnation, this had been the Southern Cross station on the edge of the Central Business District. Not so long ago, it had been the terminus for Victoria's regional rail network and one of the stations on Melbourne's City Loop underground system. Three or four months ago, it had been a bustling metropolitan transport hub. Now it was a military compound.

A large area of the bus terminal had been fenced off, and the fence surrounded by a barricade. There were several wooden huts, clearly intended as temporary but which looked liable to become permanent fixtures. Some of the larger huts looked like dormitories or storage facilities. There was also a pile of canisters, each about a metre long, half-covered in tarpaulin, the skull-and-crossbones decals obscured, but unmistakable nevertheless. He saw lines of army lorries of the kind he'd been brought in on, and a number of civilian buses that had been repainted in khaki colours. There were two more Abrams tanks, along with four Humvees, all of the latter in various states of disrepair. Other armoured carriers were being attended to by mechanics. Presumably the military were only sending out the heavy armour one at a time to conserve fuel and spare the hardware.

He saw troops drilling. Some looked like they knew what they were doing, but most were amateurish and ill-disciplined. He supposed that the military, like the rest of the world, had lost the majority of their people in the epidemic. When the soldiers from his patrol pulled their gas masks from their faces, they proved to be a mix of young and old, only a few of them carrying themselves like professional military. A largely volunteer army, presumably enticed by the promise of food, shelter, and the modicum of authority that a military uniform might afford them. Enticed, too, by the desire for order and instruction, for certainty in an uncertain world. Useful to know.

"Oi, daydream believer," said a sudden, vaguely familiar voice in his ear. The child captain who'd kneed him in the bollocks. McGuire detected a change in the commanding officer's tone, as though he were trying to ingratiate himself. "You're with me. We're gonna have a chat."

The captain was accompanied by an armed escort, a young man and a young woman, carrying submachine guns, with gas masks slung around their necks. Like the other soldiers, they looked distinctly ill, whey-faced and tired. He guessed that the gas masks served not only for intimidation, but as an alternative to sun block. Many of these soldiers were probably suffering from vitamin D deficiency.

McGuire was pushed toward a temporary-looking wooden cabin with blacked-out windows. He mounted the decking and was shoved through a misaligned door. The building—a single room, really—contained a desk, a hat stand, a round meeting table surrounded by mismatching chairs, a chest of drawers and a couple of dented filing cabinets. The walls were adorned with maps of Melbourne and its environs, and the states of Victoria and NSW. A tatty Australian flag was pinned to a propped-up corkboard at the far end of the room. McGuire noticed an old-fashioned kettle, camping stove and porcelain tea-set. He could also see his assault rifle and battered canvas backpack in the corner of the room. It looked as though the armour was still inside.

"Have a seat," offered the young captain. McGuire shrugged and took up the invitation, although the captain chose to perch on the edge of the desk, his hands spread on his thighs. "My name is Captain Bennett. I'd like very much to know who you are."

"Would you now?" McGuire crossed his arms and viewed his captor with disdain.

A pause ensued while the captain marshalled his thoughts. "A few of my people say they recognise you. In fact, they've stirred a few memories of my own."

"Is that so?"

McGuire examined the captain more closely. He seemed better fed, more rested, than his troops. There was a faint lustre to his skin, and a smell McGuire struggled to identify. A flowery, vaguely perfumey whiff. Moisturiser.

Bennett arched an eyebrow. "Shall I tell you who I think you are?"

"I reckon you're going to."

"There was a news story, probably seven or eight months back, some time before the Cull. A heist at Melbourne Airport. A gang of bikers attacked a plane with a bulldozer. They were after a haul of gold bullion, I think, that was about to be transported. The thing of it was, someone in the gang had tipped off the cops and they in their turn tipped off the media. The whole thing went wrong, and it was broadcast to the nation."

McGuire chuckled, "Aw, yeah, I think I remember that. Bad business. The bulldozer was a fucking stroke of genius, though."

"It was a complete and absolute massacre, as I recall." Bennett's eyes narrowed. "Of course, the media *fucking* loved it. They loved it even more when the ringleader scarpered into the Bush, because then they could carry on the story. For fucking *months*, while the coppers failed to find him." He blinked hard each time he swore, as though the obscenities were somehow painful.

"Reality TV. Can't beat it."

"His name was Kelly McGuire. The ringleader."

"Clever bastard."

Bennett shook his head. "Stop jerkin' me about, McGuire. I know it's you. You were all over the TV and internet for months on end."

"I think the guy you're thinking of is dead, actually."

"Yeah, well, you wouldn't be the first to fake their death."

McGuire shook his head and sighed impatiently. "What d'you want from me, captain? Or is this what you mean by 'torture'? Boring the fuckin' arse off me?"

Bennett sucked his teeth. "Listen to me, McGuire. The world you've stumbled back into has radically altered."

"So people keep telling me," McGuire said.

"But I have rather a lot of power in this new world, mate. Melbourne's under martial law, in case you hadn't guessed. In fact, the whole fuckin' country is."

"You could have fooled me." McGuire cast a meaningful glance toward the window. "I didn't see much evidence of law out there."

Bennett shifted his stance, evidently eager to explain. "No, you see, that's the thing. We're gradually restoring order, but we need people like you. An experienced man. Someone who's seen some stuff, who knows how to handle himself."

"You want me to *enlist?*" The grin was already creeping across McGuire's face.

Bennett nodded enthusiastically. "Why not? Our troops are a ragbag mix of bank tellers, school teachers, bricklayers. A few educated types, some middle classes, rather too many bogans for my liking, but you know, we're all in this together. Hardly the ingredients for an efficient army, you might think, but we do okay. But if we had you, a *real* warrior, well, that would be marvellous. For one thing, morale would go through the roof, let me tell you."

McGuire viewed Bennett with a look of disbelief. "It'd be *marvellous*, would it? Really fuckin' spiffing, what?" He cracked his neck from side to side, his arms still crossed, thoughtful. "But hang on a mo', Blinky. If I'm who you say I am, then I'm a violent criminal. A murderer and an armed robber."

Bennett clicked his tongue. "Well, yes. But these are tough times, McGuire, really they are. I told you, I have power. I could exonerate you of all your crimes, as long as you promise to work for me."

McGuire shook his head, incredulous. "You're off your fuckin' trolley. You want me to join your tin-pot little army? Fuck me, things must be in a bad way." He suddenly rose to his feet, his huge bulk bearing down on the gawky Bennett. The two armed guards readied their weapons, and Bennett waved his hand at them impatiently.

McGuire regarded the guards witheringly, then returned his attention to Bennett. "Do you know who I fuckin' am, Bennett? I mean, really? Do you know the things I've done? Do you know the *details* of my crimes?"

Bennett looked up at the bigger man. "I've got a fair idea. That's why I am asking you to join us," he said with a small smile.

McGuire continued to shake his head in disbelief, laughing and pacing the room. The guards exchanged uncertain glances, tightening their grips on their weapons. McGuire stopped suddenly, and stared directly at Bennett. "This has been very informative, captain. Thank you very much."

A look of confusion creased the captain's features. "What do you mean?"

"You'll find out."

Bennett looked genuinely hurt. "Am I take it to mean you're refusing my offer?"

McGuire swivelled his head around, clicking the bones. "What do you think, dickwad?"

Bennett nodded. "Okay." He turned to his guards and announced, "This man is a looter and probably an arsonist. Take him outside and shoot him." He leaned in to the male soldier and said in a stage whisper, "Make sure you have an audience."

The guards nodded, the man stepping forward to grab McGuire. "It's okay," said McGuire, raising his hands, then changing the movement into a punch. The male soldier fell backward into the woman, blood and cartilage exploding from his face, his momentum pulling both him and his comrade to the floor.

McGuire dodged past the suddenly terrified-looking captain, making for the ill-fitting door. He stepped outside into a forest of gun barrels. The furore inside had clearly attracted some of Bennett's more alert people.

"Nice try," said a relieved-looking Bennett, emerging behind him and clapping a hand on McGuire's shoulder. The guards followed, the one McGuire had struck trying unsuccessfully to stem the flow of blood from his wrecked nose.

A WIND HAD got up from nowhere. McGuire closed his eyes and felt the cool air on his face. When he opened them, it was to see a ring of desultory civilians—including some handcuffed prisoners who had travelled into the base alongside him in the lorry—and a similarly motley-looking gathering of soldiers, their pasty faces blinking in the severe sunshine. A few of the bystanders wore other kinds of uniform: a portly woman dressed in chef's whites, a couple of mechanics, a man in medical fatigues. McGuire noticed that Bennett had emerged from his wooden cabin onto the decking outside. The captain sipped at a delicate porcelain cup of tea perched on a saucer, as though he'd goose-stepped right out of some colonial fucking photo.

McGuire's hands were once again bound, this time to a makeshift wooden pole. A soldier—the flabby sergeant from earlier—stepped forward to blindfold him, but McGuire dodged his head out of the way. The man shrugged and stepped back.

The two guards who had led him away from Bennett's wooden cabin had been joined by another three soldiers, also equipped with submachine guns. The soldier whose nose McGuire had broken—a bizarre-looking, hastily applied bandage now obscuring much of his face—seemed to be particularly relishing his role in the firing squad. The sergeant stood to one side, a look of resignation etched into his features.

"Take aim," he intoned half-heartedly.

The soldiers inexpertly raised their weapons, their guns buffeted by the wind. McGuire half-wondered whether they would actually hit their target, even from this close range. The idea of being repeatedly wounded but not killed did not appeal to him. He looked down, his fingers working frantically to pull apart the inept knots around his wrists.

A burst of rapid gunfire made McGuire look up, expecting to see one of the soldiers holding a smoking weapon, but the firing squad were looking to one another in alarm. A second and a third burst of gunfire rang out, followed by a sustained burst of machine gun fire. The portly woman in chef's whites looked down in surprise at her chest, which had been ripped open like an unbuttoned tunic, and collapsed backward in a juddering, ungainly heap of exposed innards. Suddenly the firing squad and the ring of bystanders were scattering in terror. Bennett's cup and saucer toppled from his hands.

The compound was under attack.

CHAPTER FIVE

THEY NEVER TELL you this about shrapnel, reflected McGuire, as he dropped to the ground, shielding his face with his arms. Shrapnel isn't just spinning fragments of glass or metal or brick or wood, though there was plenty of that. It isn't just bits of shells or grenades or bullets, though they're in there too. On the contrary; it's bits of people, humans turned inside out, wrenched apart or atomised and flung about at speed. That and wedding rings. Wedding rings kill a fuck of a lot of people in battle.

Once the mass of spinning debris had finished cascading down on him, he pulled himself to his feet. A whizzing noise filled the air and one of the parked lorries exploded, flinging out another wave of twisted, flaming debris, thankfully some way distant. A second mortar erupted in the midst of a squat-looking building that was being used as a canteen, tearing through the roof and sending the windows billowing outwards. Soldiers, civilian workers and prisoners scattered in terror, some clutching burned and bloody injuries, many screaming. The injured sat or lay curled up, sobbing, or trembling and silent in pools of blood.

The soldier whose nose McGuire had smashed rounded on him, seeing his opportunity to execute the prisoner slipping away. McGuire had used the distraction to finally loose his bonds and was already coming to meet the man. He grabbed the barrel of the soldier's gun and pushed it under his chin just as the man pulled the trigger. The top of the man's head erupted in a spout of scarlet, and McGuire pushed the gushing body aside.

"You've got visitors," he said as he pushed past Bennett into the wooden hut, crunching over the remnants of the delicate porcelain cup and saucer. The captain was barking orders, his voice hoarse, desperately trying to corral his troops into ordered lines of defence.

McGuire reappeared moments later, clutching his assault rifle and backpack. Bennett whirled around, bringing up his pistol, but before he could loose a bullet McGuire had flipped his rifle butt into the captain's face, sending him crashing to the ground. McGuire dropped to a crouch beside the moaning figure, flipping open his backpack and pulling out Ned Kelly's armour. Of course he could have killed Blinky Bill, but somehow he felt he needed an audience for what was about to happen. Bennett watched with dazed incredulity, his puppyish face running with blood, as McGuire proceeded to strap the metal shoulders, back plate and breastplate to his body. Finally he lowered the iron helmet over his head, shifting it so that he could see properly, and turned toward the battle. He would leave Bennett to bear witness.

McGuire marched through the confusion, assault rifle at the ready. A grenade exploded nearby, flinging out a further wave of shrapnel. This time he walked through it, the debris bouncing harmlessly off his armour. The military largely ignored him, intent on repelling the attackers. Only occasionally did one of Bennett's soldiers catch sight of him, recoiling in amazement or horror. Inside the helmet, McGuire smiled to himself; he could have been Ned Kelly's ghost, as far as any of them knew.

McGuire passed a group of soldiers clustered behind one of the dormant Humvees, struggling to get a bead on their assailants. The same could not be said of the attackers, who seemed able to pick them off with impunity and impressive accuracy. As McGuire passed, one of the soldiers spun around, much of her shoulder missing. McGuire saw the perpetrator, a wiry-looking kid sporting an epic facial scar, swinging his sniper rifle and sprinting to a different vantage point.

"The fuckers are headed for the food store!" yelled one of Bennett's soldiers. McGuire watched as a squad of quad-bikes bounced across the compound *en route* for an anonymous red-bricked building, engines shrieking. The quad-bikes received covering fire from the groups advancing on foot, some with mortars hoist on their shoulders. McGuire observed that the attackers seemed considerably more disciplined than the 'professionals' defending the compound.

A familiar grinding noise rose above the cacophony. McGuire whirled around to see the tank from earlier coming to sluggish life, its turret swivelling toward the quad-bikes. The tank gun erupted, the recoil sending the vehicle lurching backward, and one of the quad-bikes was flung into the air, crashing down on one of its fellows in a miasma of twisted, burning metal. The attackers on foot launched a furious barrage against the Abrams, but their efforts were largely wasted as the bullets and grenades scudded harmlessly off its metal skin. Meanwhile the troops defending the compound took heart and renewed their counter attack, breaking from cover to launch rocket-propelled grenades that sang and zipped through the air into the midst of their assailants.

McGuire had dropped behind a pile of rubble. The front gates were wide open; presumably the attackers had either stolen a military vehicle and used that to gain access, or simply waited for a genuine army vehicle to enter and followed it. That'd teach the soldier boys to be a bit more careful in future. Either way, this was clearly McGuire's escape route. But it wasn't time to leave the party yet. From his vantage point he could see the twisted body of one of the fighters who'd broken into the compound. McGuire dodged out from cover and rolled beside the figure, and then turned the man over. Half his head was missing, but McGuire ignored that and began to remove the homemade belt of hand-grenades from around the dead man's waist. As he fumbled the belt free, he noticed that the man's upper torso and part of his right shoulder and lower neck were adorned with an extraordinarily intricate tattoo, like the scales of a lizard.

The belt released, McGuire scrabbled upright. The air was rife with the smell of cordite and drifting smoke. Keeping low, McGuire dodged from cover to cover, ducking behind industrial-sized refuse bins, overturned vehicles, even piles of bodies as necessary. Eventually he'd executed a tight arc around the back of the slow-moving tank. Judging his moment, he broke cover, running to scrabble up the machine's rear, bullets bouncing around him as Bennett's troops realised what he was doing. McGuire turned and let off a few blasts from his rifle, then pulled himself up onto the vehicle's turret and wrenched up the hatch.

He ripped one of the pins from the hand-grenades and dropped the entire belt into the hatch then leapt, with all his might. As McGuire fell to the ground and rolled for cover, he heard the first of a rapid succession of dull *crumps* and saw the tank shuddering ferociously, as though it had swallowed something untoward, which it had. When he looked again, it had come to an abrupt halt, and smoke was belching from the open hatch. Someone was screaming.

Bennett's furious soldiers were bearing down on him now, gunfire cracking the ground all around him, occasional pieces of debris pinging off his armour. As he struggled to steady his weapon, a searing pain coursed through his shoulder and down his arm, the cost of his leap from the tank. He was vaguely aware of a buzzing approaching, like that of a gigantic insect.

"Come on!" yelled a voice close by, strong hands grabbing him by the arms and dragging him upright and into a seat.

McGuire looked up dazedly to see that he'd been pulled aboard the rear of one of the quad-bikes. "Hold tight!" bellowed a female voice. McGuire wrapped his huge hands around the bike's frame as it shrieked into life and leapt forward, bouncing across the compound toward the gateway. The driver let rip with a machine gun, tearing into the soldiers bearing down on their position.

He could see the rest of the quad-bike squad roaring after them, some of them carrying pillion passengers shooting at the advancing soldiers. One of the quad-bikes was suddenly ripped apart by something, probably a bazooka, the machine tumbling in a chaos of flames and metal, the rider and passenger crushed in the bike's unstoppable momentum. McGuire could see the soldier carrying the bazooka readying for another shot. Wincing from his dislocated shoulder, McGuire pulled his ACR into position and opened fire. The bazooka-wielding soldier's chest erupted in a fountain of flesh and cartilage, her weapon spinning from her grasp.

They shot out of the gates of the compound, skidding across the rubble-strewn street before coming to a lurching halt. The pause was momentary; once the rest of the squad caught her, McGuire's driver twisted the accelerator and the quad-bike shot off again, the squad in chaotic pursuit.

HE LIFTED THE iron helmet off his head, blinking away the sweat, appreciating the cool breeze on his sweltering face and matted hair. He took in the sandstone building before him, its spire rendered in silhouette by the midday sun. The Cathedral's gothic edifice was implacable, dominating, and untouched, which surprised him. Surely angry or reproachful believers would have wanted to take out their feelings on God's House? After all, He had let them down somewhat. Someone was clearly looking out for it; perhaps the Lord Himself. Or perhaps the high walls fashioned around it from wrecked cars, purloined fences, bricks and barbed wire, guards patrolling the makeshift walls, had something to do with it.

By now the noise of the quad-bike had subsided. "Thank you," said McGuire's saviour, pulling the motorcycle helmet from off her head. McGuire guessed Korean descent. Above the neckline of her singlet he noticed the same lizard-scale tattoo he'd seen on the dead man back at the compound.

"For what?" replied McGuire warily.

"For saving us from the tank."

McGuire smirked. "That. That was me saving myself. Don't get too fuckin' excited."

McGuire swayed unexpectedly and she moved to steady him. "Are you hurt? Your armour looks very old..."

McGuire pushed her away. "The armour protected me."

"It's your shoulder," said the woman, concerned. "Let me—"

"I can do this," said McGuire determinedly. He straightened up, then smashed his armoured left shoulder with his right hand, popping his arm back into place. He gave a grunt of relief.

By now the other quad-bikes were parking up, riders and passengers disembarking, including the wiry kid with the sniper rifle, who couldn't have been more than fifteen. A burnt, dented mini-bus followed, presumably transporting the foot soldiers who'd provided support for the quad-bikers. People from inside the barricade—including, McGuire noted, children and teenagers—rushed to push a repurposed military lorry in front of the gap. He was intrigued to see that the vehicle looked to be equipped with flamethrowers. Probably one of the lorries they'd used to dispose of corpses, that the guy from the crashed Cessna had rambled about.

He'd swapped one compound for another.

"Who are you people?" growled McGuire.

"We are God's Children, just like you," answered the woman, smiling at McGuire's scowl. "But my name is Cho Hee." She held out her hand, which McGuire reluctantly accepted.

The returnees were busy unloading boxes of food from their quad-bikes. "You attacked a military compound," observed McGuire. "Isn't that a bit, uh, foolhardy?"

Cho Hee laughed. "You'd rather we starved?"

"There must be other ways of getting food."

"What do you suggest? Cannibalism?" she said, her smile unrelentingly fixed. "But you're correct. We did have an ulterior motive."

"Which was what?"

She shook her head. "I'm not sure I can tell you that. I'm sorry." Still fucking smiling.

McGuire shrugged and looked around himself, at the individuals carrying boxes of food, at a scruffy group of kindy-aged ankle-biters receiving a school lesson from a matronly-looking woman with her hair in a bun, at the laughing, happy people. "God's Children," he mused.

"Exactly," said Cho Hee excitedly. "The day of the gun and the bomb is coming to an end. God wills it."

McGuire spat a trail of bloody saliva onto the ground. "Does He now?" he said, wiping his mouth. "You could have fooled me."

"Yes," said Cho Hee, blinking in surprise. "Why don't you ask Him?"

MᴄGᴜɪʀᴇ's ꜰɪʟᴛʜʏ ʙᴏᴏᴛs echoed across the ornately patterned floor. He'd returned the pieces of Ned Kelly's armour to his backpack, and he felt them scraping impatiently against one another as he strode. He hadn't entered a church—let alone a cathedral—for many years; not since his parents' funeral, in fact. He was half-surprised he hadn't simply burst into flames as soon as he set foot inside. As with the exterior, it was clear that someone was looking out for the place. Even the fragile processional doors through which they had entered, formed chiefly from a stained glass rendering of the story of Paul's Damascene conversion, were intact. Occasionally he spotted kneeling parishioners engaged in prayer or other reflective supplication. They all wore the same self-satisfied look that had crossed Cho Hee's face when the pair of them had entered the building.

"No sign of God," observed McGuire.

Cho Hee glanced at him. "You'll see Him soon enough. All you have to do is open your heart." She closed her eyes as she walked.

McGuire grinned. "Of course."

They continued in silence, eventually reaching the altar. A figure clad in dog collar and black pulpit robes, who had been filling the stone font with stagnant-looking water, turned at their approach. She was portly, rosy-cheeked and elderly. McGuire watched as she reached reflexively for a shotgun propped against the altar.

"Who the fuck is this?" she said, levelling the gun at him. He could see a portion of the lizard-scale tattoo peeking over the edge of her dog collar.

"Reverend Sarah, this man is McGuire," said the younger woman firmly, bowing slightly. "He single-handedly destroyed a tank. Without him, none of us would be here."

"He looks familiar," said the woman. She was frowning, staring at him intently with azure eyes. "In a bad way."

"He is a valiant, honourable man, Reverend," responded Cho Hee.

Reverend Sarah continued to view him sceptically. "What does he want?"

"He wishes to commune with Our Lord."

"No shit?" The Reverend gestured with the gun. "Door."

The three of them made their way around the far extent of the pulpit to a heavy oaken door. This led down an oak-lined corridor, terminating at several more doors. A burly guard blocked their progress, a bandolier strung across his bare chest, Uzi in his hands. McGuire wasn't surprised to see the tattoo again.

"Reverend." The guard bowed and leaned over to open the door behind him, and they stepped into a wood-panelled room. McGuire took in a mahogany chest, luxuriant leather armchairs and an extraordinary oil painting of a magpie rendered in shades of reds and blacks. A pool table had been shoved against the furthest wall.

A group of greasy-looking men and women dressed in denim and leather were gathered around a muscular figure on the floor, clapping and whooping. The man on the floor was performing press-ups, the veins on his enormous, exposed biceps throbbing with each push. The spectacle was all the more impressive because the man wore articulated braces on his legs, which creaked with each push-up.

"...Ninety-seven, ninety-eight, ninety-nine, *one hundred!*" yelled a bloke in a bandana, snapping a stopwatch to a halt. "Three minutes and five seconds."

The figure on the floor pulled himself to his feet with the help of some of the onlookers. One of the men handed him a towel, with which he proceeded to wipe his face and shaven head.

"Here is Our Lord," said the elderly Reverend, gesturing to the muscular man.

The figure turned in surprise, his glistening chest and shoulders dominated by the tattoo of the lizard scales.

"Hello, Trex," said McGuire.

"Oh, for fuck's sake," said the man.

*   *   *

"THEY THINK YOU'RE GOD?"

"Uh-huh. Pretty much." The room had been cleared of Trex's henchmen and women, and Cho Hee and the Reverend had bowed solemnly and departed. Now Trex sat behind the enormous mahogany desk, toying idly with a Newton's cradle. Behind him, mounted proudly on the wall, was Trex's notorious hand scythe, with which he had won many arguments quickly and effectively, if not eloquently. McGuire paced the room, struggling to contain his incredulity.

"Fuck me. How did you do it, Trex?"

Trex leaned back in his chair and rubbed his chin ruminatively. "Well, y'know me, always one for the business opportunity."

"What's with those lizard tattoos they've all got?"

Trex's eyes glittered. "Do you like 'em? It's my logo, mate. I use it as a mark of, y'know, *fealty*. So people know who they follow, and I know I can trust 'em. I am Trex, the fearsome Tyrannosaurus Rex—hear me roar!" He chuckled to himself.

McGuire rubbed his scar through the grimy bandage. "Tell me how you did it, Trex. I'm intrigued."

Trex puffed his cheeks. "That last job at the airport. Fuck me. My legs got fuckin' shot to fuck." He moved the wheeled chair so that McGuire could see the braces on his legs more clearly. "Gotta wear these fuckin' things now, like some fuckin' cripple. Doesn't impede me overmuch, though. As you saw."

"Fuckin' annoying nevertheless," observed McGuire.

"Fuck yeah," acknowledged Trex. "I only got away 'cause Big Foot shoved me on the back of a fuckin' luggage cart. The gang was just a mess, loads of 'em dead, you AWOL." He sniffed. "I just laid low. Fortunately for me, you went and turned into some sort of fuckin' celebrity villain out in the Bush. Really took the heat off the rest of us, thank fuck. Gave the cops and journos something to concentrate on."

"And then the epidemic happened?"

"The Cull. Decimated the Melbourne gangs, us included. In the end there was just me, Spider, the Kendalls, a few others." Trex fixed him with a steely gaze. "Ritzo."

McGuire smiled sweetly. "Yeah, we met up. Chewed the fat."

"You had a fun barbie, by all accounts. You should meet my man Rudy, he likes fire a lot. And I mean, *a lot*. Useful bloke, as it goes."

McGuire raised an eyebrow in surprise. "You heard about our little tête-à-tête at the museum, then?"

Trex chuckled. "It's a small city, McGuire, and there aren't many people left. Word gets around. Dead Kelly *walks*, for fuck's sake. How long were you out in the Bush? Eight months? Hunted by every fucker from here to fucking Katoomba? If I hadn't known you for years, I never would have thought it possible. But here you fuckin' are. In the flesh. Unbelievable."

McGuire nodded impatiently. "Whatever, mate. I wanna know the rest. How did you set this up?"

Trex shrugged. "Figured if I was gonna start a religion, I needed a church. You gotta look the part, don'tcha?"

"A big fuckin' church."

Trex seemed surprised. "No point in thinking small." He smirked. "Isn't that what we always said?"

"And it worked? It looks like it worked."

Trex frowned. "What is it the Bible says? If you build it, they will come?"

McGuire grinned. "That's *Field of Dreams*. It's a fuckin' Kevin Costner movie. But I get the gist, mate."

Trex gestured expansively with his enormous, calloused hands. "Whatever. People were desperate, searching. There's been this almighty global catastrophe. There's no food, no water, no TV, no internet. It's all gone. And when something like this happens, a figure is meant to emerge, y'know? A religious figure."

McGuire couldn't help but snicker. "A saviour?"

Trex leaned forward in his chair. "That's it exactly," he said, waggling a finger. "A *saviour*. That's what I am. They're my, uh, *flock*. I look after 'em. Make sure they're protected, fed, that they've got shelter, warmth." He motioned vaguely towards the window. "You saw the school?"

"Yeah, I saw the fuckin' school, Trex. Fuckin' mental. And in return they worship you?"

Trex pursed his lips. "I think it's a pretty good deal, don't you?"

McGuire shrugged. "Looks good to me. You're making enemies, though."

Trex waved his hand dismissively. "You mean the fuckin' military? They're a right fuckin' mess, mate. You saw 'em yourself. Barely any of 'em are professional soldiers. Few nice toys, I'll give you that—but most of 'em are shot. That posh dweeb that leads them is about fourteen. But yeah, they're a pain in the arse, that much is true."

"What about the other gangs? There must be others. Couldn't just be you and Ritzo."

"Well, you very kindly eliminated Ritzo's little outfit, but then that was hardly anything to write home about. A few spotty adolescents. The Kendalls have fucked off somewhere else, so they're not an issue. But you're right, there are others. Thing is, I'm driving the competition, if you get my meaning. It'll just be me eventually. No worries."

"Uh-huh."

"Yeah. The mission you blundered into the middle of. It wasn't just about grabbing food. It was sort of a recce. We were looking for information. Weaknesses, that sort of thing."

McGuire smirked. "Didn't feel the need to be more discreet, then?"

Trex sighed. "Yeah, well. That's not the way we roll. You gotta think *big*. Anyway, turns out there's some canisters in the compound. Nasty ones."

McGuire nodded. "I know the ones. Draped in a tarpaulin like they were trying to cover 'em up, but the skull-and-crossbones are a bit of a fuckin' give-away."

"Cho Hee reckons it's nerve agent. Hit 'em, and that'll be the end of the compound."

"Oh, yeah, Cho Hee. One of your more devout followers."

"So what d'you think?" enquired Trex, his eyes glimmering with enthusiasm.

McGuire looked baffled. "About what?"

"My plan," said Trex, a look of disappointment creeping across his broad features.

"Uh, yeah. Great plan."

Trex beamed. "Glad you think so, dude." He relaxed back in his chair again, putting his humungous hands behind his head. "So, the issue now is you. Do you want in? We could use someone like you."

McGuire licked his lips, amused. "You're offering *me* a job?"

Trex nodded. "I know it's difficult, mate. You're no longer Top Dog. Things got shifted around a bit. That's a hard call. But it doesn't need to be weird. You could be my lieutenant. I'd give you a lot of power, mate. It'd be pretty cool, trust me."

McGuire smirked. "I didn't realise the post-apocalyptic world would be so jam-packed with fuckin' career opportunities."

Trex laughed. "For men of our talents, the world is now officially our oyster, mate."

McGuire continued. "'Cept, the thing is, like you I'm really just interested in information. Knowledge is power and all that."

"Oh, yeah?" Trex looked suddenly suspicious.

"Yeah. I wanna know who betrayed us. Who betrayed *me*."

Trex laughed unconvincingly. "The heist from Hell? The fuckin' thing with the bulldozer? Jesus, mate, that's pre-history now. Didn't you notice? It's the fuckin' Day of Reckoning out there. Events have moved on, bro—you should too." He rapped his hands playfully on his braces. "Look at me. I could be fuckin' bitter, but I'm not." He gazed steadily at McGuire, his grin rigid. "I just get on with it.".

McGuire returned his stare. "Ritzo said it wasn't him."

Trex narrowed his eyes. "You believe him?"

"He was negotiating for his life."

"I wouldn't believe anything that little shit said. Especially if you had 'im on the rack."

"So you know he was lying to me? You know that for certain?"

Trex stood up, his braces squeaking. "Is this what this is, McGuire? A revenge thing?"

McGuire held up his hands, palms outward. "I didn't say anything about revenge."

"I've got my own army, in case you didn't notice," said Trex angrily, pointing out the window. "Half of them are former gang members, the rest think I'm fuckin' God. Any attack on me and they'll tear you limb from fuckin' limb."

"Whoah man," said McGuire, his tone managed, eyes scanning Trex intently. "Why're you so sensitive?"

"What did Ritzo say?"

"He said he didn't know who betrayed me. But that there were rumours..."

"Rumours?"

"About Lindsay."

Trex's expression abruptly transformed from fury to incredulity. Then he clapped his hands together triumphantly and smiled. "I knew it—this is what this is really about, isn't it? Fuckin' Lindsay."

McGuire swallowed hard. "Is she alive? Where is she?"

Trex shook his head. "Lindsay. I should have known."

"I need to know where she is," said McGuire. He couldn't keep the urgency out of his voice.

Trex leaned on the desk. "I'll tell you what. I'm a magnanimous God, as it goes." He took a walking stick from a hook on the wall and swaggered toward the door. "Let's have ourselves a little deal. Yes, I know where she is. And I'll give you someone to take you to her."

Trex leaned out the door and called out, "Mate, can you come in here a second?"

A squat, thickset man entered, the top of his sweat-stained shirt unbuttoned, revealing the familiar scaly tattoo.

"Baxter," said McGuire quietly.

"Fuck me," said Baxter incredulously, a grin spreading across his compact features. "So it's true. Dead Kelly walks."

"Fuckin' hell," muttered McGuire.

Trex clapped his hand on Baxter's shoulder, looking for all the world like a proud father. "You know what, Kelly? The thing about Baxter here is that he's completely and utterly unique."

"Is that right?" said McGuire in low tones.

"Uh-huh." Trex nodded emphatically. "His life hasn't been altered one jot by the apocalypse, has it now, Baxter, old son?"

A looked of confusion rippled across Baxter's face. "I don't understand, Trex."

Trex flashed a grin. "Don't worry, mate. What I mean is, you're the go-between. The messenger, moving between different gangs, between different tribes. Just like you always were."

"Oh, yeah," said Baxter with relief, grinning ruefully. "Our man on the ground."

Trex laughed and squeezed Baxter's shoulder with synthetic affection, "That's what we always say, isn't it, mate? *Our man on the ground.* I'm telling you, Kelly, we've got every angle covered."

McGuire was shaking his head. "For fuck's sake, Trex. Just tell me where she is. I'll go on my own."

"Uh-uh," said Trex, with mock sternness. "You go without him and they'll kill you as soon as look at you. You need Baxter. He's your passport, mate."

"For fuck's sake," said McGuire, *sotto voce*.

"Baxter, I want you to take McGuire to see Spider."

Baxter's puzzled expression had returned, his gaze shifting between Trex and McGuire and back again. "Really? Uh, okay, boss."

"Spider?" responded McGuire, askance. "What the fuck is she doing with that fucker?"

Trex looked steadily at McGuire, all humour gone. "Listen, Kelly. I told you. Things have shifted. That's who she's with now."

McGuire's eyes flashed. "You've got to be fuckin' kiddin' me."

Trex shook his head. "I'm sorry, man. It's just the way it panned out. It's a different world."

McGuire had unconsciously picked apart the bandage on his hand, exposing the curved scar. "The fucker," he said disbelievingly, staring at the wound.

Trex nodded emphatically. "Yeah, well. No argument here. That sap has been a pain in my backside for as long as I can remember. An *irritant*, know what I mean? Little things. A raid here, a raid there. And that's your side of the deal, mate." He made a dismissive gesture with his hand. "I want him gone, I want his gang *wasted*."

McGuire nodded slowly. "Maybe."

Trex chuckled. "You can't lose, mate. This way you can knock off Spider *and* get your lady love back. Revenge and romance, you gotta love the combination."

McGuire continued to stare at his scarred hand for a moment longer, then offered it to Trex. "Okay. You got a deal."

Trex clasped it. "You have my word, mate. And my Word is Law."

CHAPTER SIX

"THIS IS SO fucking cool."

Baxter was grinning from ear to cauliflower ear as he gunned the X-Trail down Flinders Street and right onto Batman Avenue. In the old days the journey probably would have taken ten minutes by car; now, what with negotiating the rubble and abandoned vehicles, it took three times as long. Baxter kept looking excitedly to McGuire like some fucking cocker spaniel, then making lame-arse attempts at conversation. McGuire countered now and again, but otherwise maintained a stoic silence, his eyes playing on the fragmenting world around them. Eventually Baxter ceased gabbling, but the adoring grin remained.

The SUV was well-suited to the uneven terrain, but being around the quad-bikes had made McGuire pine for his beloved Harley. He'd ridden three different Harleys over the past twenty years, maintaining them with care and attention, delighting in seeing his reflection in the polished chrome. They'd been more important to him than anything else—at least until Lindsay came along. He remembered her riding pillion, the feel of her breath on the back of his neck, her loving hands gripping his waist. Melbourne to Sydney, the Snowy Mountains, the Victoria High Country, the Great Ocean Road. McGuire and Lindsay at the apex of the gang, and Trex, Baxter and the others trailing behind.

He remembered the mayhem of that day. The bulldozer smashing into the newly-loaded airliner, just like they'd planned. McGuire, Big Foot and the Kendall twins gleefully pulling out those chests of bullion, loading them on the back of the wagon, while Trex and the others dealt with airport security. McGuire's sudden misgivings about the lack of police sirens or airport alarms, wondering why everything was so fucking quiet. The sudden dryness in his mouth as he spotted the glint of sunglasses and saw the snipers on top of the control tower. Suddenly seeing sharp-shooters all around them, hidden in the airport terminal, ensconced in the hangar, behind the fucking catering wagon.

The shouted warnings to drop their weapons, McGuire and Trex exchanging glances, the words they didn't need to say. Turning to rake the coppers with bullets, the buzzing torrent of their reply. His gang members ripped apart by snipers, blasts of automatic fire, grenades—the quicker ones, the cleverer ones, running for their bikes, returning fire all the while. Trex being hit in the legs but carrying on regardless, whirling his treasured hand scythe in the air like a nutjob, Meg Kendall loosing one lethal shot after another from her crossbow, Baxter dashing for the exit with an animalistic shriek of fury, Ritzo atop the mobile stairway, pistol in one hand, Uzi in the other, laughing.

McGuire remembered leaping aboard his bike, making for the exit, the police wagon coming from nowhere and side-swiping him, he and his Harley parting ways. The bike slaloming under its own momentum until it flipped spectacularly and skittered to a standstill, sparks cascading in its wake. McGuire himself flung through the air, crashing down and rolling over and over until he too came to a halt, exposed flesh ripped to fuck, his ACR still gripped tight in his hand. Lying face-up as the cops bore down on him, biding his time like a clever boxer riding out the count. Then rolling over at the last possible moment, ACR blaring, blowing apart legs and abdomens and chests.

Trudging over bones and body parts and the half-alive, past the remnants of his beautiful bike, the cacophony of battle dying behind him. Tearing through a wire fence like a wild beast, and then out into the open.

He remembered the blood in his mouth, the scraping of his bones. Lindsay being led away by police, the fleeting, pained look she threw in his direction. The barking of police dogs, the shouts and the gunfire, the car he stole and later abandoned. He remembered running, hiding and surviving amidst the rocks and the gum trees and the bushes. That fuckin' helicopter. Jesus. But most of all he remembered the realisation he'd been betrayed, and a thirst for revenge that grew in him like Japanese knotweed, its gnarled, reaching tendrils choking everything in its path, until it *became* him. Just like before, like that time with his parents—

McGuire snapped from his reverie to see the overgrown mayhem of Darling Gardens flashing past, Baxter bringing the vehicle to a rumbling halt on Alexandria Avenue. He planted a boot onto the rubble-strewn bitumen, and Baxter led him across the bicycle lane down toward the Yarra. The sky had become a dull grey mantle, threatening rain. They pushed their way through the tree line and down the grassy, overrun embankment, coming to an arched opening into a tunnel. Immediately adjacent was Church Street Bridge, its concrete supports festooned with the usual cryptic graffiti, including the word 'Eternal,' executed in giant, curving scarlet and black letters.

"What is this place?" said McGuire suspiciously as they approached. "You're taking me down a fuckin' sewer?"

"Not a sewer, Boss," corrected Baxter. "It's a storm drain. There's a whole network of 'em beneath the city. Not many people know they're here." He immediately corrected himself: "Not many people *knew* they were here."

"And the fucker's down here, is he?" replied McGuire sceptically.

"Yeah, Boss. But listen, we have to be quick." He gestured a stubby hand toward the menacing grey sky. "Storm's coming. We get caught in there when the river's up and we're liable to have a big problem."

McGuire nodded; it was already specking with rain. "Why here?" he asked warily.

Baxter had resumed his dreamy grinning as his booted feet clanged over a metal grille and into the tunnel. He switched on a torch, its beam playing off the curved red brickwork. "I guess they figured the streets are too dangerous. All sorts of things up there." He waved his torch beam at the ceiling.

All sorts of things. McGuire thought of the polar bear. "Fair fuckin' point," he acknowledged, following Baxter in. They advanced down the tunnel, accompanied by a steady drip-drip of water and the intermittent chirrup of crickets. McGuire turned his own torch on and picked out scuttling forms on the walls and floor: cockroaches.

"How'd you end up with Trex's gang?" said McGuire abruptly, as they walked.

Baxter turned back to him, his brow corrugating. "You disappeared, Boss. After the heist. Then the Cull happened. Loads of us died. Those of us that were left, well, we sort of got mixed up, y'know. Stuck with whoever we could find." He struggled to articulate himself. "People came together in different ways..."

McGuire stopped. Baxter did the same, turning toward him. "You okay, Boss?" he asked anxiously.

"Someone betrayed me," McGuire said simply.

McGuire's beam played on the squat man's face. Baxter's illuminated his in turn.

"It wasn't me," said Baxter contritely. "I swear, Boss."

McGuire let the sound of the dripping water and scuttling of cockies dominate for a moment. "Of course," he said eventually, letting a broad grin creep over his features. "I know it wasn't you, mate. Guess how I know."

"I, uh, dunno, Boss." Again with the stupid grin.

McGuire tapped his forehead. "You're too fuckin' smart, mate." He clapped Baxter affectionately on the shoulder. "Let's carry on, you fucker."

Baxter laugh nervously, flashing his yellow teeth. "Thanks, Boss."

They resumed walking, this time in silence, passing occasional daubs of graffiti. Overblown tags, cryptic names and messages, some of the most striking in red and black. Most of them looked far more than a few months old, as though people had been coming down here for some considerable time. McGuire noticed that the older red brick was left alone; only the newer concrete elements of the tunnel were considered fair game for scribbling on. Down here, at least, the past was evidently still respected.

"The problem is," said McGuire suddenly, apropos nothing, "when there's no fuckin' society, who the fuck do you rebel against?"

"Up here, look." Baxter gestured to a piece of graffiti indicating that 'The Chamber' was thirty-eight metres distant. Then he turned back to McGuire. "That's what Trex said. That's why we're trying to build a new society." Again the furrowed brow. "Maybe that's *why* we need a new society?"

McGuire let out a low laugh that echoed off the brickwork. "So now *we're* society? And Trex is God? What the *fuck?*" He'd stopped walking, and placed a restraining hand on Baxter's arm. "How come you know the way? They just let you in, do they?"

Baxter sighed. "It's just the way it is, Boss. Like Trex said, it's like it always was. I move around, y'know, between the different factions. Our man on the ground, remember?"

McGuire let go of Baxter's arm. "Our man *underground*."

Baxter nodded. "That's it, Boss." They walked on, and very soon it became apparent that the tunnel was opening out. McGuire could see natural light through cracks in the Chamber's wall, and wondered what was above them.

A sudden noise made them both halt. The figure of a woman was just visible in the darkness beyond, fleetingly visible in a dancing pool of light. "Hold it there," she said. They heard her footsteps closing in and she emerged into the light, a gas lantern clutched in her hand.

"Baxter," she said, face taut and scowling against the beam from his torch. She was a statuesque woman: a blonde pony tail, gaunt, high cheeks, into which crosses had been scored. Late forties, probably. An extraordinary bow-shaped meat cleaver hung from her belt. "You're late," she said through a mouthful of gum, reaching out a hand to lower Baxter's torch. "Spider doesn't like to be kept waiting."

"Sorry, Nancy," replied Baxter. "We came as quick as we could."

"Either of you carrying?"

"We're visitors here, Nancy," said Baxter emphatically. "We know the rules."

The woman moved toward McGuire, the lantern swinging in close to his face until he felt the heat on his cheek. "Is that him, then? The one they've all been talking about?"

"Yeah, that's him." Baxter nodded.

The woman cocked her head to one side. "Dead Kelly, eh? I remember you from way back. I don't fuckin' buy it myself. I think you're a fuckin' charlatan."

"Pays to be suspicious," McGuire said, returning her hostile gaze.

Baxter intervened hurriedly. "Uh, Kelly McGuire, meet Nancy the Nun."

"I remember you too," said McGuire. With her height and the scars on her cheeks, she was hard to forget. As was the meat cleaver. The story went that she'd been an orphan in one of the church-run homes around Sydney, forced to work in the kitchens. When she tried to protect some of the younger orphans from the advances of a kiddie-fiddling priest, he'd held her down and 'crucified' her face, in order—apparently— that he might cleanse her soul. Nancy's response was to bring to bear the nearest thing to hand, which turned out to be the meat cleaver. Figuring he was clearly experiencing difficulty with his vow of celibacy, she generously removed the offending appendage.

McGuire's eyes played on the meat cleaver glinting in the torch light. "You used to run with Lenny and his lot. What happened?"

"The fuckin' plague," snapped Nancy. "What do you think happened?" She gestured with the blade. "After you. And mate, I don't give a fuck if you are gangster royalty—if you fuck about, I'll slice you in half. Get it?"

Exonerated by the courts by dint of her age, Nancy slipped easily into gang life, finding increasing use for her skills with the blade, the meat cleaver having become her signature weapon. She kept herself to herself and most gang members afforded her a wide, respectful berth. That, with the crosses either side of her face, earned her the 'Nun' appellation.

"Yeah, I think we got it," said McGuire, following Baxter and Nancy into the Chamber. They had to be careful to avoid the recessed path bisecting the room, through which flowed a steady stream of bubbling water. The cracks of daylight reflected off the water and cast jittering patterns on the ceiling, and the walls were adorned with vast murals depicting animals and people. Clearly this space had been known about a long time prior to the Cull, although Spider's gang must have adopted it only in the last few months.

Crowds of people broke around them as they entered, their whispers fading to nothing. McGuire saw some reaching for their weapons or just staring suspiciously, their faces caught in the glow of manifold candles and gas lanterns. People were sitting on raised platforms either side of the gully. He was surprised to see a few kids amongst them, and could even hear a baby mewling, its sporadic cries bouncing off the walls and ceiling.

"What is this place, Baxter?" hissed McGuire.

"I told you, Boss. Storm drain. There's dozen of 'em under the city. This is just one of the more accessible ones."

McGuire grunted. It wasn't the answer he'd been looking for.

The crowd in the centre of the Chamber had begun to join their fellows on the makeshift seating, subdued, almost reverent. McGuire looked to the men and women, a few of them hardened gang-members he recognised from Back in the Day, but mostly civilians who had had to learn brutality in order to survive. Their eyes glittered in the candlelight.

At a sound behind him, McGuire went for his rifle, before remembering he didn't have it with him. After a moment, he realised someone was clapping, albeit weakly. He turned to see a figure slumped in a wheelchair, wizened face caught in a rictus grin, slowly and inexpertly applauding. The candles near him cast a shifting, elongated shadow, altogether more animated than the emaciated man in the chair.

"McGuire," rasped the newcomer. "I mean, *Dead* Kelly. What a performance."

"Spider," said McGuire, incredulous and amused. "The virile, square-jawed Spider. The bloke that banged every woman he ever met. Isn't that what you always reckoned? Not looking so well, mate. What's eating you?"

"Laugh it up, mate," Spider said, sneering. He coughed, spattering his collar with yellowy spittle. "It ain't got me yet, though."

McGuire regarded the slumped figure with smiling disdain. "Spider, mate. I think that may only be a matter of time..." He trailed off as he picked out another figure in the gloom, a short way behind Spider. It was a woman in another wheelchair, clearly unconscious, wrapped in a tartan blanket. She was greying at the temples, but there was no mistaking her auburn hair.

"Lindsay," McGuire breathed, moving toward her.

"No," said a severe voice behind him. He felt the cool blade of Nancy's meat cleaver caressing his ear and the back of his neck, and froze.

Spider exhaled a guttural laugh. "You. You fucker. Seems like you've been making waves, Kelly. Ritzo, the army compound. I heard you paid Trex a visit, too. How's the, uh, God business working out for him?"

McGuire grinned ruefully, casting a glance around the Chamber. Sure, his audience was suspicious, but there was something else, too. It was as though they were *expecting* something. Spider, like most of the old gang, enjoyed theatrics, so he could have planned a show of some kind, prior to McGuire's inevitable execution. Although given Nancy the Nun's evident distaste for him, the performance might well be a whole lot shorter than intended.

"What is this?" said McGuire mockingly. "Amateur dramatics down the sewer?"

"It's a storm drain," muttered Baxter churlishly, but McGuire flashed him a warning look.

"We're survivors," snapped the figure in the wheelchair venomously.

"Survivors?" echoed McGuire. "Barely."

Spider paused before replying. "You know, when Baxter sent word you wanted a meeting, I thought to myself, 'I know what this is about.'"

"Yeah?"

"You want revenge, and you want Lindsay. Am I right?"

McGuire sniffed. "Correct on both counts."

Spider snorted derisively. "Right. You think someone in the old gang dobbed you into the coppers. Yes?"

McGuire nodded. "You pretty much got it. You don't get fuckin' police snipers turning up accidentally. The heist was blown because someone squealed."

"And you think it was me? Having exhausted all other possibilities?"

McGuire chuckled. "I've yet to exhaust all other possibilities. You just happen to be next on my list."

"Let's get this straight," said Spider, shaking his head. "You killed Ritzo 'cause you could, 'cause he was weak? But you let Trex off the hook 'cause you couldn't beat him? How very *selective* of you. Some might say *cowardly*."

McGuire shook his head. "It's all about timing, mate. Everything comes to he who waits."

Spider's bloodshot eyes played across the audience opposite him. "And so I'm next in line for a good talking to?"

McGuire absently rubbed the scar on his hand. "You know, man, that *would* make some sorta sense." As he spoke, he noticed the audience's weapons becoming altogether more prominent. Some had pulled pistols, others hefted submachine guns or blades of various descriptions. Clearly audience participation was part of the show.

Spider chuckled. "So that's the plan, is it? Kill all the old gang members? Fuck me, mate. I was expecting something a bit more fuckin' intellectual from you, McGuire. Very disappointing, mate."

McGuire kept his gaze locked on the emaciated figure in the chair. "As my old Papa was fond of saying, you'll get what you're given."

Spider grinned lopsidedly. "Is that what you said to him before you chopped his head off?"

McGuire could feel Nancy's cool breath, felt the blade flat against the nape of his neck. "I'm here for Lindsay."

Spider's grin remained fixed as he turned to face the woman slumped in the wheelchair beside him. "Oh, you mean my Queen?"

McGuire shook his head. "What the fuck?"

Spider nodded, as vigorously as he could manage. "Yeah, that's right, mate. I'm King and she's *Queen*. Cool, eh?"

McGuire ignored that. "What's wrong with her?"

Spider waved his hand dismissively. "Oh, I don't know. The birth, I guess. Really took it out of her."

McGuire's eyes flashed. "What the fuck d'you mean?" he growled, clenching and unclenching his fists. He felt the curved scar on his hand opening up, warm blood in the palm of his hand.

Spider squeezed his eyes shut, his body quivering. At first McGuire figured he was in pain, but then he realised the cunt was laughing. "Fuck me," he said eventually. "You're in for a treat, mate. You really are. *Frieda!*"

McGuire followed Spider's gaze to the seating and saw a figure rising, clutching something to her breast. The girl— little more than a child herself—made her way down from the platform, occasionally assisted by the audience, until she reached the centre of the Chamber. She gingerly stepped over the gully, presenting herself to Spider with a curtsy. Spider smiled a crooked half-smile, which McGuire imagined was supposed to be benevolent, but which just looked deeply sinister. Then Frieda approached McGuire. In her hands, wrapped in a piece of cheesecloth, was a newborn baby, probably a few days old. Presumably it was the one McGuire had heard crying as they entered the Chamber. He looked to the teenage girl, unable to disguise his bafflement, and she shyly returned his look and smiled. She very carefully lifted the cheesecloth aside so that he could see the baby's auburn hair.

McGuire stepped back from Frieda and the baby in shock, almost backing straight into Nancy's cleaver.

The sickly semi-grin was still on Spider's face. "What do you think, Kelly?" he enquired mildly.

"It's mine," McGuire whispered.

Spider flourished a withered hand. "Hmm. Hard to say."

McGuire rounded on the man in the wheelchair. "Of course it's fucking mine. I've only been gone eight months, mate. Your brain isn't that fucking addled."

Spider nodded. "Yeah, well. Maybe I'm misremembering. Or maybe, just maybe, she wasn't quite so *committed* to your relationship as you like to think." He smirked. "I am Spider, after all. You know my reputation."

"Fucker," McGuire growled, his body tensing, stopping only as Baxter gripped his arm. Baxter nodded toward Nancy the Nun, right behind McGuire, her meat cleaver poised.

Spider, meanwhile, continued to speak. "Could be yours, couldn't it? But then again... It could be mine. The problem is..."—he licked his thin lips—"you just can't be certain."

McGuire was quiet a moment. "A boy or a girl?" he said at length.

"A boy," nodded Spider. "I know what you're thinking, Kelly. I know you too bloody well. Sure, you want to be in command, you want to displace Trex and fuck the military and take over the city. Maybe even the whole fucking country. Sure, you want the power, the glory, the drugs, the pleasure." Spider's watery eyes wandered about the Chamber. "But most of all you want yourself a legacy, for your name to become the stuff of legend. And you think this baby boy will give you that, don't you, Kelly?"

"The baby's mine," said McGuire, blood trickling from his hand and onto the damp ground. "I know it."

"I'm glad you're so fuckin' certain. The thing is, I'm dying. I'd quite like a legacy too, as it goes." He beamed at McGuire.

"Fuck you."

Spider sneered and made a jerky gesture with his hand. McGuire was suddenly aware of a dozen or so submachine guns and pistols pointing directly at him. Spider shifted awkwardly in his wheelchair. "You can't take him unless you kill me. And if you kill me, my people will kill you. What *are* we gonna do, eh?"

McGuire looked to the people on the seats, to the few gang members he recognised, the ones he didn't. The civilians who'd joined up with Spider's gang just to survive. They all looked exhausted, many of them afraid. And still they looked expectant.

McGuire nodded slowly. "I don't think so, Spider," he said at length, and in measured tones. "Trex sees you as an *irritant*, you know that? But you're not even that. You're a useless pile of skin and bone. And this place, your lair—this isn't a headquarters. This is a *hole*, where a Spider crawls away to die."

"You fuckin' idiot, McGuire. You've got no idea the power I wield. I saved these people from oblivion." He pushed on one of the chair's wheels and spun about. "Barbara!" he called suddenly, his scratchy words echoing off the brick walls.

"Here," said a portly woman in her sixties, shotgun quivering in her red, peeling hands.

"What were you doing when I found you?"

"Eating out of a bin, Spider!"

Spider nodded, spinning his wheelchair around. "And you, Sam Mei—what were you doing?"

A young Chinese man responded, "I'd been arrested by the military for looting, Spider." He was holding a pistol on McGuire, sideways, like something out of a fuckin' Tarantino flick.

Spider smiled grimly at the memory. "And what were they going to do to you?"

"Shoot me, Spider."

Spider nodded his understanding. "And what did I do?"

"You sprang me, Spider. You saved my life"—he clutched the hand of the girl beside him—"and my sister's."

Spider wheeled around to address Nancy. "And you, what about you?" he said tenderly. "What were you doing when I found you, Nancy?"

Nancy moved in front of McGuire, then wordlessly lifted her head. McGuire saw the serration across her throat and the neat stitching that had saved her life.

"You see?" said Spider, rounding triumphantly on McGuire. "These people owe me their very existence."

"Some existence," replied McGuire, his voice rising in volume to be heard by the crowd. "A half-life, hiding beneath the city?"

"Nancy," intoned Spider.

She straightened to attention, meat cleaver glinting in the candlelight.

"Spider," she acknowledged. "You want me to cut 'im down to size?"

"Oh, you'd love to do that, wouldn't you, my dear? Chop-chop, eh?" Spider grinned. "But not this time, Nancy. No, I thought we might call on your Biblical expertise, my dear."

"What're you up to, you fucker?" demanded McGuire. He waved his arms angrily at the Chamber. "What is all this *shit?*"

"Come here, Frieda," Spider instructed the girl, who reluctantly stepped forward. "Ah, the dear ickle baby," he cooed, reaching out a gnarled, blood-stained hand to caress the bundle. Abruptly he looked back to Nancy, staring intently at the meat cleaver and licking his lips. "You see the problem, dear Nancy. We can't decide who should have the baby. Should it be Mr McGuire here or myself?"

Nancy blinked. "Yes," she said simply, "I see the problem."

"What would be the best way of deciding, do you think? Or is there a way of satisfying both parties?"

Nancy frowned, and wiped her mouth with her free hand. "I don't..."

"King Solomon," admonished Spider. "Don't tell me that your religious indoctrination has left you completely, my dear? That *would* be disappointing."

Nancy gazed at the enormous blade in her hand.

"You remember," said Spider, delighted. "A compromise solution, intended to satisfy all parties?"

"Nancy," said McGuire urgently, "he's fuckin' insane. You're not. You don't need to do this." His eyes darted back and forth to the audience. A dozen or so guns were still trained on him, but he could swear some were beginning to waver.

"Don't be ridiculous," hissed Spider. "Nancy here has cut more people than you can fuckin' imagine. She's even cut herself, for fuck's sake." He giggled, wheezy and high-pitched. "What difference is one more little *fuckin'* child going to make?"

"Yeah, you know the Biblical story," growled McGuire, this time to Nancy. "And you know your own story. Why don't you remember that instead?"

Spider let out a shrieking giggle, "Ooh, that's underhand. It really is." He tugged hard on one of the wheels of his chair, rounding on Nancy. "Slice the fuckin' baby in half. *Now.*"

Nancy blinked. "No," she said.

"What do you mean, 'no'?" responded Spider furiously. "I'm fuckin' telling you to do it. I saved you, you owe me."

"No," repeated Nancy, staring at Frieda and the baby.

"Fuck you," spat Spider. "*You've done much worse.*

Remember those things. All the blood and suffering you've caused with your mighty fuckin' blade."

"Not to children," said Nancy woodenly. She had lowered her blade. "Not to children."

"You fuckin' bitch!" bellowed Spider, leaping from his wheelchair. He grabbed for the meat cleaver, but his ruined body was too weak to reach it. He fell awkwardly at Nancy's feet and writhed on the floor, wailing brokenly in agony and rage, the most his atrophied lungs could evidently manage.

McGuire flashed a look at Baxter, who nodded at him.

"Listen to me," said McGuire suddenly and urgently, raising his voice so that the whole Chamber could hear him above Spider's yowling. "Is this the world you want? Where fucked-up monsters try to take the lives of innocents?" Spider's people exchanged looks. Many of the guns were pointed away now. This, it seemed, was the audience's expectation: they wanted him, McGuire, to *release* them from Spider's web.

He pointed at Spider, scrabbling helplessly in a heap on the floor. "Your leader—this sick fuck—is dying. That he's lasted this long is a tribute to his tenacity, to his bull-headedness, fuckin' whatever. But you lot—what are you doing? Skulking down here, living half-lives in the gloom and filth, occasionally sneaking up into the daylight to scavenge for food and drink, taking the occasional pot-shot at Trex's people?" He heard whispering from various corners of the Chamber, and watched as still more of the guns were lowered.

"He's fuckin' insane!" yelled Spider, his body twisting with the effort of calling out.

McGuire ignored him, continuing his address to the Chamber. "*Listen to me*. There's a world up there, and it's new born. It's unformed, undecided, full of potential." He paused, eyes scanning the rapt audience, milking the opportunity for all its worth. "Spider's time is at an end and he knows it. You can't skulk down here anymore. If you join me, we can make this world afresh."

An echoing silence descended, broken only by the steady drip-drip of water and by a gentle pitter-patter from outside. The rain had begun. Even Spider's sporadic wailing had subsided to nothing. The group continued to gaze at McGuire, all of their weapons now lowered. He saw in their eyes relief, but also uncertainty.

McGuire's nostrils flared, and he smiled broadly at the assembled mass. "You must go *up*," he proclaimed.

The dripping water was coming faster. Suddenly one of the crowd—Barbara, the large woman—broke away from the mass, beckoning emphatically to her companions. Then someone else did the same, and then another, and another. Abruptly the Chamber erupted into a flurry of activity, individuals making their way down from the seating, heading back along the tunnel, or for the exit in the far wall.

McGuire turned away, satisfied. Nancy was watching him, a stunned expression on her face.

"You know the Cathedral?" he said. "Trex's compound?"

"Yes," she said slowly, "I do."

"Come there in three hours. Say you're with me."

Nancy looked at him in initial confusion, but slowly nodded. "Okay." And with this, she turned on her heel, stepping over Spider's prostrate form and heading up the tunnel, away from the Chamber, bloodied meat cleaver dangling from her hand.

By now the Chamber had largely cleared of people. Frieda stood, wide-eyed and watching, the baby in the crook of her arm, uncertain what to do. McGuire dropped beside the figure of Lindsay, clutching her by the hand. It was clammy. He gently caressed her hair, her head lolling into his strokes.

"Can't be..." he heard her mutter.

McGuire looked to Baxter. "She needs medical care."

"Boss?"

McGuire spoke urgently. "Listen. Enough of Baxter the go-between. For the time being you need to choose sides. I need a squire."

"What, Boss?"

"You know, like in days of yore."

Baxter blinked. "Oh, a *squire*, Boss."

"Yeah, you fucker. A helper. You *capiche*?"

"Yeah." Baxter nodded slowly. "Yeah, I got you."

McGuire nodded, moving to the back of the wheelchair. He released the brake. "Good. Take the baby."

"Boss?"

"The baby," urged McGuire.

Baxter stepped forward, and Frieda pulled away, but then she fixed on Baxter's intent face. He nodded and she allowed him to carefully extract the infant, cooing as he did so. Pausing only for a final, longing look, Frieda disappeared through the exit in the far wall of the Chamber.

"We'll take them to the cathedral. They'll have a doctor there."

"You fucker," hissed Spider. He was sobbing silently and rolling back and forth on the floor, arms and legs waving, unable to right himself. Tears were rolling down his face. "They don't know you. They don't what you're capable of."

"They'll find out soon enough," snapped McGuire, wheeling Lindsay past him.

"But Boss," said Baxter, hurrying after him, the baby resting in the crook of his massive, muscled arm. He gestured back to Spider, at his quivering body. "What about the deal with Trex? You were meant to kill Spider. That was the deal, wasn't it?"

McGuire looked around the echoing, empty Chamber, felt the moisture in the air on his face. Through the cracks in the far wall he could see the rain falling ever more heavily. The water in the gully had already begun to rise. Soon the Chamber would be flooded.

"I think someone's gonna get himself flushed down the fuckin' plughole," he said. "What d'you reckon?" Without waiting for an answer, he began wheeling Lindsay down the tunnel and toward the light. Baxter followed, the child cradled in his arms.

CHAPTER SEVEN

"WHAT THE FUCK are they doing?" he asked, pulling up his fly as he emerged from the bushes.

Lindsay grinned. "Probably playing sandcastles. Boys will be boys."

McGuire snorted in agreement. He could see Trex, Ritzo and some of the others in the distance, swigging on beers, a few of the girls gyrating to some sort of heavy metal. Their bikes were parked on the rocky outcrop above.

"Forget 'em, Kelly. We don't need 'em."

McGuire nodded absently. He lowered himself back onto the sand and leaned on his elbows, gazing out toward the Bass Strait. Cobalt blue waves rose majestically before crashing into frothing nothingness on the shoreline.

"What is it, hon?" Lindsay shifted onto her side and gazed at him, head propped on her hand. Much of her auburn hair was tucked under a headscarf she'd fashioned from one of his bandanas, her emerald eyes hidden behind a huge pair of sunnies. Earlier he'd helped lather her porcelain skin with sun block. A person of her rarefied complexion couldn't outstay her welcome on Bells Beach.

He stared at her, remembering the first time he'd seen her from astride his Harley. The gaggle of high school girls were headed for St Magdalene's, chattering and giggling and throwing him and his gang furtive glances. All apart from her. She'd kept her head down, the faint blush on those pale cheeks only making her more alluring. It had been easy to begin an affair, harder to keep it secret from her friends and inevitably her family. He didn't give a fuck about that, felt no guilt that he'd corrupted her. Her beauty would never survive the suburban marriage and motherhood her family had planned for her. No stiff of a man with a business suit and a dull job would cherish her like McGuire would. With him, her beauty would never fade, because he would make people see it.

When her relationship with a gang member was exposed, her parents threatened to cut her off. It wasn't a threat that was ever liable to work. She loved him as he much as he loved her. 'Infatuation,' her parents called it, but they could go fuck themselves, a sentiment he expressed to them repeatedly as he and his gang smashed their delightful, cosy home to kingdom come. Five years later and she hadn't so much as breathed a word about her parents or her old life. They were gone; not even forgotten, but *erased*. Lindsay would always be with him. To all intents and purposes she always *had* been with him.

She handed the spliff over with an inquiring look. "Everything's fine," he said, pulling the smoke deep into his lungs. "*Everything*."

"Uh-huh," she nodded, one eyebrow curling sceptically. "What next, then?"

McGuire paused before replying, the roiling surf filling their silence. "I've got an idea for a raid."

"Tell me." She smiled dreamily, pulling the sunnies away from those startling eyes.

"A big one. An airport." He took an extended pull on the joint, watching it flare and subside.

"Sounds peachy."

Pot smoke billowed from his half-open mouth. "Uh-huh. The clever bit is the bulldozer." He smiled, more to himself than anything. "Wait for them to load the plane, then smash it with a bulldozer." He illustrated the plan by crashing his fist into the palm of his other hand. "I fucking love bulldozers."

Lindsay let her hand play on his bare chest, curling his hair. "*Awesome.*"

"Yeah," he breathed. "It'll be fucking beautiful. Just as long as..."

Her brow furrowed. "Just as long as what?" Her hand had flattened on his chest, unmoving, rising and falling with his breathing.

"Forget it," said McGuire, turning and smiling at her. He mashed the spent spliff into the sand. "I told you. Everything's fine."

She cocked her head. "You're sure?"

"Don't worry," he smiled. "It's nothing I can put my finger on." He lifted his hand to his forehead in mock salute. "Scout's fuckin' honour."

"You could put your finger on me," she said winsomely, flashing him a grin. She leaned over and kissed him on the mouth.

This one time it was different. This one time, everything worked as it should. Perhaps it was the roar of the ocean or the feel of the sun on their naked skin, but this time she didn't seem to mind the deformity, and he didn't feel ashamed. For the first time ever he felt the thing she had inserted for him—as a sign of her devotion—with something other than his hands or his tongue. The golden stud that only he and she would ever know about it. A symbol of their love, hidden from view. Only the two of them knew she had mutilated her innermost body for him. Only the two of them knew why.

When they'd done, McGuire looked up to see Baxter watching, stubby fag in mouth, his face expressionless. McGuire scowled and Baxter staggered backward across the sand-dunes to the rest of the gang, like a scared dog.

"What the fuck are you doing?" McGuire had pushed open the door to find Cho Hee bent double by the bed, hands clasped together. Lindsay lay curled on the mattress, semi-conscious, wrapped in a sweat-stained sheet. On the way back from Spider's subterranean base he'd noticed her clutching at her swollen belly. She did the same now, her grey face contorting with pain. Rain thrummed inexorably against the window, rattling the peeling casement. The storm had well and truly come.

Cho Hee turned, smiled, and stood. "Asking for God's love."

"God's playing pool down the corridor," muttered McGuire sardonically. "You could ask Him in person if you wanted."

Cho Hee continued smiling, bowed, and departed. She had to sidle past the doctor who'd entered behind McGuire and was now kneeling beside Lindsay, checking her pulse. McGuire looked over at Baxter, sat in the corner of the wood-panelled room nursing the baby, an expression of delight playing across his swarthy features. To give him his due, this was nothing more than he'd asked of him, and at least it gave the simpering, arse-licking toad another focus.

"How is she?"

The woman didn't look up, but instead rummaged in a cracked plastic case rather like a mechanic's toolset. She sighed. "Her body's gone into shock. She's malnourished, and gave birth without any medical assistance. She's lost a lot of blood."

"So she needs a transfusion?" demanded McGuire.

The quack stared at him, her hair wild and her eyes bloodshot. "We need a means of giving her a transfusion."

"Baxter will get you what you need."

Baxter looked up, surprised. "Boss?"

"Put the baby in the crib," instructed McGuire.

"Yeah, sure, Boss. Will do." Baxter hastily stood and gently laid the baby in an ancient-looking wooden crib before turning expectantly toward the doctor.

Two burly figures had appeared in the doorway, arms folded.

"Trex wants you," said one of the men.

McGuire inhaled. "Yeah. Sure he does."

"GOOD MAN," ACKNOWLEDGED Trex as McGuire entered the room, looking up only momentarily from the pool table. "I hear you stamped on our arachnid friend good and proper. Fuckin'-A." McGuire didn't reply, his attention captivated by the red and black oil painting of the magpie on the far wall. It smelled strange; he wondered what kind of paint the artist had employed.

"Cool picture, eh?" Trex's rumbled. "Vivid, uh, colours. Exchanged a crate of wine for it. Really makes the place come alive, don't yer reckon?"

McGuire grunted sceptically, turning to see Trex smacking the cue ball into a cluster of stripes. The rest of the balls spiralled around the table, but nothing was potted. Trex scowled good-naturedly as a bearded biker in wrap-around shades and a bandana stepped in to take his shot.

"Heard you found Lindsay, too. And a surprise something else to boot." He hobbled toward McGuire using his cue as an improvised walking stick, pulling a cigar from out of his shirt pocket. "Congratulations—I'm sure you'll make a magnificent daddy. The McGuire dynasty continues, eh?"

McGuire waved away the offering. "Whatever, Trex. Now you and me can go our separate ways."

Trex shrugged and thrust the cigar back in his pocket. He leaned on the cue and peered at McGuire. "That what you want?"

McGuire shrugged. "I got what I wanted. So did you."

Trex shook his head in disbelief. "Fuck me, Kelly. What about your revenge? You're not telling me you've gone soft? That you're gonna go grow melons or some shit like that?"

McGuire sighed impatiently. "I'm all about the revenge, don't get me wrong. But Ritzo is dead, Spider's been flushed away. You say you didn't betray me and I believe you. The Cull dealt with everyone else. There's only two people left I need to sort."

Trex frowned. "Two people? Who's that, then, fella?"

"Who'd you think? The fuckin' Kendalls."

"Oh, yeah," said Trex, thoughtfully. "The Kendalls. Right fuckin' weirdos, the pair of 'em. Not seen hide nor hair of 'em for a long time. I told you, they skipped town."

McGuire nodded. "Yeah, I heard that too. But I'll find 'em. Once Lindsay's well enough to travel."

Trex clicked his tongue. "Big country, mate," he observed. "Sure you don't want some help?"

McGuire arched an eyebrow. "In return for what?"

Trex beamed. "Remember those canisters back at the military compound? What d'you reckon would happen if we hit 'em?"

"You wanna bring it to a head?"

"Fuckin' yeah. We need to clear this town out, make it obvious who's in charge, yeah?"

"Yeah, I get it."

Trex cocked his head to one side, staring wistfully into the middle distance. "Those Abrams, mate! Imagine what you could do with those tanks."

"So you blow up the canisters. Then what?"

Trex laughed again. "That oughta do it, don't you reckon? Get 'em on the run, straight into our guns."

McGuire shrugged. "Could work." He was vaguely aware of a commotion in the corridor outside.

"Yeah, couldn't it just?" Trex puffed out his chest proudly. "I got the idea from World War One."

"Great precedent."

"So you'll do it, yeah?"

McGuire viewed him doubtfully, "Maybe. And in exchange you'll help me track down the Kendall twins?"

Trex nodded, "You got it. We'll be waiting in the streets all around. Just chase 'em into us and we'll do the rest."

"Okay," said McGuire, licking his lips. "But I wanna choose my own people. None of your fuckin' religious fruitcakes. I want gang types. Hardcore."

Trex extended his lower lip reflectively, "Yeah, okay. Maybe we can do a deal. Who've you got in mind?"

The door was flung open, and McGuire turned to see Nancy the Nun entering, struggling free of two of Trex's beefier henchmen, one of them sporting a fresh bite mark on his cheek. Nancy was drenched, strands of her swept-back hair falling in bangs around her dripping face. Her scowl transformed into a lopsided smile upon seeing McGuire.

"She's one," said McGuire.

"HOW IS SHE?"

The doctor turned around dazedly. "A little better, maybe. She needs to rest." Lindsay still lay curled on the bed, but she seemed to have drifted into a deep sleep. Her face, though, was cast in a seemingly perpetual, pained frown. A winding plastic tube extended from her arm to a bag of blood hanging from a metal pole that quivered every time she moved.

"She can't."

"What do you mean, she can't?"

McGuire shook his head. "She can't rest. It's not safe here."

"What's up, Boss?" Baxter had turned away from the baby. A stubby fag hung out the side of his mouth.

"Keep your fuckin' fag away from the baby," snapped McGuire.

"Sorry, Boss." Baxter ineffectually tried to conceal the cigarette before finally giving up and dropping it to the floor, mashing it into the carpet with his colossal boot.

"Trex wants a big push against the military. We're going to attack the compound."

"Right." Baxter looked at him expectantly.

McGuire sighed. "So we need to move Lindsay and the baby."

"Oh, yeah. Yeah." Baxter nodded.

The doctor looked outraged, at least as far as her exhaustion would allow. "I don't advise it. I'm telling you, this woman really needs to rest and recuperate."

McGuire towered over her. "Yeah, well, if the soldiers get their shit together and get this far it'll be fuckin' bad, trust me. She has to be moved somewhere safe, and so does the baby. It's a precaution."

"I know somewhere," said Baxter momentarily. "I mean, it's temporary, right, Boss?"

THERE WERE TWELVE of them in total, including McGuire. He and Nancy the Nun were the only ones lacking the lizard-scale tattoos. Most of them McGuire knew from the gang days, some very well, others only vaguely. The few exceptions included Cho Hee, who Trex had insisted join them on the mission. She was completely committed to Trex; McGuire figured she was besotted with him. He found her annoying, but he had seen her in combat and the woman had rescued him, so she clearly had some fire in her belly. Each of them carried a battered walkie-talkie, although some were little more than children's toys. It was a tribute to the importance of the mission that Trex had authorised the issue of the batteries, an increasingly rare commodity in the post-Cull world. They'd also been given gas masks, which hung from their necks, in anticipation of the release of the lethal gas once the canisters were blown.

McGuire had meanwhile instructed Baxter to take Lindsay and the baby to the safe-house Baxter had picked and to stay with them at all costs. The 'safe-house' turned out to be a container at the port, but Baxter was adamant he could defend it against any attack. His fawning earnestness made McGuire's skin crawl, but truth was, Baxter was the nearest McGuire had to someone he could trust. McGuire had insisted the exhausted doctor join them too.

The storm had lasted a few hours, but the familiar azure sky was gradually breaking through. They plunged through the puddles, McGuire letting Cho Hee lead them a circuitous route through crumbling buildings and away from the main thoroughfares, lest one of the military's frequent patrols spot them. This had been Trex's idea, but McGuire agreed with it, even though it effectively doubled what would have been a twenty-minute journey. McGuire's experience of Bennett and his tin-pot soldiers was that they were paranoid in the extreme, determined to defend their space rather than enlarge it. That was what the patrols were about, spotting and neutralising potential threats instead of extending the military's sphere of influence.

They ascended a pile of rubble and the compound rose into view. Cho Hee motioned for them to take cover. The squad sank behind a further pile of smashed bricks, Cho Hee pulling out a pair of cracked binoculars. McGuire lowered his clanking backpack to the ground.

"They've upped the number of guards since our last visit," she said, excitedly. "Seven by the front gate, all with machine guns. More along the perimeter, too."

McGuire accepted the binoculars from her. She'd missed out a detail. "Tanks," said McGuire, sniffing. "The couple that are left—they've positioned them to repel an attack."

"You think they know we're coming?" asked Mikey, a wiry kid with a vicious-looking scar running from ear to nose. McGuire had remembered him from the original raid on the military compound and asked for him specifically. He clung to his sniper rifle like it was a cherished toy. He could have been clutching a teddy bear, he was so fucking young.

McGuire shook his head. "I don't think they know about this attack, if that's what you mean. But these fuckers are afraid of us. In fact, they're afraid of everyone."

"But they're the military," said Cho Hee incredulously.

McGuire shrugged. "There's a few professionals in there, but the bulk of them are just stiffs in uniforms with minimal training."

"Then this should be easy," said one of the other gang members, a shaven-headed black guy called Wilcox. Like Nancy he'd been one of Lenny the Fish's people. McGuire had spotted him wandering around the cathedral and renewed their acquaintanceship. McGuire recalled him being a bit of a whizz with machinery, which he thought might come in handy.

McGuire rubbed his chin reflectively. "Yeah, except they're still wandering around with automatic weapons and grenades and shit. And being scared and paranoid means they're also fuckin' unpredictable."

"So what do we do?" asked Nancy the Nun distractedly, sharpening her meat cleaver with a rounded stone she carried with her. The sound it made was very close to being fucking annoying.

McGuire lifted the binoculars to his eyes again. "The cylinders are stowed beside the dormitory building."

"That's it, then," said Nancy, looking up and grinning. "Bung in a couple of grenades, 'bang' goes the canisters, and all Hell breaks loose. Then we can herd them out the front gate into Trex's waiting arms. Fuckin'-A."

"Sure, that's the plan," McGuire said, thoughtfully, "but if they get those Abrams moving, we're fucked. I totalled one of 'em but they've still got two to play with. Make no mistake, those two are gonna be primed and ready for action. After last time, they're liable to be a bit more protective of them, too."

"Imagine if we brought a tank back to the cathedral," said Cho Hee cheerfully. "Imagine how pleased our Lord would be."

"Yeah," said McGuire. His mocking eyes connected with Wilcox, who flashed him a smirking look of disdain.

"What do we do then?" asked another one of Trex's men, an older bloke called Rudy. He carried a bizarre-looking weapon, hooked up by tubes to a pair of canisters on his back. It looked to McGuire like he'd cannibalised a flamethrower from the ex-military lorry back at Trex's compound. A pervading smell of petrol accompanied him wherever he went; Rudy was clearly the 'useful pyromaniac' Trex had mentioned.

"First of all, we need to take out those canisters from out here," said McGuire.

"The boy here is the best shot I've ever seen," observed Wilcox, clasping Mikey on the shoulder.

"Too right," said McGuire. "That's why I chose the fucker."

The youngster looked sheepish, his cheeks colouring slightly. "Yeah, I'm pretty good," he said, his hand playing distractedly with the strap of the rifle. "Actually, fuck that—I'm shit hot." He smirked at Wilcox, who nodded encouragingly.

"Good." McGuire nodded. "As soon as they realise you're trying to hit the canisters, they're liable to come after you big time. You're gonna need to be somewhere you can get off repeated shots without them instantly fucking you over. You get it?"

Mikey nodded, looking around. He pointed to a tall, partially-redeveloped building a little way off, the yawning windows at its base smashed to buggery but the rest of the edifice largely intact.

"First floor," said Mikey.

"Cool," said McGuire. "Keep low, wait for our signal. As soon as the canisters go up, we'll make our move."

Mikey nodded his assent and took off back the way they had come, dodging from cover to cover.

"What about us?" said Nancy.

"I think you're right," said McGuire grimly. "As soon as those canisters are hit, chaos will break out. As soon as it does, start taking out the guards on the gate."

"We still need a way *through* the gate," objected Wilcox, who'd taken the binoculars. "Look at all that crap behind it." He was right: the military had piled car wrecks two and three high, along with girders and piles of bricks. Bennett's response to Trex's previous incursion: dig in. Blinky Bill was more paranoid than ever.

McGuire rose to his feet, slinging his backpack over his shoulders. "Stay here," he said suddenly, and then he *ran*.

HE ARRIVED, HEAVING for breath, to find that the driver was still *in situ*. Perhaps he'd been trying to escape the city when the virus had overtaken him, perhaps he'd just clambered into the driver's seat in sheer delirium. Fucking whatever. McGuire heaved at the mummified remains, which eventually came free with an extraordinary tearing noise, leaving the man's leathery hands steadfastly attached to the steering wheel. McGuire was forced to smash them off with the butt of his rifle. The key was still in the ignition; the engine erupted fitfully before petering out. A wavering needle on the dash confirmed what McGuire had already suspected.

He found some fuel, to his mild surprise, in the overturned ambulance a short distance up La Trobe. The looters must have been more interested in drugs. Using a discarded bucket and some indeterminate piece of medical apparatus he was able to siphon off the petrol and transfer it. On the third turn of the key, the engine sprang into life and the machine shot forward, evidently still in gear, tipping dramatically as it did so. He wrenched on the brake and picked up his walkie-talkie.

"I have a way into the compound," he announced as he grabbed his canvas backpack from where he'd slung it in the rear of the driver's cabin, over the colossal din of the engine. He began extracting the armour. "But I'm not exactly discreet. Mikey, when I give you the nod, take out those canisters. I'll be a few minutes. Over."

The walkie-talkie hissed with Mikey's reply. "No worries, over."

"Ready and waiting, over," came Cho Hee's voice.

"Over and fuckin' out," said McGuire. Once he'd pulled on the bulk of the armour and a pair of leather gloves, he paused, momentarily, to turn the helmet around in his hands. Baxter had done just as he'd been instructed. The iron helmet now featured a fetching skull and crossbones, rendered haphazardly but effectively in white paint. McGuire nodded to himself, satisfied, and lowered it over his head.

The bulldozer trundled down La Trobe, then on to King Street. McGuire shrieked with joy inside his helmet; he fucking *loved* bulldozers. Moments later he was on Spencer Street and approaching the compound. "Okay, Mikey. Take a shot at those fuckin' canisters. And for fuck's sake, make it count." He had to bellow at the walkie-talkie to be heard.

"Will do, over."

By now McGuire could see both the compound and the building opposite, where Mikey was ensconced. He watched as a shot zipped across the street. Immediately there were shouts and hectic activity from the compound.

"I hit it!" screeched Mikey over the walkie-talkie, barely discernible through the static and above the bulldozer's engine. "I fuckin' hit it!"

"Nothing happened!" crackled Cho Hee.

"Hit it again," growled McGuire.

Another shot shrieked across the street and into the compound. Again, there was no explosion, just yells of consternation. A staccato blast of machine gun fire emerged from the compound toward the building, then another, then another, all from different sources. They'd worked out where Mikey was.

"I hit it!" burbled Mikey's voice over the walkie-talkie, his mounting desperation tangible. "There's nothing in those fuckin' canisters!"

A calamitous *bang* sounded, and a shell arced across the street from the compound, smashing into Mikey's building. For a heartbeat there was nothing except the gaping hole, before the shell erupted outward and upward, the air suddenly full of spinning debris, tumultuous smoke and furious fire. When the smoke dissipated, it became clear that a huge lower section of the building had been decimated. The building teetered, the few remaining walls struggling to support upper floors. There was no way Mikey would have survived the onslaught.

"They're using the tank!" came Cho Hee's urgent cry. "What shall we do, over?"

McGuire grimaced. "Just follow my fuckin' lead!" he roared at the walkie-talkie. By now he was directly parallel with the compound. Bullets started to ricochet off the driver's cab, sparks glancing off McGuire's helmet. With a snarl he wrenched at the bulldozer's steering wheel, turning the machine hard right, its engine bellowing in protest. The tracks came down with a crash just as the bulldozer ripped through the reinforced fencing around the compound, careening through the barrier of old cars, rubble and steel poles.

The bulldozer hurtled forwards, bullets sparking off its raised scoop. The tank that had destroyed the building opposite was swinging its still smoking gun in McGuire's direction. McGuire leapt from the driver's cab, firing as he went, the bulldozer rumbling inexorably onward. The tank let rip, the whizzing shell smashing into the bulldozer's scoop, exploding on contact and sending fiery metal cascading down on the compound.

The predicted chaos had arrived even without the canisters. By now Trex's people were engaged in a firefight with the guards. Bennett's soldiers ran to and fro, chaotic and undisciplined, hitting targets seemingly by chance. Grenades blossomed, atomising glass, metal and people. McGuire saw Nancy creating gleeful havoc with her meat cleaver, machine gun clutched in her other hand, and the old bloke Rudy barbecuing all and sundry with his Heath Robinson flamethrower. As he watched, Wilcox charged the tank that had hit Mikey's building, shooting and scything his way through the cordon surrounding it and clambering up its front like a berserk animal. He was watching Wilcox drag the tank crew out through the hatch, when his attention was abruptly dragged elsewhere.

A familiar figure had emerged through the melee, clutching an Uzi and heading straight for McGuire.

"What the fuck do you want from me?" Bennett shrieked.

"I want your people," said McGuire matter-of-factly. "Tell them to surrender."

"You fucker!" screamed Bennett, coming to a halt a few metres distant. His face was a mess, poorly stitched together after his encounter with McGuire's rifle butt. The stitches looked like they might split open each time he shouted.

McGuire strode towards the boy, smirking beneath the helmet. "You're a fucking joke. Captain, my arse."

"Keep back!" Bennett raised his gun. "Keep back or I'll fuckin' kill you!"

"Who are you really, Bennett?" demanded McGuire. "Tell me who you are." As McGuire reached the boy-captain, he lunged for him and wrested the submachine gun out of his grasp. As McGuire pulled the weapon free, Bennett slipped to his knees, blubbing.

"I'm no-one," he was muttering. "No-one."

"Bit of a disappointment, were you, Bennett? After Mummy and Daddy lavished so much money on your education? What were you *meant* to be?"

"Daddy ran a merchant bank," mumbled the captain. "He said I wasn't up to working there, but that maybe he could get me a commission. Please don't kill me."

"You're a fucking joke and so is your phony fucking army," said McGuire, bearing over Bennett's pathetic figure. He crouched down and hissed, "Listen to me. You could do one thing to give yourself a trace—the merest hint—of dignity. There's an outside chance your rabble could be of use to me."

"Anything..." A trail of snot dangled from his nose, and he smeared it across his uniform sleeve.

"Surrender."

Bennett was wide-eyed. "Surrender? I can't tell them to surrender. We're the military. We're the last bastion of civilisation, the..."

McGuire motioned with a gloved hand toward the Abrams, and Wilcox glaring out from the turret. He'd apparently single-handedly taken control of the machine. The bodies of the crew lay beside the tracks, their scarlet innards sparkling in the bright sunshine.

"We have one of your tanks," said McGuire flatly. "If your people continue to resist, we'll blow the fuckers to fucking Paradise and back. They need to surrender." He jabbed a finger at Bennett. "*You* need to convince 'em."

"Okay, okay," muttered Bennett as McGuire hauled him unceremoniously to his feet. "The tannoy, I have to get to the tannoy..."

"Run along, then!" said McGuire, kicking the kid up the arse. Bennett stumbled, arms and legs flailing, for the wooden cabin. McGuire could hear him babbling to his soldiers: "Ceasefire! Ceasefire!"

McGuire turned and strode back toward Wilcox's tank.

"Reckon you can work this beast?" he bellowed.

"Fire it, you mean?" responded Wilcox, wild-eyed. "Fuck, yeah. I'll work it out."

McGuire pointed. "Take out that wooden hut over there. Quick as you fuckin' like."

Wilcox disappeared inside the tank and McGuire found himself having to duck as the turret whipped around to point at the cabin. McGuire could hear some tinny little PA system whining into action, Bennett's desperate voice pleading with his troops to stand down. It was short-lived. McGuire jumped aside as the gun barrel roared into life. Even with the helmet covering his ears, the roar was terrific. The hut exploded into a burning cloud of wooden fragments, human tissue and bone. Although probably not *back*bone, McGuire wryly reflected.

And with that, the defence folded. However incompetent Bennett might have been, he'd been their commanding officer; and one of the two Abrams was in enemy hands to boot. Wherever he looked, beyond the dead and the dying, beyond the debris and bits of bodies, McGuire could see hands raised in surrender. The twelve of them had taken the compound, with only one casualty: the boy sniper Mikey. It had been a rout.

Cho Hee bounded up to him. She was bloodied but otherwise unhurt, her hair matted around her oily face. McGuire had removed his helmet, and now ran a gloved hand through his own greasy hair.

"McGuire!" she called breathlessly, grinning and waving her machine gun triumphantly. "We beat 'em!"

"Huh?" McGuire grunted, his attention elsewhere. He was estimating the number of prisoners, helmet dangling from his hand.

"McGuire!" she yelled again, more insistently this time.

"What the fuck is it?" growled McGuire, turning to look.

"This." She'd levelled her machine gun at his chest. He laughed involuntarily. His one-hundred-and-thirty-year-old iron breastplate wasn't liable to provide much defence against a modern machine gun, destiny or no destiny.

McGuire snorted. "What a fuckin' surprise."

"Our Lord doesn't trust you," she said, sadly. He couldn't tell whether she was genuinely remorseful or not.

"You don't say," nodded McGuire. He deliberately turned his back on her, continuing to gauge the strength of Bennett's defeated force.

"He thinks you might try and displace Him," she explained. "I'm sorry—you saved us, before. That was a holy thing to do. But the Lord's will be done."

"One thing," McGuire said suddenly, turning back toward her, a thin smile playing on his lips.

"Anything," Cho Hee replied, her expression earnest. She looked like she might cry, for fuck's sake.

"This," said a voice behind her. A sudden crack sounded; Cho Hee's eyes widened in shock as she reached a free hand up to her forehead, where she found a trickle of blood. McGuire watched as her hand reached the meat cleaver embedded in the middle of her skull, gingerly testing the edge of the blade. She fixed a reproachful gaze on McGuire and pitched forward.

"Fuckin' nutter," muttered Nancy. She placed a boot on the back of the woman's head and heaved at her weapon, now firmly wedged in the skull.

"What the fuck?" Wilcox was out of the tank and running toward them, slowing as he approached. Some of Trex's other people turned to look, disbelieving. Some couldn't decide whether to train their weapons on McGuire and Nancy or to continue marshalling the prisoners. Rudy approached, flamethrower still smoking. He was muttering to himself in Polish, laughing and shaking his head.

McGuire addressed them, "Think about it. We took this place with twelve people. We captured an army with twelve people. We suffered one fatality."

"Fuckin' yeah," acknowledged Nancy.

"Trex is in charge," snarled Wilcox. He was a big man, bigger than McGuire even, and bore down on him. "We work for him."

"Consider yourself headhunted, mate," smiled McGuire. He nodded at Rudy. "You too, twisted firestarter. Fuckin'-A."

Rudy beamed appreciatively.

"We work for Trex," insisted Wilcox. "Why'd you go and whack one of his fuckin' acolytes?"

"Trex tried to get Cho Hee to nail McGuire," said Nancy angrily, finally extracting her meat cleaver from the young woman's skull with a jarring, scraping noise and a loud, sucking squelch. "He's not to be trusted." Wilcox regarded her with suspicion.

"Nancy's right," said McGuire. "I want a new fuckin' world, not a replay of the cosy old one. Join in or fuck off."

Trex's people looked at one another, uncertain. Cho Hee had been the only true believer on the mission; the others were all gang members from Back in the Day. Their decision would rest on who they respected more: McGuire or Trex.

"Okay," nodded a woman with an eye-patch. "I'm in."

"Me too," piped another.

"Yeah, fuck it," said someone else.

"*Tak, ja też,*" said Rudy with an absent smile, blowing a curl of smoke from the nozzle of his flamethrower.

Others hesitated, then one by one threw their lots in. Only Wilcox held back, his eyes playing on the figure of Nancy as she lovingly wiped the blood and brain tissue from her blade with a rag. Without looking up, she said, "There was nothing in those canisters, Wilcox. Trex set us up. Mikey died for nothing."

Wilcox stared at her for a moment. "Okay," he said eventually. "Count me in."

"I know Trex," said Rudy thoughtfully. "He will not go without a fight."

McGuire nodded. "That's what I'm counting on."

CHAPTER EIGHT

"NICE ONE," CALLED Trex. "You done got me a tank!" He stood at an awkward angle, leaning heavily on his cane. Ranged behind him was the motley rabble of his army. To one side, the massed ranks of gang members, clad in variations on a familiar uniform: beards, shaven heads or long hair, ripped denim, bandanas, motorcycle boots and tattoos, automatic rifles, shotguns and knives. On the other side, the civilians of Trex's cult, all with the same glazed expression as the late Cho Hee, also brandishing a miscellany of weapons. McGuire even spotted the aged Reverend Sarah, shotgun propped languorously against her shoulder, a faint smile playing on her lips. Against a sea of incongruity she still managed to stand out. Behind them all rose the cathedral, its sandstone spire reaching for some other, better realm.

"And an army," added McGuire, striding toward Trex, exuding bonhomie, his iron helmet clasped under one arm like a returning general. "A shit army, but an army nevertheless."

Behind McGuire, Trex's former accomplices—the nine who had raided the compound and now switched allegiance to

McGuire—shepherded rows of battered, bloodied soldiers, guns at their backs. The uniformed men and women trudged into the compound, their hands above their heads, some looking defiant but most defeated, perhaps even relieved. There were about forty in total. A dull rumble accompanied their desultory approach: one of the liberated Abrams, Wilcox's head visible in the turret. McGuire led his squad to a standstill some twenty metres from Trex's ranks, the tank coming to a peremptory halt shortly after. Wilcox signalled for one of his comrades to cut the Abrams' engine and a pregnant silence descended, broken eventually by the distant laughing of a kookaburra.

"Trouble is," mused Trex, hobbling toward him, braces shrieking with each step. "This looks a little bit, uh, *confrontational*." As he approached, McGuire saw Trex's familiar hand scythe dangling from his belt. "Not planning something disloyal, are you, mate?"

McGuire stared him down. "I told you, Trex," he deadpanned. "I'm all about the revenge. Plain and simple."

"Fuck me. How many more times?" returned Trex, seemingly genuinely exasperated, but also undoubtedly playing to the crowd. "*I didn't betray you.*"

"Maybe you didn't," ruminated McGuire. "But let's be honest, eh? You used me to neutralise the military compound. And my reward? One of my 'team,' brought along at your insistence, turned out to be a swivel-eyed assassin intent on blowing my head off. Not to mention those canisters containing precisely fuck-all. Thanks a fuckin' bunch, mate."

Trex waved his hand dismissively, "Yeah, well. The canisters were a genuine mistake, mate. Empty, were they? Well, there you go. As for Cho Hee—well, maybe she got a bit overzealous and misinterpreted my instructions."

"Like fuck she did," McGuire sniffed. "Anyway, she got a meat cleaver in the brain for her trouble. I think she finally achieved enlightenment, mate, let me tell you. Nice bit of, uh, *trepanning*, I think they call it. Perhaps you should try it too."

Trex laughed, gesturing behind him to his acolytes. "Easy come, easy go, mate. There's plenty more where she came from."

McGuire nodded. "Whatever. Let's cut to the chase. I want your unconditional surrender. It's over, Trex. I fuckin' won. Lay down your weapons, walk away from here and we'll say no more about it. You'll have a fine fuckin' time out in the Bush, trust me." He flashed Trex a wide grin. "I know I did."

"And what're you gonna do if we don't play ball, fuckwit? Blow us up?" Trex laughed for the ranks, but nobody particularly joined him, even the perpetually sycophantic acolytes. Every set of eyes was transfixed by the tank.

McGuire exhaled theatrically. "Yep, that is pretty much the idea."

Trex called out to Wilcox. "Don't listen to this fuckwit, mate. He's off his fuckin' rocker."

McGuire shook his head. "He's not interested, Trex. That kid Mikey paid the price for your little game. They've all had enough. Back in the Day, we were the rebels, don't you remember? We *fought* against the shit, we didn't fuckin' give into it, let alone try and fuckin' duplicate it, or whatever it is you think you're up to."

Trex snorted, then projected his voice to the masses. "How the fuck would you be any fuckin' different, tell me that? You're full of shit, mate."

McGuire looked around him, at the crowd in front of him, the mob at his back. "People don't want churches and schools," he said. "They're no fuckin' use any more. They want order, they want control, they want certainty. That's what I'll give 'em."

"'Certainty'?" echoed Trex. "Do you wanna know how I was *certain* you were up to something?" There was a look of manic glee on his face.

McGuire's grin became fixed. "Tell me, fucker."

Trex gestured to his people. "Bring 'em out. All of 'em." A ripple went through the group behind him and Lindsay emerged, stumbling, held tight by two of Trex's minions, still dressed in her torn, dirty shift.

"You *cunt*," breathed McGuire.

She was brought forward, blinking confusedly in the sunlight and struggling to walk. A further ripple spread across the crowd as the bedraggled doctor emerged, the baby in her arms. Behind them came Baxter, head bowed, hands secured with twine, his squashed face a mass of congealing lacerations and pulsating bruises.

"They were caught heading for the docks," announced Trex cheerfully. "Fortunately, you'd put Professor Baxter here in charge." Some snickering from Trex's troops as Baxter bowed his head still further. A gobbet of spit flew out of the crowd in a high arc and hit Baxter squarely in the side of the head. It dribbled down his pockmarked, bleeding face. Trex's people seemed more confident, now, despite the tank. McGuire would have to be careful; the situation was becoming unpredictable.

"I thought to myself," continued Trex, "why the fuck is a sickly woman and her tot being moved? And then it occurred to me that my dear old mucker Kelly McGuire must have plans, and that said plans must involve fucking with me and my people. Hence moving his nearest and dearest to a place of safety, lest I decided to turn them into hostages, or perhaps get a little ruthless with 'em." His bloodshot eyes met McGuire's. "Am I warm?"

McGuire's eyes narrowed. "Wilcox's just waiting for my word, man. If I give the signal, he'll destroy the whole motherfuckin' lot of you."

Trex pulled Lindsay to her, one arm still resting on his cane as the other clutched her fast to him, his massive bicep wrapped around her head. Sunlight caught off the hand scythe hanging from his belt, briefly dazzling McGuire. "I'll tell you what. I think the blade is faster than the tank. What d'you think? Shall we see?"

McGuire's gaze switched to the men and women standing behind Trex. He spoke loudly, rapidly: "You'd sacrifice all of your followers, all of your men and women, just to slice a woman and her baby? Some fuckin' God you are."

Trex smiled a lopsided grin. "How does it go? *Suffer the innocents* or something?" Suddenly he let Lindsay go, and she collapsed to the ground, moaning.

McGuire started forward, but thought better of it. "So this is it, then? A fuckin' stalemate?"

Trex looked surprised. "Fuck, really? I fuckin' hate stalemates."

"Me too," McGuire said. "What's the alternative?"

Trex grinned at McGuire, baring his teeth. "We're like, um, a couple of bucks, you and me, ain't we? Struggling for control of the herd?"

"If you say so, Trex."

McGuire watched as Trex unhitched the hand scythe from his belt and hold it aloft. "Remember this? Remember what I've done with it?"

McGuire shook his head in disbelief. "Look at you, mate. You walk with a cane and you've got fucking leg-braces. Hardly a fair fight."

Trex emitted a low grumble. "All it does is even it up a little. I mean it, you fucker. You and me. Toe to toe."

McGuire rubbed the back of his head. "And the winner gets everything?"

Trex laughed. "I think that's a fair bet, don't you?"

McGuire's eyes played across the tranquil faces of Trex's acolytes, weapons at the ready. He wondered how serene they would remain if he gutted their deity. "One thing. The ones who really think you're God..."

Trex smirked. "Not liable to be an issue. But yeah, I see what you're getting at." He pivoted awkwardly on the spot and addressed himself directly to his faithful. "Listen to me. I am your God; you know that. I am about to battle this man. I will win. But if I do not, my spirit will move to the body of the man who triumphed over me. He will henceforth be my vessel. You will obey him in my stead, in all matters. You understand?"

Some of the acolytes looked uncertain, but most smiled beatifically, nodding their understanding.

Trex turned back to McGuire, smiled at him, and let the cane clatter to the ground at his feet, swaying for a moment. He passed the scythe from hand to hand, feeling its weight, focussing himself.

Trex watched with amusement as McGuire lowered the iron helmet gently to the ground, pulled off his leather gloves and with measured movements removed his armour, placing each piece in turn beside the helmet. He bent to remove the Bowie knife strapped to his shin, and before he could straighten, Trex was on him, swinging with his own blade. It struck McGuire's shoulder, piercing his battered canvas jacket and plunging into muscle. He grunted with pain and threw Trex over his shoulder, the scythe ripping flesh as it pulled free. Trex landed heavily, cracking the tarmac.

McGuire staggered backward, torn jacket flapping, blood cascading down his arm, and roared. Trex pulled himself awkwardly to his feet, the dripping scythe in one hand.

"Sneaky bastard," spat McGuire.

"Faster than you, mate," retorted Trex, leering. "Even with these fucked legs, I'm still faster than you." He leapt forward, swinging the hand scythe, leg-braces buckling with the impact of the landing. This time, though, McGuire was ready for him, and sidestepped the manoeuvre.

Behind him now, McGuire swung his boot into Trex's calf. The braces on Trex's left leg splintered completely under the force of the blow, folding him backwards. McGuire plunged his knife into Trex's side, ripping down and forward, and Trex fell to his knees and desperately shoved McGuire away.

The gash in Trex's side ran deep, right across his abdomen. The colour seemed to have drained from his body, perspiration coating his face and torso. He tried to rise but couldn't; his free hand moved to the tear, scrabbling to keep his innards from escaping.

"You fuckin' killed me, you bastard," he said. Still on his knees, a look of abject shock on his features, he swayed gently to and fro, the remnants of his braces creaking with the movement.

"Face it, Trex," hissed McGuire, staunching the flow of blood from his ripped shoulder. "You're a fuckin' dinosaur, mate."

"You fucker!" One of Trex's lieutenants, the massive bloke with the bandana and wraparound sunglasses, stepped forward and brought his submachine gun to bear. McGuire, too far away to stop him, braced himself for the inevitable, but the man was turning away, training the weapon on the doctor and the baby. He saw the doctor desperately trying to leap out of the way, her precious burden clutched to her breast.

And abruptly the man's head exploded, in a torrent of skin, skull and brain. His headless body fell to the ground, revealing Reverend Sarah, smoking shotgun clutched in her pudgy, wrinkled hands and a look of supreme satisfaction on her lined face.

She turned to the people around her and shrugged. "They had a bargain," she protested. Nobody spoke.

McGuire had dropped to Lindsay's side. She was covered in brain and blood, but otherwise she seemed unharmed. She stared at him in bafflement.

"You're dead," she said simply.

"Look after her," whispered McGuire to Baxter, swinging his Bowie knife through his friend's bonds.

In the silence that had settled, McGuire heard a gun being primed, and then another. He glanced at Wilcox aboard the tank, who nodded in readiness. McGuire spun, pulled his submachine gun and let rip, filling the air with the noise, spent cartridges bouncing on the road at his feet. With his other hand he snatched up Ned Kelly's iron helmet. "Listen up!" he yelled, leaping onto the front of the tank, grasping hold of its gun barrel.

"Trex is gone. Bennett is gone. In the last few days I've dealt with others, too. They were fuckers, all of 'em; chancers, miscreants. And there are more to come, biding their time, hiding, waiting for the moment to strike. Scum, wanting to fuck you over. If you do as I say, we will root 'em out. We'll fight 'em, and together we'll fuck 'em."

From his vantage point atop the tank, he saw someone he recognised, emerging from behind a teetering brick wall. It was Jess, the girl with the pink Mohican, hair slightly singed but otherwise going strong. She was with the blonde girl from Ritzo's gang, and a smattering of Spider's people. As he watched, McGuire saw others emerging from their hiding places, some he recognised, some he didn't. In their eyes he saw wonderment, but something else: he saw hope.

"First, we must have order. There will be law, and it will be *my* law." McGuire pointed at one of Trex's men, a bearded hulk of a bloke with a Kalashnikov. "You," he said. Then he pointed at Nancy, who raised her eyebrows in surprise. "You." Finally he thrust a finger toward one of Bennett's burlier soldiers, whom McGuire recognised as one of the few professionals amidst the remnants of the military. "And you."

"The three of you are the beginnings of our police force. Find others, people you trust. There's a building—you might know it—called Parliament House, at the intersection of Bourke and Spring Street. That's our base, from this point onwards."

"Who the fuck made you leader?" said the bloke with the Kalashnikov. He'd stepped out from the crowd, cradling his weapon.

McGuire looked at Trex, lying face-down in the dirt in the midst of his death throes. The God's final thrashing movements, it seemed, were anything but mysterious.

"*He* did," said McGuire, pointing to the bloodied heap. Then he lifted aloft Ned Kelly's battered iron helmet for all to see. "And so did *he*."

Silence dominated. The crowd looked to him, blinking, trying to comprehend what was happening. Then he heard a single voice—Baxter's—chanting. The cry was taken up by a second voice, and then a third. Just the old gang members to begin with, pumping their fists in the air each time, then joined by the others: Trex's acolytes, Bennett's soldiers, the remnants of Ritzo and Spider's gangs, a few random survivors who had simply joined the throng. Soon the words folded into one another, becoming a beautiful paean, and the air was a sea of thrusting fists.

Dead Kelly.

SHE SHOOK HER head, feeble, but still incredulous. "I thought they'd killed you. The newspapers said..."

McGuire knelt beside Lindsay, her hand in his. Blood was oozing from the wound in his shoulder, but he ignored it. "The fuckers couldn't catch me. No-one can catch Kelly McGuire." Around them, his followers from the raid on the military compound barked instructions. For now, at least, the disparate factions seemed willing to accept their authority, Bennett's former soldiers particularly eager to prove their allegiance to the new order. McGuire would establish more disciplined chains of command once he was ensconced in Parliament House. He would build structures, implement protocols, construct rituals. In short, he would impose order.

He stared at Lindsay searchingly. The tatty shift she was dressed in was ripped to fuck, her face swollen. But she was still the woman he loved. "Why were you with Spider?"

Lindsay hugged her knees to herself. "Don't be angry with me," she said. "I thought you were gone. After the Cull... There was no-one else."

McGuire reached out to gently touch her cheek, and saw her flinch. It was probably the scar on his hand.

"Where's Liam?" she said.

"The baby," said McGuire. "Baxter!"

Baxter emerged through the crowds, holding the child tenderly in his arms. "He's here, Boss."

"He's here," echoed McGuire, as Baxter handed the bundle to Lindsay. McGuire watched the relief on Lindsay's face.

"She needs rest," said a weary voice at his shoulder. The doctor. "So does the baby. They need to be away from here. From this..."—she cast about herself despairingly—"whatever this is."

"Of course," said McGuire. "Reverend!" he called.

Reverend Sarah wore a broad grin as she approached, swinging her open shotgun.

"What can I do for you?" she enquired mildly.

He pulled her aside, while the doctor checked the child. "I need your help again, Reverend," he said. "Can I trust you?"

The Reverend shrugged. "I saved your life. Isn't that good enough?"

"The tattoo," said McGuire, gesturing to the base of her neck, just above her dog collar.

The elderly woman chuckled, spat on her finger tips and rubbed the tattoo, pulling her hand away to reveal a smudge. "It's pen ink," she said. "I have to reapply it every day. Just above the dog collar, you understand."

McGuire cocked his head to one side, impressed. "I think that makes me *less* fuckin' likely to trust you."

She returned his smile. "Not sure you have a choice. You want me to give Lindsay and the babe sanctuary in the cathedral?"

McGuire nodded. "Until our headquarters are ready, yes."

"Very well," said Sarah at length. "I'll do a deal with you. In return for saving your life, and in return for protecting the life of your child, *you* will protect the cathedral. Yes?"

"So that's your game. Protect the cathedral at all costs. Was that your arrangement with Trex?"

Sarah shrugged. "More or less. It worked, too." She beckoned for Lindsay to pass her the child. "Of course, the real question should be, why should *I* trust *you*? Why should any of us trust you?"

McGuire returned the shrug. "You've no choice either."

The old woman cradled the baby. Without looking at McGuire she said, "Ah, that's where you're wrong. My allegiance is to God, not to fuckin' butchers like you and Trex."

"You saw what happened. I kill only when I have to. Just like you."

Reverend Sarah cooed at the baby, not looking at McGuire. "What you're doing is different. There's no *necessity* for revenge, McGuire."

"An eye for an eye and all that."

"Don't give me that Old Testament bullshit," she snapped, suddenly locking eyes with him. "The thing is, you want to be *certain*, don't you, McGuire? So you go after each and every one of 'em and then you kill 'em. The only problem is, that won't tell you *who* betrayed you. Will it now?"

He glowered at her without answering, until she returned her attention to the baby.

"This child needs changing."

McGuire watched as together with the doctor she powered Lindsay and the baby into the crowds, Lindsay throwing him a bewildered look over her shoulder.

"You did it, Boss," said a familiar voice in his ear. "This is your world now."

McGuire turned to see Baxter, features drawn wide in a grin. "Not yet," he said. "There are still scores to settle." He stared into the crowd where the three women had disappeared.

"You mean the Kendalls?"

McGuire ignored that. "You almost got Lindsay and the baby killed."

Baxter shook his head. "Yeah, I'm sorry, man. There was too many of 'em. I couldn't get away."

"You heard what I said, Baxter. I want certainty in all things."

Baxter's eyes were wide with innocence. "I'm sorry, Boss, really I am," he protested. "It won't happen again. Honestly it won't."

McGuire licked his lips, his eyes playing on the lizard-scale tattoo across Baxter's neck and shoulder. Unlike Reverend Sarah's, there was no doubting its permanence. "I need a sign, mate. A token of your loyalty."

"Anything," insisted Baxter.

McGuire smiled slightly, then beckoned toward Rudy. The old man made his way through the milling crowd, still clutching his homemade flamethrower. "Rudy, Baxter here needs your assistance. He needs something *removed*."

CHAPTER NINE

THE MULTICOLOURED TOWER swayed but did not collapse. "Red one," piped a child's squeaky voice.

"It'll fall," said McGuire softly. "It's too much."

"Red one," insisted the child.

"Okay," responded McGuire, picking another chipped red block from off the floor. He bit his top lip as he placed the block gingerly on top of the tower. The auburn-haired child giggled as the tower swayed one way, then the other, before inevitably collapsing.

"I told you," said McGuire. The little boy simply laughed, clapping his stubby hands together. McGuire pulled himself awkwardly to his feet and left the child alone on the hessian mat. This was why he seldom played with the kid.

"Little fucker doesn't know when to stop," observed Lindsay, with a faint smile. "Maybe it's hereditary." She was sitting on the window sill, painting her toenails.

"Uh, Boss," said a gruff voice. Baxter stood in the doorway; McGuire could see Wilcox and Nancy the Nun beyond him, making eyes at one another. The thought that the two might do something as normal as hook up fair made him wince.

McGuire took a swig from a tinny of flat lager, grimaced, and placed it back on the wobbling table. "What is it? Better be fuckin' good, mate."

Baxter's hand played involuntarily across the enormous burn scar travelling from beneath his neck all the way down the left side of his body. McGuire recalled his screams as Rudy went to work. The bearded mountain men of Katoomba probably heard the fucker, he was so loud.

"It's Zircnosk," blurted Baxter.

McGuire nostrils flared. "You got him?"

"Sort of. We've got a, uh, lead."

"A lead? Is that it?"

"The thing is, Boss," said Baxter hesitantly. "The thing is, you'd better come."

HE SAT, GRIM-FACED, as Wilcox powered the Humvee down Lonsdale. Food, shelter, fuel, armaments, vehicles. McGuire controlled all of these things, and from all these things arose the one thing he cherished above all else: certainty.

The Humvee slowed as they passed one of the work details. McGuire looked out of the tinted window at the ashen faces of the people, of all ages and ethnicities, their clothes tattered, faces bloodied and battered, spirits fractured like the fragments of rock and metal they sought to collect. He saw, too, the well-fed guards. In the midst of this chaos he had imposed an order, with him at the apex, his guards managing discipline, the people being helped to build a new world. It was an exchange: their toil in exchange for protection, for food. There was no hope in their eyes anymore, because no-one needed to hope anymore. They had what they needed, as far as this world was concerned. Certainty had been delivered unto them.

There were exceptions, of course, the occasional blip that tested the system. In the year and a half following Trex's demise a number of individuals—even a few groups—had arisen to mount a challenge. Most of them were known quantities, minor figures with some sort of gripe who'd mistakenly thought they could mount a successful challenge to his power. There was the occasional chancer, too, who'd blown into town and fancied taking a pop. Whatever their MO, they'd been dealt with, ruthlessly and with precision. Some of Trex's people, in particular, found adjusting to the new regime problematic. Not the religious ones, of course: Trex had told them his spirit would inhabit McGuire on his death, and they weren't the type to question.

No, the most serious threat to his authority had been initiated by hardened former gang members, the ones McGuire knew of old, the ones who had been part of Trex's army at the cathedral. McGuire could have gone fuckin' ballistic at the mutiny, but he chose not to. This, he felt, was a sign of true leadership, something he had learnt from watching TV biographies of tyrants, back before the History Channel itself became history. In a way he didn't blame the revolutionaries: they were programmed to be rebels, and he, McGuire, had become their enemy simply by dint of being in control. Funny how things turned out.

Even so, they'd still had to be dealt with. When the conspirators were rounded up he'd utilised some techniques he'd read about in an old library book—a heavily singed copy; one of the few tomes to survive the fire in the State Library— about the Great Leap Forward. He'd even gone so far as to stage his own show trial and public executions, picking off a few other individuals he thought might prove problematic into the bargain. In the end, all very satisfying.

So Ritzo had been wrong: the past wasn't so easily dismissed, and could be of use if properly—that is to say, *selectively*— employed. All the same, though, there were elements of his own past that he wished he could erase. Not the murdering or the brutality or the drug-taking or the stealing, of course. Those were the things that made life worth living, and made an otherwise wild and unpredictable world manageable. What worried him was his need for revenge, which remained as intense as ever, even if the actual details of the heist had become hazy after all this time. What he needed, he realised, was *closure*. To be certain. Though it was a wrench to admit it, the elderly Reverend had been right: eliminating all of the potential suspects was not sufficient. He needed to know who and why. He needed the cop, Jack Zircnosk, the man who'd dealt directly with McGuire's betrayer; the man who'd alerted the media to the heist, including but not limited to twinkling talk-show host Danny Kline.

Wilcox swung the Humvee to a halt, and McGuire stepped out and pulled the iron helmet over his head. Today, the helmet would be sufficient. Baxter emerged from a second Humvee, driven by Nancy.

It was a children's play-park. Several motorcycles rested beside the park, polished chrome blinding in the morning sun. A gaggle of leather-jacketed men stood around them, smoking and laughing. A short distance away McGuire could see a boyish woman with spiky purple hair, dressed in leathers, head down, swaying on one of the children's swings. Megan Kendall.

"What is this?" breathed McGuire. His eyes flitted between Meg and one of the men, a rotund guy with a goatee. He recognised him too.

"McGuire!" yelled Goatee, approaching with a wide smile. As he walked, he pushed his jacket aside so that his shoulder holster and automatic pistol were easily visible. The gaggle of men fell in behind him, grinning.

"The Kendalls," growled McGuire, looking at Baxter. "What the fuck is this?"

"No, I promise," said Baxter hurriedly. "They wanted to *talk* with you, Boss. That's all."

The man stopped some short distance from McGuire, his broad smile intact. "How you doin', mate?" He gestured vaguely at McGuire's helmet. "Nice look. Tell me, are you Ned Kelly the hero or Ned Kelly the villain?"

"I'm both," McGuire said from within the mask. "It all depends on who *you* are."

Bobby smirked. "Must be hot, though, wearing that thing..."

"I heard you'd left town, Bobby."

"We did," said Bobby Kendall. "Things got a little, uh, excitable here. Decided we needed to lie low for a while. Gather our thoughts, that kind of thing."

McGuire nodded towards the woman on the swing. Her face was turned to the sky, wearing a distant grin. She seemed to be giggling to her herself. "How's your sister? Still playing with her bow and arrow?"

"You know Meg. She always was a bit of an eccentric."

"I'll fuckin' say," said McGuire. "This is all fine and dandy, but you still haven't explained what you're doing on my turf, *mate*."

Bobby laughed. "Yeah, I heard that, man. You control most of the fuckin' city now, don'tcha? Not bad for a dead man."

Without looking, McGuire knew that Wilcox and Nancy's hands were resting on their weapons.

"I think you'll find," he said, "we control the *whole* city."

Bobby laughed again, and raised his palms. "Of course. I didn't mean no offence, Kelly."

"What do you want, Bobby?"

Bobby nodded. "Okay. You know me, Kelly. I'm a businessman. I seize opportunities when they arise—"

"I've got things to do, mate. Enough of the spiel. Fuckin' hurry up."

Bobby's smile vanished. "Okay. We want you to leave us alone."

McGuire chuckled, turning to his own people. "So you come here to tell us that? Mate, you're screwier than I thought."

Bobby stared at him. "Yeah. Simple as that. We supply a lot of people with fuel. We want to carry on doing that."

McGuire considered a moment. "Okay, I get that. How do you propose securing such an arrangement?"

Bobby nodded. "Yeah, well. Through information, Kelly. Specifically, regarding Jack Zircnosk."

McGuire tensed. "Where is he?"

The smile had returned. "I'll take you to him. I just need an assurance from you that you'll leave us be. Forever." He held out a stubby hand. "Okay?"

Now McGuire smiled, under the helmet. "Yeah, why not?" He reached out his scarred hand and clasped Bobby's. He saw Bobby's sister Meg gazing straight at him, head cocked curiously.

THEY MOVED IN convoy further into the city, the two Humvees flanked by the gang's motorcycles. Meg rode pillion on Bobby's bike, crossbow and quiver strapped to her back. Occasionally she came parallel with McGuire's window, and seemed to stare straight at him, as though her eyesight could penetrate the tinted glass.

Bobby's bike peeled off toward the River Yarra, and Wilcox followed. Above them rose the decaying towers of the Crown Entertainment Complex, their windows cracked, vast portions of the buildings scarred with fire and, as per usual, spidery, largely meaningless graffiti, much of it in red and black. McGuire struggled to make out the words *Everlasting* and *Ceaseless*. The great gas brigades that used to shoot enormous fireballs into the sky every evening had died when everything else had.

A sudden burst of automatic fire blossomed from one of the windows of the Crown Metropol Hotel, ricocheting off the roof of the Humvee.

"Fuck," muttered Wilcox, turning the vehicle into a skid which momentarily lifted its left side in the air before it crunched back down. Wilcox slammed his foot on the accelerator as more bursts of gunfire raked the ground around them.

McGuire could see a laughing Bobby slaloming his bike to avoid gun shots. Meg had her crossbow in her hands and was shooting at the hotel, mouth wide with glee, laughing like a fucking kookaburra. The rest of the Kendall gang opened up with their submachine guns as well.

Bobby came to a halt beside the Yarra, a safe distance along from the Complex, the rest of his gang arriving right behind him. McGuire leapt out of his Humvee as soon as it stopped, and marched directly up to Bobby, heedless of the Kendalls' weapon-wielding heavies.

"What gives, fuckwit?" he snarled, grabbing the chubby man by the shoulders of his leather jacket.

Bobby shook his head, half-laughing. "It's him, mate. It's Jack Zircnosk."

"Like fuck it is."

"I'm telling you. He came to us. Wanted to do a deal."

"A deal," breathed McGuire. "A deal to do what?"

Bobby grinned again. "To bring you down, mate."

"You fucker," growled McGuire. "Are you fucking with me?"

"No, mate. Honestly." He raised his hands. "I'm telling you. Your man Baxter had put the word out. We were gonna hand him straight to you, but he ran when he realised what we were up to. We chased him here, but you can't get near him. He's holed up in a hotel room, got the whole fuckin' place booby-trapped. The fucker's mad, mate. He's totally lost his mind."

"I need him," whispered McGuire.

"Yeah, well. Good luck. I've done my side of the bargain." He motioned to his people to mount their bikes. "You gotta keep away from us now, Kelly. That was the deal, mate."

"How do I know it's him?"

"You know it's him," Meg said dreamily, long hands caressing her beloved crossbow. "You're Dead Kelly. You *know*."

"Good luck, man," said Bobby, mounting his bike. Meg swung her legs over the pillion and leaned forward on the bike. Bobby turned in response to her touch and kissed her hard on the lips.

Bobby grinned at McGuire, then revved the bike and pulled away. The other bikers followed suit, throwing up a wave of dust and old newspapers in their wake.

McGuire pulled the iron helmet off, scowling. He turned to Nancy and Wilcox, handing them the mask. "Follow 'em," he rumbled. "Take some people and wipe 'em out."

Wilcox nodded. "We're on it."

McGuire placed a hand on Nancy's shoulder, stopping her, his eyes playing on the cleaver strapped to her thigh. "I want evidence—you understand?"

"Sure thing, boss."

As the Humvees pulled off in pursuit of the Kendall gang, Baxter looked to McGuire. "What next, boss?"

"Fuckin' Zircnosk," replied McGuire grimly.

McGuire HELD UP his hand in warning, and Baxter came to a stop. They had approached the hotel from behind, taking cover from the carcasses of rusting vehicles and overturned street furniture, and come to a halt near the corner of the building. With luck, the awning over the ground floor of the hotel would hide their approach from Zircnosk's overhead viewpoint, but it was still a risk; from the nearest cover to the edge of the awning—a length of about twenty metres—they would be out in the open.

McGuire picked up a half-crumbled brick from the gutter, drew his arm back and launched the brick at a pile of rubble near the awning. The brick smashed into the rubble, sending debris skittering outward across the pavement. McGuire looked up, to where he remembered the automatic gunfire coming from. Midway up the wall, the reflection of the sun on one of the hotel's windows rippled, barely perceptibly, but enough to catch his eye. McGuire nodded to himself. Halfway along the sixth floor. While it was clear that Zircnosk could hear, McGuire didn't think he could see the approach. They would soon know for certain.

McGuire turned to Baxter and placed his index finger on his lips; Baxter nodded. McGuire, rifle in hand, ran into the sweltering sunshine, dodging silently along the edge of the building to the awning. Then he turned back and motioned to Baxter. Baxter sprinted to his side, his face a mask of sweaty determination, Uzi clutched to his chest.

The entrance was barricaded; working as quietly as they could, McGuire and Baxter had to heft aside filing cabinets, sink units, and wardrobes. Beyond these obstructions stood two sets of jammed revolving doors, their frames bowed out of shape and much of the glass fractured or missing. Baxter went to climb through the jagged glass, but McGuire held out his arm.

"Carefully," he whispered, and Baxter nodded dumbly. Why had so little effort been made to block the doors? Clearly Zircnosk—or whoever else was in the building—had other defences further inside the building.

Baxter followed him through the wreckage of the doors. The foyer beyond was covered in rubble and dust, where parts of the high, arching ceiling had collapsed. Bullet holes scarred the walls, the marble-tiled floor, and even the huge teak desks that populated the reception area. A foul stench hit them as they entered. McGuire looked about and spotted the remnants of a human body protruding from a set of half-open lift doors. It looked like an arm and a head, although the extent of the decomposition made it difficult to say for certain.

McGuire wordlessly gestured to the staircase and Baxter nodded. Amidst fallen masonry they came across more corpses, or more accurately *parts* of corpses, blood and entrails coating the steps and rendering the climb slippery. Unlike the body decaying in the lift, these bodies were mostly fresh. He wondered whether there was something in the building worth taking, or whether they'd just been seeking refuge. As they ascended, McGuire saw blood trailing up the walls, as though bodies or portions of bodies had somehow been dragged upward. McGuire peered up, and saw something yellow and plastic dangling down the stairwell several storeys above them.

McGuire stopped suddenly as they rounded the corner, reaching out a hand to grab Baxter. Perched on the very next step was a row of odd-shaped green plastic devices. There were more on the next step, and so on, travelling all the way up this flight. The bloodstained walls were festooned with cracks and craters, while tiny flecks of ripped human gristle and bone dotted the staircase.

"Fuck," he muttered.

"What are they, boss?" asked Baxter.

"Butterfly mines. Fuck. One probably wouldn't kill you, but all these together..."

"What do we do, Boss?"

McGuire clicked his tongue, then pointed. "Up there."

"The banister?" Baxter blinked. McGuire watched him scanning the narrow handrail, then saw his eyes flicker to the landmines. "Really, Boss?"

"Any other suggestions warmly fuckin' received."

"'Kay," replied Baxter slowly. An extended pause ensued, then eventually, "No, sorry, Boss. No ideas."

McGuire flashed him a withering glance. "Me first," he said, and grabbed hold of the banister, placing a booted foot on it and hoisting himself up. The banister creaked under his weight. Raised mosaics in the wall afforded him sporadic purchase. Painfully slow, the banister protesting with each footstep, he began to edge up and past the landmines. Then the banister groaned even more loudly, and he looked around in horror to see Baxter placing a foot on it.

"Wait until I'm across, you fuckwit," he spat.

Baxter, wide-eyed, nodded, and took his boot away. McGuire continued to pull himself upward, until eventually, awkwardly, he stepped off the banister on to the next clear flight. He looked to Baxter, and gestured impatiently.

"*Now*," he said through gritted teeth.

Baxter began his own ascent. Under McGuire's weight, the rivets supporting the banister had already begun to bend. Fortunately Baxter was a smaller man than McGuire, and he didn't hang about. Only as he was nearing the safety of McGuire's flight did he slip, his flailing foot inches from grazing one of the tiny landmines.

There was little sentimentality in McGuire's next act. He knew that at this distance, he would himself be consumed in the blast if Baxter fell. He reached out, grabbed Baxter with one arm and lifted him back onto the banister. Baxter wobbled before reasserting his balance and edging the final half-metre or so to safety.

He stared at McGuire, sweat dripping from his pronounced brow, and panted. McGuire said nothing, instead turning and resuming the ascent up the stairs.

CHAPTER TEN

The sixth floor. McGuire and Baxter emerged from the stairwell and into the corridor. As they'd progressed, they'd encountered more of the mines, presumably appropriated from some stolen or otherwise mislaid military shipment. McGuire dimly remembered hearing about how the Soviets had used them in Afghanistan, of how they'd eventually been banned because children thought they were toys. Even by his flexible moral standards, these were nasty fucking devices. They were often deployed out of helicopters; someone could have happily dropped them down the staircase, replenishing them once they'd detonated. The higher they went, the fewer body parts they encountered. Clearly only the most intrepid, careful intruders had managed to sneak up to the higher levels, until finally their luck or skill had deserted them.

The pair paused momentarily while McGuire, intrigued, examined the yellow plastic object he'd seen from below. It seemed to be a modified cleaner's bucket, its top half hinged, the lip crudely cut into jagged teeth. The bucket was suspended from a pulley made from the fire-hose reel, the makeshift guide rope wrapped securely around the banister several times. He gingerly lifted the jawed lid of the bucket and was greeted by a horrific stench. Scraps of human entrails and blood slopped in the bottom of the bin. Clearly the claw was used to grab body parts following encounters with the mines. Fuck knew why.

McGuire let the lid snap shut and turned toward the corridor. Motes of dust whirled in the occasional shafts of sunlight through missing or smashed doors. After the stairwell he was still cautious, although the hallway looked pretty innocuous. McGuire couldn't see any rubble from exploding mines, nor indeed bodies or bits of bodies. There were, however, huge blood stains across many of the walls, which looked as though they'd been scrubbed. It seemed someone was making a concerted attempt to keep this part of the building clean and tidy, as far as was humanly possible.

McGuire stopped suddenly. Baxter looked to him questioningly, and he raised his free hand to his ear. Baxter frowned and listened, and a look of wonder crossed his face as he, too, heard the music.

The lyrics were crackly but distinct nevertheless: '...*shooting arrows in the blue*...' McGuire recognised the tune from when he was a kid. It was called 'Little Arrows,' but he couldn't recall who sang it. An American bloke, he knew that much, probably in the late 'sixties. As a child he remembered stumbling, bleary-eyed into the lounge late at night, hearing the song as he approached, watching as his parents swayed to it. They would feign outrage as he entered, before one or other—or sometimes both—would laughingly scoop him up, and return him to bed with a soothing lullaby and good-night kiss. Then they'd close the door and he'd hear another easy-listening classic saunter into life, before falling into a contented slumber.

The memory had brought tears to his eyes. They were good parents, Lucy and Joe, despite what they gave him, despite what they did to him. Looking back, he often wondered whether, if things had turned out differently and he hadn't hacked them to death with that axe, they might have made good grandparents. Probably. Still, as his dear old Papa was wont to say, if wishes were horses then beggars would ride.

The song had come to an end, giving way to hissing nothingness. The door was ajar, and he could hear someone shambling across the floor and the sound of the needle on an old record player being lifted. McGuire had readied his weapon, and now pushed the door open with his foot before stepping through.

A gangling woman of about fifty with a misshapen bob of a haircut and a heavily-powdered face stood by a table upon which sat an ancient wind-up gramophone. She carried a cigarette in an old-fashioned holder, and looked thoroughly bemused. On the other side of the room, an elderly man sat in an armchair, a shotgun levelled directly at McGuire's chest. He leered at McGuire. A pair of false teeth sat on the scuffed metal cabinet beside him.

Baxter stayed out of view, listening.

"I'm looking for a policeman," said McGuire.

The woman looked to her companion, a smile cracking her lipsticked mouth, before drawing on her cigarette. She and the man began to laugh.

"Bit late for that, boyo," said the man in the armchair. "I think the situation's a bit beyond the plods, if you take my meaning."

McGuire's eyes flickered around the room. Another door led off. An assault rifle was propped on a tripod at the window. Unused cartridges and magazines littered the floor.

"Oh, my goodness, sorry about the mess," said the woman through a fug of smoke. "We do try and keep the place tidy, but you know how it is..."

"His name is Jack Zircnosk," said McGuire. "It's imperative I find him."

"*Imperative?*" parroted the man in the chair, guffawing. "*Imperative?* What're you, boyo, some sort of *ponce*, is it?"

"No-one here 'cept us, old chum," said the woman at the gramophone, gesturing around. "But bravo on making your way up the stairs. Those butterflies can be really quite hazardous. Really excellent work. In fact, you're the second person to breach our defences in as many weeks—we'll have to review our approach." She flashed a meaningful glance at the bloke in the armchair, before switching her attention back to McGuire. "The thing is, you're really no good to us in *one piece*, dear chap."

McGuire's gaze flicked to the inner door. He could hear muffled noises, sounds of movement.

He gestured with the gun. "What's through there?"

"Nothing you need worry your pretty little bonce about, boyo," said the man in the armchair, caressing his shotgun, to which he now looked meaningfully. "Now fuck off out of it."

"Nice weapon," acknowledged McGuire. "I reckon something like that could cut through a wall no problem."

"Probably, boyo," acknowledged the man with a snort, "but I'm not shooting you through a wall, am I now?"

"No, of course not," said McGuire, licking his lips. "But my colleague is."

The wall ripped apart as Baxter opened fire, gunfire exploding across the room and into armchair man's chest, flipping the seat backward. The man's shotgun fired involuntarily into the ceiling, dislodging a torrent of plaster. The woman at the gramophone produced a Beretta from a drawer on the underside of the table, and McGuire slammed the butt of his gun into her shoulder; she fell backwards, pulling the gramophone down on her own head. The woman's limbs spasmed briefly before falling still, a dark pool of blood spreading out rapidly from her cracked skull.

Baxter entered, grinning, and McGuire put his index finger to his lips and gestured toward the inner door. He reached out and carefully pushed the door open.

On the far wall hung an enormous canvas, depicting a silhouetted eighteenth-century clipper atop a blood red sea, black seagulls circling it. In the centre of the room, his back to them, stood a stubby, middle-aged man in spectacles and shorts. A pair of orange headphones trailed into a cracked Sony Walkman resting on his thigh. Periodically he would dab a paint brush on the palette in his hand, then dart forward to daub at the crimson sea. Now and again he would tut, reach over to a blue plastic freezer box and pull out a handful of something thick and reddish, which he then massaged into the canvas. The floor was covered in the mess.

McGuire's gaze drifted to other canvases of varying sizes

dotted around the room, all in the same distinctive red and black, though the subject matter varied from animals to landscapes to portraits, including what looked like the man and woman from the other room.

He recognised the style from the magpie hanging in Trex's inner sanctum back at the cathedral. He also recognised the stink, which in here was overwhelming and unmistakable: raw human flesh and blood.

He heard Baxter retching behind him.

The painter turned, pulled the headphones from his ears and blinked at them. "Can't stand their bloody music," he explained. "They call it camp and ironic, I call it shit. What do you want? I am *working*, you know. I'm in the *moment*."

"What the fuck is this?" McGuire murmured.

"This is art, mate," responded the painter. "What the fuck do you think it is?"

"You're using corpses," McGuire observed. "People's innards. As paint."

He heard Baxter spewing again.

"Of course," smiled the painter. "You like it? Well, of course you do—otherwise you wouldn't be visiting our collective."

McGuire viewed him steadily. "You blow 'em up, collect 'em in your bucket device and then make them into..."

"*Art*," interrupted the man. "Yes, of course."

"And why the fuck," said McGuire slowly, "do you do that?"

The painter blinked in surprise. "Isn't that obvious? We *immortalise* them. You've obviously not read our manifesto."

"You immortalise them," echoed McGuire blandly.

"The Cull will wipe us out, you see," explained the painter. "Humanity, I mean. Eventually. What better way for people to live on than in the work of our collective? I mean, who doesn't want immortality, eh?" He let out a shrill giggle.

Suddenly McGuire remembered. All across the city. The statue outside the museum. All those buildings he passed. Even the storm drain. "The graffiti," he breathed. "The black and red graffiti."

"That's right," nodded the painter enthusiastically. "Although to be honest, that's more Karen's thing. She's very into public art. I'm a bit more old-fashioned, as it goes. I prefer galleries." He looked suddenly worried, as if he'd finally realised something was awry. "Are Karen and Tony there, by the way?" he added, craning around McGuire.

"No," said McGuire quietly, his shock subsiding. "My colleague and I immortalised them."

"I'm sorry, what—?" began the painter.

"This," said McGuire simply, and let rip with the rifle. The painter was thrown backwards against the canvas, his face a mask of surprise as he gradually slid to the floor. His innards left an enormous tidal splash in the middle of the sea, one that threatened to engulf the ship. McGuire cocked his head appreciatively, impressed with his own artistry.

A low moan dragged his attention to the ensuite bathroom leading off. McGuire made his way across the slippery floor and pushed open the door. An obese, naked man lay on the filthy floor, pudgy hands and ankles secured behind his back with twine, mouth gagged. With some effort McGuire pulled the fat fucker into an upright position and used his Bowie knife to slash the man's bonds before removing the gag. The bloke looked at him dazedly, his swollen face wobbling with a mixture of gratitude and incredulity.

"I've been looking for you," said McGuire.

THEY SAT ZIRCNOSK in an armchair and stood back. Judging by the state of him, he and Baxter had arrived in the nick of time. His body was covered with lurid, bleeding welts, where he'd been repeatedly punched and hit. There was presumably an artistic rationale, but McGuire was fucked if he could think what it might be.

McGuire's own tolerance for horror was profound, but he could see how staying in that room of obscenities would not be conducive to questioning. Besides, Baxter's stomach was clearly not on a par with his own. They didn't dare move far from the collective's apartment in the trapped hotel, so McGuire opted to relocate to the nearest room without a locked door, or—it turned out—any door at all.

Baxter had found a stained duvet from somewhere and wrapped it around the policeman, presumably in an effort to restore to him some sort of dignity. McGuire watched him with a raised eyebrow.

"What the fuck are you doing now?" he asked, as Baxter rummaged in a dusty linen cupboard.

"Looking for a pillow," replied Baxter innocently.

"For fuck's sake," said McGuire. "Enough. He's a fucking copper, remember that."

"Sorry, boss," said Baxter sheepishly. Traces of heave had dried on his stubbly chin, and he absently began to pick them off.

McGuire pulled up a tatty pouf and sat on it, facing Zircnosk.

"You know me?" he growled.

"You fucker," croaked Zircnosk, regarding him through puffy, black-rimmed eyes. "How the fuck did you survive?"

McGuire shrugged. "Easy. I had to die first."

"I was looking for you," gurgled Zircnosk, struggling to sit upright so that he could better see McGuire. He gasped with pain as he shifted position. "Couldn't get close. Surrounded yourself with a fucking army, haven't you?"

"If you'd knocked on my door I'd have welcomed you with open arms, Zircnosk. Believe me."

Zircnosk snorted. "It wouldn't have been a social visit."

"Is that so? What were you gonna do to me if you found me?"

"What do you think?" smirked Zircnosk, and then winced with the effort. "You're psychotic. A multiple murderer, a vicious armed robber and fuck knows what else. I'd have put a bullet in your brain, mate. At the very least."

McGuire gestured at Zircnosk's broken body and let out a throaty laugh. "Looks like your plan went a bit fuckin' awry, mate."

Zircnosk grimaced. "The Kendalls sold me out. Incestuous fucking tosspots."

"And then fuckin' Andy Warhol and his mates decided to get all creative on your arse?"

"Fuckers," muttered the cop. "They normally let the landmines blow people apart then use that weird fucking contraption to pick up the remains. 'Cept I was better than that—I got as far as this floor, then they ambushed me. Fucking *avant garde* bastards."

McGuire puffed out his cheeks. "I'm impressed—we had a hard time getting up here. Had to balance on the fucking handrail."

"Ah well, I thought laterally about it. There were some kids hiding out in the lobby. A blonde bogan and some tart with a pink Mohican."

McGuire snorted. "So you sent them up ahead of you—how fuckin' nice of you. I reckon we probably trod in them on the way."

Zircnosk grimaced. "Yeah, well, they were vermin. Like the way you and him are vermin."

McGuire looked to Baxter. "Fuck me. And this bloke's meant to be the good guy."

"Boss?"

"Never mind." He returned his attention to Zircnosk. "Listen to me. I need something from you."

Zircnosk gave a low, rasping chuckle. "Why the fuck would I help you?"

"I can make your pain a lot worse, Jackie Boy. I really can."

Zircnosk shook his head fractionally, opening a sore on his neck as he did so. "Look at me, mate. There's fuck-all you can do to me."

"You'd be surprised. Trust me."

"You'd have to kill me. And then where would you be?" He stared at McGuire, his chins rippling.

McGuire's features darkened. "Don't fuck with me, mate."

But Zircnosk continued thoughtfully. "Now, let's see. It's obviously something very, very important for you to come looking for me. Let me guess..." He blinked. "Of course. The heist. It's gotta be."

"Bingo."

"You wanna know who dobbed you in?" Zircnosk asked. "You wanna know who was it, out of your gang, who came to me one fine summer's day and fucked you over?" Zircnosk's eyes flitted to Baxter. "Am I right? Is that what this is all about?"

"Tell the boss," said Baxter firmly. "Otherwise things will go badly for you."

"Things will go fuckin' *badly* for me?" Zircnosk shook with laughter, blood trickling from one eye. "You don't know, do you?" he said gleefully. "You've got no fuckin' idea."

McGuire towered over him, grabbing the arms of the chair. "Who was it?" he hissed, leaning toward him. "Tell me now and I'll make the pain go away."

"Pain?" responded Zircnosk, suddenly thoughtful, a dreamy, idiotic grin playing on his flaccid features. "Yeah, pain."

"I'll make it all go away," repeated McGuire.

Zircnosk nodded eagerly, as far as he was able. "You'll take it from me? My pain?"

"I promise," whispered McGuire.

"Okay," said Zircnosk quietly. "Come closer."

McGuire leaned into Zircnosk's wrecked visage.

Zircnosk closed his eyes. "I'm trying. I just can't remember her name."

McGuire gripped the arms of the chair still harder. "*Her* name?"

"Just that she had red hair." Zircnosk's eyes snapped open again, and glittered.

"What?"

"Yeah. Auburn, really," said Zircnosk, with the faintest hint of a smile.

"You're fuckin' with me." McGuire stepped back from the former cop and glared. "It wasn't her."

Zircnosk, though, had closed his eyes, a dreamy grin playing on his face. "What was it now? Began with an L."

"He's fuckin' with you," said Baxter, eyes fixed on Zircnosk. "Don't listen to him."

"Lorraine? Laura? I forget."

McGuire turned on Zircnosk, face twisted with rage. "You *fucker*."

"You know, you're right." Zircnosk smiled. "You've done it. You have actually taken my pain from me. I do hope you enjoy it."

"You're lying," said McGuire.

"Am I?" said Zircnosk, sounding almost surprised. "Do you really think that? Did it never occur to you why you were *really* killing all your old chums? Trex, Ritzo, Spider? I'll tell you why. It's not that you want to know the truth. Quite the contrary, mate. It's so you don't have to hear what you've already guessed."

Through gritted teeth McGuire said, "Why the fuck would she do that to me?"

"Perhaps because she was going to have your child. Perhaps because you're a fuckin' psychopath." His stubby fingers had clenched hold of the duvet in his excitement. "We protected her. At least, until the fuckin' Cull hit. Then she had to fend for herself like the rest of us. She ended up with Spider, by all accounts."

McGuire lunged forward in a fury, smashing his rifle into Zircnosk's skull, knocking him and the chair over. The cop lay on the floor, panting curiously. It took McGuire a moment to realise he was laughing.

"I forgot her name," Zircnosk laughed, greasy blood pouring off his face. "But I'll never forget the *stud*."

"What did you say?" McGuire's voice was slow, stunned.

Zircnosk looked up to him, still panting. "The golden stud, mate. You know what I mean." He stopped laughing for a moment, and a thick tongue emerged to lick his swollen lips.

McGuire stood over him, struggling for control. "It was a good idea," he said suddenly, grabbing Zircnosk and heaving him to his feet, so that the duvet fell away. He powered the enormous, naked man out of the hotel room and down the corridor. McGuire could hear Baxter struggling to keep up.

As they reached the stairwell, McGuire gripping him by the folds of fat around his neck, Zircnosk tried to turn his head and look at McGuire. "What was a good idea?" he said, still grinning manically.

"Letting someone else deal with the landmines," replied McGuire, heaving Zircnosk forwards. McGuire and Baxter watched as the cop fell, grabbing desperately for the yellow claw. He seized it, and for an incredulous moment it looked like the claw might prevent him pitching forward, but his weight betrayed him. The guide rope wrenched through the pulley, ripping the banister from its moorings, and Zircnosk fell, still clutching the claw.

The former cop's enormous bulk tumbled hectically down the stairs, bones loudly cracking at each impact, until eventually he smashed into the midst of the landmines at the bottom of the next flight. The resulting explosions bowled McGuire and Baxter backwards, lumps of human blubber and plaster cascading down on them. A few moments later there was another flurry of explosions, as the remainder of Zircnosk landed on the next set of landmines; and again, and again. The hallway around them vibrated, until eventually the noises subsided.

"Ought to make leaving the hotel a little easier," observed McGuire, as he hauled himself to his feet.

A dazed Baxter nodded as he struggled upright. "Y'know he could have been lying, boss."

McGuire paused momentarily from wiping the human detritus and dust from his clothes. "No," he said simply.

Baxter averted his eyes, and they headed down.

CHAPTER ELEVEN

"WHERE IS SHE?" The words resounded in the great hall, sending ripples across the dank, still water in the stone font. He saw a couple of faces look up from their prayers, terrified eyes peeking over the backs of the walnut pews.

Reverend Sarah returned his gaze calmly, drying her hands on a mouldy towel. Already an imposing woman, here in the depths of the cathedral she seemed indomitable. She smiled beneficently at him, her eyes flitting between McGuire and Baxter. McGuire saw his shifting reflection in the font's water. He noticed a trickle running down the font's fluted side, where it collected in a growing puddle at its base.

"I don't know," she said patiently. "Perhaps she's at Parliament House? Or perhaps you'd prefer if we called it your *palace*."

McGuire rubbed his scarred hand. "Don't fuck with me, Sarah," he hissed. "I know she came here."

"Yes," conceded the Reverend, cocking her head and nodding thoughtfully. "She brought the baby here."

"Why, though? Why did she come here?" McGuire glared

at Baxter, who started from his reverie, his thick, veiny neck flushing.

The Reverend laughed. "Why do you think?"

McGuire shook his head. "To pray?" He remembered the graceful high school girl with the porcelain complexion and auburn hair he'd seen heading for St Magdalene's all those years ago. For fuck's sake. That other life was meant to have been wiped away, to have never existed.

Sarah rubbed the palm of her own hand, either unconsciously mirroring him, or mocking him; it was hard to say. She said, "You can't control this world, McGuire, any more than Trex could, or any of those other hoodlums. This world is bigger and more complex than you think. Only one person can see it fully, and He isn't you."

McGuire snapped, "I see all I need to see."

Again the loving smile that made his stomach boil. "Is everything about revenge, McGuire? Everything?"

McGuire grabbed Sarah by the wrist and shook her. "*Everything*," he whispered into her ear. "Tell me where she's gone." He wondered where her shotgun had got to. It was unusual for her not to have some means of defending herself and her parishioners.

"Dead Kelly," called a woman's voice. McGuire released his grip and the elderly woman collapsed to the floor. He turned to see Nancy and Wilcox approaching. Nancy was holding something that dripped a dark, continuous line along the intricate mosaic floor.

"Got something for you," Nancy called. There were gasps and shrieks from the parishioners as they realised precisely what this woman had brought into the House of the Lord. This was the new world; nothing—*but nothing*—was sacred anymore.

Nancy lifted her prize up for McGuire to inspect it: Bobby Kendall's head, his flaccid face frozen in a look of astonishment, neck cartilage and tissue hanging in ribbons from where it had been hacked off.

"As you requested," said Wilcox, stifling a snigger. "He ran for it, but didn't get far—fat fucker."

"Most of his gang are dead," said Nancy, chewing gum as she stared, fascinated by the decapitated head, watching as rivulets of blood trickled to the floor. "A few scarpered. The petrol dump is ours."

"You've done it, boss," exclaimed Baxter in an intense, excited whisper. "That's it. You've won. The Kendalls, Trex, Spider, Ritzo. Even fuckin' Zircnosk. You beat 'em all."

"Not all of them. Not yet," McGuire shook his head, his bloodshot eyes fixed on Reverend Sarah as she struggled to pull herself to her feet. "Now I know who betrayed me. She has to pay. She knows she has to pay. Isn't that right, Reverend?"

"You're the Devil," spat Reverend Sarah. She'd used the font to pull herself up; he noticed the puddle of overflowing water had reached the tip of his boot. "But your reckoning will come. God will deal with you, you fucker."

McGuire regarded her defiance with a pained smile, which abruptly vanished. "What did you do?" he said suddenly, fixing his gaze on her again. "What did you do to the baby?"

"What do you think I did?" she said, perplexed. "I blessed him and I named him."

McGuire shifted his stance, slopping the puddle. "Why?"

"You know why. He will be in the Lord's hands if anything happens to him."

"She wouldn't..." he hissed.

"She plans to deny you everything," responded Sarah calmly. "She knows how to do it."

"I want my revenge. I want my son." Suddenly furious, he bellowed, "I want my *fuckin' legacy!*"

"We saw her," said Wilcox unexpectedly. "Lindsay, right? Gunning down La Trobe."

McGuire rounded on him. "You fuckin' *saw* her?"

"On one of those quad-bike things. Ten, fifteen minutes back."

McGuire spun back to Baxter. "Grab the armour," he said urgently. "Meet me by the bikes. No-one else, just you."

"But Boss," protested Baxter, "we don't know where she's gone. Unless..."

McGuire towered over Baxter, clenching and unclenching his fists. "*Unless* what?" he snarled.

Baxter stared at McGuire, a familiar look of consternation on his thickset features. "Unless she's taken him back. Y'know, to where it began."

*   *   *

HE RELAXED HIS hand on the throttle, clambering off the machine before the motor had stopped, and felt the sandy breeze on his face. The animal growl of the engine faded, and the roar of the wild ocean flowed into the void. He saw the quad-bike Lindsay had taken, a child's seat and assorted abandoned toys visible in the rear of the vehicle. Despite the wind, their footprints—hers and the toddler's—were easy to spot. He apparently wasn't too far behind them. With a grimace, he pulled his ACR from its straps on the side of his bike and started down the narrow wooden walkway. He'd barely begun the descent to the beach when the sound of a second quad-bike approaching reached him, and he heard Baxter's familiar, stumping footfalls crunching on the stony terrain. Baxter's arrival sent a wallaby bouncing back into the trees.

McGuire stepped onto the beach, onto that fine, familiar yellow sand. There was only one set of footprints now; she must have picked up the child when she heard the approach of his bike. He walked steadily, not changing pace at all. By now Baxter had caught up with him, and crunched alongside with the backpack, as if they were heading out for a fucking beach holiday.

The squat man grinned. "Perhaps we should just leave her, boss. Forget it and move on."

"Fuck off," muttered McGuire. "When we reach them you'll need to take the kid. You've gotta keep him safe. That's your job. You got it?"

Baxter frowned. "Sure, boss. You really think she'll harm him?"

"You heard the Reverend," he responded. "She plans to deny me everything. There's only one way she can do that. You've got the armour?"

Baxter patted the backpack. "Uh-huh. Sure thing, Boss."

Lindsay's footprints drifted to the right before disappearing amidst an outcrop of rocks at the edge of the sea. Above them towered the sheer, jagged cliff face. As McGuire and Baxter rounded the corner, McGuire saw her desperately picking her way over the slippery rocks, the wriggling child clutched under one arm, Reverend Sarah's shotgun in the other. Somewhere high above them, a kookaburra laughed.

"Why?" called McGuire suddenly, almost despite himself. The echo of his voice threw his own desperation back at him, and he detested it.

Lindsay turned in horror, stumbling to a halt on a stretch of sand. She hesitated, clearly unsure what to do. Sure, she could cross this section of beach, head for the next bluff, but she was a smart girl. She must know the situation was hopeless. McGuire would catch her without breaking a sweat. He just needed to get to her before she could harm the child.

"I had to," she shouted. She lowered the kid to the ground and backed onto the sand as McGuire and Baxter continued their approach, ushering Liam in front of her. She half-heartedly raised the shotgun, clearly unsure how to wield it. He'd never seen her lift a gun, not even in jest. "Life with you was *fucking* insanity, Kelly. I couldn't carry on anymore. Not with a child."

McGuire lifted his hands up, palms outward, as he stepped off the rocks and onto the wet, compacted sand. "You could've left me without betraying me," he said calmly.

"Look at what you're doing now," she responded, struggling to keep the gun level. "You'd have come after us. Of course you would. I betrayed you to the cops because I figured they could protect me. I didn't know they were going to leak it to the fucking media, to Danny Kline and all those bastards. I'm so sorry. If it wasn't for the fucking Cull..."

McGuire shook his head. "But you didn't run this time. Not till now. Not till I found out."

She laughed weakly, shaking her head. "There was nowhere to run to. And besides..." Her voice trailed off, caught by the wind.

The toddler had become fascinated with a rock pool. McGuire gestured to him. "Lindsay, let me have the child and you can go. I promise. Just don't harm him."

Lindsay looked baffled. "Harm him? Why would I harm him?"

McGuire sighed, turning to Baxter, dropping his assault rifle to the ground. "Give me the armour."

Baxter nodded in surprise. "Sure, boss," he said, sinking to one knee. He began pulling the helmet and breastplate out of the backpack, passing them reverently to McGuire.

McGuire held the two pieces of armour up, then resumed his steady, unflinching approach. "Don't you see, Lindsay? This is my legacy."

"Stay back!" hissed Lindsay, steadying the gun.

McGuire ignored her, continuing his relentless approach, "When I'm gone, someone has to wear them. My son. It's... it's *destiny*."

A shot rang out and McGuire instinctively shielded himself with the armour. He felt a jolt, enough to stop him walking. He looked down at the armour; unsurprisingly, the bullet had passed straight through the breastplate. With a pained grunt, he looked to his arm and saw where the bullet had grazed him. The smell of his own seared flesh reached him through the salt-tainted air.

"I told you to stop," cried Lindsay. "It's old, that armour, a thing of the past—it can't stop my bullets. How's it gonna protect him?"

"That doesn't matter. It's a symbol. He has to wear it," insisted McGuire. "He's my son."

The kid glanced up from his endeavours with the rock pool, his face lighting up as he lifted a quivering finger and pointed. "Daddy," he said.

McGuire looked at the green-eyed boy with the porcelain complexion and the auburn locks, at his button nose, at his squat, podgy frame. He looked at his chubby hand and realised the finger wasn't pointing at him at all, but past him, to his squire. McGuire smirked, and shook his head, gesturing toward himself.

"Daddy," he corrected.

"*Daddy*," insisted the kid, frowning, pointing still at Baxter.

McGuire began shaking his head, irritated, when he caught sight of the look on Lindsay's face. Those pale, delicate cheeks were flushing, ever so slightly. McGuire's mouth went suddenly dry, and he gaped at her. She turned her head to look out to sea.

Kelly McGuire felt something cold and round nudge the back of his exposed neck. It was the nozzle of a submachine gun. "Sorry, Boss. Smart kid. Just like his daddy."

"No way," breathed McGuire. His gut screamed.

"Way," confirmed Baxter.

"You fucker."

"Quite literally," Baxter said. "But thank you, mate. You did it all for us. Built us a fuckin' empire, you might say." He was calm, self-assured. "Killed everyone that needed killing, knocked off all the competition, enslaved the rest. Created an infrastructure. Invented systems, protocols, rituals. Only a man as obsessed with control as you—with certainty—could have done it. Thank you so very much."

"Bullshit."

Baxter cleared his throat. "Not really. All we needed was the last piece. We were just waiting on the Kendall gang. When I saw Bobby's decapitated head I could've jumped for joy. Once he was accounted for, that was it. Time to bring you somewhere remote and wrap the charade up."

"I knew you'd follow me here," said Lindsay absently, still staring out toward the Bass Strait. "And if you didn't, Jonnie would have made sure you did. That's why I didn't run. I didn't have to, this time. I had to bring you here."

"Jonnie?"

"She means me, *mate*."

"You fuckers don't have the balls for a putsch," hissed McGuire. "Let alone the *brains*."

Baxter caressed the back of McGuire's head with the cold barrel of the gun. "Fuck me, I wouldn't talk about *balls* if I were you, McGuire. Besides, this is no putsch, mate. You never were in control of this to begin with. It was always me. I worked every fucking angle, took every fucking opportunity. I *owned* it."

"I'm telling you it's bullshit."

Baxter gave a rumbling laugh. "Think about it. I was always in there, keeping tabs on things, manipulating things when I had to. Before the Cull and after it. Baxter the messenger? 'Our man on the ground'? Now *that's* bullshit, comrade."

"You're not clever enough. Neither of you. It's beyond you."

"You think? I'll tell you what. I'm going to explain it to you now, because I want you to know just how comprehensively we fucked you over. Then we'll see how clever you think we are."

"Tell me."

McGuire heard Baxter draw a deep breath. "Originally, back before the Cull rearranged the chess board, we just wanted to take over the gang—y'know, a sort of Bonnie and Clyde-style arrangement, only minus the bloody denouement. To do that we had to make sure you were either dead or in jail. Didn't quite work out like that, as you know. You did a runner and then the fucking Biblical plague hit. Everything looked like it was fucked for a bit, but then lo and behold you came walkin' out of the fuckin' Bush like the answer to our prayers. We couldn't fuckin' believe our luck. So we hatched a bigger plan, one where we let you do all the work for us, and the prize is all the greater. Because the prize is, like, *everything*. Y'know. Control of *everything*. Still think we're not clever?" He'd brought the gun around and was caressing McGuire's face with its nozzle. "Not just an incy-wincy bit?"

"It's mine," murmured McGuire. "I made this world. I fought for it."

Baxter leaned in to him. "Oh, does diddums think it's unfair? You know your problem, McGuire? You're not *anything*. You're just a fucking *void* where a person ought to be. The media gave you a name, so you stole a dead man armour's and thought that would make you a hero, a rebel, a proper villain or some shit. Then we let you think you had a son to continue your legacy. But the hilarious truth is there won't *be* any legacy. Not for you. No immortality. Nada, zilch. Not even a graffiti daub of your blood and guts." He kept the gun trained on him as he stepped backward, pulling the helmet from McGuire's slack fingers, moving to join Lindsay. "That's the point of telling you all this. I want you to understand that, when you're dead, no-one will remember you even existed. 'Cause you, see, Kelly, I'm erasing you from history." Baxter beamed triumphantly. "Now tell me. Do you *capiche*?"

McGuire swallowed. "How long?" he said at length.

"How long have we been fucking?" Baxter chuckled, then paused. "Let's not worry about that. You can do the math, though, mate. I mean... well, the thing is. You couldn't do it, could you now? Not with that crippled thing between your legs?"

239

McGuire watched Lindsay flinch, her face still turned from him. He clenched his jaw, froze his expression, let it all wash over him.

"They tried to fix it, didn't they?" continued Baxter, his gimlet eyes searching McGuire's face. "The surgeons, I mean. All the way through your childhood. And each time they made it worse. How horrible. How painful. How *humiliating*."

Baxter gestured with the gun towards McGuire's crotch. "What must it have been like growing up with that? The torment. The teasing. The first time a girl ever saw you down there, felt down there. What must it have been like, eh?"

McGuire blinked slowly, but still he did not speak.

"Is that why you killed 'em, mate? Is that why you axed dear old Ma and Pa? Yeah, I did my research, mate. I've known about your little secret for longer than I care to remember. Long before the fuckin' Cull."

A flurry of fractured images flashed in front of McGuire. His Papa desperately trying to protect his Mama. The axe in his hands. The hoarse screams, the spraying blood, the splintering cartilage. Staring at what he had done. The brain and bone and blood, some of it brightest crimson, some of it deepest scarlet. The red and the black. "They said it was beyond their control," McGuire said simply, his voice little more than a whisper. "They said they tried to fix me, that they were sorry, but they couldn't. But it wasn't good enough. Nothing is beyond control. *Nothing*."

Baxter lowered his voice, "You did manage it once, though, didn't you? To fuck, I mean. Just the once. Here on this beach. I watched you. That's why we thought you'd be keen to return, to where it all began. The thing is... me and Lindsay were at it like jack rabbits. All the fuckin' time, whenever your stupid back was turned. Take it from me, the golden stud was never, ever for you, mate." Baxter lifted his head, inhaling the sea air appreciatively. "Which is more likely, do you think? That you're the kid's dad or that I am?"

The three of them stood in front of him now, the happy, triumphant family. Or some shit like that. Lindsay watching the crashing sea, the toddler preoccupied by his rock pool. McGuire looked from the child to the man and back again.

The shape of the face, the physique. The brow, furrowed in concentration. There was little doubt that Baxter was his father.

McGuire watched as Baxter pulled the iron helmet over his own head. "The others won't accept you," he said evenly. "Wilcox, Nancy, Rudy. They won't trust you."

"They'll trust us," riposted Baxter, his head covered. He tapped the iron mask with his free hand. "It's a fuckin' brand, mate. Think about it—no-one will be able to tell the fuckin' difference."

"You fuckers," growled McGuire. He flexed his hands impotently, felt the rough skin of his curving scar. "*I'm* Dead Kelly."

"Yeah, you always were," conceded Baxter, his voice muffled. "Dead to the world. But you've been replaced. Now it's my turn."

"You covered every angle," said McGuire hollowly.

"You got it, mate," acknowledged Baxter, finger poised on the trigger, eyes just visible through the slit in the helmet, the painted, peeling skull leering at him. "*Every* angle."

The kookaburra's staccato laughter reached McGuire suddenly on the breeze, and he looked up at the cliff-top. "Except that one."

A fleeting, streaking blur, a solid thud. Baxter pitched backward, the bolt emerging from the eye slit. Lindsay spun in horror, no idea where the shot had come from, her own gun useless in her hands. McGuire heard the kookaburra laugh again, melancholy above the roar of the ocean. The second bolt hit Lindsay in the side of her head, spinning her around, emerald eyes staring, auburn tresses floating, before she collapsed in a heap beside Baxter.

Liam had started to cry. McGuire watched the boyish silhouette of Meg Kendall, crossbow raised, silent now, no longer the laughing kookaburra. He wondered whether she would kill him, or the child, or both of them.

He watched intently as she gradually lowered her weapon. From her perspective, she'd executed Dead Kelly and his lover, and in doing so avenged her brother and her lover. Evidently that was enough. After a moment more her silhouette vanished.

He stepped over Lindsay's corpse and reached down to Baxter's helmeted head. With a loud squelch, he extracted the bolt from the eye slot, then prised the helmet off Baxter's bloodied head. He placed the helmet and other pieces of armour into the backpack, before stepping away to consider Lindsay and Baxter's corpses.

He tried to find within himself the appropriate emotional response, finally discovering it as he scooped the crying child up into his arms. It was satisfaction; of that he was certain.

McGuire picked his way back along the beach, soothing the boy with promises. Eventually the child stopped reaching for his parents and began to smile, and then to nuzzle into his shoulder. Dead Kelly smiled too.

THE END

THE BLOODY DELUGE
ADRIAN TCHAIKOVSKY

With thanks to Jarek Rybski, Michael Czajkowski, Shane McLean and Irene Bock for their assistance in researching the world before the Cull.

PART ONE
BETWEEN THE EAGLES

CHAPTER ONE
AMIDST THE BONES

THE VAN HAD taken them as far as Wrocław before running out of gas. Katy had been driving two whole days and half a night by that time, running on fumes herself. She had barely been able to see the road by then, dusk and her own leaden eyelids making the obstacle course of abandoned cars into a deathtrap.

"That's it." Her voice came out as a dead croak. "Emil, that's all I've got in me. We'll hunt some fuel tomorrow, when I can see straight." There was a tight fist of a headache dug in between her eyes, like she always got if she drove too much, or stared at a computer screen...

Oh, yes, staring at computers. When did we last do that?

"Miss Lewkowitz, they're still out there," came that cautious, measured voice from the back.

"Listen, Emil." She had her eyes closed. They were on the outskirts of the largest city in Western Poland, and surely there were still people here, but the night was silent. No shouting, no screaming, no gunshots, no vehicles on the move. They might have been in some other world entirely from all those things. *Makes a change from where we came here from.*

"There might be... looters, cannibals—or more fanatics. Please," pressed the soft voice of Dr Emil Weber. He had two modes, she knew of old: very, very polite, and his sudden rises to impassioned rhetoric. And his cringing embarrassment after the latter, she supposed, made three. But he had been polite all the way since they fled the executions at Forst.

"There's going to be a road accident right here if I don't sleep. Car crash, right? Ah, *Autounfall?*"

"Miss Lewkowitz, my English is perfectly—"

"And the car's out of diesel. Argue with *me* all you like, but—"

He hissed through his teeth. "Then you may by all means sleep for precisely such time as it takes for me to siphon some fuel out of any of these vehicles that still have any."

"They won't. Why d'you think they're abandoned?"

"You don't know that. Arguing from a position unsupported by evidence—"

"Oy, Emil, not *now*. Save it for the show trials." She settled back in the driver's seat as best she could, reflecting that his patient, almost accentless tones became incredibly annoying after prolonged exposure. It was something she had never noticed when he was her tutor.

SHE DIDN'T IMAGINE anyone would be studying to be a biochemist any time soon. She might as well have gone to the Brandenburg Technical University to be a wizard or a Disney princess: the ambitions were just as realistic, had she only known.

Her German had been rusty when she came over from the UK, and learning the language and the science at the same time had almost broken her. But she had trained and studied, under Emil Weber, and thanks to his meticulous assistance she had passed, and secured a starter position with a GMO lab in Kolkwitz nearby. Her golden future as a bona fide scientist was right there waiting for her.

And then the Culling Year had come and everyone had died. Everyone at the lab but her. She had stumbled out into a country that had degraded shockingly fast into somewhere she could not even recognise. She had only survived because she was often the closest thing to a doctor that anyone could find. Practical medicine was another thing she had to learn fast. Those first few years had made all of her study at Potsdam look absurdly leisured and simple. Every day had taught her something; every day had confronted her anew with the fate awaiting those who failed to learn.

She had thought that she had found a new life for herself, by then. Not a good life, most certainly not the life she wanted, but unless someone had a magic wand, then she was never going to get that. She had set up shop as quack and sawbones in a walled community and fended off the advances of the local young bucks.

And then the first word had come from Emil. He, too, had survived. More, he was working. He had gathered up students, colleagues, everyone he could find with a pulse and an education. Faced with the oblivion of everything he had ever known, the deaths of almost everyone he knew, Dr Emil Weber had got to work. She had pictured him, a short, stocky man, grey peppering his dark hair and stubbling his cheeks, pushing his glasses back up his nose and reducing death from the apocalypse to just another problem for science to solve. And every little death had its own nemesis. The letters she got from him said he was working on the biochemistry of the Cull virus. He was after a cure.

And of course he had asked her to join his little community, and of course she had meant to, but there had been people close at hand who had needed her—or who would have tried to stop her leaving. She had never quite broken away.

And if she had, they would both be dead by now. Procrastination had saved her, and she had saved him.

SHE WAS STARTLED awake by him banging on the side of the van.

"Miss Lewkowitz! Miss Lewkowitz!"

He would never just call her Katy.

"Seriously?" She took a deep breath in which the last few exchanges between them replayed in her mind. "You've filled the tank? Already?"

"No!" And still maddeningly polite, but there was an edge to it now, a man strained towards breaking point. "They have found us."

"How do you know?" Because she thought he was just overreacting to something. He was a man of infinite calm, in his laboratory kingdom. Take him out of that, and he jumped at every shadow.

But then she heard them: the growl of the bikes.

Emil jumped into the passenger seat. "Drive us!"

"Doc, still no diesel!" she snapped. "We're going to have to make it on foot."

"No, that is not acceptable."

"Just follow me." She kicked the door open and was out, scanning the dark road, the strewn debris of dead vehicles. *How did they find us?* But then the enemy had been on their trail since Forst, never far behind, never catching up. That had lulled them into a false sense of security. *And taking the biggest, straightest road east might not have been the best move. So what now? Can we hide?* Surely the ruins of Wrocław offered a thousand boltholes. How many were unclaimed, though?

Still: "Into the city," she told him. although she had to drag him by the cuff. He was still wearing one of those pinstripe shirts he had never been without, though it had gone through at the elbows, and hadn't seen an iron in a year. They had taken his lab coat off him when they caught him, though. White was their colour, and they were jealous of it.

Emil and she should have made it, she would decide in retrospect. They should have melted away into the ruins. All those houses with vacant-eyesocket windows, all those hollow shells cast up by the tide of the Cull, moulded around the vacant impressions of their lost owners. She and Emil should have been able to hide there forever.

The dogs betrayed them, in the end. She had not thought about dogs, but of course the Cull was like some message from a green messiah. The innocence of the natural world was not the target of its sermons, only sinful mankind. There had been a lot of dogs in Wrocław. Most of them had not long survived their owners, probably, but the biggest and the strongest had growled and clawed and snapped their way to some sort of supremacy. They ruled the streets there, and in the utter absence of human moral guidance they had made their own society.

From the look of the pack that loped into view, they had recruited some wolves along the way. They were big, scarred beasts, and there was no recognition in their eyes that they had once bowed their heads to masters. Only the moon gleamed back from their fixed gaze. *No collars, no chains,* that stare seemed to say.

"Just keep still," Katy hissed, but Emil was already shuffling backwards. Dogs were just one of a long list of things he was not fond of.

"They're just—" she started, and then the growling started: a low, deep sound that seemed to reach her through the ground more than through her ears. It spoke to something primal in her, something that had hidden up trees and trembled when the pack gathered to greet the moonrise.

She dragged the pistol from her pocket. There was a look in the dogs' eyes—or it was her imagination—that said they *knew* what it was, and what it could do. The growling grew steadily louder, and then they were barking furiously, first one, then all of them. Compared with the silence that had reigned moments before, the sound was deafening.

Emil ran, and she was backing away right after him. The dogs advanced a few steps, and kept up their savage racket. *Go away! Go away! This is our place now!*

And that was how the enemy found them. She almost ran straight into Emil at the far end of the street. Three bright orbs confronted him: headlamps. The growling yammer of the dogs gave way to the thunderous rumble of the bikes.

The moon caught them: they wore old leathers, painted up white so that they shone like broken angels, the colour flaking away at the joints and creases as though the darkness within was leaking out. Only one had a helmet, in the same livery, painted with a dark cross. The others had shaved heads, pale faces, the whitest of the white, with that black bar across their eyes, that stripe from forehead to chin. Black cross on a pale field; the ghosts of history.

She was behind Emil. The thought came to her that they had not seen she was armed.

One of them reached up high, arm thrust into the air. He had an air-horn there, the sort of noisemaker she remembered from the football games her dad had dragged her to. Even as she recognised it, he let out a long, piercing hoot that echoed out across the broken rooftops.

It was answered almost immediately, and from not far away.

"You're going to have to run now, Doc," she murmured.

"Not without you." He had actually squared himself, as though ready to put up what miniscule amount of fight he had in him.

"Oh, I'll be right behind you, only I'm going to put some bullets their way first."

"That will only antagonise them."

"Doc, they were going to hang you. I don't figure pissing them off is going to make things worse."

"A good point."

The man in the centre was lazily guiding his bike forwards. He had a hockey stick over his shoulder, its inside edge studded with sharpened coins. They would have guns as well, but she had seen the way they worked. Given a victim who could not fight back, the soldiers of the Order preferred the personal touch.

"Good girl," he murmured, grinning. Jarringly, his accent hailed from London, still flying the tattered flags of Chelsea and Fulham, but then the Order was happy to take in anyone who was male, white and bigoted as hell. "You come quietly, good girl. Step away from your friend there, nothing bad's going to happen to you."

One of the others made a suggestion in German about precisely what might happen to her. Probably he didn't consider it 'bad.' Perhaps he thought it would be an honour.

The Englishman's eyes glinted as he inched his bike closer. "That's it," he said softly, but the same desires were plain on his face. Neither she nor Emil were getting out of this, if they were caught.

So: "Run," she said, and then gave Emil a shove when he didn't move. He stumbled to one side, but then he was dashing off almost at random, leaping and clambering over a bank of blackened rubble where one house had come down, where the bikes couldn't follow.

English Bigot gunned his bike forwards, and perhaps he didn't see as she brought the pistol up. His two friends did, certainly. Would-be Rapist dived off his machine, letting it clang heavily to the ground as he scuttled for cover. The man in the helmet went straight for her, practically demanding to become her primary target.

There was a moment when her finger was on the trigger and she could not make herself pull it. Then she must have done, because the weapon bucked in her hand, the recoil jarring her wrist, and Helmet was lying flat back across his saddle, hands ripped off the handlebars by the impact. His bike slewed sideways, spilling him off and almost scything her legs from under her. She jumped aside, and was already pelting after Emil.

She got to the rubble just after English Bigot, and he turned on her, lashing out with that doctored hockey stick. As she reeled back out of reach, he dragged his own gun out of his waistband. She froze. For a long second she had no idea what to do, and if he had been able, he could have shot her there and then. He was fumbling with the safety catch, spiked motorcycle gloves making a fist of it, and she forced herself to raise her gun again, even as she scrambled up the scree of bricks and broken tiles.

He brought his pistol up, saw that she was ahead of him, and threw himself down the slope. The weapon thundered in her hand again, the shot going who knew where. Then she was off after Emil.

She *hoped* after Emil. He had shown a surprising turn of speed. She could only hope that if she lost his trail, so would the Order.

The sound of bike engines was loud across the barren skyline of Wrocław.

She darted through the ruined house, boots crunching and skidding on stray detritus, and then she was out in what had been a garden once, now a bristling nursery for weeds. These had been good houses with big gardens. For a moment she entertained the thought of simply hiding in the new-minted undergrowth, stalking the Order soldiers like a Viet Cong veteran.

Except she had one bullet left. One.

She hit the fence at the back of the yard, already rotten with too many untreated winters. Here was Emil's trail; he had frantically kicked through it to get out. It couldn't be more obvious if he had left an Emil-shaped hole in the wormy wood like Wile E. Coyote. She followed after, waving the gun behind her in case it might give the hunters even a second's more pause.

There was another garden beyond, in the moon-shadow of a house that had weathered the fall rather better. The back door was open: Emil again. The building would provide no shelter, given even a cursory search. She only hoped he had kept on running.

He had got as far as the street out front, she discovered, and had stopped there. Two more Order bikers had turned up. They had him pinned between them, circling slowly, revving their engines. One was swinging a chain lazily, the other had what looked like a shotgun levelled crookedly over his handlebars.

She burst from the house's front door like an avenging angel, gun thrust out towards them. *One bullet. Two men. No chance they'll line up, is there?*

Emil flinched and dropped, covering his head with his hands. She caught the startled looks of the Order men, seeing her. Mr Shotgun swore and almost lost the weapon under the front wheel of his bike.

Her gun went off at point blank range. She was still running, her aim veering madly between them. She had not even decided to fire; her finger had twitched as she ran and taken the decision from her. The bullet struck sparks from Chains' bike, making him yell in shock. Mr Shotgun was juggling his weapon, bringing it up, and she was looking right into the barrels. He had gone for heavy spiked gloves too, and she was close enough to see him trying to jam his finger through the trigger loop.

She was close enough to grab the weapon's end and whip it upwards into his face; the report as it went off sounded like the end of the world. Mr Shotgun screamed and fell backwards off his bike, clutching at his face. Katy was hardly better off, half-deaf and with one hand bruised and seared from the gun's discharge.

Someone yanked at her. She swatted wildly with her pistol before she saw it was Emil. There was shouting from behind them: English Bigot and company catching up.

Adrenaline had her springing away fast enough to win sprint medals, still waving the useless pistol. She heard a bike behind her roar, and realized she had forgotten Chains. Her own shadow fell away into the night ahead of her as she was caught in the headlamp.

Look left, look right: no convenient side alley, but that house ahead had a good stretch of garden in front. Another second's safety from the bikes. Every moment was becoming increasingly precious.

"Emil!" she gasped. "Left!"

He was already running out of strength, she saw, stumbling and lurching. He had never exactly been a jock, and the privations of the Culling Year had not strengthened him. He cut left, trying to vault over the garden fence, and tripped, falling flat on his face. He crammed his glasses back on.

The bike had caught Katy up. She felt the roar of it up her spine, heard a whistling whip that must be the chain in motion. Something flickered past her face and she flinched back, turning just as the bike spun past her on its side and smashed the wooden fence panels to splinters.

Chains was on his back in the road. The transition was as sudden and inexplicable as if he had suffered a freak heart attack, until she saw the slender shaft that stood proud of his chest. He was still alive, apparently, twitching and gasping, but he was not about to threaten anyone any time soon.

The horse's shoes on the grass-cracked tarmac of the road were very loud. The beast was sleek and lean and beautiful; if it had come with a horn Katy would not have been more surprised. The woman riding it wore a grab-bag of denims and leathers, with a scarf over her hair. Her face was closed and dark, maybe five years older than Katy's own late twenties. There was a quiver hanging from her saddle, and she had a short, recurved bow in her hands, and was guiding her steed with nothing but her knees.

English Bigot and Would-be Rapist spilled out of the ruined house down the street, finding Mr Shotgun first, who was in no position to advise them. She saw Helmet there as well, making heavy going of it, but obviously not badly hurt.

"Listen," Katy said in German, low and urgent. "This man, he needs to get out of here."

The horsewoman regarded her impassively.

"He's important. He's a scientist. These men—they're—" She had been going to say *religious*, but then maybe this woman was just the same. It seemed to be a disease sweeping the world, from what Katy had seen, with people taking refuge from the global tragedy in the most hate-filled sects and dogmas. "He is trying to help people, to protect them from the plague," she went on. "Please, these men, they'll kill him, for no more reason than that. Is there somewhere you can take him?"

"Katy, what about you?" Emil asked plaintively.

"I'll take my chances. Doc, I'll do better without you slowing me down."

He complained about that, but the rider had come to her decision. She spoke to Emil, something Katy could not follow, but then she was reaching for him, dragging at him. Katy had to help coerce his protesting form onto the saddle, but then he was there, somehow, magically, and the woman was bending down to speak.

"Bless you," she said in awkward German. "These men we know. We fought them. Fight them. I will come back for you. Have faith."

Katy did not know what to make of it, but then she heard a shout from English Bigot. Their time was up: they had been spotted.

The horsewoman turned her mount and it coursed off, not at a gallop that would shake Emil from his tenuous seat, but faster than anyone on foot could have kept up with.

That just left Katy to figure out where she could run now.

CHAPTER TWO
HISTORY'S REPEATERS

With hoofbeats ringing in her head, she jumped on Chains' groaning body, scrabbling at his leathers, because he *had* to have a gun, surely he had a gun, surely she couldn't have here the only Order soldier who had some kind of fucking *oath* not to have a firearm on him when she needed one...

If he'd had one, it had come loose, skittered off into the thousand shadows of Wrocław. He had a big serrated knife, and he had his stupid chain, a weapon that was probably the quickest way for Katy to strangle herself if she tried to use it.

She took the knife. Why the hell not?

English Bigot had shoved Mr Shotgun off his bike, and was now approaching with caution. Behind him followed his two mates, Helmet still limping, one gloved hand pressed to his shoulder.

Katy was backing off: not a conscious decision, but her feet had made it for her. Three steps, four. The moonlight gleamed on English Bigot's grin and he revved the bike engine ferociously.

"Run, girl! Why don't you run!" he shouted at her, and some madly calm part of her mind thought that he was a fantastically unimaginative man. Of course he wanted her to run. He wanted to ride her down like a knight of old. All very well as long as she ran down the road.

She bolted through the jagged hole in the fence that Chains' bike had made, dashing across the overgrown tangle of the garden. From behind there was a chorus of shouts as the Order realized she was not interested in playing fair, and then the big-cat growl of the bike as English Bigot gunned it forwards.

She made to go round the side of the house, but abruptly there was a cast iron gate in the way, one that the night had hidden from her. Shoving knife and empty pistol in her belt, she leapt at it frantically, failed to gain purchase and ended up sitting at its base. Spitting fear and frustration, she started scaling it more carefully, soles slipping on the elaborate curved flourishes.

She heard English Bigot come into the garden when she was halfway up, and that gave her the motivation to double her speed. He yelled something at her—it might have been "I'll shoot, you mad bitch!"—and then she was folding over the top of the gate, for a moment snagged on it, wrestling to get free.

She heard the *bang*, and the gate shuddered, sparks flying as the bullet ricocheted back from it. Then she was over, falling heavily to the ground beyond, hard enough to knock the breath out of her. Breathless, she lurched to her feet, stumbling away. English Bigot took another shot and the gate fielded it for her again and sprang open.

She ran, pelting into a back garden. Was there a gate out? There was. Was it locked? She fought with it, got it open with a furious wrench of the rusted latch. Then English Bigot was on her. He got a hand on her shoulder just as she was about to go through, dragging her back. She whipped her pistol out, meaning to threaten him with it, and smashed him across the nose by happy accident.

He stumbled back, sneezing out a jet of blood that was black in the moonlight. When he looked up, it was into the barrel of her weapon.

"Give me your gun," she told him. *Because your gun probably has bullets in it, and then I won't need to keep pretending that mine does.*

His teeth were bared like an animal's. "Luv, you are in so much trouble right now."

She wanted to say something very suave like, *I'm not the one with a gun up his nose,* but all she could do was just stammer, "Give me the *gun!*"

He was buying it. With exaggeratedly careful movements he reached down and placed the pistol on the ground between them. His eyes never left her gun. She could hear his mates somewhere behind him, but she didn't care about them. They weren't going to do anything while she had their leader by the balls.

Then someone grabbed her from behind, dragging her arms down, and her finger closed on the trigger. The loud and non-explosive click of the hammer was like the punchline to a very bad joke.

She struggled, but the grip was firm, and then something hard struck the back of her head, a headbutt from someone else sharp enough to be wearing a motorcycle helmet. Even as the pain flashed through her head, English Bigot slammed a fist into her gut, the spikes of his gloves ripping her clothes.

"You *bitch!*" and a lot more like that, English and German invective, and what sounded like it might be Italian from one of them. After the third punch she was dropped to the ground, curled into a foetal position and covering her head as a couple of them put the boot in. Not too much, though. English Bigot called them off soon enough. He had other ideas.

"I want her," said one of them, quite distinctly, and she gritted her teeth against the thought of it. She tried to take comfort in Emil's escape, but right then comfort was another country.

But: "No," from English Bigot. "She's got a lot to answer for. That means she goes to the Grand Master or to the Reverend. And neither of them like their meat spoiled." He reached down and hauled her up by her collar, racking every bruise they had just given her. "Make camp," she heard him say in his accented German. "The main force will be here soon. Lukas, Anatoli, go hunting. I want that bastard doctor brought in."

Ride far, she thought, hoping that the strange horsewoman could be trusted. That the rider might actually come back for her as promised was nothing more than a fantasy.

BACK THEN, THE word that had come to her about what was growing in Brandenburg had been fragmentary, contradictory at first. The world after the Cull was still in its death throes. Every community fended for itself, and the world beyond the hastily-raised walls was not to be trusted. People looked to themselves and their known neighbours for survival. And yet, at the same time, the dream of the world that had passed was strong in everyone's minds. Early on, there had been plenty of talk about it. Surely the government was still functioning, over in Berlin. Surely the military had held itself together. There would be helicopters any day, with food, with medicine. This was a disaster, but it couldn't be *that* bad. It couldn't be the end.

And of course the months had turned into a year, and then two years. The brave got supplies together and drove out to the erstwhile capital. The lucky came back, without any good news. Too many people had died—enough that in their own little community there were hardly two people who had known each other before the Cull. Katy remembered something she had read or watched about the Native Americans on their reservations, Jack Wilson and the Great Ghost Dance, after the systematic extermination of a people and a way of life. She remembered the testimony of a survivor, that in their memory the faces of the dead vastly outnumbered those few they knew who were still alive. So it was for everyone, now. Not the government, not the military, not nations, not cities, nothing of the grandeur of the old world could survive with so few hands at the pumps. The horizon shrank.

But still people dreamt of an authority. They dreamt that someone would come and tell them what to do, just as people always had.

And so the word came, at last, and in the beginning people welcomed it: that there was a new order rising, men who were banding together to bring law and unity to the world, or at least this part of it. Men who spoke of a nation reborn, under justice and under God. And nobody, not Katy, not any of them, had so much as harboured the thought, *Surely there's no precedent for this turning out badly?* At the start, when the rumours had come, she had felt a need in her own heart for that old lie: stability and security.

But it was always a lie, just one that crept up on them. Word travelled unreliably between those isolated towns. The new power gathered itself, won some allies, kissed a few babies, until it was established. Then it showed its true colours: the white flag and black cross.

And there were people who welcomed them even so, but by then Katy had heard enough to know she wanted no part of them.

They called themselves the New Teutonic Order. They styled themselves as knights, guardians of the Fatherland. Order was what they brought, too, but they brought it by ruthlessly suppressing everything that did not fit in their Brave New World.

By then, she knew that they had established themselves near the university, and she knew that Emil would be too short-sighted and too much of a rationalist to run. He would try to argue with them.

The Order did not argue. It enforced.

She had left her community that night, because Emil Weber was the sole person left in the world whom she had known more than a few years, and she had to save him from his own naivety.

When she got to the university itself, it was burned out, with a dozen blackened corpses dangling from the trees. There had been prisoners, too—she found a few survivors who confirmed that. Yes, Doctor Weber had been amongst them.

The Order had their main camp nearby: they moved about like locusts, but only once they had beaten down all opposition in a region, seeded it with their people, put on a bit of a show. It was that last part they were engaged in, when she arrived.

Getting inside was no problem. They had no walls, and they were actively encouraging everyone from the surrounding communities to come visit. They had plenty of food, tools,

alcohol, all sorts of plunder that they were open-handed with—
to those who met their criteria; to those whom they considered
properly human and worthy to inherit the Earth. And the best
way, the absolute best way to worm yourself into the heart of
the Order was to bring them your neighbour and accuse them
of being less virtuous, less pure, less human than you.

The soldiers of the Order were all of a certain type, she saw.
They were men, uniformly men, and mostly they were young.
They had their heads shaved down to a stubble, and their
faces painted. None of them looked overly virtuous to her,
but then she reckoned they were probably little different from
any warrior elite throughout history: they took what they
wanted and rewrote morality to give them the right. Many
of them were native Germans, but truly they had collected a
pan-European band of the righteous. She heard Dutch and
Italian in their voices, Scandinavian tones, Slavic and French
and familiar English accents, from London and Birmingham
and Newcastle. These men had drifted across Europe after
the Cull, looking for somewhere to belong. They had banded
together in packs, living each day on what they could take,
fighting where they found weakness, fleeing where they found
strength. Then the bands had begun to join, she guessed, the
strong becoming stronger. Then had come a man with a dream
of nationhood and power, of a new feudal age where they
could be the first estate, those who ruled.

That was the secret, of course. Katy could watch them
holding a mirror up to history. Rule by strength is not rule
by right. Rule by strength and you look over your shoulder
always, in case someone is stronger. Convince others that you
rule by *right*, though. Convince them that this is the way things
are, and that a great supernatural beard in the sky wills it so...
well, humanity had only just started shrugging *that* fairy tale
off when the Cull came.

She was unsurprised when, within an hour of her arrival,
there was a sermon.

God's judgment. That was how the Order described the
Cull, and surely they were not the only ones to leap to that
conclusion. More, it was God's *just* judgment, another page of
the same book that had brought Noah's flood. The world had

been cleansed of so much evil, but it was for the Order—for all right-thinking people—to finish that work. Only then could the new Kingdom of Heaven be made on Earth. Only then could the true spirit of the nation rise, pure and strong.

The sermon was bellowed through a loudhailer by a man in a grey suit that looked freshly laundered. He was shorter than Katy, but up on the stage he could have been ten feet tall. His hair was groomed back in a bouffant wave, and his smile was bright as the sun. He spoke German with a Midwest twang, and she understood he was the Reverend James Calumn, Jr. Judging from his fiercely charismatic delivery, she guessed he must have been a big-time evangelist back home. Standing in the press of the crowd, listening to him exhort and cajole, she almost became caught up in it. He spoke with a blazing hot sincerity that promised hope and succour and all good things.

And then he strode back into the big white tent behind the stage, and they began bringing the prisoners out.

There were a round dozen in that first batch, bruised and bloodied and with their hands behind their back. They each bore a placard hung about their necks, written in plain, clear script. '*Schwul*' said a couple, with 'faggot' added in another hand on one man's plaque for the Order's more Anglophone homophobes. Several men and women sported the legend '*Zigeuner*,' though whether they were genuine Roma or just travellers, Katy could not tell. Three young women were labelled as '*Hure*,' which barely needed translation. A black man was simply '*Neger*.' Two others were given as 'heathens'—'*Heide*'—and the last was Emil Weber. About his neck they had hung a word that transcended any linguistic boundaries here: '*Atheist*.'

And, she had to admit: guilty as charged. Emil had always been a fierce, almost a crusading champion of humanistic atheism. The fierce fires of his unbelief would have made Richard Dawkins proud. The slightest sniff of organized religion, new age superstition, astrology or homeopathic medicine would get a rise out of him reliably enough that his students ran sweepstakes on it. It was not surprising to find him up on stage with the other enemies of the Order. What was surprising was that he had lived that long.

She knew with bitter certainty that the idea of simply keeping his mouth shut and mumming along would never have occurred to him. Like many brilliant men, he could be extremely stupid, in a lot of ways.

The crowd were encouraged to yell and jeer and throw things. Anyone who had come here hoping for a handout would want to be right at the front; others were probably thinking that a poor showing here could see them on the stage the next time this pantomime was enacted. And of course there would be a few for whom this was what they had been waiting for all their life. There always were.

The Reverend Calumn was back, smiling like a lighthouse, speaking in his US-accented German. "Brothers and sisters, you will now see God's work performed right before you. This is what back home they call a 'lynching,' you know that term?" The English word leapt out at Katy with the terrible understanding that she had come too late. Trapped by the crowd, she could only wait, hands clenched into fists, bottling up her fury because it would only get her a placard of her own.

But it turned out the Order was rationing its prisoners. The Reverend picked two of the Roma and one of the *Schwuler*, and they strung them up, right there on the stage. They did it the hard way, too: no trapdoors and sudden drops, but teams of straining Order soldiers hauling them from their feet by their necks, letting them kick and gasp, swing and jerk and mottle over agonised minutes, before the crowd, before the other prisoners. Everyone was very quiet for it, and she saw a kindred horror in many of the people there—watching this spectacle, and seeing how many men there were, with guns and cudgels and black-crossed white faces. They were watching a coup; a *fait accompli*. It was time to cheer along or to flee and never come back.

The balance of the prisoners were taken back inside the big tent, and the Reverend was introducing a new man, some leader of the Order, a tall, broad-shouldered thug with cropped peroxide hair, long-limbed as a spider. He started to talk about the Teutonic spirit, about God's mission for a chosen people. Katy sloped discreetly off during that. She had no idea how long before the lynch mob would be ready for a second helping.

At first she despaired of getting near the tent. There were plenty of Order soldiers about, not exactly on guard, but very visible. She made a circle of it, as innocuously as possible. Behind the marquee were a host of other tents, looted from a dozen outdoor living and army surplus stores, together with a motley host of vehicles. *I can't just walk into their camp, though. They'll catch me in an instant. I can hardly dress up like a soldier and hope.*

And then she saw it: that she had been guilty of thinking like the enemy. She was never going to pass as an Order soldier, no: they were all men. She had already worked out that this new dawn for Brandenburg had very definite ideas about a woman's place.

And that was it: a woman's place was everywhere. The camp was *full* of women—cooking, cleaning, darning, mending. They had been put back in the kitchen by their new overlords, and at the same time, nobody was paying much attention to them.

She walked straight in. She kept her head down, her shoulders a little slumped. She had her backside slapped a couple of times, and once a lurching soldier slapped a stinking, boozy kiss on her lips, mumbling endearments. Enduring all of that took her to the side entrance of the main tent, though, and she stepped in with two mismatched mugs and a pitcher of beer, entirely invisible.

They kept the prisoners strung by their arms to the ridge pole of the tent, and there was a single man guarding them. He was a lean, bony youth, probably very low on the pecking order to draw this duty. He was young enough to be her kid brother, surely no more than eighteen. Under the white, his face was a minefield of acne.

"All right, yeah?" His eyes lit up when he saw her. From beyond the tent came the sound of the Order's leader ranting himself into a fury. "And two mugs also? You and me, yeah?" The guard spoke German badly, but she could not identify the accent.

"Yeah," she said, giving him the pitcher and one mug. She held her own out to be filled. In her other hand was the knife.

By then, she had killed twice, but both times had been in self-defence, her actions forged in the fires of fear and adrenaline.

Standing there, watching this near-boy pouring a cup of beer for her, she suddenly knew she couldn't do it. Not in cold blood. Not like this.

And of course it was Emil who came to her aid, squinting at her through the spectacles he had somehow retained, and saying, "Katy?"

The guard's eyes went wide and he looked from Katy to Emil, mouth opening. By the time he glanced back, she had driven the knife down past his collarbone with more strength than she thought she possessed.

He hacked a mouthful of blood over her and she stabbed him again, and then four times more, teeth gritted against the sensation, a wholly unanticipated fury driving her hand.

Then she cut them all down, starting with Emil.

The escape was ragged and desperate, but she liked to think that most of them had a good chance of getting clear of the camp at least. She slit open the back of the tent and raced for the slew of vehicles.

And from there to the eastbound road, with the motorcycle outriders of the Order always behind them, until she simply could not understand why they had not given up. What was it that they saw, in her, in Emil, that they would go to such lengths, cover such distances to regain them?

And at last, in the empty shell of Wrocław, regain her they did.

CHAPTER THREE
THE MASTER AND MAGDAYEVA

THE LITTLE BAND of Order hunters made camp in one of Wrocław's vast supply of abandoned houses while they waited for their scouts to return. Katy had never been given to prayer, but she came close: if the bikers came back with Emil riding pillion, then it would all have been for nothing.

But at last, they came back empty handed. The strange woman, whoever she was, had out-ridden them.

Then the English Bigot who led them seemed to remember the prisoner he had been ignoring for hours. She had been lying, bound, in an upstairs room. But now he came kicking the door open, his hockey stick in one hand.

"Where did you send him?" he demanded, and when she did not answer, he hooked her about the head with the jagged inner curve of the weapon and hauled her upright. "Where?" he demanded again.

"Away," she said, with a defiance that lasted precisely until he cocked the stick back to strike. "Away! I just told him to—he got on her horse. I don't even know who she was."

"Then why did you send him with her?" he demanded.

Because she wasn't you! But she just cowered, and that seemed to pacify him a little. He plainly liked a woman who cringed.

"Woman, the Grand Master is on his way with our army. The Reverend, too. They'll want to speak with you, be sure of it. They'll want to have a *real* long talk with you. But if there's anything left of you after that, if you don't cause them to destroy you, then I'll ask them to give you to me. I'll be waiting for you, girl."

Spit, I spit on you. But she didn't. She was disgusted by her own cowardice, but she could not make herself antagonise him.

She tried to get some sleep after that, for some imaginary future in which being rested and alert would be in any way useful. The engines woke her at what felt like past midnight: bikes, cars, the *basso profundo* of trucks. The vanguard of the Teutonic Order was drawing to a halt at the outskirts of Wrocław.

There was a lot of shouting after that. She supposed she was in no real position to take satisfaction from the sound of the English Bigot getting a chewing out in acerbic German, but it lent a tiny spark to her, that someone else was having even a shadow of her bad night.

She hunched over to the window, dust-slathered and streaked, but she could just peer through it if she twisted her way to her knees. The view was mostly of the back garden, but she could see a little of the street through a stand of trees, and there were plenty of headlamps out there jostling for position. She could hear the sounds of a lot of men bitching at each other and heavy objects being unloaded. No doubt the tents would be going up soon.

Something moved in the garden, just a fleeting suggestion that caught in the corner of her eye. She stared out desperately into the dark, trying to recapture it. A cat? A fox?

For just a moment, she thought she saw an upturned face lit briefly by the moon.

Then heavy boots were clumping up the stairs, voices nearing, and she flopped back down to the floor, innards freezing up in fear.

"I don't believe it," she heard that sharp German voice. "Your men have just been sloppy. They're in hiding. We need to draw them out."

Then English Bigot, struggling a little with the language. "There's not a one, Grand Master. We have searched many streets. No single person can be found living here. Can they have all died?"

"God has not spared us the work elsewhere," the Grand Master replied as he gained the landing. "And there must be some righteous men in Breslau who would join with our crusade and form a chapter." Breslau was the German name for the city, Katy recalled.

Then the door was opened, and there was the wide-shouldered, long-limbed man she had last seen ranting at the crowd back in Forst. Behind him, English Bigot held an oil lamp that threw his master's shadow across Katy's prone form.

He regarded her with disappointment. "This is all you have for me, Edward?"

Edward the English Bigot hung his head in shame. "I am sorry, Grand Master."

The big man took a deep breath and then crouched down on his haunches next to her. "Do you know who I am, child?"

She shook her head.

"My name is Josef Danziger, and I am God's chosen." He spoke softly, almost gently, eminently sane. "I am tasked with establishing the Lord's Kingdom in His new Holy Land, in these the End Times."

She decided to nod, this time.

"Tell me, where are all the people?"

"I don't know. We only just got here when your people found us."

Danziger's expression was best described as vexed; a man discovering the milk is off in his tea. "The Reverend will be disappointed not to put on a show. But perhaps we may still be able to purify the world of a few more sub-humans." *Untermenschen*. The word sent shivers down Katy's spine.

"Speaking of which," Danziger went on, "Edward here tells me you were the last to see Doctor Emil Weber."

Her bad feeling was only getting worse. "Why come all this way? Surely the world's full of people you want to hang?"

"We would have come here eventually. These lands are part of the new Fatherland, as they were of the old. And the world is a little emptier of those people, day after day. I make it so." And he smiled: such an engaging expression, as though he expected to awake an answering grin in her. "But Doctor Weber is more than just a sub-human, he is the Enemy of God."

She stared at him. *Because he's an atheist? No, he means something more...*

"I want you to spend some time in earnest contemplation and prayer while I order my camp," Danziger told her, almost avuncular. "Then you will tell us where you were fleeing to, and where you have sent Doctor Weber. Or I will punish you, as wilful women must be punished."

Away, there was nothing else to it but away. But she knew that answer would not satisfy, so she said nothing.

The Grand Master straightened up and put a hand on Edward's shoulder, lightly at first, but then he obviously ramped up the pressure, making his subordinate twitch and hiss.

"More scouts," he ordered. "Find the people of this place. Find out who this rider is. Find *something*, Edward. Sometimes I doubt your faith."

The door closed behind them, and Katy heard them thumping down the stairs. Right about then, she was considering whether she could somehow break the window glass and try to cut her throat on the shards.

But then the window rattled: once, twice, and then it was sliding open and a woman was slipping in. Not *a* woman; *the* woman. She stared at the closed door for a moment and then said something fast that Katy didn't catch. Seeing her blank expression, she added in her poor German. "Thought they would never leave."

She crouched by Katy and slit her bonds, hands moving with swift economy. "You will keep quiet now. Follow with me and quiet."

The window was still open, and the woman peered out, pressed against the wall to minimise her silhouette. Katy took a moment to study her: small-framed, lean and leathery, her tan skin weathered brown, her features not quite Germanic or Slavic, but something else.

"You will drop," she told Katy flatly, leaving no option to demur, and then she was out of the window, hanging by her fingertips. There was almost no sound when she let go and hit the ground. Faced with that example, Katy felt she could only follow it. She did not look down. Events were handing her this path. Loosing her grip on the sill, she dropped into an unseen abyss, terrified of breaking an ankle, of getting so far and then no farther.

Strong hands caught her, the woman falling back with her to break the last of her fall, then springing immediately to her feet. No broken German now, just a beckoning gesture.

The garden was dark, overshadowed by trees. Strips of light from the house's lower windows scarred it, briefly busy now and then with the shadows of the soldiers inside. Katy's rescuer stepped carefully from shadow to shadow, unhurried, stopping and starting to a rhythm entirely within her head, leaving Katy to muddle along behind her. The Wrocław night, that had been so bone-silent, was raucous now with fifty or more of the Order setting up camp, breaking out the drink. From somewhere came the cries of a woman doing her utmost to convince someone she was having a good time.

At no time did Katy hold any belief whatsoever in the reality of an escape. Part of her was waiting to reawaken bound in that room. Of course the rider had not come back for her.

And then there was a flash of white ahead, at the garden's end, and she froze, seeing a pale face quartered by black. A huge man stood there, leaning on what looked like a sledgehammer. The horsewoman had stopped as well, crouched low and waiting. She did not have her bow, Katy saw: probably it would have been too cumbersome and noisy to sneak about with.

Kill him, she willed silently. *Creep up on him and cut his throat.* Except that the rider would have had to stretch to tip-toes to even reach; would have to sit on Katy's shoulders, possibly.

More movement: another two soldiers slouched up, on patrol and plainly not too happy about it. The moon caught them for a moment, and then they were in the big man's shadow. After a couple of words, they moved on, talking in low, discontented voices.

The big man watched them depart, and Katy thought, *Go now! Now, while he's distracted!* But the horsewoman stayed utterly still, and without her example Katy did not dare try it.

Then the Order soldier was looking back towards the house— no, he was scanning the garden, eyes raking the shadows. What had betrayed them? A noise, a furtive movement. And now the rider was darting forwards, right into his line of sight. Katy hissed desperately at her, reached to snag her belt and missed.

She met with the big man, brushed fingers with him momentarily, then glanced back for Katy.

"Now we go," she explained. The big man nodded and shouldered his hammer.

THEY WERE CLEAR of the camp soon after, but they were an hour crossing open country, moving swiftly off-road and away from Wrocław, before they reached the horses. There was a second woman there, fair-haired and thin-faced, who must have had an arrow directed at them long before they saw her.

"Jedziemy do domu," she said, or something like it.

"We go home," Katy's rescuer explained, for Katy's benefit.

"Where's home?" Katy demanded. "Where's Emil? Who even are you people?"

At their expressions, she grimaced. "I mean, thank you. Thank you for getting me out of there."

The big man nodded. "Is good," he said simply. "Home is good also."

"Your man, he is with my people. They take him a safe place," the horsewoman confided. "We go there now also."

Katy felt that tide of destiny again, carrying her along whether she wanted it or not. "Please, just tell me who you are. I..." *For all I know you might be just the same as them.* It seemed impolitic to say it. "My name is Katy Lewkowitz. I'm—I was a biochemist, like Emil, the man you rescued."

"Magdayeva," the rider announced, pointing at herself. "Is Karel," the big man; "Is Jenna," for the other woman, pronouncing it as a Slavic 'Yenna'. "And your Emil is safe, if there is safe in this world now."

"Jenna Casimir," the fair-haired woman agreed. "Ride with me, Lewkowitz, so Magdayeva can scout."

THEY RODE ALL night to put distance between them and the Order—not the mad gallop Katy had expected, but a careful cross-country progress. Magdayeva, by far the best rider amongst them, came and went like a ghost in the moonlight, sloping up with her bow in one hand, the reins loosely held in the other, then vanishing away into the night again.

At dawn they rested, and Katy, who had nearly slid from the saddle twice, slept like the dead until they roused her at noon to eat wheatcakes and drink weak beer. A booze breakfast had been something that post-Cull life had inured her to: better to stress the liver than die of cholera. Karel was washing the paint from his face with great enthusiasm.

"Please tell me where we are going," she asked at last. "I'm in your debt, I really am, but..."

"You want to know if you need to start running from *us*," Jenna finished for her with a dry smile.

"No, no." *Yes*.

"My people are camped near here still," Magdayeva said, between mouthfuls. "If we reach them before they move, you will see your friend also. After that, to take you to Jasna Góra. That is near to safe."

"Until the Order gets there," Katy put in.

Karel grimaced and spat something unintelligible.

"We will let the Abbot decide what to do about the Order," Jenna decided.

"I... don't think Emil needs to go anywhere there's an Abbot..." Katy said uncertainly.

Karel chuckled deep in his massive chest. It was not a particularly welcome sound.

"But the Abbot will want to see him, and you," Jenna explained.

So the answer is yes, I should have run. But she could not outrun the horses and she still needed to recover Emil. The reins of her future were still firmly in the hands of others.

THE NEXT MORNING—before the dawn—she was woken roughly. There was a fourth there, a small, dark man already ahorse and obviously on the very point of leaving. He was a relative of Magdayeva's, Katy gathered, and he had come to warn them.

Firstly, that her people were already on the move. There would be no safe haven with them, and the stranger—Emil— had already been passed on to Jasna Góra. In Katy's mind the name was starting to conjure up something medieval and fortified, some Tolkienesque stronghold blighting the land with its shadow.

The other warning was unnecessary by the time they had her awake and stumbling towards the mounts. The sound of bikes was already in the air. The Order outriders were pushing east.

Karel had been all for stopping to fight them, but more sober heads had prevailed. They would ride for Jasna Góra.

The next few nights and days were a jolting, headlong nightmare for Katy. She was already sore from the saddle, and now they had doubled their speed, so that every part of her was bruised, and her legs were stripped raw by constant chafing. None of the others seemed to care. Even big Karel kept up a solid, competent pace on a steed that must have been descended from carthorses. Magdayeva could have been born to the saddle, riding ahead or out to one side, always keeping an eye out, reading the countryside even as it coursed past them.

Katy wanted to stop. She did not know these strange, fierce people, and she did not trust them. She had a horrible feeling that Emil would need rescuing from this Abbot just as much as he had from Josef Danziger and the Reverend Calumn. She entertained mad thoughts of headbutting Jenna, taking the horse, leading the others in a breakneck chase over the countryside that would require her to somehow pick up a decade of riding experience in moments. She reckoned the utmost rebellion she might actually effect would be to fall out of the saddle and break her neck. That would show them.

They barely stopped to rest, in that mad dash—and when they did, it was for the benefit of the horses, not the riders. Katy's world contracted to a tight knot of weariness and rubbing pain. Even though every step was now shooting agony through her, sleep still clawed at her. She sat before Jenna like a zombie, falling in and out between wakefulness and lurid, confused dreams of black-crossed white faces, of foreboding high walls.

And she must have slept, in the end, if only because the next time she became aware of herself and her surroundings, both she and they were still. She was lying on a pallet bed, in a darkened room. Stone walls loomed on every side, rising to a vaulted ceiling. A crypt; a tomb, a cell.

Eyes wide open in the gloom, she tried to understand what had happened to her.

CHAPTER FOUR
A TOUCH OF THE GOTHIC

VOICES DRIFTED TO her, echoing. She caught no words, but enough to guess they were speaking Polish or something similar, not German.

Katy stood up, feeling every part of her ache, and hobbled to the door. The room had nothing but a lantern and a row of makeshift beds in it. Outside was a cramped antechamber: a few more doors and some steps, with the promise of daylight above.

For a moment, she was going to look in the other rooms: perhaps Emil was right there, and after all, she was only in this mess because of him. The light was irresistible, though, as to a moth. She needed to know where she was. She needed to see the sun, if only to give a sense of reality to her strange, gothic surroundings.

"Going where, I wonder?"

She spun, seeing that Jenna Casimir had been sitting right

beside the door, so still that Katy had missed her entirely in the poor light.

"What do you people want with me?" she demanded, backing towards the stairs, reaching for a knife she didn't have.

Jenna raised an eyebrow. "Aside from taking your friend with the glasses in, and then rescuing your backside from the fascists? Well, some idea of why we've gone to all of that trouble, maybe."

"We don't want to be trouble for anyone. We just want to..."—she stuttered a bit there, because the plan had not gone much beyond rescuing Emil from the Order—"be on our way," she finished awkwardly.

"Be careful what you wish for," Jenna told her, standing up smoothly. "Let's take you to your friend, and then take you both to the Abbot. It's time for everyone to get some answers."

She was springing up the stairs in the next moment, every easy movement confronting Katy with her own arthritic rawness. Every step seemed a direct attack on her joints, so that by the time Jenna led her out into the open air she was ready to complain vociferously about everything she had been through. Until she saw where she was. She stared, dumbfounded.

They had come out into the courtyard of some sort of grand house. It could have been an unostentatious Ducal palace or a particularly fancy prison, three storeys of regimented windows on all four sides—some broken and boarded up, but most intact—capped by a steep-sloped roof covered entirely in verdigris. The space within the walls looked as though it had been a garden or a park, once, but right now it had been turned into a cross between an outdoor workshop and a renaissance fair. There were men and women everywhere, carding wool, clacking away on looms, sawing wood. The sound of patient, steady hammering rang from one corner, where a black man was tending a little forge. Beside him, a woman had a pot of glue on the boil and was carefully splitting feathers with a little knife, ready to fletch arrows. In the centre of the courtyard, a couple of lean young men in masks and padding were fencing, or whatever the equivalent was when the swords were four feet long and double-edged.

"What the hell is this?" Katy demanded, louder than she had

intended. Her English seemed to make little impression on the people around her.

"Tomasz, Paul!" Jenna called.

The duellists parted, and one of them pushed his mask back, exposing a lantern-jawed, bony face. There was a brief discussion in Polish, then Jenna gave them some sort of instructions and they loped off.

"I told them, if they've nothing important to be doing, they can go get your friend," she explained for Katy. "Come on then. The Abbot's on the walls."

I don't want to meet any Abbot. But it was plain she was not really being given a choice.

She had not quite registered Jenna's 'on the walls' before she took her out of the courtyard of that grand, grim building, and then up on what she could only describe as broad battlements. She found herself atop a great wall that enclosed not only the big house, but the looming spire of a church and ranks of humbler buildings as well. *A castle, a fortress.* It was not quite either, but she could not quite think what it actually was. The surrounding wall stretched off away from her in two directions, forming what must be a square compound, with great spear-head shaped projections butting out from the corners she could see. Beyond...

She had expected something craggy, mountainous even, or perhaps a dark forest straight from the Brothers Grimm, stretching impossibly to the horizon. Instead, when she reached the wall top and looked over the edge, she saw a great, silent city. The castle, or fort, or whatever it was, stood in a swathe of parkland, stubbled with the stumps of felled trees, but beyond that sprawled the interlaced streets of another monument to the terrifying scale of the Cull. *Wrocław, all over again.* For a moment she just stood there and stared out past all those empty homes, some whole, some fallen into ruin, to the far skeletal strands of the railway lines.

And, like Wrocław, an oppressive quiet hung over the place, clogging the air with absences, so that she spoke out loud: "Where is everyone?"

"There were many who wanted to stay here in Częstochowa, in the first days," said a new voice, in Slavic-accented German. "Perhaps some have. I hope most have listened to us and found other places. Why stay in a dying city, no way of feeding yourself, no clean water? All those we spoke to, they took what they could and they left to find somewhere they could *live*, not just survive."

And she turned, and set eyes on the Abbot.

He was not as big as Karel, who stood at his shoulder, as out of scale as a bad photoshop, but this newcomer was still broad-shouldered and powerfully made. His short-cropped hair was gun-barrel grey, and his face was set between two scars: a jagged old twist at his chin and a livid flash over one eye that looked more recent. His eyes were grey-blue and hawk-like. He wore a simple dark robe, but his belt looked modern, as did the combat boots beneath it.

Her first impression was *dangerous*—both in himself, and because these people round him evidently did his bidding. She thought about Danziger and Calumn—was he a rival warlord, or would he sing from their hymn sheet, or was he something different again?

When she made to speak, he held one hand up—almost a benediction—and tilted his head down the line of the wall. Tomasz and Paul were on their way, and between them was a familiar figure.

"Emil!"

She saw him start, then pick his pace up, outdistancing his escort. As he approached, she scanned his face for signs of injury, finding he had added a striking black eye to his mementos of the Order.

For a moment, she thought he was going to hug her, but that would not have been the man she knew. Instead he slowed as he approached, visibly recalling his dignity, and managed a businesslike nod. "Miss Lewkowitz, I am..." He shrugged. "I hadn't thought..."

"You and me both," she confirmed. "Emil, who are these people?"

"Introductions, then," the robed man broke in smoothly. "You have met our Jenna, of course, who commands our scouts.

Paul and Tomasz are my captains here, under whose guidance the order of Jasna Góra is maintained." He spoke carefully, pausing on and off as he found the words. "And here is Karel, our champion, who styles himself the Golem of Prague."

Katy looked the vast man over. He looked less Jewish than she would have expected, for the nickname.

"We're very grateful for your rescuing us, sir..." she started, and stuttered to a halt in the face of the Abbot's stern regard. Apparently nothing but frank introductions were going to be good enough. There would be no quick talking her way out of this.

"My name is Katy Lewkowitz." *Name, rank and serial number.*

"English?" Paul asked. He was smaller and stockier than Tomasz, and more suspicious, too, from his expression.

She shrugged. "It doesn't seem to matter anymore."

"And this is Doctor Emil Weber," the Abbot finished. From the way Emil started, Katy saw it was information he had not volunteered. "Doctor Weber, it's hard to be famous at the end of the world, now we who remain live in such reduced ways. Yet here you are, and there are people who have travelled a long way to meet you."

Emil's eyes twitched to lock gazes with Katy. *No need to ask who that is.*

"Come with me." The Abbot made a curt gesture and set off along the wall. With Karel and the rest forming behind them, it was hard to say no.

He stopped, looking out over what Katy guessed was the main entrance to the complex: a bridge rising up gradually through the near edge of the parkland. Beyond it, she could see a great stretch of open tarmac, still clogged with the rusting hulks of cars, edged by what might have been the rotting remnants of cafés.

"Tourist central," she murmured.

"It was," the Abbot confirmed. "You are standing at the heart of the faith in Poland. Pilgrims came here from all over the world."

She saw Emil squirm at the talk. Overt displays of religion always made him uncomfortable, and she guessed recent experience had done nothing to alleviate that.

"Our problem is *that*," Paul put in, pointing out past the ramp.

There were some tents set up there, and although she had been expecting them, Katy's heart still sank to see them. This was not the Order's great circus of preaching and punishment. She counted eight tents, along with six vehicles that had plainly been driven in recently. A scatter of motocycles were there too.

"So you have more pilgrims," Emil said harshly. "You must be pleased."

"We know the New Teutonic Order," the Abbot said thoughtfully. "When the Rom travel west, they meet them sometimes. When you two were saved from them, my people were scouting out the limits of their presence. But they are far west, out beyond Wrocław. We know they are on the move, spreading their doctrine from community to community. But now they are here, a long way from their usual haunts. Perhaps you can tell me why."

His gaze raked Emil, who squared up to it as best he could.

"Because they're madmen, fanatics. Or perhaps you see that as their good points."

"Emil," Katy said, warningly. "Abbot, I don't know who you are or what it is you're doing in this place, but if you've seen anything of the Order, you'll know the sort of people they are. I rescued Emil from them, when they were about to hang him—and not just him. They have quite a list of people they don't like." *But then, maybe you have one too.* She searched his expression for some clue, found nothing.

"Lewkowitz," the Abbot pronounced, and hearing her own name on his lips sent a jolt of sudden fear through her. "Jewish?"

She didn't answer, but apparently she didn't need to. He just nodded thoughtfully. "You're brave, then, to go into their camp for your friend. You're surely on their list."

"I'd be a 'Heathen,'" she confirmed flatly. "It's a sort of catch-all category. And you?"

"They don't need a reason!" Karel snapped suddenly. "It's not like this hasn't happened before. They say they're here for him? They're here because they're Germans. This is what they *do*. It's what they've always done."

Katy was just trying to get her head around having the huge man as an ally when Emil attacked him furiously.

"They are not German! How dare you say that's what this is about? My friends at the university, that the Order killed, *they* were German. *I* am German. Those men out there, they do not even deserve to be called human. Faced with a global disaster, *humans* do not seek to turn their backs on the world and indulge in the worst excesses of history. There is some other word for what they are, and it is not 'German'!"

Karel stared at him as though Emil had gone up to him and personally asked to be punched in the face, but then Paul put a hand on his arm.

"Karel, *I'm* German."

"No you're not." The big man frowned.

"Seriously, he is. What did you think?" Tomasz put in, and Katy felt a weird sense of surreality, because of course the whole argument was even being conducted in German: the Czech and the Poles probably had no other common language.

"Enough." The Abbot spoke quietly, but he had everyone's attention. "Our guest is quite right. It isn't national pride that has brought them to our door. Nations are dead. With what has happened in the world, the only people still flying the flags of Nations must be the mad or the wicked. They came here for you, Doctor Emil Weber, and I want to know why."

"So you can decide whether to hand me over?"

"Yes, exactly that." The Abbot looked him in the eye as he said it. "These are just the first. There are more on the way, and I am responsible for all the souls within these walls. The Order wishes to talk, and I will hear them out." At Karel opening his mouth, he held up a silencing hand. "Just because they are bad men, does not mean they cannot also be wronged. I will go. Paul, assemble a dozen of our fighters, enough that the Order will mind their manners." And the Abbot's eye flicked over to Katy. "And I suppose you should come, too."

"Me?"

"If I took your friend, I feel the temptation to break the truce would be too great for the hunters out there. But I assume that he would prefer someone present to represent his interests? Who else is there but you?"

CHAPTER FIVE
OLD DOGMA, NEW TRICKS

THE ESCORT THAT Tomasz and Paul put together consisted of eight men and four women, ranging in age from twenty to twice that. Apparently Karel the Golem of Prague was not coming, possibly because he was nobody's idea of a natural diplomat. They sported a motley of studded leathers, Kevlar vests and pieces of metal armour that were archaic of design but weirdly new-looking. Some had bows, or in one man's case, a modern high-power crossbow. Others had shotguns or hunting rifles, and one carried a stubby assault rifle slung on a shoulder straps. There wasn't one of them lacking a sword or hatchet or long fighting knife.

"It's *Mad Max*," Katy said before she could stop herself. She hoped that nobody had been close enough to hear, but then Jenna was at her elbow with a sharp laugh.

"I saw that movie. We had a copy. The dubbing was horrible: one man, reading all the voices."

"Who are you people? What is this place?" Katy demanded, almost desperately. She felt as though, somewhere during their frantic ride from the Order, she had gone down a rabbit hole and ended up some place where history documentaries went to die.

"Come back from the meeting, I'm sure the Abbot will have all the explanations you need," Jenna told her coolly.

"If he doesn't just hand me over."

"If that." Jenna shrugged. "No point me filling your head with useful information if that, eh?"

They were all mustering in a narrow, crooked courtyard, the gates of which opened onto the bridge she had seen earlier. The mood amongst the locals was serious, a little nervous. The odd snatch of laughter from amongst the makeshift soldiers sounded forced.

"You've not had to fight much around here, I'd guess," Katy remarked.

"Not yet," Jenna confirmed. "But history taught us that the day would come."

Then there was the sound of hooves on stone, and the Abbot appeared, alongside a familiar horse. In the saddle, Magdayeva was bending low to speak to him.

He nodded at her words, then looked up with a glint in his eye, making some approving comment in Polish to the troops. Then he had a little spiel for Tomasz, who had turned up with a longbow in hand, every inch a Robin Hood. Katy assumed the long-framed man was going with them until he nodded sharply and took off for the walls, full quiver rattling at his belt.

Because of course that's going to help. Katy was becoming increasingly convinced that she was surrounded by crazy people.

Then the Abbot had a meaty hand on her shoulder, and the escort was forming up around them. A handful of people unbarred the gates and hauled them open—and Katy could not help but notice all the recent reinforcement that had gone into them—and then there was nothing but four hundred feet of ramp and car park between her and the Order, dotted with the hulks of failed cars at the near end.

There were a fair mob of Order soldiers watching them emerge: perhaps half with guns of some kind, the rest with a menagerie of close quarter weapons. Their uniform facepaint made them into something more dangerous than the people from the fortress, though: one creed, one face, one mind.

They were most of the way down the ramp when the Abbot waved a halt.

"Just you and I, now. We'll show them how things will be done." His voice was light, but the hand on her shoulder was heavy. The escort had spread out to either side, not actually pointing weapons at anyone, but arrows were on the string, guns were directed not quite at the ground. A few had stepped into the cover of the picked-over chassis that had been abandoned towards this end of the ramp.

No, not abandoned, dragged there, Katy realised: another home-grown attempt to make this place more difficult to just drive up to.

She saw quite a stir amongst the Order when she and the Abbot came to the very edge of the ramp on their own, out into the horrible open ground beyond. For a moment it was not clear what their response would be, but at last a small group of them peeled off: four soldiers backing the one man amongst them who didn't paint his face, and who wasn't overtly armed. God had apparently sent His own mouthpiece to seek the recapture of Emil Weber: the Reverend James Calumn, Jr was leading the charge.

Magdayeva said something then, some caution or farewell, and then she was guiding her horse away, past the Abbot and off at an angle, away from both groups and off into the ghost-town that was Częstochowa. A few Order rifles twitched a little at that, but apparently everyone was still very much on their best behaviour for the diplomacy.

"Where's she going?" Katy hissed. She had liked Magdayeva: anyone who would do what that girl had done for her was something to be counted on. She did not have the same feel about Jenna or any of the rest of them

"She's carrying word to her people," the Abbot murmured.

Her people. The Roma? That was the impression Katy had got. She had seen how the Order treated gypsies, but at the same time she had a feeling they hadn't fared that much better in Poland, or anywhere else, historically. Nobody liked perpetual outsiders.

Then her eyes were drawn to the Order delegation, and she realised with a sinking heart that she recognised more than just Calumn, and that this other man would know her.

"That one, at the preacher's left shoulder," she murmured to the Abbot. "He's"—she almost said *the English Bigot*, but that would hardly have been constructive—"Edward, his name is. He's a second to their Grand Wizard, or whatever they called him."

"Danziger," the Abbot said softly, and Katy glanced at him in surprise. "Oh, yes, we have heard the name, despite the distance between us and him. A distance I suspect is shortening rapidly."

But then he was raising a hand as the cross-faced soldiers approached. "Dzień dobry, Pochwalony Jezus Chrystus! Welcome, in the name of the Father, the Son and the Virgin Mary!"

Calumn and his cronies had stopped, somewhat startled by the address, but at last Edward said an awkward "Same to you" in his rough German. Katy wondered for a mad moment whether she would have to act as his interpreter. She had forgotten the Reverend's gift for languages, though. The preacher strode forwards with smooth assurance, hand thrust out until the Abbot had to either take it or declare de facto war by way of poor etiquette.

"Good day to you, sir," the American said, his smile gleaming, "and may I say, it is a pleasure to find more of His servants in this blighted world!" Behind him, his escort was uncertain: to follow up into arm's reach of the Abbot would look as though they were about to attack him, to hang back was plainly counter to their pugilistic instincts. In the end three of them milled, and Edward obviously reckoned Katy's presence was enough to allow him to regain the Reverend's shoulder once again.

"My name is Calumn, sir,"—*Mein Herr*, but Katy translated it to the American idiom unconsciously—"James Calumn. I consider myself a servant of God in these latter days. I do His will."

The Abbot nodded soberly, plainly giving this all due consideration. "I am the Abbot Leszek of Jasna Góra. I do what I can."

"I'm sure you do, sir," Calumn agreed sunnily. "Now, sir, I'd wager word of the New Teutonic Order has come to you, even here." At Leszek's cautious nod, he continued. "And perhaps you'll have heard some stories that would lead you to be suspicious of their good intentions? It can't be helped that the Devil has a quick tongue, wouldn't you agree? It quite outpaces the Lord's truth, sometimes."

The Abbot grunted.

"I'll tell you, sir, I was in Berlin when the last days began. I was booked in to preach to packed studios, sir. I sure as damnation had not seen the way my future was about to take off. I'm certain you remember those days clear as I do: how the deaths came, and more and more of them. Bodies in the streets, sir—not enough left to even give them a decent burial. The police, the hospitals, doing what they can, and none of those good people realising that this was not a matter for their hands any more. This was not just some new virus out of China, no sir. It was the end of the world. Well, sir, I don't mind telling you, I had my moment of doubt. I was sore afraid, you can be sure. I reckon there aren't many who wouldn't say the same."

He could certainly talk, could James Calumn, Jr. Katy found herself nodding along, remembering how it had been for her and recasting those memories in the Reverend's words.

"It was a testing time," the Abbot agreed curtly.

"It surely was." Calumn paused philosophically. "When the worst of it was done, when God had sent so very many to their judgment, I found myself still breathing, and with not an idea of why I had been spared."

"That was when you heard of the Order," Leszek put in.

"It was, sir. You're absolutely right. They were few in those days, just a handful who were asking the same questions I was: why have we been kept on this Earth? Where is the New Jerusalem, as was foretold? And so I joined them, and we found others—some believers, others who *wanted* to believe— and we set out on what I believe to be the final Crusade, the final expression of God's will, to open the way for the Second Coming, and the founding of God's Kingdom on Earth."

"Do I gather that this way involves the removal of those who are not part of God's plan?" There was no judgment or condemnation in the Abbot's voice; precious little of any emotion at all, in fact.

For a second, Calumn's eyes flicked from Abbot Leszek to Katy and back, trying to work out which way the wind was blowing. "Sir, it does, for Christ's new Kingdom cannot be established on Earth while there remain sinners who have escaped judgment. That is the task that God has given to us."

"You have come a long way to reach our doors. Are there no more sinners left between here and Berlin?"

Katy frowned: she had been asking herself exactly the same thing.

Calumn smiled. "There are sinners and sinners, Abbot Leszek. Some simply have no place in Christ's new Kingdom, but there are a few who are active servants of the Devil, men who will try to undo the Lord's work! In the face of such hubris there's no distance too far to go, don't you think?"

"We come now to the matter of Doctor Weber."

"We do indeed, sir." The Reverend's expression suggested infinite regret at the wickedness of Man. "Do you know what he and his cohorts were about, when we discovered their little nest of heresy? They were using the tools of the Devil to study the instrument of the Lord that had sounded the last trump for the world. They believed that they could interfere with its effects, to prevent souls from being reaped by it. God has sent this judgment onto the world, Abbot Leszek, and it is not for Man to scheme against that Divine work. So yes, we have come here to bring judgment to this man Emil Weber, because he is an avowed enemy of the Lord, a man who before the fall spoke out against me and you and all other believers, and now has cast off his mask and works as the Devil's right hand. I put it to you that it is your duty as Christ's representative in these parts to pass him to us, so that the Lord's justice may be done." He took a deep breath: a compassionate man with a tear in his eye. "Sir, I know that folks hereabouts have looked to the great city of Rome for their inspiration, and I know that you and I might not, in other days, have seen eye to eye on that fact. I'll warrant you've had no news from that quarter any time since the fall, but I can say this with one hundred percent conviction: I believe that if the Pope were here now, he and I would be singing from the same hymn sheet. After all, what has the great organisation of Christ's Church on Earth, of whatever sect or flavour, been preparing for, if not for this?"

Leszek's expression was... was almost absent, Katy realised, as though he had retreated inside himself. "You make quite a case," was all he would say.

"So may I go back to my fellows and tell them that we shall see the heretic Weber shortly?"

The Abbot grimaced. "I will have to speak to my people. They are a varied lot, from many backgrounds. They are not perhaps as united in purpose as are your friends."

Calumn nodded, with an easy smile that failed to encroach much on his eyes. "Of course, sir, of course. But, I pray you, remember we are all on the same side—*His* own side. You wouldn't want us to have a disagreement over this."

"I am sure many would regret it." Leszek took a deep breath. "Do widzenia, Reverend Calumn. I am sure we will speak again shortly."

As he spoke, Edward had leant in to murmur in the preacher's ear, and the American nodded unhappily.

"Sir, there is one other matter: that woman who stands beside you, you'll know she's a confederate of this man Weber?"

"That is known to me, yes."

"Well I'm sure that she has told you many slanderous things about the Order and its cause. Perhaps she hasn't told you that she's a murderer. The blood of Christ's soldiers is on her hands."

I may have neglected to mention it. She had not thought of the man in the tent, whom she had knifed when freeing Emil, for what seemed like an age. Now she saw the Abbot look sidelong at her, with a slight twitch of his eyebrow.

"It is true that this has not been said to me," he confirmed.

"I don't doubt it, sir," Calumn stated. "I'd urge you to weigh that fact, when you listen to her lies. I have no doubt she's a follower of the same Satanic cause as Weber himself."

It seemed that Edward wanted to press for more—probably for Katy to be handed over—but Calumn cut him off with a sharp gesture, and then the Order delegation were trekking back to their camp, and she and Leszek were returning towards the walls of Jasna Góra.

CHAPTER SIX
DINNER AND INQUISITION

KATY FOUND HERSELF not quite a captive, when they returned, but most certainly not free to wander. She was back in what she had taken for either a stately home or a prison, but which she now understood to be the actual monastery building that Jasna Góra was built around. It didn't seem to quite be fulfilling that function now, despite the presence of an Abbot. Instead, it seemed to house a surprising number of people, of all ages and both genders, all of whom had a great deal to be getting on with. She wandered the limited fraction of the building she could access—always with someone or other dogging her shoulder— and saw carding, weaving, cooking, cleaning, even teaching: a class of children repeating by rote something in Polish, that might have been doctrine or trigonometry, for all Katy knew.

She did catch various scraps of a running discussion between Paul, Tomasz and Karel as to how they might go about making a sortie to attack the Order camp, if it came to it. The topic turned sour towards evening and she gathered further reinforcements had arrived for the Reverend Calumn and his martial flock. It was evident that the fighting compliment of Jasna Góra was not large.

Later, Jenna tracked her down again. "Do you wish to go to the service, now?"

Katy blinked at her. "As in a church service?"

"Yes."

"I guess you're all avid churchgoers around here," Katy remarked, and then had to restate the sentiment so that Jenna could follow.

"Before the dying started, I would take any excuse to avoid going to church," the woman told her solemnly. "Even on a Sunday. Now... now things are different. It is what binds us together."

Just like the black cross binds the Order, thought Katy sourly. "You just go ahead. My family were about as unreligious as it's possible to be while still being Jewish, but I reckon becoming Catholic's still a step too far, personally."

Jenna shrugged. "Our smith, Hamid, he comes, and he's hardly taken the sacrament, but it's your choice. After that, the Abbot has requested to dine with you, and your friend, too. He wants to decide what to do with you."

THE ABBOT'S QUARTERS were lit by candles and rank-smelling lanterns, and a single bright star of electric light that seemed somewhat less miraculous when Katy discovered someone had to wind it briskly every quarter of an hour to keep it shining.

There were just the three of them at the table, although no doubt a dozen tough survivalist monks were within earshot waiting for the call. Besides, the Abbot could have broken both his guests over his knee without breaking a sweat. Underlit by the jumping flames of candles, his face had a positively villainous caste to it.

The fare was coarse bread, beer, pickled cabbage and slices of heavily cured sausage that Katy stared at mournfully but could not bring herself to touch, no matter what she had said to Jenna about her upbringing. Emil had gone right for it, but then stuttered to a halt under the Abbot's stern gaze, and fumed silently while the man said a quiet grace.

"I trust we do not fail as hosts," Leszek addressed them, when at last he had allowed them to fall to eating.

Emil's look was baleful but his mouth was full, and so Katy said, "What is this place? Who are these people? And why is this city and Wrocław, why are they so deserted?"

The Abbot smiled slightly. "It's not so, west of here, then? Perhaps not. East of here as well, no doubt. What can I say? This is the monastery of Jasna Góra. For a lot of people, in the world we once knew, this place was Poland. This was the heart of our land, and every believer would make a pilgrimage here, at least once in their lives. How is that, Doctor Weber? You have come to shelter in the very bosom of the church!" The Abbot's smile was mischievous. "This place was freedom from oppression, from conquest. I should tell you about the Deluge, some time—no, not the Biblical flood, Doctor Weber, but our own local tide of destruction—that broke against the walls that stood here, and came no further. But enough of that. Today, Jasna Góra is no more and no less than you see. Because of its place in the hearts of so many, many came here after the great dying began. Many have stayed: we take those who will teach or who will learn."

"And who will pray," Emil noted flatly. Katy tried to kick him under the table, but could not reach.

"The Reverend Calumn had much to say about you, Doctor Weber," Leszek noted. "You and he are old enemies, I think?"

"I took him down a few pegs, when he dared to come on German television with his particular brand of nonsense," Emil said hotly. "His absurd lies about the age of the earth, about 'God's plan,' so he said. I took every argument and tore it apart, him, and some fool of a chemist who'd defected to the Intelligent Design camp, and I think there was a Bishop of some place I can't even remember, one of your co-religionists. I took them all on."

"Emil," Katy snapped warningly.

His eyes found hers and for a moment he struggled with himself, but in the end he shook his head. "I'm sorry, Miss Lewkowitz. Feel free to disassociate yourself from everything I say." He tore a loaf of bread in half, savagely. "Abbot Leszek, I have lived my entire life believing only in those things which can be demonstrated, consistently, by scientific method. I have fought tirelessly against quacks, charlatans, homeopaths, fraudulent psychics and men of the church, any church, who believe they have the right to insist that people honour and respect their stale dogma simply because some primitive fool wrote some lies down millennia before—" Just then, Katy, by dint of hunching half under the table, managed to connect with his ankle, cutting him off, and he glared at her. "I'm sorry," he said again. "This is the only confession you'll get from me, Abbot. I will eat no wafers, I will mouth no platitudes. Not even if it means my life."

The Abbot's hooded gaze regarded him for a few long seconds. "You are ready to be martyred for your unbelief."

"Mock all you want," Emil said fiercely, although he drew his legs up as he said it. "I am not a brave man. I am not a strong man. But I have my limits."

The Abbot ate a little in silence then, as Katy tried and failed to catch Emil's eye. At last, he said, "The Reverend Calumn claims that you have been trying to undo, as he says, God's work."

Emil scowled. "That... *barbarian*. Before he and his brigands destroyed my laboratory and murdered my fellows, we had been trying to understand the method by which the blood-disease operated: how was it made—for believe me it *was* made, not sent by any man's God. How does it kill? Why are some blood groups unaffected? How might it be prevented?"

Leszek made a dismissive little gesture. "And yet the deaths happened. Or are you also researching a conveyance for going backwards in time?"

"Emil—!" Katy tried again, but the scientist stood up abruptly, knocking his chair over with a thunderous bang.

"You don't understand!" he snapped. "You're as blind as Calumn, as any of them!" He was angrier now, at this affront to science, than personal threats or insults ever made him. "Perhaps you truly believe that every living thing came into this Earth in its current shape, unchanging and *designed*, but it is not so! Life changes, Abbot Leszek. And if natural life changes, so does the artificial plague that human hands have unleashed upon it. What happens when the disease *mutates* so that the surviving blood type is not immune, tell me? What happens then, when a further, say, seventy percent of the surviving human race dies off? If we are to survive, we must develop a means of countering this thing before natural selection selects *for* it and *against* us!"

Big Karel and a stocky, short-haired woman had burst in, but Emil hardly seemed to notice them, even the pistol the woman had aimed at his head. He was breathing heavily, like an athlete just off the track. The candlelight caught the glint of tears in his eyes. "It's not over," he said hoarsely. "Life is never over. If human life, with all that it has created and discovered, is to survive, then we need the rational power of scientific thought more now than ever. Superstition and blind ritual will kill us all."

The Abbot had barely reacted to the tirade, and now he waved the guards away with the smallest of gestures. Another motion of his hand sufficed to get Emil to right his chair and sit down again.

"To return to Miss Lewkowitz's original question," he said, as though Emil hadn't spoken at all, "when the Cull came to these lands, there were many among the survivors who formed communities and had plans for the future. Given where we are, not a few of these were men of the cloth, or otherwise devotees of the Mother Church. Others were not: there were warlords, little parliaments, men who set themselves up as the ziemianie, the nobility of old. And there was fighting, and hardship. Many who survived the plague starved, or died from other infections. It seemed that mere chaos and human dissent would finish what the disease had started.

"But matters fell out that the leaders of all these communities could meet even though they did not trust each other. Here, they could meet. There was a summit, within these walls. They travelled many miles, some of them, to be here. Jasna Góra casts a long shadow."

"I don't believe it," Emil broke in bluntly. "Or are you telling me someone kept the Polish cellphone network up somehow?"

"There was a way. Not as fast as all the modern conveniences we remember, but more reliable, more resilient. Sometimes the old ways are the best. But they came. Because the church called, if no other reason, they came. Many of the local leaders held sway because the survivors had come to the church in their time of need." His lips twitched at Emil's immediate sneer. "I wonder how matters might have gone, if you had found yourself at that gathering. Everyone there was frightened, as you can imagine. Anyone who had an answer—a future they had foreseen—they had an audience. People wanted to be told what to do."

"That is an old excuse for the abuse of power," Emil said curtly.

"And you can imagine some of the futures that were described. Yes, there were enough who wanted to revive the fortunes of the church, to return these lands to a time when religious law was a rod of iron. There were many ready to drive out any who refused to obey the strictures of the Mother Church. They argued that this was a new dawn, an opportunity literally God-given. If Reverend Calumn had been present, he would have found more than one kindred spirit in that gathering.

"And there were others who saw in this catastrophe the moment for our pride to resurface. They flew the red and white flag, or the eagle of old, and they told us that this was when Poland must be reclaimed for the Poles—that foreign influence must be cast out, hounded from our borders. Whichever borders they were using: we have had a remarkable variety over the years, depending on who was drawing the maps. There were great dreams, in those days. There were men who ruled communities of a thousand, two thousand people, wanting to re-establish the Commonwealth, each seeing himself king of a land that stretched from Berlin to Moscow, seeing himself Pope of a Polish Rome. There were men who had made themselves warlords, dreaming of becoming Emperors out of Warsaw, out of Poznań, gathering the desperate and the lost to themselves."

There was something in the Abbot's face. The candle-flame gleamed on it as though burning those past days like so many old newspapers. Even Emil had no words to take the moment from him.

"But other voices were heard," Leszek said, at last. "There were some men—and yes, men of the cloth—who held their own council, and framed their own future. I cannot say that I was the leading voice, but mine was amongst them."

"And you expect me to believe it was all peace, love and understanding?" Emil asked acidly.

"That is what Christ preached, after all," the Abbot said softly, and in bringing his voice down, he seemed to summon silence into the room, that only his words could break. "But also this: each of these other futures relied on drawing borders: the church and the heathen; Poland and those who were not Polish; *us* and *them*. And so it was said: have you not seen what has happened to the world? Is it not the case, that every one amongst us knows more who have gone to God, than remain? Do you think we shall prosper, by drawing these divisions, and driving away those we see as not like us? And as for building empires—whether united by church or nationality or the size of a man's shoe... these are dreams. These can be nothing but dreams. I am aware of what is going on west of here: the Order are not even the only warmongers whose names have come to us, and to the east there are more Tsars and Khans, more Alexanders and Peters and Terrible Ivans than I can count. And they shall pass, all of them. They shall pass, because while they make war and steal from one another and from those weaker than they, they build nothing. They do not plant, nor do their harvest. They see only their own tomorrows. Their ambition is to be the king of mankind's ruin for a handful of years, and then pass from history, leaving the world only poorer. Those who seek to restore or even to maintain the dreams of yesteryear shall accomplish nothing, save to lessen the common lot of mankind. We cannot be the nations of old, any more than we can be the empires of ancient history, the heroes of myth. This we saw, when the clamour of voices in these halls reached its peak."

"So what did you tell them?" Katy asked, in the hush that followed. "What was your solution?"

"Leave the cities," Leszek revealed, "for the cities will not feed you; the cities will grow nothing but plague as the water turns foul, as the survivors live on top of one another and in each other's filth. Poland has more than enough land for every man and woman to till the earth. Leave the cities and go to the villages, the farms. Learn what you can of the old ways, for the years of industry, of electricity and wonders, are dead or dying, and they will not return in our lifetimes. And although there were some who would not hear us, who returned to their strongholds to plot the conquest or conversion of the world, the majority came to see things as we did. And so anyone who could shoe a horse or tan leather, work wood or draw a bow, they were invited to come here, where their skills could be taught, passed on. And for the rest, so long as they can be a good neighbour, there will always be a place for them."

"So your local warlords who aren't good neighbours...?" Katy prompted, seeing that Emil had lapsed into sullen silence.

"Those who shared our dream helped one another. And those who chose instead to hold to their own dreams of exclusion and elitism, they did not. And there are not so many of them left, now. Now that the petrol is used up. Now that they must count each bullet for the guns they love. What was it that Goering said? 'Guns will make us powerful; butter will only make us fat'? It was the death knell of the old fascists— you can have all the guns in the world and starve from lack of butter."

"So what this boils down to..." Emil started, and then looked at the Abbot with a curious expression, hostile and plaintive all at once.

"Is we will not hand you to the builders of Empire, either of you," Leszek finished. "Jasna Góra will hold out against the invader, as it has before. We will weather this Deluge as with all the others."

"And I?" Emil demanded.

Leszek spread his hands in a beatific gesture. "Welcome to the bosom of the Mother Church, Doctor Weber. I'm sure we'll find some use for you."

PART TWO
BRINGING THE STORM

CHAPTER SEVEN
THOSE WHO DEFEND

Jenna Casimir leant on the wall top, watching the soldiers of the Order. Since the Cull, the walls of Jasna Góra had been sporadically re-edified whenever there had been people without more urgent tasks at hand. Nobody had the skills or the materials to do the fortifications justice, and so what had been put up was mostly a motley of doors: front doors, interior doors, car doors, along with sundry pieces of wood and the like that could be spared from the cooking fires. The monastery had inherited people who knew their history, and a lot of the bigger pieces had arrowslits sawed into them, which was just as well, since the monastery boasted more archers than gunmen.

The Order had waited a day for Emil Weber to be handed back to them, after which they had begun offensive manoeuvres. By that time they looked to have around a hundred under arms in their camp in the car park. If Weber was as important as they'd said to the Abbot, then doubtless there were more on the way. Nobody was quite sure how many roving bully-boys the New Teutons could field, but Katy Lewkowitz claimed there had been a couple of hundred just in the camp she had sprung Weber from. Likely there were three times as many—have gun, will travel—able to drive the vacated roads from the border to Jasna Góra.

The total fighting strength of the defenders was about the equal of the mob currently at the gates, certainly not enough to make any sortie into the barrels of their guns an attractive prospect.

That first day, the enemy had simply scouted out the place. They had been given a look at the main entrance, the John Paul II gate, but there were other ways in. To the side, two narrower paths climbed to the Jagiellonian Gate, that had been solidly barricaded, and that a handful could defend. Everywhere else was similarly barred, so that anyone who didn't want to have to make an assault straight up the wall was going to have to try the ramp and the gate.

There had been a few shots exchanged, on the next day. Men with rifles had tried to make the defenders' lives difficult, but they had few targets, and from the bottom of the gradient, they were out-ranged. Still, there had been little return fire from the walls.

"We want them overconfident now, before there are enough of them that they can afford to be," she explained, for Katy Lewkowitz's benefit. Weber's sidekick was a minefield of questions about Jasna Góra, and it was Jenna that she tended to dog.

"Why not just gun them down?" Katy wanted to know. "Every one you can."

"You're a bloodthirsty one, aren't you?" Jenna noted. "This is not a good range, for them or for us. Shoot now, we waste most of our bullets. We don't have so many. Neither do they, we hope, but we can make arrows and they cannot manufacture ammunition."

"Back where I was, people used bows to hunt. Hunt rabbit, that is," Katy stated. "You seem to think they're a weapon of war."

Jenna gave her a frank look that hopefully concealed how annoying she found that sort of talk. "When it comes to it, you'll see. Probably the Order think the same as you. I hope so."

"But who... who are you people, to sit here turning the clock back a thousand years? Shouldn't you be... trying to preserve everything you can of our world?"

"Why, yes, every evening we gather in the refectory and re-enact reality television shows so that future generations will know the beauty of the art of the ancient world," Jenna told her acidly, but she said it in Polish, which the girl didn't speak a word of. More patiently, she went on, "I was one of the first to come here, after the Cull. I was nearby, with Tomasz and Karel and some others of ours who survived. Most of our friends died. Most of the monks had died. Leszek gave us a place, and he could use our skills." Seeing the inevitable question bubbling up on the other woman's face she went on. "They call it 'living history.' We would get together at places like this, places of great heritage, and we would re-enact battles and do crafts and show how people lived. For some it was a hobby, for others, study. These skills we are teaching, they were a thing of academic interest once. Now they have saved many, many lives: they clothe people, feed people, prepare people for the simpler lives we must lead."

"Re-enactors," Katy repeated leadenly, with a clear, unspoken *who I am trusting my life to?* "You must be loving this."

"Really?" Jenna gave her a level look. "It was a game we played. I was a film extra, for money—over in the Czech Republic, mostly. I got a lot of work because I was a good rider. They were always doing historical epics, cut-price Tolkien pieces. I loved the internet. I loved television. I loved my family and friends, most of whom are all dead. So no, I am not loving this. I am surviving this, and helping others. That is what I am doing." She brushed over the mumbled apologies. "And what do you do, Miss Lewkowitz?"

"I've done some medical work, if you have supplies..." A panicked look came over her face. "I don't know crap about how they used to do that back when, what, Galen was around, so—"

"We have some painkillers, anaesthetics, antibiotics," Jenna broke in. "Get it in your head: we're not wilfully ignorant. We're facing the fact that nobody is *making* these things anymore."

There was a staccato crackle of gunfire and everyone around them froze for just a moment. Jenna leant out a little and her eyes narrowed.

"Right. I think we're going to see their teeth. Hamid!"

The dark man who had been serving as smith earlier bounded over to her. He was a big, broad character with an easy smile, but unless he was some deadly martial artist he did not look ready to fight anyone.

"Go down the wall to Paul. Make sure he's seen this. Then get Lewkowitz to the medics in case she's any use."

THE ORDER HAD three score soldiers mustering to advance along the bridge. Tomasz Osinski rested his binoculars on the wall top, seeing a good showing of rifles—sports guns, a few nasty-looking hunting pieces, a handful of ex-military automatic weapons. The Order had certain priorities, he guessed. They rated being well-armed more highly than being well-fed the year after next. The Abbot's strategies—which had become their common strategies—were longer term: years and decades. Of course, to win in the long term you had to survive in the short term.

He had gone against the Abbot's orders only once. Just a month after their community at Jasna Góra had got its direction—a month after everything had started working out—he and Paul had piled into a flatbed truck they still had fuel for and taken off for a place Tomasz remembered from his army days. He had done his time in the services, when not playing at being a medieval archer or a renaissance hussar. He had worn the blue beret and driven armoured vehicles and been spat on in fifteen different languages for trying to make things better. He had decided he was owed something, for all that.

The details of what he and Paul had done had stayed out there, where they had gone, or at least no word of it had yet crept to the walls of Jasna Góra, save in Tomasz's own confession. They had not been the only ones trying to lay claim to the quartermaster's stores, that was for certain.

They had come back to the monastery with a handful of rifles, ammunition, grenades, some armour vests. They had come back and stood before the Abbot and borne the brunt of his anger: that they would just go off and do such a thing without asking. Because Tomasz believed in his heart that the Abbot was a good man, and a wise man; but sometimes wisdom needed help from fools.

The word was already going out, to gather the bulk of the defenders on this wall. There would be enough eyes around to keep watch in case this was a diversion.

He hefted his own bow. He could have had his pick of the modern weapons, but there was a sense in his arms and in his mind when he drew the string back, that spoke to him as a gun never could. He had joined the army for the same reason he had taken up with the living history mob. He was a man who had always been lost in time: all the complexities of the lost modern world had eddied around him, understood but incapable of connecting with him. He might have become a drug addict, he might have become a killer. He had skated near the edge during psychological assessments in the army. It was just as well that Katy Lewkowitz never got round to accusing him that he was loving what the world had come to. In his heart he would know that she was right.

The Order made their move towards the John Paul II gate. There was a prolonged rattle of automatic fire as a handful of them opened up on the makeshift crenellations. At this range they could barely hit the walls like that, let alone anyone on them. Tomasz felt a moment of satisfaction. Military men would not be doing that: wasting ammunition on little more than noise.

He took a good view of them past his barricade, which had once been some suburban Częstochowan's front door. A moment later he had the bowstring back by his ear and loosed a ranging shot, which arced high before it fell down amongst the enemy. He saw the shaft rebound from the tarmac, the Order soldiers scattering in momentary surprise. *You are in reach*, he thought, grinning to himself.

The enemy were advancing more cautiously. He let them have another few shafts, not really trying to hit anyone at this range, just amusing himself. A rifle bullet chipped the stone ten feet from him, sending some of his fellows ducking. He waited, and then waited some more, seeing the Order's progress speed up as they covered more than half of the distance towards the gates.

Then he reckoned they were close enough, and yelled out the signal. In a ragged attempt at unison, two score archers, crossbowmen and snipers opened up, close enough now that at least a couple of the Order went down. The attackers grabbed what cover they could and returned fire, but there were too many of them crammed together down there, and they were bunching up more as their progress stalled. Tomasz just watched them; Paul would be dealing with the tactical work, passing along the wall and giving orders.

The Order stuck it out for another couple of minutes, unleashing a storm of ammunition against the walls. The defenders pot-shotted back at them, single shafts and shots, and the occasional short burst, just as Tomasz had taught. One of the defenders took a bullet through her upper arm. Another sprained his ankle coming up the steps to the wall too fast.

One, a former plumber from Wrocław, was killed. Tomasz did not see it happen, but the ripple of shock went down the wall, and he knew they had lost a defender long before the name came to him. Matteus Brodzinski, he was called. He had been with them for several years, a hard worker and a good man. Not the best of archers, though, and he had been leaning out, trying for a good shot after sending several shafts frustratingly wide. Whether enemy skill or his own poor luck had finished him, nobody could say. He had been shot in the chest and, by the time they had stumbled him down to the medics, he was in shock, heart pushed too far, past saving.

The Order had taken another handful of casualties by then, and abruptly they were on the retreat, entirely ignorant of the victory they had won over a forty-two-year-old former plumber. Tomasz watched them scurry away, taking their fallen, the odd arrow still falling amongst them. He drew his own string back, entirely still and steady and cold.

They were at the far end of the ramp, regrouping, arguing. He took a deep breath, held it, loosed.

The arrow leapt to the sun, then dropped back earthwards,

lancing into the enemy even as they threw their recriminations. One man dropped, clutching at his leg, his thin cry just reaching Tomasz's ears. Not a killing shot, but it was something to remember him by.

PAUL STEINARDT HAD checked in at the field hospital, assuring himself that Hamid was coping with the few injuries the first skirmish had turned up. The Lewkowitz woman was genuinely of use, apparently, which surprised him. She was trouble, by his estimation, and her friend the doctor was more so. Paul had a deep and abiding faith, not so much in God as in people. He believed in the Abbot and his comrades and the community that had built itself up in Jasna Góra. He would just as soon the outside world had not come to intrude.

But now it had, and his job was to soften the blow. While his opposite number Tomasz was out amongst the troops, clapping them on the shoulders and telling them they'd done well, Paul was counting. He counted the medical supplies after Hamid was done. He counted off the bullets the defenders had fired, the arrows loosed. He went to the fletchers and told them to make more, and from others within the monastery he asked for more bandages. He called up two dozen who had expressed an interest in learning to fight and told them their time was at hand, noting those whose expressions—now that fighting could easily mean dying as well—were suddenly less keen than they had been.

Then he went and made his report to the Abbot, finding him in his private chapel where the monastery's greatest treasure had been set. Kneeling before Leszek, he heard a sound, and saw that the newcomer, Weber, was there too. The man was looking at the respect gesture as though it was a Satanic rite.

Paul did not want to report while Weber was present: the man was hardly going to betray them to their mutual enemies, but it still felt wrong. The Abbot had that expectant look on his face, though, so there was nothing for it. He rattled off his observations, his projections, the current numbers of the enemy, the weaknesses he saw in the monastery's defences: nothing to worry about just yet, but depending on what the

Order could muster... Paul was a worrier by nature. Back before the end of the world he had been a very successful civil lawyer, winning cases through meticulous preparation rather than impassioned rhetoric. Right now, someone who lost sleep over the small details was just what Jasna Góra needed.

"What supplies do you have?" Weber broke in.

Paul glared at him, but the Abbot seemed to think it a reasonable question from an outsider. "Of water, beer, wine, more than enough. Of food... Paul?"

Their monastery had cured meats, pickled vegetables, a small store of grain. Hundreds of people called Jasna Góra home, though, and until now the monastery had lived by actively trading skills and finished goods for food. That avenue was closed to them until the Order gave up or was decisively defeated.

"I have put some rationing in place," he confirmed. "We can live for perhaps six weeks, I think, without resupply. After that... I need to recount the cans." Years back they had harvested what canned goods could be found in Częstochowa. Paul had been meaning to inventory them for far too long. Now that unattended task called to him in a voice of pure guilt.

"I have faith in you," the Abbot told him.

This seemed to annoy Weber no end. "And that's it? Where does the faith go when you've run out of food?"

"We must hope that God will provide," Leszek told him mildly. Paul caught his mischievous tone: the Abbot loved playing the Devil with people, and this Weber seemed exactly the type to have his tail pulled. The good doctor himself took the words at face value, sure enough, and seemed fit to explode. Seeing the Abbot in good spirits, despite all the grim news—despite having a funeral to attend—lent a great deal of heart to Jasna Góra's quartermaster right then. But then, Leszek was always one to rise to a challenge, never in better spirits than when God had laden his shoulders.

The next morning, the Order unveiled its new weapon, and began an entirely different assault upon the monastery.

CHAPTER EIGHT
THE LOUDHAILER WAR

MOST OF JASNA Góra's complement were up with the dawn and so, the day after the abortive attack, she was woken rudely at daybreak by what seemed for a moment to be the voice of God. In those sleep-blurred minutes, if she had staggered outside to find a burning bush personally haranguing her, she would not have been remotely surprised.

But it was a human voice, though greatly magnified, and a voice she knew.

"*Good people of Jasna Góra!*" it trumpeted, echoing back off the walls, "*I know you are a God-fearing and virtuous people at heart! You are those who have survived into the End Times, when so many of the wicked and the heathen have been cast down! You are those whom the Lord has chosen to build His New Jerusalem in this land, when it has at last been cleansed of evil!*"

The Reverend Calumn, of course, but from the sound of it, he had grown forty feet tall and was looming over the monastery.

Katy struggled into some of the rough homespun that she had been given and staggered outside, blinking in the early light. The usual bustle of the place was stilled, everyone stopped in their tracks at this prodigy. She bumbled about, still bleary, before finding her way up onto the walls where she could see the Order camp.

There was the Reverend James Calumn, Jr, standing on top of a truck for greater stature and holding something to his mouth.

"I forgot he had a..." And she could not think of the word for 'loudhailer' in German.

It turned out she was overthinking it. "*Lautsprecher,*" Tomasz supplied. He stood beside her, arms folded, while Calumn went on praising the godliness of the denizens of Jasna Góra in a way that seemed uncharacteristically full of Christian meekness. Now, however, the worm of his rhetoric turned.

"*People of Jasna Góra, you have been deceived. There is one among you, one to whom you are giving shelter, who is no friend of Jesus!*" he warned direly. "*You have taken within your walls a serpent, who wishes nothing more than to destroy all love of the Lord in this world, and remake it as a playground for the Devil, where nobody prays or worships, and where your faith would see you reviled and spat upon.*"

"Uh-oh," Katy murmured mildly. Tomasz just grunted.

"*This man, this servant of Satan,*" Calumn went on grandly, "*he has beguiled your leaders into sheltering him from the Lord's just retribution! But I tell you, it is not too late for you to do the Lord's work, and give him up to justice. I speak of none other than the man Emil Weber—you will have seen him in the counsels of your leaders, I have no doubt. He is a creature of lies, an enemy of the Lord in every fibre of his being! He styles himself 'doctor,' but his only wish is to dismantle the Church of the Lord, to destroy its very foundations—your church, my church, all the churches of the world he has sworn to tear down.*"

All of which would all be hilarious if it wasn't fairly close to true. Katy ground her teeth. "How many of your people here know German?"

"Most know at least some," Tomasz said flatly. "Those who don't will ask those who do."

Katy thought about all those people who, when the world was tottering on its axis, chose to flee to a monastery. How soon before they started making demands of the Abbot that Emil be thrown to the wolves? Probably before noon, by her estimation. *And me, too. If he goes, I guess I probably get the boot as well.*

"We need to do something," she said, looking for agreement in Tomasz's long face. What she found there was a calculating regard. He went to Mass like the rest of them, of course. She had made the mistake of thinking he was *on her side.*

"Tomasz." For a moment she felt a stab of fear that he would throw her off the wall: ludicrous, but reflective of a greater and far more reasonable concern.

"It will be the Abbot's decision." And he was the Abbot's man. What *he* might do, if he had command of Jasna Góra, he did not enlarge on.

CALUMN KEPT UP his vitriolic sermon for a good two hours, before retiring in obvious good spirits, his holy work done for the day.

The next day at dawn, he was back, dispelling any thought that his bullhorn had run out of batteries. Of all the miscellaneous pieces of technology to still be in working order, that squawking amplifier was fast overtaking guns and motorcycles as Katy's least favourite. If Calumn had just been some hate-spreader, then she would not have minded so much: that kind of invective would have done more to unify the defenders than to split them. The Reverend was a strong and eloquent speaker, though. He quoted scripture readily and well; he had mastered an impassioned tone that made one imagine tears of love for the divine in his eyes. Worse, he had plenty of material to work with when it came to setting the devout against Emil Weber.

If Emil had been willing to bend even a little, then perhaps he and Katy could have fought some manner of rearguard action: he could have gone to church, mouthed a hymn, done a turn in the confessional, been baptised. He would not, though Katy argued ferociously with him. He would not fake devotion, any more than the most Catholic of the defenders would spit on a crucifix.

"This is who I am," was all he would say.

The Reverend's tirade continued for four mornings before the Abbot himself was forced to put in a showing on the walls. In that time, the attitude of many of the defenders had changed markedly towards both Emil and Katy. Black looks were given and backs were turned. Conversations stopped when they approached. Even those who were not so religious as to be swayed by Calumn's rhetoric were being constantly reminded that the unwelcome visitors on their doorstep were entirely the fault of one man.

On the fifth morning, Katy found herself on the wall—she always did, as though her presence could somehow blunt the Reverend's sermonising. She had looked at Tomasz, because he seemed like a good touchstone for the general mood. His expression had little welcome in it. He and Jenna had both grown subtly more distant as the verbal assault had continued, and Paul had never been friendly to begin with. Katy's only unexpected ally was Karel, the 'Golem of Prague,' whose personal dislike for the Order outweighed any sectarian considerations. He would keep Emil safe for the sole reason that if you gave him a rope with the Order on the other end, he would pull in the opposite direction.

Calumn was in fine form that morning, speaking in glittering terms of the new Kingdom of God that was just over the horizon, if only the last of the wicked was purged from the Earth. To hear him, Emil might actually be that last sinner, whose death alone would usher in the golden age of piety and plenty.

"Can't you shoot him?" The words got out before she had properly vetted them. Tomasz glanced at her with a raised eyebrow.

"With your bow," she added unnecessarily. "They keep putting that truck closer. I saw you get an arrow that far when they came."

He kept on looking at her, and she had a sudden sense of

herself through his eyes: the stranger in their midst, advocating bloodshed against...

"A man of God," she finished the thought. "Is that it?"

Whatever Tomasz might have answered she never knew, for, a moment later, the Abbot was up beside them, staring out over the wall's edge. Tomasz's whole attitude changed immediately, though Katy suspected the man didn't realise it. He was, abruptly, all dutiful attention.

Abbot Leszek stared down at Calumn as the Reverend's amplified voice washed over him. His weathered face was expressionless. Two or three times, Katy made to speak to him, but his forbidding demeanour put her off.

At last he straightened up, rubbing his hands together to dispel the chill of the morning. He made a sidelong remark to Tomasz in Polish, and the lean man's lips twitched a little before he replied.

A moment later, Tomasz was off, perhaps on some errand the Abbot had just given him. If Katy had hoped to see him come back with a quiver of arrows to make target practice of the Reverend, though, she was disappointed.

A moment later she had the heart-freezing thought that perhaps he had been sent to get Emil.

"What did you tell him to do?" she demanded. The look the Abbot turned on her was veiled, but she thought there was just a tweak of humour about his eyes.

"I only said, so much of a nuisance this is," he remarked, and then: "Miss Lewkowitz, you and Doctor Weber will dine with me tomorrow evening, if you please."

THE NEXT MORNING, she was jolted awake by the loudhailer again, just the same. She spent a minute cursing Calumn under her breath in English, German and Yiddish, as inventively as the hour allowed, before realizing that something had changed.

She lurched out as usual into the unwelcome proximity of dawn, the walls of Jasna Góra's buildings ringing with words boosted to the echo. This time she did not know the words, though. The Reverend Calumn's smooth German had been replaced with...

Polish? she wondered. *Has he been visited by the Gift-of-Tongues fairy in the night, or...* But, of course, it wasn't Calumn's voice. Now she was fully awake, she recognised the Abbot's tones, whatever language he was speaking.

He was up on the wall, and she couldn't get up there to join him because most of Jasna Góra had turned out for him, and she was just one more in the crowd. He was up there, with Paul and a handful of others keeping a watchful eye out towards the Order's camp, and he was conducting some kind of service. Through a loudhailer. Through the Reverend Calumn's loudhailer, to be specific.

"You've got to be kidding me," she said, to nobody in particular. A moment later she was looking around the crowd, searching for one face.

There was Tomasz, at the crowd's edge, and she approached him almost angrily.

"You, you did this," she accused him.

He turned his cool look on her, raising his eyebrows. For a moment he almost had her, that she was mistaken, that the whole thing was some larcenous miracle the Abbot had brought about. Then she saw the traces of paint about his face, a little white caught in his stubble and eyebrows, and gritting his hairline. There was only one reason that Tomasz Olinski of Jasna Góra would be going about in whiteface, and it wasn't mime.

"You did this," she repeated, almost wondering, and at last his lips quirked a little. Even with that confirmation, she could not imagine how the business had been accomplished.

BEING HELD IN high regard by Katy Lewkowitz was not something that Tomasz had been seeking, particularly, but he had to admit that seeing the sour woman impressed was a pleasant bonus. A nod from Abbot Leszek had been the main reward for his night's work, that and his own personal satisfaction at the exercise of his skills. A little baffled admiration from the English girl couldn't hurt, though.

He had told only Jenna about the scheme: he needed someone watching for him on the wall, and he knew he could talk her into helping him without her trying to dissuade him or insisting on coming too.

Back before the fall, he had been a man without an idle moment in his life. The time his squad mates had spent drinking and watching movies and arguing about the football, he had used to recapture the skills of a lost past. He had not known at the time that he was also honing the skills of a terrible, devastated future. As well as archery and medieval longsword work, he had beaten every climbing wall he had ever seen, could hit a bull's eye with a thrown knife and pick a lock like a master cracksman. None of these skills had ever been of *use* to him, back then. Simply knowing that he *could* was the point; that and finding new theatres to test himself in. Life had never challenged Tomasz in the way that he had wanted. He had been forced to up the stakes on his own.

So, with Jenna on the wall top with a rope in case he needed to get back up quickly, he had descended the wall of Jasna Góra by hand, face painted up in the monochrome livery of the Order.

He had spied out their camp by the light of their own fires, noting that their discipline was not of the best, their watchmen were too thinly spaced, and few of them had their minds on the task. After all, the people of Jasna Góra had made no move against them. Any initial vigilance had been worn away by inaction.

Reconnaissance accomplished, he had found the weakest point in their perimeter and crept in. Once inside, it had been a matter of walking with the confidence of an Order soldier within his own camp. There were few about, and nobody challenged him.

The morning before, he had taken a glass and, at the end of the Reverend's sermon, seen exactly which tent the man had retired to.

The next step had worried him: something he could not readily plan for. Perhaps the Reverend would be up late entertaining? Perhaps he was a light sleeper, woken by every sound or his own nightmares?

But the Order camp was hardly silent—even past midnight, there was plenty of murmur, laughter and argument from the tents. More, there were a good many empty bottles stacked fastidiously outside Calumn's personal domain. Abstinence was nowhere near godliness, it appeared. Tomasz could probably have brought Karel along to search the man's tent, without any fear of waking the Lord's chosen.

He had stood over the sleeping Reverend then, loudhailer in one hand, the other itching for a hilt. *If it was just me...* because Tomasz was bitterly aware that there were key parts of being a Christian that ran against his natural instincts, and that he had to fight them down on a regular basis. In another life, he knew, he might have been a different and darker man, perhaps even worn the facepaint for real.

Even now, listening to the Abbot speak, feeling the tension in his fellows unwinding after five days of Calumn's proselytising, he wondered if he might regret staying his hand.

KATY HAD EXPECTED the Abbot's table to be somewhat plainer than before, as Paul's rationing measures began to bite. Instead, she was treated to an abundance: meat, fruit, fresh vegetables. It was all they could not preserve, she realised. The monastery had salted and dried and pickled everything it could. This bounty was to be enjoyed now, or it would pass beyond the reach of men into rot. The thought made her shiver: rationalist though she was, she had begun to see omens everywhere.

The Abbot had called all of his officers to the table this time, and whilst she saw Emil mirroring her own gloom, everyone else seemed in great high spirits, as though the theft of a bullhorn signalled the end for the Order.

They all took their places: she saw Jenna joking with Tomasz—he shaking his head and grinning at some suggestion of hers. There was Karel, already munching on an apple even before anyone had been served, and Paul was bringing in platters of food along with an older woman Katy didn't know. Another woman—Anya or something like that, she seemed to be in charge of various weavers and makers—was knitting determinedly at the table: what looked like a child-sized glove. Hamid was next to her, passing on a wine bottle without pouring a glass. Katy made a beeline to grab the seat on the other side of him: he was something of an outsider himself, and so he made her feel less alone.

Emil had taken the place at the far end of the long table from the Abbot himself, which had probably been intended as a way of staying out of the limelight, but had the unfortunate result of putting him in prime debating position. Or perhaps that had been his intent all along. By then, everyone else was finding a seat, the air filled with chatter in Polish and German. A single place was left empty when everyone was settled, like a reverse game of musical chairs. For a moment, Katy wondered if this was some remembrance of the dead thing they did. Was that a Catholic tradition? She had absolutely no idea.

Then, just as the Abbot was lifting his hands to call for quiet, a woman slipped in, peeling back a fur-trimmed leather coat: Magdayeva in the flesh. Katy stood up abruptly, feeling an unexpected flash of delight. She hadn't thought to see the woman again since she rode off.

"How did you get in past the Order?" she asked, belatedly aware that everyone else had gone quiet, so that her voice rang out across the room like an actor's declamation.

Magdayeva smiled a little. "Not so hard, not on foot for one," she said. Her eyes flicked to the Abbot and she muttered something in Polish. Katy had the impression she had come to speak to him, and had not expected to walk in on a formal gathering.

Leszek's reply was obviously *later,* and at his gesture, she took the last seat, fidgeting through the Abbot's sonorous grace. It was a strange, exclusive feeling, to see most of the heads bowed sincerely as the litany washed over them, while Emil scowled, and Hamid kept a polite smile on his face.

She had asked the smith, just the day before, what had brought him to Jasna Góra, the stronghold of another faith. He was Turkish, she learned. He had been an archaeology postgrad, working with the living history crowd on a doctoral thesis comparing European and Middle Eastern metalworking.

"Didn't expect I'd need to *do* it," he had told her wryly. "But these days—no, *those* days—if you studied the past, they expected you to recreate it. That's where the grant money was." He had a good line in self-effacing grins.

With grace apparently said, everyone set to work on the food with relish, and for a while there was no sound but chewing and the occasional request for one dish or another. Katy ate too, feeling somehow as though she was stealing, an imposter at the feast.

"Now, Doctor Weber," the Abbot said at last, and Katy's heart sank as the table quietened. "I have been having some thoughts on your future."

Emil's jaw stopped moving, and then he forcibly swallowed. "Oh?" he got out, tensing up. Cued by his mistrust, for a moment Katy expected the Reverend Calumn to sweep in like Darth Vader to take possession of him.

"I understand that there are men and women of education who have come together near Kraków," Leszek went on genially. "They have what there is of the university there. They would be interested to continue your researches."

Emil's expression was still eminently wary. "Is that so?"

"You are not enthusiastic, Doctor Weber," the Abbot noted, and Katy could see that he was amusing himself at Emil's expense. "When it is safe for you to leave here, is this not what you want?"

"Under whose auspices is this team working?" Emil demanded. Everyone else at the table was looking from one speaker to the other, plainly not sure where this was going. "Or can I guess? This is your church?"

Leszek smiled. "I do not think the church exists as you imagine it, in our new world, but these men are men of faith, yes, as well as of science."

Katy almost put her head in her hands at that, because scientists who 'defected,' as Emil had it, were the Doctor's particular hatred. *Tact, please, Emil; tact,* she thought, as though she could crowbar the words into his head by telepathy.

The expected explosion did not come. Emil took a deep breath and occupied himself with a piece of carrot until he could say, with clipped decorum, "You will forgive me for saying that I have never observed faith to be the friend of science."

Leszek took no offence at that, for which Katy was glad, for plainly most people at the table would follow wherever he led.

"I correct you, Doctor Weber. For many centuries there were few men of science who were *not* men of faith. After the fall of the Romans, what learning there was, in the lands of Europe, was a flame kept alight by the church. To know the workings of the world was to know God."

Emil was about to hotly dispute as much of that as he could, but the Abbot put a hand up, that mild gesture that was a cast-iron injunction when he wished it to be. His sleeve slipped a little as he did it, and Katy was startled to see a mess of scars about the wrist. *Pretty sure the church is against that.*

"Until these difficulties are ended, no answer can be given," Leszek said, "but I wish you to know the choice you have. You would be welcome in Kraków; you would be honoured for your learning, and assisted in your quest for the good of all. There is nothing in the Saviour's teachings to disapprove of that. But you would be living under God's roof, whether you believe in Him or not. That is the choice you will have to make."

"You would test me?" Emil asked him, belligerently.

"Test, tempt." The Abbot shrugged easily. "As you will. Perhaps God wishes to see the manner of the man you are."

Emil's fuse was well and truly lit, and so Katy jumped in to stop him saying anything unwise, or possibly blasphemous.

"These men in Kraków, Abbot. How did you hear of them?"

Leszek turned his challenging smile on her. "Perhaps, mysterious ways, Miss Lewkowitz?"

She took a deep breath. Here was something she had been wondering whether to throw at him, and now probably wasn't the time, but: "I'd believe you have a radio."

The table went quite quiet, even Emil stilled in mid-splutter, so she pressed on, "You were saying that there were ways you had, of communities talking to each other, and I was thinking... and seriously, once I started looking, I saw it: there's an aerial right outside this room, or maybe it's the next room here, your chambers. It's new—not something from before the Cull. It's been bolted on too roughly for that."

Into the silence that followed, Paul muttered, "It was a good job of work," which served to defuse any tension that had been growing.

"You must have batteries, a transmitter," Katy pushed on. "So... all your little villages and farms have them? How is that even possible?" She had begun to wonder if all this medieval-ness was a sham, and that they were hiding some high-tech survival beneath the woollens and the chainmail.

But Leszek shook his head. "You're very observant, Miss Lewkowitz. And yes, we have a transmitter. No batteries, though."

"Then how...?"

At a look from the Abbot, Paul spoke up. "When we wish to use it, we have to wind a lot of handles. Our only way of powering it is..."—he mimed turning a crank—"dynamo. However, many of the other communities have radios they can listen with—wind-up ones, again. They're all UN-issue, meant to be distributed wherever the troops went. They receive very well. There are transmitters also at Kraków, and a place outside Warsaw. Two others that are mobile." Another glance to Leszek, for a permission that was given, and he added, "This is not mostly how we talk, though. Too few transmitters, too hard to use and maintain."

"Then how?" Emil broke in. His annoyance was completely gone; he was fascinated.

"Magdayeva, of course," Leszek explained, bringing all attention back to the horsewoman.

CHAPTER NINE
THOSE THAT BESIEGE

AND OF COURSE everyone else at the table knew the story, and conversation turned to other topics, and so it was that Katy and Emil found themselves that evening in the Abbot's own quarters, along with Leszek and Magdayeva, and the secret came out.

"When the plague came," Leszek started, and then shrugged. "You know how it was. It was the same everywhere. You tell me, Doctor Weber, this is a thing made by human hands. That is a thing I wish to believe, far more than the Reverend Calumn's divine judgment." He took up a half-bottle of wine that he had somehow saved from the meal, and poured out four small glasses.

"But it did not lay an even hand on everyone, that we discovered," he added. "Some there were, who lost fewer, though all lost some." Seeing Emil regarding the wine dubiously, he added, "This is lay alcohol, Doctor Weber. It will not become the blood of Christ."

Emil drank very little by habit, but he obviously took that as a challenge, for he downed the glass.

"Amongst those who suffered less were Magdayeva's people."

"The Roma," Katy put in, and Leszek nodded.

"It's possible," Emil allowed. "There were reports, before we stopped getting reports, that some ethnicities were more resistant to the Cull. Certain blood types, yes, but also genetic markers that promoted a resistance to the disease. It was what we were working on when..." He blinked, ambushed by memories.

"When." The word from Leszek bestowed finality, releasing him from having to put the deaths of his colleagues into words. "Yes, the Roma, or at least some families of them, were left far more intact than most of us. So it was that, when emissaries from across Poland gathered here, they were greatly represented."

"I imagine that might have become ugly," Emil said. "Antiziganism was alive and well in Germany, at least, before the Cull."

"England, too," Katy put in, remembering hysterical headlines in the tabloids from her youth.

Leszek shared a look with Magdayeva, a window onto shared tribulations past. "Yes, well," he said, after a thoughtful pause, "I will not lie. That there were those who, despite all that had been lost, still wished to have nothing to do with the Roma, that is true. That there were Roma who wanted to shun the *Gadzie*, this also. That there were those who claimed the Roma had brought the plague, had carried it from town to town, yes."

"And some of those from within the church?" Emil put in archly.

"Magdayeva is a good Catholic, and so are most of her kin... but yes. I am ashamed for it, but yes," Leszek said frankly. "But in the end the last voices speaking were those arguing Christ's message, to love our neighbours. And arguing reason, Doctor Weber."

"Because there were too many of them to push around?"

"Because we needed them, and they needed us," Leszek explained. "The settled and the travelling. The Roma cannot grow or harvest as settled farmers can; we cannot travel as they do. In this world where all the fuel and power of yesterday is draining away, we are fortunate that enough of the Romany kept up their husbandry of horses. They allow each community to trade with the next. And they carry our news. They are our little lights, in the great darkness that has descended on the world." He smiled at Magdayeva fondly. "I have come to be very glad of our friends the Romany." There was a lot of history in the look he gave the horsewoman: history, and perhaps apology.

After that, it was plain that Leszek and Magdayeva had other matters to discuss, and Katy and Emil went to their respective beds with much to think about.

THE SIEGE CONTINUED unabated, and unchanging, for seven days. In that time, the Order soldiers kept a watch over Jasna Góra, preventing any large-scale exodus or resupply. Although Katy would not have trusted herself to get out unseen, there were a few sufficiently stealthy that they would risk leaving at night, under the guns of the soldiers. Magdayeva was gone the morning after she arrived, creeping away with the last hours of the night to ride back to her people. Tomasz himself came and went as he pleased, testing the piecemeal Order perimeter, and once bringing back a black-crossed banner to hang from the monastery walls.

Shots were exchanged infrequently, between opportunistic snipers atop and outside the walls. There were no injuries on either side, or not from the guns. With foodstocks still carefully rationed, the greatest test of the defenders' mettle was a widespread outbreak of constipation.

All that changed on the evening of the seventh day. As the skies above were shading into evening, the Order's reinforcements arrived. The hundred-odd who had been camped out before the gates of Jasna Góra were abruptly swelled by a motorcade of vehicles: Transit vans, two large lorries, a cattle truck, a ramshackle fleet of sedans and estates and hatchbacks, and a tank.

It ground in at the back, a lumbering, tracked monster,

drab green and brown paint flaking away from grey metal, a camouflage made perfectly pointless by its colossal grumbling roar. Behind it, the crumbling tarmac of the Częstochowa roads was left dented and mauled. It was a muscular, brutal implement of warfare, dented and scored, every line of it focused towards the stubby barrel of its great gun.

Leszek came out to see, as the newcomers were setting up their new swathe of canvas.

"Tomasz?" he asked.

"Leopard 2A4M CAN," came the immediate reply. "From the way it's handling, they've had good use of it before bringing it here." Tomasz stared down at the thing, nestled within the expanding Order encampment. "I worked with them, years ago," he confirmed. "Not easy to keep running. They must have some military on hand." He was trying to think about fuel and ammunition—how much had the Order scavenged, to bring this monster to their door?

"Ah." Leszek leant on the wall, staring out. Tomasz tried to follow his line of sight, and saw a large tent being raised, with another black and white banner flying proud over it: this one showed, with some artistry, a black eagle grasping a crossed white shield.

"I rather suspect that this signals the arrival of this Grand Master Danziger that Miss Lewkowitz spoke of," Leszek noted. "We have achieved something, Tomasz. We have the full attention of the New Teutonic Order."

"They will attack soon."

"It seems likely," the Abbot agreed.

"If they have shots for the tank gun, then the gate will not hold. The walls may not. They weren't built with this in mind."

Leszek took a deep breath. "These walls have held off a great deal that they were not made for," he remarked mildly. "When the Swedish King swept his bloody Deluge across Poland, destroying with his cannon all who would not pledge themselves to him, the walls of Jasna Góra held. When the blood-plague cast down church and state and common humanity in our land, here was where that tide turned. Shall we not stand our ground one last time?"

Tomasz did not trust himself to speak. He knew the history

as well as anyone, but there were a lot of men with modern weapons out there, and a great many civilians behind the walls who had no ready means of defending themselves. And still the Abbot stared out over the darkening tents, over the hollow rooftops of Częstochowa, as though searching the face of God for answers.

"YOU HAVE COME here to do the Lord's bidding," the Reverend Calumn told his congregation. "Within those walls is penned up one of the Great Deniers, a man whose every breath has been to spit on the good book, to spread lies about the faithful, to work against the Second Coming of Christ!"

These were not the ragged band of scouts and bruisers who had first pitched up before Jasna Góra's gates. Here before him was a true crusading host, surely every spare body the Order could muster. Calumn had sent word back to the Grand Master, that the work of the Lord required a true gathering of the faithful. He had not been sure how Danziger would respond. The two of them had masterminded the rise of the Order from what was little more than a street gang into their current nascent empire, but Danziger was his own man. He took no orders from Calumn, nor from God. Danziger's faith was in himself and the destiny of the Order, and it was unassailable.

"It is not just that the man Weber denies Christ," Calumn told the assembled faithful. "We know from the confessions of his fellows that Weber seeks to undo God's work! We all know that the great plague was sent by God. You and I, my brothers, we knew this end was prophesied, that the Lord had His plan for this world. Yet there have always been those who fought the Devil's fight to turn back God's clock. When the first signs of the End Times were felt—when storms and disasters and floods racked the world—did these wicked men seek absolution and bow to the Lord's will? They did not! They turned to their false science and spun their webs of lies about melting ice and global warning. They claimed that the hand of Man was behind God's work, just as they have always sought to deny the Lord, claiming His majesty for mere humanity or for some senseless, unfeeling cosmos. Where are they now, these so-called men of science? I'll tell you, my brothers: Hell! Burning in Hell, almost all of them, and only a few left to trouble the world."

There had been a time, before God's judgment had come to the world, when Calumn's own faith had known its ups and downs. The temptations of a material world had all too often lured him from the righteous path: women, drugs, all the wickedness that money brought. When the first news of the Cull came, he had been in a hotel room in Berlin with three prostitutes. The Lord would have been well within His rights to strike down James Calumn, Jr along with all the others, and he had waited for it. As so many others had died around him, he had knelt and prayed and readied himself to be gathered to God.

And yet he had lived, and wondered if it was only by Christ's mercy had he survived. Surely the Lord therefore had a purpose for him. When he found Danziger whipping together the beginnings of an army under the black cross, he knew that he had found that purpose as well.

"Why did the Lord spare men like Weber, you'll ask?" he told the rapt crowd. "Why did the Lord's justice not light upon him, as it did for so many? I'll tell you, brothers, though the answer may pain you. God is testing us! God knows that you and I and all of us, we did not do enough, back before the End Times. Our faith was weak, when it should have been strong as iron." And passion leaked into every word he spoke, and fired them all up. "When we should have stood for God's will, we bowed to Man's law. We made accommodation with the Devil, when the Adversary spoke through the mouths of politicians and environmentalists. We let ourselves be led from the path, my friends, and for that the Lord will test us. We must prove to Him that we are worthy to witness the Second Coming! It is for that reason that God spared men like Weber. It is for that reason that the world is still a home for homosexuals and heathens. Because the Lord has set us the task to cleanse this world of the unworthy, before He will build His Kingdom here! We are the instruments of that cleansing, my brothers! We are the sword of the Lord!"

*   *   *

EDWARD GUYER, UNTIL recently temporal leader of the Order's mission to Jasna Góra, had not been looking forwards to making his report to the Grand Master. He had been dispatched with one mission: catch and kill Emil Weber and his accomplices. In this he had singularly failed. Now Danziger was here with most of the Order, and it was reasonable to assume that he would not appreciate being put to the trouble.

Order soldiers came from a variety of backgrounds, but a good proportion of them had known both violence and the hard hand of authority back before the Cull. There were some soldiers amongst them, some police, a fair number who had been in and out of prison more than once. Beyond them, there were those who had lived their lives twitching for a certain kind of violence, but had never indulged in it for fear of the strictures of law and state. They had read the reactionary news and ground their teeth about the foreigners who had moved in three doors down. They had snarled and threatened on the internet. They had told each other that life had been better way back when...

And then the world had fallen, and all that they had was lost, and they had found in themselves, these men, two great needs: for someone to tell them what to do, and for someone to blame.

Edward was one of these. He had been an investment banker for a London firm, seconded to the Berlin office on an assignment that was supposed to last a month but ended up lasting until the end of the world. He had lived for demolishing his rivals on the squash courts and scheming in the boardroom. After the Cull, when it was clear that he was out of more than just commodities futures, he had lost all sense of what to do with himself. He would almost certainly have got himself killed if he had not found the nascent Order. Amidst its initial roster of hooligans, thugs and petty malcontents, Edward was ideal second-in-command material.

Of all the things that scared him in the world, Josef Danziger scared him more than most. Edward mummed along to Calumn's services without being won over, but Danziger put the fear of God into him right enough. And now an angry Danziger was exactly what Edward was expecting.

The Grand Master's tent was a full-size furnished marquee. Danziger did not care to live in a field like an animal, as he put it. The interior was curtained into a twilit gloom, then lit with a rank of hanging lanterns back to something approaching daylight. The extravagant use of their oil supplies was pointed; it was important for the ranks to know exactly who was in charge. A third of the tent was hidden by drapes, concealing the double bed that Danziger's menials assembled wherever he stopped. The rest was dotted with folding chairs, a battered table liberated from a restaurant and a narrow bookshelf with a handful of books. Edward ducked in to find Danziger at his desk, a big antique piece pillaged from who knew where. A handful of messengers were waiting, their bikes outside ready to roll. Danziger finished each missive in his jagged, spiky handwriting, giving each man a one-word destination and sending him out. From the foot of Jasna Góra they would be heading west, back to the communities that the Order had stamped its mark on.

Reverend Calumn was already there, sitting incongruously in a deckchair. He was a welcome sight: perhaps the Grand Master's ire would be split between the two of them.

But when the messengers were all sent on their way, Josef Danziger looked up with a disturbing absence of expression.

"So, you didn't get your man yet," he noted.

"If it were that easy, it would be no test of our virtue, Grand Master," Calumn replied. The relationship between the two men was a shifting one. Calumn's sermons gave the soldiers of the Order a strength of purpose beyond the simple need to loot and control. He spoke for God, after all, a venal Pope to Danziger's would-be Holy Roman Emperor. At the same time, it was the Grand Master who gave the orders. They had come close to falling out before.

"And you, Edward, what have you to say for yourself?"

Edward swallowed awkwardly. "The fortress resists us. Our assault"—*and why did we only try the once? Surely that makes me look weak and uncommitted*—"was thrown back with losses. Since then... since then, we have been unable to make any progress. I am sorry, Grand Master."

He waited for the angry reprimand, but for a moment Danziger just looked at the two of them—looked *past* them, really. Every second that ticked by was a stay of execution. Danziger's anger didn't need to bide its time before striking: the Grand Master of the New Teutonic Order treated failure summarily and harshly.

But now Danziger's eyes were hooded. "What motivates our soldiers, do you think?" he asked, surprisingly mildly. "James? Edward? What do you think?"

"Faith," said Calumn after a moment. His tone suggested he was testing the waters with Danziger, not sure where the man was going.

"God is our standard bearer," the Grand Master murmured. "There are enough, it's true, who follow because they have faith this is God's plan. Because turning to a vengeful God makes sense of this world we find ourselves in."

"The Lord is just—" started Calumn, but Danziger spoke over him.

"Let Him be vengeful. We need a vengeful God. How else to explain so many lost to His disease? And a vengeful God motivates our soldiers far more than a God of love. Do you think God loves us, James?"

Calumn opened his mouth, paused, closed it.

"Our God, the God who has done this, He doesn't love us," Danziger said, and at last Edward understood he was in the backswing of his mood, wrestling with the dark strength inside himself. Soon he would be standing before the soldiers, spitting destiny and purity of purpose at them, but for now the Grand Master was brooding. It made him more dangerous; it built a pressure in him, so that when his mood switched—always abruptly—back to action, it would be with plans full formed and ready for violence.

"We are the Lord's instruments," Calumn essayed.

"Yes." A spark of anger flashed in Danziger's eyes, a signal that he was approaching the flashpoint. "We are not loved like an ornament. We are *used* like a sword. So long as we are useful in destroying His enemies, He tolerates us. So that is what we do." He blinked, long and slow. "You haven't said anything, Edward."

"I..." Edward started, his mind a blank.

"What motivates our soldiers, would you say, those who are not as strong in their faith as the three of us?"

A brief ransack of his brains brought some of Danziger's rhetoric to mind. "We have a destiny, Grand Master. We, the pure, have inherited the world, free at last from those who would dilute our heritage with mongrel blood..."

Danziger stood abruptly, and Edward stuttered to a halt as two long strides brought the Grand Master right in front of him.

"Everything you say is true." The man's voice was like flint. He was on the turn for certain, now, rising from the black reaches of his soul on flaming wings. "We *do* have a destiny. We are the chosen people. The laws and borders of the old world, that were the bars of our prison, have been broken. We are free to take our place in the world. But do they see it? Do they *believe*? Precious few. I shall tell you what motivates too many of our soldiers. They march with us because in our wake they have their pick of the spoils—the food, the power, the women. They march with us because it is better to be behind the sword than before it. Despite all my efforts, despite every sermon James has given, there are too many who follow our strength because they are fundamentally *weak*." And he was staring right into Edward's face as he said it, eye to flinching eye.

"But this is what I am given, to hammer into our new Empire. This is the dross I must forge into fine steel." He turned away sharply, staring towards the tent flaps, towards the wider camp hidden beyond. "I knew we would come east eventually," he said, and by now his voice was twanging with that nervous, bludgeoning energy that had allowed him to gather this band of cutthroats to him in the first place. "I had thought we would spend more time consolidating our position within the Fatherland, but we would have to come here. You've forced my hand, you two. When Weber escaped, that was a slight, an insult that demanded answer. But now you have brought us before a whole fortress of mongrel heretics who defy us. What are we to do?" He swung back to them, eyes gleaming in the lamplight. "If we turn away now, if we return to our work back west, we will lose the heart of the Order. The men who have come here, they will remember that we looked to the East, that we stood in the shadow of this place and then turned back."

Danziger breathed a long sigh, fists clenched. "But if we crush this place, if we defeat and humiliate and destroy those who dare to oppose us, will they see at last that we have a destiny? Will they stop thinking of themselves as men with human frailties, and see themselves as heroes? As supermen?" And now he was back: the leader of warriors, returned from the lonely places. "They might, Edward. And so I thank the pair of you, in a way. You have given the Order the chance to become what it should be." And, with a fierce smile, he cuffed Edward hard across the side of the head, enough to send him down to one knee. Danziger fired up was prodigiously strong.

"But you've failed still," the Grand Master snapped, and he had a grip on Edward's shoulder now, keeping him kneeling. "You've risked it all, forcing us to this point before we're ready. So you can do something for me, Edward, to help get us out of this mess."

"Anything, Grand Master." Because anything other than total subservience was a mistake, at times like this.

"We will take this fort of theirs," Danziger stated. "We have superior numbers and superior weapons, and superior blood. But there are ways to weaken them first. If we cannot get an army across the walls without a fight, we can get a handful, eh? Just a few. Just enough."

"Grand Master...?" Edward didn't like where this was going, but he was being dragged along for the ride anyway.

"We have amongst our soldiers men who have scaled walls, men who have scaled mountains. This fort of theirs is a big place, and there do not seem to be so many defenders that they could watch every scrap of wall, not if they had some other distraction to hold their attention. Your time has come, Edward. This is your penance. I will muster the troops. You will enter the fort."

"And do what, Grand Master?" Edward's voice shook a little. The prospect of being at the head of the spear for once was not pleasing to him.

Danziger's smile was icy and uncompromising. "Kill Weber. Kill Weber's woman. Kill this so-called Abbot. Open the gates."

CHAPTER TEN
LONG KNIVES

KATY HAD HOPED to eat a quiet dinner in the refectory, but the Abbot was having none of it. He was a busy man with plenty of demands on his time, but when the routines of the monastery gave him time to himself, he seemed to spend far more of it trolling Emil than in prayer. Now here he was, planting himself on the bench beside his victim with a satisfied sigh, as people hurried to serve him with what fare there was.

Emil was eking out a bowl of stew and a heel of hard black bread, and he flinched as the Abbot had his beaker refilled with the watered beer everyone drank there. Emil loathed beer, Katy knew, but at the same time he loathed dysentery, and he was a rational man.

The Abbot started off mildly enough, praising the food and the cooks, thanking God for the bounty, and each sentence punctuated with a "Do you not think so, Doctor Weber?" When Emil mustered only a few grunts of acquiescence, not rising to the bait, Leszek stepped up his campaign, asking if the good doctor had ever seen Kraków before. "The brothers there, they work out of Wawel castle, the cathedral there. Plenty of space for your experiments under that roof." He became mock-solicitous. "Or you will live on the streets, perhaps. Kraków has seen its share of hermits."

Emil twitched at that, and glowered up at him, meeting Leszek's hard grey stare.

"Or perhaps," the Abbot said sternly, "you are ready to admit that living under the Dominion of God is not the hell you always believed it to be."

Emil closed his eyes for a moment, and just then he was exactly how Katy remembered him from his televised debates, his defence of evolution and humanism in the face of the smooth disdain of creationists and men of God like the man before him.

"I know," he said quietly to the Abbot, at last. "You are all very virtuous here. So very open-minded." A deep breath. "A world away from the persecuting church that I have always fought against, you say. There are no gibbets on this side of the wall, after all." But he was conceding nothing. For Emil Weber, this was fighting talk. "Back in Forst, they hung homosexuals, did you know? Does the church have a comment on that, Abbot?"

Leszek met his gaze levelly. "God's love is for all His children." Katy wasn't sure, but perhaps the Abbot's gaze flicked to where Tomasz and Paul sat, discussing something animatedly over their own meal. If so, it was a moment's break in his concentration. "Nowhere in His book does He withhold it for the act of lying with another man. So long as such matters are kept behind closed doors."

Weber nodded, a fencer's move, exploiting weakness. "So long as they deny who they are, when asked? So long as they stay in the closet. Yes, yes, of course, you are not like the Order. Given how many died in the Cull, you know how precious is each human life. But if two men—two women—were to love one another within your walls, well, if they can't hide it from God, at least you prefer they hide it from you. And if Hamid was to give the call to prayer from your walls?"

"Hamid is a valued—"

"So long as he keeps his head down and doesn't rock your boat," Weber put in, cutting him off. If he noticed the hostile audience he had acquired by now, he did not show it. "And believe me, you are a man of enlightenment and tolerance." The words were almost insults. "Because I know full well there are many of your faith who would take a far harder line, end of the world or not. You see yourself as the opposite of those men out there, Abbot, but you're not. You, they, you're on a continuum. Because the world you live in is determined by arbitrary faith, and if the logic of that faith took you to the terrible place where they are standing now, what then? And don't say it couldn't happen. History tells us it can happen. History tells us it has happened."

Tomasz was standing, with a hand to his sword hilt, and Katy's breath had caught in her throat, waiting to see how badly this would go, but right then Jenna burst in, half out of breath.

"They're mustering!" she spat out.

TOWARDS EVENING, THE troops of the Order began to muster, breaking from their tents and fires to form rough ranks before the monastery walls. Tomasz watched them thoughtfully, seeing the tank, of course, front and centre.

Paul was beside him, studying the enemy through field glasses.

"They have mustered rifles on the flanks," he reported. "I think the men behind the tank have pistols and close weapons." The bulk of the Order's men were packed in an unruly mob in the centre, obviously hoping to follow the tank through the gates and then disperse for mayhem. "You think this is it?"

Tomasz frowned. He felt inside himself for the spark of atavistic anticipation he would have expected, and found it wanting. "I'm not sure. Where's the Abbot? He needs to see, if nothing else."

By then, there were a great many people on the walls. Some were nominally defenders, at least partially trained by Paul and Tomasz. Others were just civilians, come to see, because to be left with nothing but rumour and imagination would be worse.

Tomasz opened his mouth to clear them all off the wall

top, then wrestled with the words, aware that the last thing anybody needed was a panic. Still, if the Order did make a sudden advance on the walls, he would be wading through a lot of people whose only purpose would be to get in the way.

"Are they coming, then?" someone asked him, and he turned irritably.

"Why does everyone think I know these things?" he demanded, and Katy Lewkowitz backed off, looking put out.

"I was just..."

"You're scared. They're coming for you, for your friend," he finished shortly.

"No—"

He could feel his uncertainty about what was happening outside turning into anger at her, and fought it down. "Are you armed?"

"I've got a knife."

"Unless your knife can reach a hundred feet, you're probably not much good up here, then," he pointed out.

She glowered at him. "Then give me a gun."

"Hm," he considered, and then, "No."

"You don't trust me."

"You're not one of us. We have a common enemy, but you're not ours. If they said they'd spare you and your friend, I think you'd open the gates to them."

"You think that, do you?" She had her hands on her hips, fighting her own temper. Tomasz observed himself distantly, knowing that he was pushing her solely because he could not go out and push the Order back from the walls singlehandedly.

He started to speak again, but she broke in on him. "I know. We brought them here. We're to blame. And I'm just waiting for the moment when you think it's expedient to hand us over, so the distrust is mutual, believe me." And, seeing him wrong-footed, she pressed on, "Tell me you wouldn't. All it'd take is your Abbot giving the order."

"How happy it is an order I'm not about to give." Abruptly Leszek was looming between them, the wind tugging at his habit. "So, they think they will take us, then."

At least *that* wasn't phrased as a question. Perversely, Tomasz felt drawn to answer him anyway.

"I'm not sure. There's a lot of movement, but... I don't feel it from them."

For a long while, the Abbot leant on the haphazardly-reinforced wall-top and stared out at the Order, as the skies shaded through increments of grey. A great murmur and a mutter arose from the ranks there, as they milled and shuffled, and a voice spoke over it, the words lost in the distance, but the tones of the Reverend Calumn quite recognisable.

"Are they reaching for their courage, I wonder?" Leszek murmured. "Keep a strong watch, Tomasz. You'd better have your people standing armed and ready through the night." He turned to the people thronging the wall. "For the rest of you, return to your rooms. Find your weapons. Make sure your families are safe, that you know where everybody is." And then again, in his coarser German for the non-Poles.

"Where will you be?" Tomasz asked him.

"At prayer," Leszek told him. "Send for me if it seems they will make the attempt," and he was striding off through the dispersing crowd.

"Abbot Leszek!" Lewkowitz was calling after him, and for a moment Tomasz was about to restrain her, because the Abbot could do without the distraction, She was off after him before Tomasz could snag her arm, though, and he could not go after her. His place was on the wall.

BACK BEFORE THE Cull, Edward had kept himself fit: jogging, circuit training, golf and squash, because lean and hungry was the look for a young banker on the fast track to the boardroom.

Afterwards—and especially after falling under the dominion of Josef Danziger and his nascent Order—he had been forced to turn his gym-honed physique to a whole variety of skills he had never imagined he might need. He had learned to hunt, men and animals; he had learned to shoot; he had learned to use a knife in anger, rather than just to cut his steak; he had learned to infiltrate, to sabotage, to murder.

There had been a point, standing over his first sleeping victim, when he had wavered. Danziger had run into an established commune in Lübben, whose charismatic leader had held the

Grand Master off with a fine line in rhetoric. Danziger hadn't had the numbers to just march in, but it had been plain that the woman in charge was the heart and soul of the community there.

That had been Edward's first real mission, when he had been trusted to accomplish something important. Danziger and the rest had made a great show of retreating in disappointment. Edward, a one-man Trojan Horse, had broken in and found the commune's leader. By then, a few years' sneaking and clambering about dying cityscapes had equipped him with the skills and knowledge to do it, and he had found the woman fast asleep, an easy mark. Still, he had hesitated, whilst his many futures unfurled past him like the skimmed pages of a book.

And he had struck, of course. Struck and got clean away, though more by luck than skill or divine favour. The second time had been easier. Soon he was leading scouts and punitive raids and manhunts, riding the adrenaline, bloodying the knife because it was better to be holding it than facing it.

Looking up at Jasna Góra now, he felt that this was asking too much, but there was nothing the defenders could do to him that would be worse than questioning Danziger. The place was a fortress! Every line of it spoke defiance. And yet, and yet...

As well as the entryway that the Order was camped before, there was another around the side. Edward had given it some thought: a line of ancient archways or shrines or whatever they were would give some cover for a stealthy approach. However, the final arch into the monastery was heavily barricaded, and there were people on the wall above. But then, the walls were not so very high, after all, and they were old. Time had eaten into them, gnawed at their faces until there were handholds enough. Jasna Góra was not as impregnable as it looked.

He had his picked few with him, men he had worked with before on similar missions. They were a mixed bag: two were housebreakers since long before the Cull, in and out of prison until they had outlived the rule of law and order; one had been a ski instructor once, whose interest in certain aspects of twentieth century history would have been unhealthy if it had been made public back in the day; one was, plain and simple, a killer without any emotional connection to other human beings, who found the world post-Cull infinitely more to his liking.

The five of them discussed ingress even as Danziger was parading his men about to draw all eyes. Before evening cloaked them, they had already discarded the second entrance: there were too many heads above the parapet there, at all times. Instead they found a stretch of the wall that seemed unoccupied, and then the ski instructor, Marcus, took the wall carefully, hands and bare feet, with a coil of rope slung over his shoulder. The rest of them crouched in silence, watching the man-shaped blot of darkness creep up the wall.

Then he was up, just as the light was failing them and they could hardly make him out. The rope slithered down to them, and they began their own swifter ascent. Tonight, the judgment of Calumn's God was coming to Jasna Góra.

DOCTOR WEBER WAS stirring up trouble. That was Jenna's opinion. The confrontation over dinner had got the academic's blood up, and now he was a bag of opinions looking for someone to vent them on. He was after a fight.

Not an actual fight, of course. Weber was a pacifist, she understood. Perhaps that was a genuine idealistic position that he was fervently committed to; perhaps he was just a coward. Jenna attached no particular stigma to cowardice. She knew what fear felt like. She had found it and fought it within herself, and she knew that some people just couldn't cross that line: the fear would always master them. They were strong in other ways, no doubt. However, a coward who went around picking fights was something she had little tolerance for. She had known a few, and they were bad for the community. They undermined morale.

Undermining was precisely what Doctor Weber was about, she thought. It wasn't that he wanted to bring the walls down about their ears, but she reckoned he couldn't cope with only having the church standing between him and his enemies. It rankled too much, and so he looked for victories where he could find them.

Right now, even with the Order's forces mustered and ready for an assault, he was playing his intellectual drum. He had tried to pick a debate with three people already—not defenders on the wall, but just inhabitants of the monastery, minding their own business. So far he had come across nobody who would admit to sufficient German to comprehend the lash of his attack on superstition, but now he had located Hamid, who was boiling water and readying bandages in case the attack came tonight.

He sat down companionably enough at first, and Jenna hung back round the corner, waiting for it to start. Sure enough, after a few clipped pleasantries he was back in the saddle.

"It can't be easy for you, to live amongst these people," he observed.

Hamid cocked an eyebrow at him and made a vague conversational noise.

"They make you go to their church services, I saw," Weber noted.

"They invite me."

"Really." Weber was good at putting a boatload of subtext into a single word.

Hamid dumped a batch of bandages in one bubbling pot, and then began lifting damp strips of cloth from another, rolling them deftly with metal tongs he'd already sterilised. Antiseptic was in very short supply, and infection was always a spectre even in everyday life, let alone when there were fascists at the gates.

"Doctor Weber, I know what you want me to say," the Turk told him. "Yes, I prefer to pray in my own room, because they do look, and they do talk, and some of them really don't like it. And I sit in their services because here, that's part of life. It's what they do. They don't force me to drink wine or eat pork, or try to convert me. Like you're doing."

"This isn't the same," Weber sniffed. "So, fine, they're all good civilized people. They remember how life was, before the world went mad. And their children? How will they think? Like us? Or like the children of the Middle Ages, knowing only all the invisible walls of dogma? Where will civilisation be then? Where knowledge? Where will this tolerance be, when your grandchildren want the freedoms they grudgingly allow you?"

"Tolerance." Hamid sighed. He was a man of very even temper, Jenna knew, which was just as well. "Doctor, if you had found your way to whatever's left of Istanbul, would we be having this conversation? Just because I know God in a different way to them, it doesn't make me your ally against them. Perhaps you should do as I do, and be grateful for their shelter and hospitality."

Weber twitched at that, and then made a few abortive attempts at a comeback, obviously trying to find some way to twist the conversation back to where he wanted. Silently, Jenna smirked to herself, shaking her head.

"But listen, you're a modern man. You're a man of science—or a historian, anyway," he pressed on at last, sounding desperate. "You want things to go back to the Middle Ages? Can you honestly say that when society recovers from the terrible catastrophe that has befallen it, you want it to be a feudal theocracy? You want everything that we learned for the last thousand years to be buried, because it's inconvenient, because it contradicts something some priest set down thousands of years ago, and claimed to be God's words?"

"Careful, Doctor," was all Hamid would say.

"But is that what you want?" Weber insisted. There was a quaver in his voice: the future he was seeing was one that he must torture himself with every night.

"Is that what you see happening?" Hamid asked, stopping his work at last.

"If something isn't done, yes," Weber hissed. "If men like me don't take a stand. We'll lose it all."

Hamid shook his head tiredly, not so much in disagreement as failure to understand the other man's mind. Jenna judged that was probably a good time to interrupt, to guide Weber off so that he could stop wasting other peoples' time.

She was drawing breath to call his name when she saw the intruder, just a shadow in the open doorway that Weber had entered through, but there was the gleam of a knife there, already half-raised.

KATY DOGGED THE Abbot's heels all the way from the wall. She had been trying to corner him for a few days now, and as far as she could make out he had known it, and had taken particular pleasure in always having some other matter at his fingertips every time she had tried to beard him. Now the enemy was at the gates, a moment of crisis when she would have expected him to be surrounded by his people, and yet here he was, off alone.

She tracked him to the monastery's church. Nobody seemed interested in stopping her right then, what with the Order giving out free tickets to the post-Cull world's biggest military penis-waving contest right outside the walls. So it was that she found him, a small figure in its gilded space, alone amongst the statues. There were candles lit here, but the evening, and the lack of electric light, made of the place a rookery for shadows, from which sullen reflections of Catholic gold and finery gleamed like the scales of dragons.

Leszek himself stood before the altar, looking up at an ornamented picture given pride of place on the wall, and she hurried down the aisle to him, shoes striking sharp sounds like gunshots.

"So this is where you're planning the counterattack from?" she asked his back, voice echoing about the vaulted ceiling. If she had been expecting to surprise him, she was disappointed.

"No."

"I thought that's what you were coming here for," she pressed, at his shoulder. "You're a military genius or something? You've got a plan."

"Tomasz, or Paul perhaps. They are Jasna Góra's soldiers," he said softly. "I am here to pray."

"Seriously?" Leszek was a man of action. He had a brawler's burly frame, a face that had seen more than one fist coming at it fast. And she had been a disciple of Emil long enough that the idea of actual devotion—behind closed doors, when the masks were off—was something she had a hard time believing in.

At her tone, he turned at last. With a slight smile, he tugged at his robes to draw her attention. "They did tell you I was an abbot? Prayer is something I do."

She would almost have preferred him angry; that would have been easier to react against. "You must have prayed a lot when the plague came."

An odd expression was fleetingly in his eyes. "Then, I

was not the Abbot, nor did I pray as often as I should. Miss Lewkowitz, you have sought me out...?"

"Yes, I..." And she had, and she needed to talk to him before Emil went completely mad, and here he was, but... Abruptly, cornering him in the stronghold of his faith didn't seem like such a good idea. He seemed to draw strength from every stone, impervious to her accusations. Instead, her eyes flicked to the painting he had been considering. "That's... is that Mrs Good Samaritan?" The image was of a woman in richly bejewelled robes of blue and gold, long-faced and dark skinned, shown with a similarly gilded child.

Leszek stiffened. "It is the Madonna," and, when she opened her mouth to comment, "I know you draw strength from mockery, but I would ask you, of all things, do not mock her. You do not know, it seems, but she is the soul of Jasna Góra. She protects us, protects these walls, so that they may never be taken."

And so, with the Order here, you pray. "She's..." Katy frowned. "She's cut?" There were thin lines down the woman's face, too straight and sharp for tear-tracks.

"Thieves. They could not steal her, when they tried," the Abbot rumbled. "So they tried to ruin her. But here she is. Here she stays." And he fixed Katy with his eyes. "Speak, then. Every time before now, that you have come to me, I have had my people to mind. Now I have only God. He will wait. He will understand."

"I want to talk to you about Emil," she forced the words out.

"Of course you do."

"I want you to stop bullying him."

Leszek regarded her for a moment, without expression. "Is that what you think—" he started, but now she had him, she knew she could not let him squirm away so quickly.

"Abbot Leszek, don't insult me. Every time you meet him, there's something else. You mock him over wine. You make every meal a matter of 'Christian charity' to him. This business with a lab at Kraków—he can continue his work, but only if he puts on a cassock and bows the knee. You don't understand him."

"I understand that he has made it his business to attack my faith all his life," the Abbot remarked, mildly, but with a hint of iron.

"Because he sees faith doing *harm*, Abbot," Katy told him, almost feeling the ghost of Emil in her as she fought his corner. "Because he sees people put religion above health, above common sense, above reason, and call it morality."

"And if I see people put greed and power above morality, and call it reason?" Leszek's smile was gone.

"Listen to me." Katy had her hands on her hips, fighting down her anger, and not least because she was within arm's reach of him and he could break her in half. "Emil is a good man. All his life he's worked to help people. With science. With reason. He's worked to educate them. He's worked to free them from things that were holding them down, blinkering them."

"And that is how he sees God?"

She couldn't tell if he was sad, or about to burst into a rage. His face was utterly closed.

"Everything he told you about the plague, it's true," she said, the words fast and flat. "It could mutate at any time, and then we'd *need* men of science and reason to save us. Or will you trust to prayer alone?"

And she was already backing away, but she managed one step before he lunged forwards and straight-armed her in the chest, knocking her to the ground.

JENNA WAS MOVING before she had a chance to think about it, bursting in on the pair of them and then lunging past Weber. He had gone completely still, jaw clenched, and for a moment, she realised, he thought she was attacking him.

The knifeman had begun his lunge at Weber's back, but her sudden appearance threw him and he flinched back, the knife's glittering arc clipping the doctor's shoulder. He was a big man, a stranger with his hair cut short, an Order soldier even if he had washed the black and white motley from his face.

She didn't have her bow, of course, or even a knife to fight with, but in that moment of surprise, she rammed the heel of her hand into his jaw as hard as she could, and tried to get a knee into his groin or stomach to follow it up. He reeled away, taking the second blow on the hip as he bounced into the wall.

Then he was coming back for her, even as she heard Hamid yelling for help.

The room was not large enough for fancy footwork, and her attacker was short on subtlety, just groping for her, trying to fix her in place so he could tear her apart. She yelled at Weber to help, but he was just standing there, rigid as a statue.

Her assailant's outstretched fingers caught the edge of her jacket and pulled. Frantically she spun out of it, ripping her arms free and denying him his hold, and instead he shoved her into Hamid's preparation table, spilling the carefully rolled bandages everywhere. As she sprawled there, her fingers touched something cold.

A heavy hand slammed down on her shoulder and she twisted round, jabbing at him furiously with what turned out to be the scissors Hamid had been cutting cloth with.

It was not the first time she had stabbed someone. Far from the first time, in fact. The blades buried themselves into his shoulder, rammed in partly by the strength of her arm, partly by his own eagerness to trap her against the table.

He gave a shocked sound and tried to swing the knife, but she shoved him in the chest and he dropped it as he fell backwards.

There was another man in the doorway, another clean-cropped intruder. He had a pistol out, because there were already cries of alarm, and so the need for quiet knives was past. Weber was just standing there: not fighting, not cowering, facing up to the barrel of the gun.

Then Hamid took up the pot of boiling water and hurled it over the gunman with a tortured sound, and a moment later everything was steam and screaming. The scalding water lashed across Jenna's cheek, and she saw Weber catch some as well, but Hamid had been on the mark, and the intruder got the rest of it in the face.

She was already stooping for the knife the first man had dropped. Some part of her mind had been tracking it, and it found her hand as naturally as a fencer's foil. She had been too long without the practice, but her lunge was textbook perfect and she took him under the ribs as he scrabbled at his burned face. And then again, and again, because killing someone, really finishing them, with a knife is hard to do.

By then the first man was up, and he was running, the scissors still sticking in him. Jenna went after him but, even as he got into the open air, an arrow sprang from his thigh. Another drove between his neck and shoulder as he doubled over.

There were enough people out there to take care of things. She went back inside to find Doctor Weber doing what he could for Hamid's burned hands, consumed by a calm professionalism she would not have expected.

THE WORLD SPUN wildly for Katy and she fetched up hard against the stone flags, already coiling for fight or flight, when a man tried to vault over her to get at Leszek. She had half got to her feet, quicker than anyone must have reckoned, so that he kicked her painfully in the shoulder and went headlong onto his face, a knife spinning from his hands to ring against the floor.

He was not alone. A second man had come in after him, metal glinting in his hand, and a third was lurking in the shadow of the arcades, watching the doorway. They must have been creeping through the shadows, from column to column, until they were close enough to strike.

Leszek took a solid step forwards, head lowered like a bull about to charge. The fallen man tried to scramble to his feet, but the Abbot stamped on him like a street brawler, his solid boot coming down, with all his weight, on the intruder's hand, even as it raked out for the lost knife. The sound of bones crunching was audible and the next man in said, "Fuck you, old man!" in an accent that came straight from the streets of Chelsea.

Katy kicked away from him, and the words "English Bigot!" burst from her as though she had late onset Tourette's. This utterance threw Edward completely—his knife had been jabbing forwards and now it jerked back as he looked around at her. In that startled second his face was all wounded innocence, all *How could anyone think that of me?* Then Leszek punched him, roaring mostly with wordless anger, but with some words of sacrilege mixed up in it.

The first man was curled about his ruined hand, so Katy lunged after his knife, the hilt dancing and jumping like a fish in her shaking hands. The third man had given up on keeping watch and was bundling in, too, even as Edward staggered sideways.

"This was supposed to be quiet!" he snapped out in German.

"You make *him* be quiet!" Edward snapped back, lashing about with his knife to push the Abbot back.

Katy had the knife, but its owner was on her, one hand clutched to his belly, reaching for her with the other, face black with pain and anger. Beyond him, she saw the other two backing the Abbot towards his precious painting.

She was no great fighter, but she wasn't the cringing maiden her attacker probably imagined, either. He lunched for her and she buried the knife in his arm, trying to wrench it out quickly. He was a seething riot of adrenaline by then, though, barely noticing the new wound, his hand closing on her arm. She had on a woollen jumper made by one of the locals, and it stretched and pulled in his fingers, her arm sliding up inside it as he struggled to get a good grip. She hurled herself into him like someone shouldering a door, her elbow striking hard into his broken hand.

She could see Leszek with his hands up, fending off the knives. Blood flew from his palms and fingers. His back was to the wall.

With a sudden strength, she had the knife free from the man's arm and past his collarbone, her underhand grip as brutal and obvious as a stage assassin's, driving the blade in, scoring across bone and severing blood vessels so that she arose from his body painted red.

The knife was irretrievable, truly wedged, but she took up a candlestick and brought it down on the nearest man's head and shoulders. That was the idea, anyway: the fittings in the old church were museum pieces all, far heavier than she had thought, and she almost ruptured something getting the thing aloft. When it came down, though, it struck with the weight of five hundred years of history, dropping the man with bone-shuddering force.

Edward, seeing he was the last man standing, stared a moment at her, at Leszek, the latter not the least daunted by the blood running from his hands, and fled.

His hurried feet boomed and slapped in the echoing space, and when he reached the end of the aisle, Tomasz was in the doorway, a sword in his hands, murder in his face.

Perhaps Edward could have surrendered, then, although nothing in Tomasz's expression suggested that would go well for him. Instead he reached into his jacket and came out with a pistol, trying to bring it to bear.

Tomasz brought the sword down in a cleaving stroke. Edward had a moment to throw up his arms, gun and all, and the edge bit deep into his right wrist, almost severing it. He shrieked, more in horror than pain, and Tomasz twisted the blade free, the tip circling and gathering speed to swing up into Edward's armpit, hilt high to protect its wielder's face. It keened through clothes and flesh, then turned in its owner's hands to follow its own path back, swinging past its victim's elbow to cut down into the man's scalp even as Tomasz stepped away from a notional counter-attack.

"Abbot!" Despite his performance, Tomasz's expression was agonised, seeing Leszek's condition.

"I'll live. Miss Lewkowitz will staunch my wounds for now. Go send out the word. There may be more."

CHAPTER ELEVEN
THE LEOPARD AND THE LAMB

S{.sc HE BOUND HIS} hands with strips of cloth torn from the clothes of their attackers, wincing as she did so. He had a half-dozen cuts across his palms and fingers, the sort that police would have characterised as "defensive wounds"; most often seen on corpses.

"I'm sorry," she whispered. Her own hands were shaking with sour adrenaline now the danger was past. "I'm sorry, I'm making a mess of this. I don't want to hurt you more."

"I barely feel it," he murmured, and she looked at him sharply in case that meant he was about to die on her, but he was watching her keenly. Abruptly he lifted his hands so that the sleeves of his habit fell away, and she saw the scars she had noticed before, going most of the way around his wrists on both hands. "I don't have much pain or even touch left, in these."

"I... er... I'm guessing there's a story to go with that," she noted, pulling tight and knotting and then cutting more strips of cloth. "I... they must have got to you pretty quickly, if you did that do yourself." Even as she said it, she was wondering how a man could so thoroughly cut both his wrists.

"I have many sins on my conscience," he said softly, "but not that one. The men who did this to me... yes, I was lucky that others got to me before they finished."

"Finished...?"

"Cutting my hands off. Or that was what they said they intended." His face creased: humour or old pain, she was not sure.

"This was... they were persecuting you? For your faith?" In the mad world she now lived in, it was all she could think of.

"I forgive them now, for what they did." And, despite everything, there was definitely a glint of amusement in his face. "After all, I had tried to cheat them out of a great deal of money."

She froze, trying to work that one out. "The Abbot of Jasna Góra was—"

"No, no, no. Long before. No abbot, no God-fearing man at all, then. Just a crook, a man of violence and greed." His voice grew softer as the fury of the fight and the loss of blood left him drained and weak. "You deserve to know this, to know who it is you've saved." He shook his head slowly. "The police came before my friends could finish their punishment, and we all went to prison. For many years."

"You found God in prison?"

"I did. I found God, and I lost heroin, though there were enough in that place who found it. God and the Virgin Mary touched me, in that place. Tell Weber this. Could science have done that? Could reason? I do not think so."

"Leszek—"

"I know, I know." He shook his head slightly. "I do bait him. And you, even. But you both should know that sometimes the world alone does not have enough to make a bad man good. But God..." He sighed. "And I came here, the lowest of the low, throwing myself on the mercy of the holy men who dwelled here, seeking a purpose and a life as far away from my old one as possible."

"And then they died," she finished for him.

"They did," he whispered. "They died, and so did almost all the people of the world. And, God forgive me, I made myself an abbot, and tried to do good." He craned upwards, eyes seeking the rich hues of the dark Madonna and child. There were dots and darts of blood across her face and hand, most probably his own. "So you know the truth, Miss Lewkowitz. I'm no holy man, not really. I am not a man of God. All I was, when it happened, was a man who could get things done." He closed his eyes. "I have tried, since, to be a proper heir to this place. To play-act the wise man. Nothing but an imposter, but I have tried." His voice had fallen so low that she was terrified he might die any second, but then he rallied abruptly. "And then God sent me an atheist and a Jew, and bade me protect them against those who style themselves soldiers of Christ. Have I done the right thing, do you think? Have I avoided disgracing *her*?"

By then Tomasz was bustling back in with half a dozen of the monastery's people, a pot of boiling water and a box of antiseptics and medicines, and Katy stood up and backed away, feeling herself abruptly unwanted.

Still, later that night—sleep refusing to draw near her for the duration—the captain of Jasna Góra's defenders sought her out.

"How is he?" she asked.

"Well. Sleeping." Tomasz's German was rough, and they both had to speak slowly. "He said to me what you did. We are grateful for it. I thank you."

His tone was grudging, but she managed to muster a smile anyway. "What happens now?"

"Now?" For a moment his face was blank, then he nodded sharply. "Now they attack."

EVEN THEN IN the Order camp, Josef Danziger was pacing, waiting for some sign that his assassins had hit their mark. What sign? He wasn't sure. He could hardly expect scenes of Biblical lamentation atop the walls, the gates thrown open, a general surrender from the hoi polloi once their arrogant leader was put in his place. Still, he felt he would know. The air would change in some indefinable way, as if the scent of the Abbot's blood could be carried to him all the way out here.

Danziger had not been changed by the Cull, only unleashed. Back in the day he had been a man constantly on police watch lists. A childhood spent dissatisfied and frustrated with the way the world failed to recognise him had turned into an adolescence of spread-winged eagles, of covert rallies, of learning all the wrong lessons of history: Teutoberg, the Stab-in-the-Back, the rallies at Nuremburg. He had been a man looking for a destiny to fill the hole he found inside him, grinding his teeth as he got older and older, and his cryptofascist peers just kept making the same speeches, some petty violence here, a little arson there. And still the world failed to see him as anything more than a small-time thug. In his mind, he was a wolf born to a man's shape, and he had been caged by all the rules of society, watching the Germany-that-was diverge ever from the Germany-that-should-be, the Fatherland that was more yearning imagination than history by the time Danziger got to it.

The Cull had been the hand of Fate, opening his cage and letting him loose on the world. In that time of panic, it was easy enough to find kindred spirits, or just directionless men who had been emptied by the chaos of the fall, ready to be filled by any man's purpose, so long as they *had* a purpose. Easy enough then to harken back to the birth of a fighting Teutonic nation. Easy enough to resurrect his own version of the past.

It was time, he decided. The gates were not going to open of their own accord. Edward and his fellows had failed, or they had succeeded. Either way it was time to test the Order's sword against the mail of Jasna Góra.

He called his subordinates to him and took their reports. Two were sent around the side of the fortifications to pick their way across the jumble of dead vehicles that cluttered it. The rest would be attacking up the incline to the reinforced gates. He had long-arm detachments to rake the defenders on the wall-tops, and the mass of the rest would be going in after the tank. "Make every shot count," was his instruction. The Order had plenty of guns, but ammunition was at a premium.

The tank crew he gave careful instruction to. It was a hungry beast for diesel, too, and they had only two shots for the main gun. It was a temperamental and ill-tempered monster. *Fafnir*, they called it, and the name rankled with Danziger: Fafnir was the prey of the true German hero, not its ally. Still, the myths were short on friendly dragons, and the name had stuck.

"You understand?" he demanded of all his underlings. There was a murmur and a nodding. Either they did, or they were too frightened of him to ask for clarification. It was the price of being a leader.

"ALL RIGHT, NOW they're moving," Jenna called, seeing Paul's curt nod. The New Teutonic Order had made several false starts in the pre-dawn, which might have been to keep the defenders off balance or just because they were trying to start an attack before it got light. Jenna and the other good shots amongst the monastery defenders had been on the walls since the evening, sleeping at their posts and in shifts against a night attack. And there had been the business with the intruders too, that Tomasz was spitting feathers about. After the Abbot had been hurt, he had been in such a foul mood that she was glad he was commanding the monastery's other entrance. He and Paul had drawn straws for it, and Paul had won the responsibility of fending off the main assault.

They were mostly archers like her, up on the wall. Some of the defenders had crossbows, sports and target models mostly, as the monastery smiths had not been much bothered about developing that branch of weaponsmithing. There was a scattering of rifles, too, the owners well aware of the dwindling number of bullets in their pockets. Down below, the Order was mostly just a general sense of motion as it stumbled and cursed its way into a semblance of military discipline and then pushed forwards. Except for the tank. The grumbling, growling snarl of its engine pinpointed it clearly for them, if only they had anything that might hurt it.

But that was what Paul had taken on, when he chose this front. His brains against the metal Leopard's brawn.

The first shots came, mostly from below, with a couple of

too-eager responses from the wall. Paul called for a halt, his voice clear in the still night. Then hold again, though nobody was firing. Jenna, who had been out shooting in the twilight enough to have a good sense of distance, drew back her string. Quivers of arrows were stacked all along the wall. That was one resource they were not short of.

She loosed a second before Paul's shout, the shaft vanishing away, falling towards that mostly-unseen mass of men. There were distant shouts and cries, but few, and the Order came on, the tank preceding them like the standard of their new crusade.

The defenders were all shooting now, the thrum of bowstrings murmuring up and down the wall against the staccato crack of rifles. The Order was pressing forwards swiftly, the threat of the arrows driving them to kick and shove each other, to tread on each others' feet in their hurry. Still Jenna had no targets, only the surging grey shadow, the enemy in aggregate. She could only send her shafts into that amorphous body and pray that she was doing some good.

Then the night was resounding day for one moment, as the tank's gun spoke with flash and thunder. Jenna felt the wall shudder, beneath her, and to her left a spray of stones and wood splinters peppered the defenders. Abruptly everyone's head was down, and the Order's attackers surged forwards in a tight-packed mob.

The tank reached the first of the staggered vehicles that partially blocked the ramp and shouldered it aside with a revving of its engine. The next it simply ground over, one track mashing down the rusting hulk's bonnet. Bullets and arrows alike danced from its armour. Jenna nocked another arrow, but the Order's return fire was now becoming a threat, bullets striking brief sparks from the walls, or punching into the makeshift crenellations atop them. Jenna heard more than one cry from her own people.

So how much ammunition do they have? It seemed their supply must be limitless, the way they were sending their shot up, whilst every flash and bang from the defenders was a marvel of the lost modern world that they would not see again.

"Grenades!" came Paul's cry. His hand-picked grenadiers set to work, choosing their moment to throw away the monastery's handful of explosives. One missile flashed into fire on the tank's hull without much luck. One fell into the thick of the enemy, and must have inflicted a fearful toll. Of the rest, Jenna didn't see, but she had no sense that they accomplished a great deal. The battle was lit up in brief frozen images, like a badly-tuned television showing her fragmentary moments of a war movie, nothing but the gore, the horror.

And yet too few to stay them, and now both the enemy and the dawn were close enough that she could pick her target, and yet could not afford to, lest she become one herself. She sent one shaft after another down onto them, drawing and releasing as swiftly as possible, falling back on the old Japanese techniques she had once learned, where swiftness and smoothness of action overrode the need for a careful aim.

And then the tank came before the gates of Jasna Góra, and she saw the barrel of its main gun move as though it was inspecting them.

AT THE SIDE gate, the Order had achieved an unexpected early victory. They had come first as a mob with rifles, squeezing their way through the various arches, surging up the footpath. They came shooting up at the walls, spraying brick dust and splinters and wounding a few. They came to the solidly barricaded Jagiellonian Gate, finding themselves trapped and milling, as Tomasz and his fellows loosed arrows on their heads.

Tomasz kicked himself for not spotting their true intent. He was guilty of seeing the enemy as almost mindless, just a pack of thugs who would break against the fortifications of Jasna Góra. He had applied himself to his archery, already thinking that he could go and see how Paul was getting on.

Then the attackers, having suffered a score of casualties, fell back from the blocked entryway, and he had thought they were broken. He had even said so to the others, whilst reaching for another arrow to send after the fleeing enemy.

But they had not been fleeing. They had already regrouped,

and he had the sudden thought, *Did they leave more than bodies behind?*

And then the explosives went, the charges they carried up with them, hidden in the dawn's greyness, smashing the barricade in like a fist as the defenders below yelled and screamed. And the Order—of course the Order's soldiers were rushing forwards, desperate to gain the gate.

"Karel! Ready!" Tomasz was already running for the steps. The yelling from below masked any reply he might have received.

He reached the ground just ahead of the Order vanguard. A handful of defenders was using the Jagiellonian Gate as cover, discharging rifles and crossbows at the onrushing enemy. Bullets pinged and bounced around them.

In one smooth moment, Tomasz drew back his bow, stood and loosed, the shaft vanishing into the faces of the Order's front line. A shot skimmed his shoulder as he pulled back into the shadow of the gate.

"Karel!" he yelled out again, and then dropped his bow and cut his quiver from his belt so it wouldn't trip him. His hand found the comforting roughness of his sword hilt.

He was no good at battle cries. He just went in as the Order's soldiers clambered and sprang over the wreckage of the barricade, as the defending shooters fell back.

There were riflemen in front, amongst the enemy. One dropped even as he crested the car, an arrow sprouting abruptly from his shoulder. Tomasz hacked at the next one, who raised his rifle frantically to parry him. Tomasz let his momentum carry him forwards, let his weapon pivot about the gun barrel so he could ram the pommel into that painted, black-on-white face. There was a crunch and grind of a broken nose and he kneed the man backwards, letting his blade sweep round to catch a second soldier in the side of the head. Another shot went overhead, producing a brief spray of shards as it rattled off the stonework. There were too many of the Order cramming the gateway to get many shots in without hitting their own, but if they got past the confines of the entryway in any numbers, they would probably sweep everyone aside. Tomasz simply didn't have enough firepower for a charge-stopping volley.

So it was down to the old ways, and in his heart of hearts, he was glad of it.

The Order had plenty of men coming at him, with bats and knifes, with fire-axes and cleavers. Tomasz had a blade forged by Hamid using thousand-year-old techniques and the man's own modern knowhow. Around him shoved the men and women of Jasna Góra, a fierce crowd with spears and axes and swords, and at least a handful sporting steel mail or brigandine.

He struck at the enemy; he made them fear him. He took a ragged cut across the hip and a shallow but bloody badge on his scalp. Even as he gave ground, though, something in him was singing: *Let me die now, and I will not begrudge it.* The man he had always been—the man the twenty-first century had not known how to appease—was in his element, dancing with his sword, then dropping it to grapple and twist and throw, then taking it up again.

And yet the Order was pressing, pressing in; the cordon penning them back stretched and strained, further and further...

But he heard the call, from behind him. He heard the defenders chanting, "Golem! Golem!"

Karel thundered past him like a force of nature, like a thunderstorm clad in metal. He had on his full harness: probably he had still been adjusting it when the call went out. He was all over steel, plate over mail over a Kevlar vest. In his hands he had a pollaxe, a six-foot shaft with a gimlet spike at one end, and on the other all the worst aspects of axe and hammer and spear.

He had the kind of momentum that could not be denied, striking deep into the enemy, burying the axe in one, raking the spike across the face of another, then striking about him with the scalloped edges of his gauntlets. Weapons struck lines across his armour, but Tomasz remembered the small fortune Karel had spent on all that steel, back in the day. With not an inch of skin visible, with that weight of metal, driven by the man's formidable strength, he truly was like a terrifying automaton. He truly earned his nickname.

The Order fell back before him, and the defenders seized on every inch they surrendered. Karel let the enemy break across his broad chest, seizing them in handfuls and throwing them back, wresting any weapon that crossed his narrow field of view and turning it on its wielder. Then Tomasz plucked up his pollaxe and got it back in the man's hands, and that sight was enough to break the Order's resolve. Abruptly they were falling back, the first assault repulsed.

"Get me furniture, barrels, boxes, anything to build up the barricade!" Tomasz shouted out, sending the defenders scurrying. He clapped a hand hollowly on Karel's shoulder. "Took your time," he added in German.

"Like you weren't enjoying yourself," came the voice from the helm.

THE TANK GUN spoke like a storm, so that defenders and attackers alike cringed away from the sheer physicality of the sound. The shot thundered into the gates and smashed them down as though the very fist of God was with the Order, leaving them hanging raggedly, half off their hinges, the thick bar that had held them closed snapped across. The air was full of smoke and dust and falling splinters.

And the tank ground onwards, crunching its way into Jasna Góra with eager speed.

Paul was already halfway down the steps. The defenders were rushing in to stem the tide, but the tank would not care about them. Human bodies were nothing to it, barely even noticed. The soldiers of the Order were already cheering as though the victory was theirs. Their great Leopard had triumphed so swiftly. Nothing could stand against the mechanical terror.

Or that was what they thought, or so Paul fervently hoped. How would Tomasz have dealt with this, had he drawn the short straw? Probably some manoeuvre that was one part military strategy and two parts wild daring. Paul did not have his reckless disregard for the odds; he had been planning ever since he saw the tank. Every dragon met its slayer, after all, and in the best stories it was not valour or strength of arms that killed the beast, but cunning.

The gateway was only just wide enough to admit the vehicle. The courtyard beyond was crooked, awkward to manoeuvre in. The edges of the metal monster gouged grooves in the plaster and stonework. Its engine bellowed and it surged forwards, seeking space. Pushing about the corner, the tank abruptly found itself lurching up at a mad angle, tilting queasily to the right. There was a confused eddy amongst the soldiers trying to push either side of it, finding the path ahead abruptly closed to a narrow channel either side of the skewed vehicle.

Then the real work of those atop the wall came. Those soldiers not under cover of the gateway were out of luck. Everything was coming down on them now: arrows, grenades, improvised bombs made of jars stuffed with nails and gunpowder, even big pots of boiling water. At the same time a line of defenders armed with spears below had made a fence of spikes and was pushing into the vulnerable human soldiers trying to get past the tank.

And the tank itself, modern marvel of the age? It was hoisted up, one track off the ground entirely, the other grinding uselessly back and forth and skidding without purchase on the hard ground. Its own speed had consigned it to its fate— that, and the great wooden caltrops Paul had ordered built. Each was made from strong timbers taken from the structure of Jasna Góra itself, nailed securely together so that jagged ends jutted out in six directions at once. Now the Leopard was hoisted up on a couple of them, invulnerable as ever but helpless, engine roaring and screeching as its crew tried to jerk it free. The machine gun mounted alongside the main gun abruptly stuttered out a burst, the bullets flying high over the heads of the defenders to rake the walls of the monastery. Then, as the melee about the vehicle surged, one man clambered up onto the hull and beat at the weapon with a crowbar until it fell silent, crooked and broken.

Paul had his hand to his sword hilt, but he did not draw the blade. The place of the commander was not in the press of the melee. He watched and waited, feeling the ebb and flow of the fight as though it was the blood in his veins. The desperation of the Order soldiers was in him, the fierce determination of the defenders. Every wounded cry echoed through him. And, in the end, the Order fell back—fled, even, hurrying to get out of the steel rain the archers sent after it—and left its pride and joy behind.

And the Leopard crew were still fighting, overheating the engine as they tried to work it off the spikes propping up its underbelly. The air about it was choked with the smoke of its exhaust.

They held out for a long time, and the Order made two attempts to reclaim the crippled vehicle, venturing into the defenders' shot, trying to keep them occupied with rifle fire. Their heart was gone, though. Seeing their dragon impaled thus had taken the fight from them.

In the end, one of the defenders shoved a grenade down the gun barrel, detonating with a shuddering thump within the vehicle, and then they lit fires beneath it, and on top of it, doubling and redoubling the heat of its overstrained engine until the crew were forced, choking and coughing, out of it. One man surrendered, dropping to his knees and rolling, retching and helpless. The other tried to flee, and failed to get far.

By that time, Tomasz had stood off three attacks at the Jagiellonian Gate, and the Order finally gave up the day as lost, pulling back sullenly to its camp and licking its many wounds.

"Bring me a casualty report!" Paul shouted, because a commander's work did not end with the battle.

IN THE ORDER camp, Josef Danziger received his own subordinates' reports in silence. They cringed from him, ready for his explosive rage, but this time he was calm, a core of cold steel hardening within him.

Calumn wanted to speak to him, but he curtly told the American to go preach to the troops instead, to tell them God was still on their side, that He was testing them. "Tell them whatever you like, so long as it makes them strong again," he said flatly.

Then he called for Jon Franken and Radek Majewski—Jon because he was good at following complex orders to the letter, Radek because Polish was his first language.

"I have a task for you," he told them. "Take a score of the soldiers. But it must be accomplished tonight; tomorrow we will have another way of testing these monks." And he told them what he intended, and their eyes shone with the righteousness of their cause, but mostly because this mission would give them the chance to take out their frustrations for the beating the Order had suffered today.

CHAPTER TWELVE
SUFFER THE INNOCENTS

TOMASZ HAD BEEN all for planning a sortie into the enemy camp, keen to add to their misery by spoiling their supplies or knifing a few of their leaders. Debate had swung back and forth amongst Jasna Góra's upper echelons: Paul and Hamid had been against, but Jenna had sided with Tomasz, and Karel was constitutionally incapable of turning away from a fight.

"We can't last out a long siege," Tomasz argued. "So we get them to go away, any way we can."

"The Abbot won't permit the risk," Paul countered.

"If we all agree, he will. If that's our advice, he'll listen," Jenna put in.

"We kicked half their arse yesterday," Karel growled. "We need to go tan the other buttock or they'll forget it."

Katy sat in the corner, eating a meagre breakfast of porridge and listening to them. Her opinion was not solicited, which was just as well as she didn't have one. Beside her, Emil brooded silently, hands cupped about a steaming mug of coffee. She had no idea which of the monastery's residents had felt coffee so very important, but they seemed to have enough jars of instant to see them all eating the granules raw when everything else ran out.

Emil's hands shook, ever so slightly, and there was blood drying on his jacket. The two of them had both been rolling up their sleeves to help with the injured, especially with Hamid unable to use his hands. The monastery had suffered a handful of deaths, mostly those who had fought alongside Tomasz, hand to hand against the Order's charges. More lives still hung in the balance. Medical supplies were dwindling to nothing as they fought off the threat of infection, and a score of casualties might go either way. *And there are far more scrapes and minor cuts that could just as easily go bad.* Even right after the Cull, she had not quite envisaged what the collapse of civilisation would mean. *I don't want to live in the Middle Ages. It's fucking terrifying.* Faced with the fact that the microscopic world turned every scrape into a chance of septicaemia, she couldn't imagine why anyone would ever go to war for any reason whatsoever.

Then a messenger came tripping into the room, a girl of twelve, half out of breath, gabbling something in Polish. Tomasz stood.

"Reinforcements," he translated. From his grim expression it was evident whose. He sent the girl off to tell the Abbot, and they all ended up on the wall, looking at the shambling block of newcomers as they approached the Order camp.

Jenna murmured something to Tomasz, narrow-eyed, and at Karel's annoyed grunt she clarified, "Not reinforcements."

Katy craned forwards, seeing a mass of people, perhaps fifty all told, being herded into the encampment. And *herded* was the right word: these weren't soldiers, they were unarmed men, women and children, under guard on a forced march.

"They've gone to the farms," Paul stated. It took Katy a moment to follow what he meant. As Lezsek had said, the people of Częstochowa, those that survived, had not clung on in the city, any more than the people of Wrocław. They had gone instead into the countryside, growing the new rather than feeding off the corpse of the old. This had been the plan, at the great convocation or whatever of Jasna Góra. They had been trying to look to the future.

And now the past had come to tear up their new-planted roots, carrying a black-and-white flag from a thousand years ago.

"We may need to bring them the fight sooner than you thought," Karel stated.

"They may have taken prisoners to stop us doing just that," Paul argued. "At the first sign that we are on the attack, they could kill them."

"Whatever they plan, I don't think it will involve waiting for us to act," suggested Jenna.

"We'll hear from them soon." The Abbot's voice made them all start and turn, to find him labouring up the stairs. A pair of armed defenders was shadowing him, but he was plainly refusing any attempt to help him. When he reached the top, he was breathing heavily, his bandaged hands folded into loose fists.

"Prepare for guests," he said shortly. "And remind our people we don't shoot messengers."

SURE ENOUGH, THE Order sent a man out to the gates, or where the gates had been. His face and his flag both bore the black cross on white and he halted a good ten feet from the entryway, staring at the canted tank. The defenders had thrown up makeshift barricades either side of the grounded vehicle, even as they had refortified the Jagiellonian Gate as best they could. Now they and the Order's emissary had to perform a peculiar pantomime, he passing up his flag to them before scaling the shifting wood and stone and bric-a-brac they had put in place.

The Abbot received the man in the monastery's refectory, sitting at a long table with his hands mostly hidden in his wide sleeves. All his people were there, even Hamid with his burned palms, and Katy and Emil too, staring at the shorn-headed young man with the motley face as he stood before them.

"Well?" Leszek demanded, into the silence.

The man declared something in Polish, out of which Katy just about caught the name *Radek* and a reference to the Teutonic Order, but the Abbot held up a hand.

"Yes, yes, but we're not all Poles here." His eyes flicked to Katy and Emil, as much as anyone else.

"I bring a message from Grand Master Josef Danziger of the New Teutonic Order," the man stated, his face twitching with annoyance.

"This much is obvious," the Abbot stated acidly. "Perhaps you might let us know what it is."

The man Radek's lips tightened. Presumably he had envisaged his master's name inspiring more respect. "The Grand Master sends his compliments on your valour. That you have decided to resist the righteous cause of the Order is regrettable. But your warrior spirit is to your credit." His delivery was awkward and uneven, and Katy realised he must have prepared the speech in Polish. *Little swot.*

"However, the destiny of the Order is not to be denied. God has sent us to destroy a heretic, one man. If we must tear down your fortress stone by stone, then God shall give us the strength to do it. The Order is obedient to the will of God. Many lives have been spent to do God's will already. If many more must be spent, so be it."

Emil's jaw was clenched. He flinched at every mention of the divine, and then doubly so when Radek jabbed an accusatory finger right at him.

"We came to you and demanded the surrender of this atheist, and you refused. Now many good men on either side lie dead on his account. Strong men, warriors, faithful. If it is blood that will accomplish God's will, the Order will not be slow to shed it. But the blood of warriors is valuable. More valuable than the blood of Slavic peasants. Let it be known that unless this man is surrendered to the will of God, we will execute a dozen of your people by sunset, chosen by lot. Another dozen will follow at dawn, another dozen at the following sunset. Ask yourself how much is worth the life of one who denies Christ."

Karel rumbled deep within his chest and took a step forwards, but a slight shake of the Abbot's head stopped him.

"You've spoken your piece?" Leszek asked and, at Radek's nod, "Then get out."

"I will have your answer—"

"When we are ready, and not before!" the Abbot snapped, standing abruptly. "Now get this creature out of my sight."

AFTER THAT, THE Abbot sent them all out, closeting himself away in his own chambers and brooding.

Katy found herself on the walls, staring out at the Order camp, and she was by no means alone. The sound of hammering drifted faintly up to them, blurring and scattering across the monastery walls. She didn't need binoculars to see what they were building. The row of gibbets taking shape looked all too familiar from when she had gone to Forst to rescue Emil the first time.

Running all that way, she considered morosely, *and it's just caught up with us. All that human stupidity and malevolence.* Perhaps the Abbot would put that down to original sin or something: evil was something they carried with them, no more possible to run away from than her own arm, than the heart inside her.

"You wonder what the Abbot will do with your friend." Jenna's voice came at her shoulder.

"Truly?" Katy shook her head. "Not even that. Just... this. All this."

Jenna nodded. She had her bow in hand, but no target. "I remember when they met here, all the big men, the priests, the leaders, and I thought that we would end up like that. There were some who wanted to fight—not fight the plague, because you can't, and it had already killed so many, so just *fight,* fight someone, anyone. Roma, Germans, witches, *anyone.* That out there, that's us, in some other life. That's us outside the walls of Berlin or Kiev, fighting other people because we can't fight the plague."

"But that didn't happen," Katy said carefully.

"And because of that, they come here. The Order this year. Next year one of the petty Tsars will bring their home-grown Oprichniks west, or there will be some Khan with a new Golden Horde, or Islamists coming north. While we try to survive as our ancestors did, they bring us all the mistakes of history."

Someone nearby made an approving sound, and Katy glanced over to see Emil standing there. "It's well said," he commented. There was something wrong with the way he stood, a dreadful tension wound so tight within him that, when he moved, it was like a clockwork automaton. "You, I need to see the Abbot."

Jenna regarded him doubtfully. "Do you so?"

Emil's regard didn't falter. "Whose life is it that everyone suddenly seems to have a claim on, if not mine? That gives me the right to speak for myself."

She paused a moment, wrestling with herself, and then nodded reluctantly. "Let's see if he will hear you, then."

Emil opened his mouth, and Katy knew he was about to tell her to stay put.

"Oh, I'm coming, believe me," she assured him.

THE ABBOT'S WISH for solitude had apparently been one of his few commands to be completely ignored. When Jenna brought them in, Tomasz was just coming to the end of a tir*le in fierce, rapid Polish, leaning over the man's desk and a but beating his fist on it. Seeing Jenna and her followers, Leszek raised a hand to cut him off.

"Ah," he said simply. "How did I imagine that I would have the morning of prayer and contemplation I asked for?"

Jenna explained herself rapidly, gesturing at Emil, while Tomasz glowered at the interruption.

"Well then," the Abbot considered. "I have been listening for at least an hour to the apparent necessity for our entire fighting force to rush out into the guns of the Order. I think, Dr Weber, that even you cannot tell me something less welcome than that."

Tomasz made to speak, practically spitting in his haste to get the words out, but a look from Leszek silenced him.

"Well, Dr Weber? Perhaps your science has come up with a solution to our problems?"

"Yes, it has," Emil told him, quite calmly. "You have been waving your charity at me since I got here. You have never missed an opportunity to show me how very grateful I should be to you and your church. Well then, let me say this thing now, because I won't get another chance. I *am* grateful for what you've given me, but your church and your God are not the keepers of all human morality. Some of us wish to do the right thing without a desire for reward or a fear of punishment. Some of us believe that is simply what a human being should do. So today I will go out to the Order, and your little problem will be solved."

For a long time there was no sound but what weak echoes his voice could raise from the walls.

Katy's heart clenched. "Emil—"

"No." He was terrified: she could see it in every line of his face, in his wide eyes. "This has gone on for long enough."

Then the Abbot stood, wearily. "Tomasz, Jenna," he said, and then an instruction that had them laying hands on Emil, grabbing him by the elbows and almost hoisting him off the ground.

"What, then?" Emil met his gaze levelly. "You think unless I swear to God, I'll have second thoughts the moment I step out the door?"

"You are not going, Doctor Weber," the Abbot told him.

"That is my choice to make."

Leszek indicated his captors. "Apparently not. I have sent word to the Order. Their man from the tank, I gave him a message and had Paul release him."

Watching Tomasz and Jenna, Katy was instantly sure that this was news to them.

"I have informed Grand Master Danziger that I will surrender myself, to spare the lives of his prisoners."

Tomasz barked out an uncomprehending challenge, and kept on talking until the Abbot took him by the shoulders and stared into his face.

"Come now, Tomasz. We cannot let an atheist display more Christian virtue than us, eh?" and, to the next question, "Well of *course* he may not keep his word, but, even so."

"You're mad," Emil spat, and for once he and Tomasz were actually in agreement. "Why would you do such a thing?"

Leszek sighed. "Dr Weber, I remember when you came here first. I remember you talking about your science and your plans, and about the disease that has so wounded the world. You recall?"

"Of course." Emil blinked.

The Abbot shrugged heavily. "You're right. If there is a danger that the plague may come back for us with a different face, to cull another nine in ten of the one in ten that yet remain, of course this must be prevented. I can understand the Reverend Calumn believing that the disease is God's will, but the world was always full of ways to die. Is it God's will we stand in the path of the volcano, trusting to His judgment to turn the lava aside? No. That is why He gave us feet. Is it God's will that we wait for a new plague to destroy those that remain? If He gave you a brain fit to prevent that, then no, I do not believe it is. If there is any chance at all your liberty can assist that, then it is my duty, as a Christian, to preserve *you*. It does not matter that you do not know God. It matters, I believe, that He knows you. Tomasz."

The captain of Jasna Góra stared at him mutinously, lip trembling. Katy saw tears in his eyes. The two of them exchanged brief words in Polish, and Leszek put his ravaged hands either side of the man's face and touched foreheads, as though he could impart his quiet strength to his follower.

"You will be locked up for your own safety, Doctor Weber," the Abbot announced. "If the Order comes through our gates at the last, then my people will bring you past the walls if they can, and flee for Kraków in the confusion."

And with all eyes on him, Leszek turned and went to await the Order's messenger.

CHAPTER THIRTEEN
THE STONE TABLE

WORD CAME FROM the Order before sunset. By that time, the row of gibbets was complete, a skeletal copse of crooked necks with the angular and sepulchral elegance of cranes. The victims had even been selected, a little huddle of men and women penned in full view of the monastery and guarded. Perhaps they were seeking to provoke a doomed rescue, and in other circumstances Tomasz was not the only one who would have provided one. The Abbot's word was iron, though.

And then the messenger came again, Radek, ignoring the scathing looks and the muttering, to deliver the answer. And then there was nothing left for it but for Leszek to step beyond the walls of Jasna Góra, leaving behind all of its defences, physical and spiritual, and go down to the enemy.

Katy watched them all arguing with him. Only Paul was calm enough to stand back and just let him go. Tomasz's face was wet with tears. Jenna was furiously listing all the terrible things that the Order might do. Karel had lapsed into Czech, expostulating vehemently in a language nobody else there understood. Hamid tried his turn at reason. Half a dozen of the monastery's other leading lights had their turn. None of it worked; Leszek was like a stone, letting their fears and grief and pleading wash over him. In the end, he just turned and raised his hands, calming the storm.

"Musicie mieć wiarę," he told them. "Have faith." In that moment, and only then, did Katy see the cracks in him, the uncertainty. The humanity.

They took apart enough of the barricade to let him leave with dignity, not scrambling over the top like an adulterer caught in the act. Just beyond the entryway he paused, the wind tugging at his habit, whipping his hood back from his grey head. He seemed both smaller and larger than the man she had met: not a Christ figure, but an echo of that English shadow-Christ of children's literature, the lion giving himself up to the knives in place of one he had just cause to hate.

And then he was trudging towards the camp of the Order, where the enemy waited for him.

Tomasz accosted Paul immediately, spilling over with half-thought-through plans. His fellow captain waved him off, though.

"I have work I am set," he told his friend, his sparring partner.

"What work? Work *he* set you?" Tomasz demanded.

"Yes."

Tomasz gripped his arm hard. "Will it save him?"

Paul's face was flat and expressionless. "I don't know."

Most of the people there were heading for the walls to watch their leader step into the Order's hands, but Tomasz stayed at the gate, staring out with his hand on his sword. At last he felt *her* gaze on him and stared angrily round.

"You," he got out.

"I'm sorry."

He fought down whatever first response came to his lips, and the next, and the next, until he had nothing left to say, and stalked off. Perhaps he spent the night hunting the halls of Jasna Góra, desperate for an enemy he could fight.

But late that night, Katy crept to the Abbot's quarters, and there she heard the faint, shrill whine of the radio the man had once mentioned, and Paul's patient voice heading out into the aether, trying over and over again to make contact.

THE RECEPTION LESZEK received at the Order's camp almost resembled an honour guard for some kind of state visit. A dozen of the Order's soldiers stood to either side, forming a corridor for him to walk down: big men with close-shaven heads and painted faces, like football fans gone to the bad. Leszek had been a fan, back in the day. He had stood in the stadium and cheered for Lech Poznań and Śląsk Wrocław. And sometimes there had been trouble, after a match. Not trouble like this, though; he was well and truly amidst the opposing team's supporters now.

Grand Master Josef Danziger waited for him, arms folded, a lean, long-limbed vulture of a man. He had a blade at his side, a proper museum piece, heavy with history, the hilt rich with gilded eagles. Over reinforced leathers he wore a sleeveless robe, stitched meticulously with the Order's simple, uncompromising badge.

"Good evening, Father Abbot," he called out. "We're honoured you chose to accept our hospitality." Movie-villain gloating, just as Leszek might have expected. In that moment, facing the guns and the knives and the sheer bubbling hatred of all those eyes, he felt his spirit come close to breaking. He had made a dreadful mistake. He had given away the most precious thing he had, to buy an empty nothing from liars and cheats. There was a turning instant when his heart and stomach trembled within him, and fear laid its cold hands on his shoulders and whispered in his ear.

And he closed his eyes a moment, erasing all that black and white, and felt for his faith as though it was a weapon, laying a hand on it just as Tomasz always sought solace in the hilt of his sword.

Ah, Tomasz: do I admit you were right now, and I shouldn't have come? No, I'm too much of an old fool to start listening to sound advice now. And with that thought, the shadow was gone, and he drew his faith about him, took a deep breath and looked upon the face of his enemy.

"A little wine would not go amiss," he answered, hearing his own voice calm and strong, and then he glanced at the knot of locals corralled near the gibbets. "And will you let these people go now, Grand Master?" He was going to add some taunt to that—did the Order fear to honour their obligations, some such jibe. But he had the sense that Danziger was one of those whose anger was always just below the surface: not a man to goad idly.

"That was not the agreement, Father Abbot," Josef informed him. "You have bought exactly what was offered, when you came here. There will be no summary execution. Their freedom was not on the table, however. They and their fellows will remain as servants for my people, and as surety against some act of foolishness from yours." Choosing his moment, he stalked forwards to stare into Leszek's face. "And have no fear, we will soon determine those amongst them who have no place in God's new world. We will ask close questions of them, to determine who is not of the faith; which among them is a slave to unnatural urges and longings. And those we will hang, because that is God's plan, that the world be rid of those He abhors."

Leszek blinked. "That is a plan not vouchsafed to me."

The smile of Josef Danziger was razor-edged. "Then thank God we have been sent to spread the word. You see, Father Abbot, we are all on the same side, and no doubt when you have realized that, you will assist me in ridding the world of that heretic you have been harbouring, and his witch, and we can all go on doing the Lord's work together."

THEY HAD HIM in what must have been the Grand Master's tent soon after, sat with his hands tied before him. Danziger lounged on a pirated couch, some middle manager's pride and joy, leather-upholstered and expensive, but showing the cuts and nicks where an idle knifeman had undone careful factory craftsmanship in a few moments of vandalism.

"Reverend Calumn has been looking forward to talking to you," the Grand Master revealed.

"Is that so."

"It is indeed, sir." The smiling evangelist stepped smoothly forwards. "You know, we may not see eye to eye, the three of us, but there's one thing I do know. We all of us believe we're doing the Lord's work, isn't that right?"

Leszek just looked at him.

"Abbot, good men have died here. I won't believe that doesn't mean something to you," Calumn pressed. At Leszek's grunt, he pressed on. "We are here on a mission from God, Abbot. God has charged us to prepare the world for His Kingdom. Just as a man who will build a house must level the ground, though, for God to lay out His New Jerusalem, we must remove the last stones and burrs from His creation. We must make these latter days perfect. Now you've had the man Weber in your hands for more than a few days. I'll warrant you've found him no good company, not for a God-fearing man such as yourself."

Leszek's lips twitched. "You have the right of it."

"It seems crazy, doesn't it, that we of the faithful are fighting one another over the fate of a loathsome creature like Weber?"

"Yes. Yes it does," the Abbot said with feeling.

"I'd venture to say that is the Devil's very plan here, Abbot," Calumn said. "He seeks to sow discord amongst the faithful— discord between you and the Grand Master and me. Because these are the End Times, and old Satan will do everything he can to prevent God's new kingdom arising—because that will be the Devil's final defeat."

"The last days." Leszek cocked an eyebrow at him. "You believe that?"

"The proof is all around us, don't you think?" Calumn shook his head. "So many souls purged from the world. What do you find more convincing? Some scientist's hollow prattle, or that this is the work of the Lord?"

"You make a strong case." Leszek took a long breath. "You had the radio, the TV, when it was happening? You heard the news."

"While there was news to hear," Calumn confirmed almost cheerily.

"Only, where was the Beast?"

"The Beast—?"

"The Beast!" Leszek was suddenly animated. "It comes out of the sea. It has ten horns and seven heads! Only, with all that news at the start, I was sure someone would have mentioned that. Or did it only turn up after they had stopped broadcasting, do you think?"

"There are parts of the Book of Revelations—"

"Only, if this is the end of the world," Leszek pressed on fiercely, bound hands clenched into fists, "I'd have thought Saint John the Divine would have said more about the *plague* and less about the Beast."

"There are many people who believe that our own President—"

"No, that is not what it says in the book!" Leszek told him. "I know the end of the world, Reverend. This is not it. This is a trial, perhaps, and no doubt we will all be judged."

Calumn opened his mouth, then closed it, then started again. "No, but you see—"

"I take it that you do not intend to convince your followers to hand over Weber," Danziger said lazily.

"That is correct."

"Then, if you truly think that the world will go on, you are a fool to have given up your place in it by coming here." Abruptly the Grand Master was sitting up, his sword across his knees.

"Josef—" Calumn started.

"I have done my duty, as it appeared to me," Leszek said flatly.

"Your duty was to leave your people leaderless?" Danziger kicked himself to his feet and laid the blade on Leszek's shoulder, the edge cold against his neck.

"It was to suffer for others." Leszek's voice was quiet again, his passion spent. "Sacrificing ourselves for others is our doctrine, is it not, to atone for all our sins?" He looked sidelong at Calumn again. "But you, you are all about sacrificing others for you: your power, your momentary glory."

"I'll have you know, sir, I was raised by a proper Christian family," Calumn told him firmly. "I went to church. I learned what it was to fight God's fight."

"No." Leszek's voice was low enough that the Reverend had to lean in to hear it. "You learned to fight other men's fights, who told you they spoke for God, and you never questioned them." He grinned abruptly. "What if you are wrong about God, Reverend?"

"I have faith that I am not."

"No? But it is that wager, is it not? I am too soft, you think, to let Weber live. You would be a murderer, I say, if you kill him. Which of us is judged more harshly, if he is wrong? Which of us can face God and account for his mistakes?"

Calumn's professional smile remained, but there was something sickly behind it, and he said nothing, even when prompted by Danziger. At last the Grand Master hissed with annoyance.

"I will tell you, Abbot, which of us will find himself judged and found wanting. The man who has opened his doors to all the lesser types, the godless, the Roma, the Jew. Probably you've turned a blind eye to all manner of unnatural filth, behind those high walls of yours. You think your God will turn a blind eye to that."

"I think my God wishes me to love my neighbour. Any creed, any colour, any race is my neighbour, if he comes in peace." The blade was pressing against him now, so that a shallow line of blood welled up on the side of his neck.

"And if he does not come in peace?" Danziger growled.

"Then perhaps I was never such a good Christian as that." Leszek gritted his teeth.

Abruptly the sword was gone from his skin, the Grand Master resting it on his shoulder as he paced about the tent. "You are so full of righteousness," he told the Abbot. "Look at you, sending your people to grub in the dirt, arming your soldiers with bows and sticks. You are the shadows of yesterday. You are the stain we must remove, every bit as much as Weber. For we are the future."

Leszek made a choking noise, but somehow it became something like a laugh. "How can you be the future?" he whispered. "You have no future. You build nothing. You plant nothing. You are no more than the last symptoms of the plague, before it is gone for good. You are the thrashings of the serpent, when its head is gone. You are dust, Grand Master. And in a year, in a decade, in a generation, you will have blown away on the wind. And we? We shall still be here."

Danziger turned back to him, face cold and dead, and abruptly the sword came up and he was striking, but Calumn's cry stayed his hand.

"Grand Master, wait, no! Kill him and you'll make a martyr of him."

For a moment Danziger stared at him, the steel hanging in the air, and there was enough ugliness in his expression that he might as easily have cut down Calumn as Leszek. But then something grew there, vicious and unnatural. A smile.

"Yes," he said. "That is what we'll do."

"We can still talk him round," Calumn began, but he faltered before that crooked expression.

"No talking, Reverend," Danziger said. "These ignorant peasants, they can't understand destiny. They're not part of God's plan. They never were. They won't join us, so we must break them. Break them by making an example of their leader. A martyr of him? Yes, that's exactly what we'll do."

CHAPTER FOURTEEN
CALVARY

THEN HE WAS beaten—not by Danziger's own hands, but the man watched while a couple of his men kicked Leszek back and forth with some enthusiasm. Then, spitting blood, his vision blurred in one eye, he was taken to a small tent and thrown in to await the morning.

Sleep evaded him: a multitude of pains kept him awake, and besides, he might not have another night. To sleep through his final hours seemed such a waste. So it was that the voice came to him, startling him out of sour, difficult remembrances of his early days, before God, before prison.

It spoke in a soft whisper, just loud enough to reach his ears: a voice from the aether, from the other side. Specifically, from the other side of the tent fabric.

How Tomasz had got there, he could not say, but the man always had refused to accept the limits that shackled most of humanity. Now he must be crouching at the back of this little tent, seconds away from being spotted.

"I will get you out of here," the man said.

"No, Tomasz."

"I will cut through the tent. We can run. If they try to stop me, I'll kill them. I'll kill all of them." The captain's voice sounded ragged.

"No, you won't, Tomasz," Leszek whispered patiently. "Why did I come here?"

"The—the prisoners..."

"And they're still prisoners, but not under threat of execution. Not anymore. Not for now." Speaking, even breathing, hurt. "I cannot come with you. All that sneaking and creeping. I'm too old for that."

"Abbot—"

"Go back, Tomasz. Go back and wait for Paul."

"*Paul?*"

"I have given him a duty. Listen to him. He will tell you what you must do, and when."

There was a silence, then a long, slow release of breath, and then a longer silence still, until Leszek knew for sure the man had gone. Then he did sleep a little, and, waking, was not sure what had been real, and what a dream.

When he woke up, he could hear them hammering, just as they had when they put up the gibbets. He knew Danziger's mind. He knew what they were building, and that they would have a few nails left over when they were done.

Later on, well past midnight, the Reverend Calumn was with him in the tent, or so he thought.

"You have to do what he says," the American told him. "There's still time. Tell him you'll get Weber out. That's all we want."

"Why is this man so important to you? You wouldn't go all this way for any atheist," Leszek wheezed.

"God wants to end the world," Calumn said hollowly. "He wants to bring the New Kingdom of Heaven on Earth, just like I was always taught. But this Weber, he *dares*... he dares to say that his science can defy God's judgment, that he can hold off the agent of God's work."

"That he can see it under a microscope," Leszek said softly. "Reverend, did you ever believe in God, tell me? Ever?"

"I'm a God-fearing man!" Calumn insisted.

"And is that the same thing? You were brought up amongst Christians, though? Went to church."

"Of course—"

"And then you found there was a power in it, in the pulpit and the sermon. And if God had ever been in you, He left. There was no room for Him any more."

Calumn made a couple of tries at a reply, stammering over words that would not quite come out, and Leszek wondered if, when the Cull had happened, the man had felt that emptiness inside him; whether he had gone chasing God after all, to try and cram that divine certainty back in him, because he couldn't survive or make sense of the ruined world in any other way.

At last the Reverend came out with, "It isn't my soul I'd be worrying about, Father Abbot. It's your own." He sounded glum more than triumphant.

"Even so," Leszek agreed. He had heard, once, about the speed the earth revolved at. It had never been something he could conceive of, before, but now he had a terrible sense of the dawn's swift rushing progress towards him. "Reverend Calumn, may I ask for your assistance?"

"I'm not going to release you," Calumn told him immediately, unsolicited.

Leszek laughed, then wished he hadn't. "I don't think it is a part of your doctrine, Reverend, but I would dearly like someone to hear my confession."

"Your...?"

"I have not walked with God for much of my life. I have done bad things. I do not want to see the sun tomorrow without a final accounting."

Calumn said nothing for so long, there in the dark, in the tent, that the Abbot thought he must have gone, or never been there at all, but at last his voice came, just one small word. "Sure."

DAWN WAS STILL hours away when Katy was woken by a growing murmur that echoed through the stone halls of Jasna Góra. Stumbling from her room, wrapped in a woollen blanket, she stumbled after the trail of the sound until she came out into the chill of the night; until she clambered up to the walls.

There were a fair number of people there, by then, mostly as bleary and half-dressed as she was, but a realisation was leaping from one to another. She looked about for a familiar face, and saw Tomasz, clad in dark leathers, his long features blackened up. *Just going or just back?* From his expression, she guessed at the latter.

"What is it?" she asked. Tomasz just scowled at her, but Jenna was there too, pointing out at the Order's camp.

Beside the skeletal rank of gibbets, something new had taken shape. The leaping bonfires of their camp silhouetted it, stark and uncompromising. It was leaning up against the arms of the gallows, a nailed-together construction of heavy timbers the Order must have ripped out of some old Częstochowa house. For a long moment, Katy had no idea what it was.

Then the penny dropped, and she swore under her breath.

The New Teutonic Order had built a cross. A big, unlovely, *functional* cross.

"They won't..." she started, looking around. From their faces, nobody believed her. She didn't believe herself.

"This is what they are," Tomasz said fiercely. "This is what they do. So we go. We go to them. We fight. For him."

"And what were *his* words, Tomasz?" Paul came trudging up the steps to the wall, looking like a man who hadn't slept in a week.

"That you would know," his fellow captain hissed at him. "That you would give the word. So give it."

Paul just shook his head. "I know," he said, and he gripped Tomasz by the arm. "I know how it is. But to go now would be to doom us all. Too many men out there, too many guns."

"Paul—"

But Paul was already retracing his steps. "Be ready," he cast over his shoulder, too weary even to look back.

There was no sleeping, after that. Tomasz paced and clenched his fists and clutched at his sword and snarled at anyone who got in his way. Jenna stood at the wall with her bow in hand, and plucked at the string uselessly. Karel was about by then, part-armoured, looking to pick a fight. Katy stayed out of everyone's way. She was waiting for them to remember it was her friend who was the cause of all of this. She was waiting for someone to decide to go against the Abbot's dictates; that risking Leszek's displeasure was worth saving his life. And all the time her rational mind told her, *They won't; they won't do it. They're not going to crucify the Abbot*. And despite all that, she knew they would.

And the sky had a greyness to it now, a creeping dawn-ness to it, more wholly unwelcome than any dawn she had known, for surely it was only the sun that the Order was waiting for, before putting on a show.

Then someone was looming over her, and she saw that, somehow, she was in the way of Tomasz's pacing, or he had set his course to make sure she would be. She braced herself for the ranting, and she could see that he had expected just the same, had been ready for the anger boiling inside him to vent itself on her. But it didn't come. He just stared at her, and the man who looked out on her from those red eyes was tortured by guilt and self-accusation.

He opened his mouth, not to accuse, perhaps even to ask for help. Then someone was pelting up the steps, and a sea change passed over everyone there, a sudden presentiment of purpose. It was Paul.

"It's time," he said. "Now we go. Now we bring the Deluge to them." He had his sword in hand, blade gleaming in the first leaden hues of the day.

"Yes! It's time!" Tomasz spat, and he had his sword halfway bared as well before Paul stopped him.

"Not you."

"Yes, me. I'll lead the charge."

"Not you," Paul repeated. "Karel can do that. There's something only you can do."

THEY HAD THE cross set upright, sending its dawn shadow in a long, jagged stripe across the tents of the Order camp. Then they had to take it down again, because there was no obvious way of tenanting it otherwise. The Order's usual modus operandi was lynching; crucifixion was a novelty.

Josef Danziger watched the work impatiently, glancing every so often to the walls of Jasna Góra, where the morning sun showed plenty of heads peering over the parapet. He reached for the feeling of destiny in the moment. Would it be *this* that future generations recalled, when they spoke of the rise of Josef Danziger's New Order? He knew that such a moment would arrive, when he would become the man he saw in the mirror, a man crowned by history with the laurel wreath, a man to shape the world that was to come.

Abbot Leszek's words came to him: *You have no future.* He shook them off angrily, shouting for them to bring the man out. *By the time the sun goes down, old man, only one of us will be alive to see it, or at least you'll wish you were dead. Who owns the future then?*

The Abbot stood between his guards, brooding, broad-shouldered, and yet trapped. He reminded Danziger of a caged bear, all that futile, wasted strength.

"I asked you to take a message to your people over there," he told his prisoner.

Leszek glowered up at him from the eye that was not swollen shut. "You have my answer."

"You'll *be* a message," Danziger assured him. "And your people will surrender, when they've had a chance to think on it. Or I'll do to them—all of them—what I do to you. The Order has no mercy for those who defy it."

The Abbot took a deep breath and then looked him right in the eye. "I don't know if this impresses your men, but it bores me to death. Get on with it."

Danziger felt the white heat of his anger flare and abruptly he was before Leszek, smashing a fist across the man's bony chin, sending him down to one knee. For a moment, the drive to simply kick and beat the man to death was almost impossible to restrain. He held it back, though: in the past, when he had indulged himself to that extent, he had lost followers. The sight of their Grand Master stamping and smashing a body like a child having a tantrum, spittle flecking his lips and his eyes glazed with the relish of the moment, it proved too unsettling for some. He tried to rely on others for his beatings now.

And probably the old man was baiting him to do it: a kinder and quicker end than Danziger had planned for him.

"Get him down there," the Grand Master snapped. "Where are the nails?"

They were big construction nails, the heads beaten wide and flat so that the Abbot's frail flesh would not just slip off them. There was a whole logistics of crucifixion that Danziger had never considered. As an intellectual puzzle, it was quite satisfying.

He held out his hand and, unbidden, someone passed him a hammer. "You're a strong man, Abbot," he told Leszek. "My men are making bets how long you'll last." He saw his prisoner's lips move, trying to form some mocking comeback, but no words came out. They had him stretched out now, arms and legs held down. Danziger put the point of one nail to his palm, picking a point between the existing cuts lacerating the man's hands. The hammer went up.

"Josef, Josef, wait."

Danziger bared his teeth. "Later, Reverend."

The Reverend Calumn had pushed his way to the front of the crowd, twisting his hands together. "Grand Master, there's no need for this."

"I disagree."

"Grand Master, he will come round to our point of view. I can convince him to surrender Weber to us. We can win his support."

Danziger straightened up and stared balefully at his ally. "Reverend, I don't *want* his support. I don't want to hobble our destiny by chaining it to the worthless opinions of mongrel peasants. I want to send a message to the world. I want the story told from here to Moscow, what happens when filthy slavs decide they can challenge the true masters of the world."

"Grand Master, this is... this is sacrilegious," Calumn got out. His usual smooth eloquence seemed to have abandoned him. "We may not see eye to eye, but he is a man of God. Why not keep him prisoner, use this as a threat, even—"

"I'm done with threats," and Danziger knelt back down, set the nail, and sent a single leaden blow to drive it through the Abbot's flinching hand and into the dense wood.

A moment later, he wasn't quite sure what had happened. It

seemed utterly impossible that Calumn had laid hands on him. The man didn't have that courage in him. And yet here he was, standing again, with Calumn sprawled in the dirt at his feet and Danziger's fist stinging from the return blow. Almost bewildered, he opened his mouth for a rebuke, but Calumn surged to his feet.

"I forbid it!" he snapped out, eyes wild. "You have strayed from the path, Grand Master. This is not the way to your destiny. This is not the will of God."

Danziger felt the words strike amongst his followers: the religious rhetoric, that had been so useful in forging his army, now turned against him. They were still his people, still under his iron rule, but he could feel pinprick consciences starting up in some of them. He could feel the challenge to his authority like a grain of sand under his eyelid, impossible to ignore.

The roar of the pistol was so unexpected, so out of place, that Danziger was almost surprised to find the weapon in his hand. Calumn goggled at him, out of a face suddenly white as a shroud. Behind him, men were scattering in case Danziger felt like sending another bullet their way. At this range, though, one would suffice. He had taken Calumn right above the breastbone, and when the Reverend tried to speak, there was only a pinkish froth on his lips.

There was utter silence, when Calumn dropped to his knees and then fell on his face.

"Anyone else wish to defy me?" Danziger demanded. His soldiers were silent, and he wasn't quite sure of their mood. How many of them had lapped up Calumn's sermons just that bit too much? How many of them found belief twisting in their hearts like a treacherous knife?

And then, as though the retort of the gun had finally echoed back from the walls of Jasna Góra, a roar and a rumble sounded from the monastery: thunder; a monstrous beast; the damning voice of God. Danziger froze, and for a moment even he felt that divine judgment was about to light on him.

And then people were pointing, shouting: something was coming from the monastery, crunching and thundering across the bridge and jolting down towards them. The tank.

* * *

TOMASZ HAD TRAINED as tank crew, back before, but not in a Leopard. However, the Order's crew had apparently not been professionals either, and the interior of the vehicle was festooned with labels in hastily-scrawled German, identifying the various controls. And so it was that, when he heard the signal rapped out on the hull, he sent the freed vehicle into reverse and slammed it out of the John Paul II Gate and down towards the Order camp as fast as it would go. He had no weapons to turn on them, but then the tank itself was a weapon, a battering ram. And it was a distraction. While they were watching his bumping, lurching progress towards them, the Order were hopefully not watching for the others.

DANZIGER STARED. FOR too many moments he had no words, his voice dry in his throat. His tank was coming back; his pride and joy. But, just like Calumn, it had betrayed him. It was working for the enemy now. And it was picking up speed.

He jabbed out a finger, bellowed the order to stop it, but they had nothing that could get in its way. The few who tried to shoot at it were just wasting ammunition against its armoured hide as the vehicle wove drunkenly backwards towards the camp. Already discipline was being lost, men trying to predict where the tank was going to hit, scattering from its path.

Something was wrong. There was plenty of shouting and alarmed cries, but some of them were coming from the wrong direction.

Attack!

And Danziger wheeled to see that, behind him, some of his more sharp-eyed soldiers were trying to rouse the rest of the camp's attention. The defenders had sallied out. He had hoped they would, to rescue their beloved Abbot. He had envisioned a scything hail of gunfire cutting them down as they shed the protective stone of their walls. But now they were close, far too close. They had crept from their sanctuary and were coming to him from behind, out between the vacant shells of Częstochowa. They must have been stealing out of the monastery before dawn, working their way round.

His surprise broke, and he was storming through the camp,

shouting orders. The tank could do limited damage, but here, here was an enemy they could fight, and it was almost upon them.

Even as the Order tried to make a firing line, the attackers were breaking into a run. There were rifles and pistols there, bows, swords, spears, an absurd grab-bag of human military history. Danziger saw several of them go down to the guns of his quicker followers, but not enough to stall the charge. In the lead, there was an enormous man dressed head to foot like a knight, loaded with steel and yet thundering ahead with the same unstoppable momentum as the tank. Danziger saw one rifleman shoot the giant in the chest and barely stagger him, the bullet vanishing into an impervious darkness within his breastplate.

Then the battle was joined.

KATY HAD NOT wanted to come on this suicide mission. The defenders had put together less than fifty people, and the Order had far more. There was apparently more to the plan than "run about and get killed," but nobody was telling her. She should stay behind the walls and cower there, that was plain. That would be the reasonable course of action,

And now she was here, towards the back of the mob, running into the Order camp with a pistol and a knife stuck through her belt. Because of Leszek. Because of Emil. And because the only real alternative would have been to run away, because if the monastery's warriors lost here, then there would be nobody to keep the Order out later. Paul had only a handful left for a token defence.

She had seen plenty of fighting since the Cull, but nothing like this. The warriors of Jasna Góra had used the cover of the buildings to get close to the camp, and then they had pelted across the last few yards of open ground, even as the bullets started flying. She had thought they would all die, at that point, but apparently Tomasz's antics had been diversion enough. And abruptly she was running between untidy rows of tents, vaulting bodies from both sides, following up the charge as the attacking force drove into the heart of the Order camp.

Karel was the point of their spear, laying about him with his pollaxe, striking and moving on and leaving it to lesser men to finish off any wounded he left behind. Behind him came the men and women Tomasz and Paul had trained. Most of them looked absolutely terrified, electrified by fear and adrenaline, striking out at any face that was painted in black and white. The Order were still scattering, off balance and disorganised, unable to adjust to the swiftness of their enemy's advance, but that wouldn't last. As soon as they could get enough of their gunmen in one place then things were going to get ugly.

"Where's the Abbot?" she called, completely turned around.

Jenna snagged her arm and dragged her off between two tents, stepping awkwardly over the guy ropes. The fighting was deteriorating into skirmishes now, knots of Order soldiers scattered by increasingly dispersed handfuls of the attacking force. Katy had a horrible sense of the mass of the enemy gathering itself back together again, barely scratched and recovering from its surprise.

"There!" And Jenna set an arrow to her string and loosed it, before following it towards the heart of the camp. A moment later Katy saw what she had seen: there was the cross, there the frail human form pinned to it by one hand.

The Order had first scattered outwards to meet the charge, and then recoiled away from it. The attackers were all pushing inwards, converging raggedly on their stricken leader. *Which is a recipe for being surrounded*, Katy decided, and ran for Leszek.

A moment later, she dived for cover as someone shot at her. She could hear orders being shouted from somewhere, and then she had a glimpse of the long-limbed, lean form of Josef Danziger with a fair number of men at his back. She dragged out her pistol, knowing that she was well out of range.

Then the Order men were running, scattering, and a moment later the tank ploughed through the tents where they had been, its tracks snarled with rope and canvas, oily smoke leaking from it as it slewed to a halt. Even as it stopped, the top hatch flew open and Tomasz practically leapt out, sword first.

And Katy was beside the cross, her hands reaching for the single nail, feeling it solidly set into the wood. Leszek's calm eyes were upon her. His lips moved, and she thought he said the word, "Paul."

"Yes, yes, Paul's idea, blame him," she said, looking around frantically for something to pull the nail free with. Jenna kicked her inadvertently, and Katy looked up to see the woman shooting again, reaching into her emptying quiver. The surviving warriors of Jasna Góra were pushing in, whilst around them the Order soldiers had rallied, taking up positions in the ruins of their camp, levelling their guns.

"Get him up!" Tomasz shouted.

"I'm trying!" Katy yelled back at him. She was reduced to wrenching at the nail, working it back and forth despite the ruin it was making of Leszek's hand, seeing him twist and clench his jaw at every motion.

And then it was out, but by then it was too late. The Order had found its discipline at last, all around then, and Danziger's mocking voice came to them: "I see you have a great desire to die with your leader! I grant your wish, peasants. And then I shall go to your fortress and hang everyone there from the walls. I shall show the world the price of defying the New Teutonic Order!" And he had forgotten himself enough to come to the front of his people to gloat, where any of the defenders could have taken a shot at him.

But by then Katy wasn't listening to him. "Is that thunder?" she asked, and then, "Is it an earthquake?" The ground was shaking.

"No," Jenna said, her eyes shining. "It's the cavalry."

They came swift out of the streets of Częstochowa, a coursing tide of dun and roan and grey that barely slowed as it met the milling Order soldiers. Those in the camp who had the self-possession to shoot were already using it to run. The rest went under the hooves, or were scattered left and right, to flee, or to stand and be shot down. They had rifles, the riders, and they had recurved bows of wood and horn that some driven obsessive must be crafting, east of here: skills that had waited out the turn of history until they were needed again.

The Roma had come. Called over the many miles by Leszek's radio, summoned by the urgent words of Magdayeva, they had mustered their forces: their own horsemen, and those others they had agreed to teach. They had taken up their weapons and come at the call of Jasna Góra.

And the mass of the Order, all those angry men borne here on tides of nationalism and religious hatred, broke. A few shots were fired, horses and riders brought down, but most of the men ran and, in running, were lost.

It was not over so swiftly, of course. As Katy crouched by Leszek, the world around her seemed to be filled with fighting, crackling with sporadic gunfire and the occasional hammering of automatic weapons. The Order was being forced inward by the devastating charges of the Roma, but 'inward' meant towards the cross, towards the Jasna Góra defenders. She saw Karel go down, painted with the blood of his enemies, a half-dozen bullet holes punched in his armour. Magdayeva surged past, her mount vaulting over cowering Order soldiers as she twisted in the saddle to shoot back at them. Katy saw Jenna reach for arrows in an empty quiver, and then lash her bow across the painted face of an enemy. No quarter, no mercy was asked, expected or given.

She saw Josef Danziger there, and he had a pistol in one hand and a sword in the other, but by the time Tomasz caught him, he must have run out of ammunition, for he met the captain of Jasna Góra blade on blade. He managed to fend off three furious blows, Tomasz's technique suffering under his furious need to kill the man before him. Then Hamid's steel won out against the museum-dusty metal, and Danziger's sword snapped at the quillons, eagles and all.

Tomasz barked out a yell of triumph, catching Danziger with an upswing that smacked into his ribs, gouging his leathers and knocking him sideways. Then someone shot him. Katy didn't see the impact or the bullet wound, just a sudden change in the way Tomasz stood. Even then he drove down at Danziger, but the stroke faltered and the Grand Master rolled away as the swordsman dropped to one knee. There was no awareness in Tomasz's face that he'd been injured. His murderous composure promised Danziger a thousand deaths, but his body was dissenting, and his body had the casting vote.

An Order soldier was running up, fumbling another magazine into an automatic pistol and reaching out to help Danziger to his feet. Katy shot him, arms steady against the kick of the gun so that her bullet went into the back of the man's head at five paces and spattered the Grand Master with half of his face. She had a second, then, locked eye to mad eye with Josef Danziger, in the moment when history discarded him.

Then Tomasz drove a knife into the man's foot, pinning him to the earth, and Katy shot him, and kept shooting him until she had no more bullets.

THEY GOT TOMASZ back behind the walls of Jasna Góra and they did what they could, just as Katy and Hamid and all the rest worked night and day to save all those who came back bloodied from the battle. Many lived, but Tomasz was not amongst them. Leszek himself closed the man's eyes with his good hand.

IT WAS A time of farewells.

"Are you going to keep your mouth shut and just get on with your job, this time?" Katy asked.

"What do you think?" Emil was trying to be flippant, but he didn't quite manage it. "You think anything that has happened here has convinced me that religion isn't the cause—"

"Emil."

He looked mutinous, but held his peace. "What can I say? I'll try to play nicely with the fanatics, Miss Lewkowitz. They have all the lab equipment, so I'll have to smile and pretend, won't I? It won't be so different from trying to get grant funding, I suppose. But it would be easier if I had you there to help. Surely I can change your mind?"

Katy shrugged. "I'll visit."

"Why, Katy? These people, they're mired in the past."

She shook her head. "They're planning for the future. I want to help. It's been a long time since I found something I wanted to be a part of."

A family of Roma was waiting for Emil, horses and wagons ready to travel the long road to Kraków. The animals stamped and snorted in the chill dawn. Past them, the Order camp looked like Glastonbury after the festival, a churned field scattered with all the rubbish that nobody had cared to salvage.

"Dr Weber." A shadow fell across them and Emil looked up.

"Abbot." The scientist scowled, shrugged, at last put out a hand. "I'm grateful. I suppose."

Leszek laughed at that. "Repay us by making us all grateful. I have faith in you, Dr Weber."

"Yes, yes, the humour never ends." But there was less rancour in Emil's tone than Katy might have expected.

She stood on the walls to watch them go, with Jenna and Magdayeva. They had even got Paul into the open air, though his grief for Tomasz was on him like a shadow.

"There goes the future," Jenna said softly.

"The future?" Paul said gruffly. "You know what the future is? One of the Tsars will have an army, or a Khan or a Sultan, or some Lithuanian warlord or... there's always someone."

"So long as it's someone we can fight," Jenna told him. "So long as it's not another plague."

Katy watched the little group of riders and wagons until they had vanished into the empty streets of Częstochowa.

THE END

ABOUT THE AUTHOR

Adrian Tchaikovsky was born in Lincolnshire and studied Zoology and Psychology in Reading in order to become a lawyer in Leeds. He is a keen roleplayer and sometime practitioner of European historical martial arts.

His series *Shadows of the Apt* started with *Empire in Black and Gold* in 2008 and concludes with *Seal of the Worm* in July 2014. He has also written numerous short stories for various anthologies and has a collection of short stories out entitled *Feast and Famine* from Newcon Press.

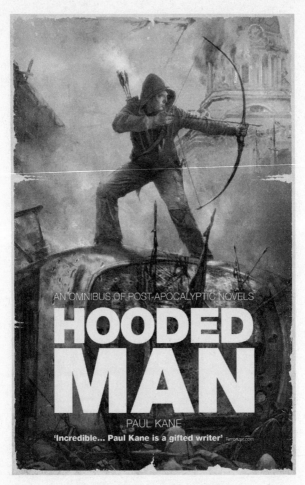

AN OMNIBUS OF POST-APOCALYPTIC NOVELS

HOODED MAN

PAUL KANE

'Incredible... Paul Kane is a gifted writer' *Terror.gr.com*

After the world died, the Legend was reborn

When civilisation shuddered and died, Robert Stokes lost everything, including his wife and his son. The ex-cop retreated into the woods near Nottingham, to live off the land and wait to join his family. As the world descended into a new Dark Age, he turned his back on it all. The foreign mercenary and arms dealer De Falaise sees England is ripe for conquest. He works his way up the country, forging an army and pillaging as he goes. When De Falaise arrives at Nottingham and sets up his new dominion, Robert is drawn reluctantly into the resistance. From Sherwood he leads the fight and takes on the mantle of the world's greatest folk hero. The Hooded Man and his allies will become a symbol of freedom, a shining light in the horror of a blighted world, but he can never rest: De Falaise is only the first of his kind.